"TELL ME, MY LORD,"

Morgana mocked as nastily as he. "If I scratched you, would your blood run blue or would it be as red as that of a common man?"

Rian's nostrils flared and his face was white around his tightened mouth. Morgana could see she'd angered him, but she didn't care. She wanted to hurt him, to get even with him and his damned arrogance.

"Don't push too hard, Morgana," he warned softly through clenched teeth, and drew her up next to him as somewhere off in the distance a clock chimed midnight.

"The witching hour." He spoke quietly, his eyes wintergreen and hard. "Shall I remove your mask and see if you really are the sorceress the villagers claim?" Before she could reply, he untied the strings and pulled the mask from her face. "Aye," he muttered. "You could cast a spell over a man with those eyes of yours." He ran his hand over her throat and down her shoulder, pulling down one sleeve to expose the whiteness of her flesh.

Morgana stared at him, mesmerized, then, recovering her senses, tried to pull away. His fingers tightened at the sudden movement, making her flinch.

"I shall have a bruise there in the morning," she whispered, her anger draining away at the light in his eyes, the pulse at the hollow of her throat beating rapidly.

"Then look at it," he answered, "and know which of us is the stronger. . . ."

Rebecca Brandewyne

No Gentle Love

LOVE SPELL ◆ NEW YORK CITY

For two sisters,
Mimi and Nanny.
In loving memory.

A LOVE SPELL BOOK®

February 2002

Published by

Dorchester Publishing Co., Inc.
276 Fifth Avenue
New York, NY 10001

First published by Warner Books

ISBN 0-505-52470-8

The name "Love Spell" and its logo are trademarks of Dorchester Publishing Co., Inc.

Printed in the United States of America.

Visit us on the web at www.dorchesterpub.com.

No Gentle LOVE

The Players

In Ireland:

Lord Fergus McShane, Duke of Shanetara

His daughter:
  Lady Rosamunde

His grandchildren:
  Lord Trevor, Earl of Shaughnessy
  Lord Gerald
  Lord Rian, Earl of Keldara
  Lord Patrick, Viscount of Blackwood
  Lady Morgana
  Lord Colin

Lady Fionna, Countess of Shaughnessy
Bridget, a serving maid, later Viscountess of Blackwood
Doctor Michael Kelsey, the family doctor
Brendan O'Hara, a clansman

In England:

Lord Braddington Denby, Earl of Brisbane
Lady Anne Winwood, later Countess of Brisbane
Sir Anthony Reginald
Lady Cecily Brooksworth
Lord Harry Chalmers
Mistress Maria Frampstead

In France:

Lord Phillipe du Lac, Vicomte de Blanchefleur

In Africa

Kassou, Chief of the Ashanti
Captain Taylor Jones

In India:

Prince Sirsi, Maharajah of Bhavnagar

His wives:
  Dhoraji
  Amreli
  Jind

His brother:
  Prince Hassan

In China:

Madame Sung
Madame Kiangsu, the Red Lady
Taian, a Chinese girl

Contents

No Gentle Love

The Emerald Isle
As the ground blossomed into greenness
With the touch of the summer sun
Matched the color of her eyes.
She gazed out over the shifting seas
And there appeared on the horizon
A tall white sail
That marked his coming.
They say he took her
Violently, arrogantly,
As was his fashion,
And made her his.
Theirs was no gentle love
Born of soft romance,
But a flaming passion
Which burned the bitter memories of time,
And set ablaze forever
The shadows of their lives.

BOOK ONE
The Emerald Isle

Chapter One

London, England, 1812

The rain drifted mistily down the windowpane as Morgana McShane looked out onto the square below. The glass felt cold against her skin, for she had her face pressed close upon the pane, but she paid no heed. She was too engrossed in her sorrow and the strange letter she had received only a fortnight ago. She watched absently as the carriages rumbled over the cobblestone street in front of her small but tasteful house. Briefly, she envied the well-dressed people inside those carriages. She smoothed the folds of her own modest gown somewhat resentfully, the drab black, for she was in mourning, depressing her even further. But the thought was fleeting, for then her conscience pricked her and she felt ashamed of herself and her self-pity. Even though the black dress she wore was the only one she possessed, it was clean and well kept, something of which no one should have been ashamed. What difference did it make if it was not the latest style? It served her well enough. She had no need of fashionable dresses and could not afford them in any event. She would never be admitted to Almack's, often called the "Marriage Mart" by many of the young dandies who frequented the rooms of that exclusive club where all debutantes hoped to catch a husband. Only the truest of bluebloods received vouchers from its sternly correct patrons.

Not for the likes of her would there be a man who claimed membership in that elite group known as the Holland House Set, that group of dandies, Libertines, and Corinthians who were close friends of George, Prince Regent; a man who patronized Watier's, Brooks's, Alfred's, (also known as "Half-Read's," having recently fallen out of favor), and White's; a man who belonged to the Four Horses Club with its blue and yellow striped jackets; a man who whiled away the evening dancing at Almack's. The highest hand to which Morgana could aspire would belong to a man of trade, or, as the nobility so vulgarly termed, a Cit; and among her acquaintances, even these numbered few.

There was the baker's son, who often pressed some pastry upon her after she'd made her small purchases, and who had once tried to kiss her in his father's shop. There was the glover, who could never remember her name as she so seldom had money enough to buy a new pair of gloves. And there was the librarian, who watched her with silent adoration and gave a prominent place in his shop to her father's books of poetry, although they never sold well.

Morgana would have had none of these men, even had they offered for her. Her mother had died of a lingering complaint when the girl was yet a child, but Morgana could still recall that sweet, gentle face well, still smell the fragrance of lemon verbena, and still hear the soft, lilting voice reciting the tale of her parents' romantic, runaway love match. This oft-told story had made a deep impression upon the child, and she had resolved that she, too, would marry only for love. And Morgana did not love the baker's son, nor the glover, nor the librarian.

Her situation in life was most peculiar. Her mother had been an untitled gentlewoman and her father an impoverished Irish baron who'd renounced all claims to his lands and title when he'd run off with the young English girl he so dearly loved. Had he not been a minor at the time of their marriage, Connor McShane and his wife would not have been reduced to the poverty in which they had lived; but he'd had no control over his estates and had been cut off without a penny for marrying without his guardian's consent. Thus Morgana had grown up in genteel impoverishment, belonging neither among the nobles nor the laborers who toiled in the filthy, sooty factories of London.

An only child, she had led a solitary life, except for the few years she'd spent at a select seminary. Her mother had wished it, and the money had been somehow scraped together. School had not been pleasant for the young girl. Her classmates, aware of her poverty, had delighted in making fun of her, mocking her manner and clothes; and the fact that she'd made the highest marks in her class did little to alleviate their cruel attentions. She took refuge in a cool dignity toward them, never deigning to give them the satisfaction of a reply, but the damage was deeply felt. Oddly enough, she did not grow bitter, but, rather, strongly resolved never to treat another human being so unkindly.

Morgana had a keen, unusual mind, and soon earned the ungracious title of "bluestocking," one of the less mean names bestowed upon her by her wealthy classmates, but nevertheless one which was meant to convey contempt.

As she grew older, Morgana developed a dry wit and a sharp, sarcastic tongue. It was better to laugh than cry, she decided; and she could not bear to be pitied. Many a well-meaning soul offering her sympathy would find her cool smile and the strange twinkle that sometimes lurked in her eyes disconcerting, and feel that he, not Morgana, was the one shockingly out of place. Indeed, worthy matrons, seeking to capture the heart of Morgana's widowed father, had puffed up with indignation at this peculiar treatment.

Still, there was a gentle, dreamy side to the girl's nature, born of the affection her parents had bestowed upon her as a child; but this Morgana never showed to the rest of the world, having learned early on at the seminary that to do so was to invite ridicule. Instead, she appeared placid and practical, with what her father fondly termed a level head on her shoulders. She had long become resigned to the fact that she would never marry. At twenty-one, she bore the mantle of spinsterhood well, accepting it calmly, dismissing as foolish her childhood dreams of runaway love matches.

Her father had tried to prepare Morgana for a life of poverty by teaching her to stand on her own two feet. Had he lived, he eventually would have realized that the world frowned on independent women, relegating them to the roles of governess and companion. He had hoped his only child might venture into literature and become another Jane Austen. He did not wish for Morgana to brave the unkindness of the world like a man, but he had wanted her to observe life and to try and expose its cruelties through her books.

The girl did not understand that the kind of life for which her father had prepared her would be generations in coming. Her one attempt at writing had been a dismal failure; and though she would never have admitted it, on this particular day she felt rather frightened, confused, and very much alone in the world.

Ah well, she suddenly returned to reality and the empty room with a sigh. It was past five o'clock and she longed to hear her father's footsteps in the hallway, the muffled sounds of his hanging his hat and umbrella on the coatrack signalling his return. But she would never hear them again. Her father had been dead for over two and a half months, a sudden heart attack the doctor had said, and only she and a few lovers of his poetry mourned his passing.

She'd closed the house and sold it, along with the furniture, keeping nothing save her own few personal possessions and her father's books of poems. Perhaps his work would have been better recognized if he had not been an impoverished Irish baron, or if he'd lived during a different time, for recently his poetry had been greatly overshadowed by that of William Wordsworth, Percy Bysshe Shelley, and Lord George Byron, who'd captured the attention of all the Ton.

Morgana knew that she would have to find work to support herself and had applied for several positions as a governess; but although she had much of the knowledge found in books, her slender fingers were clumsy on the pianoforte, and her attempts at painting watercolors would have been condemned by even the most uncritical eye. Music and art had not been her forte at the select seminary, and since it was in these that well-bred ladies of the day excelled, no one wanted to hire her.

Mister Tinsley, her father's best friend, said it was because she was so pretty.

"Aha," he grumbled when she told him of her failure to find work. "Those old cats are just afraid their sons will run off with you."

She laughed, because she did not consider herself pretty, although perhaps some might have thought her attractive. Her long hair was the color of molten copper and her eyes a brilliant emerald green, flecked with bits of gold and fringed with long lashes as sooty as the black smoke that poured from the London factories. Set under delicately arched jet brows, they were her only remarkable feature, Morgana thought ruefully. It was fashionable these days to have dark hair and eyes. She failed to appreciate the beauty of her aristocratic nose, the full poppy-colored lips which made men think that a wild, passionate nature lurked beneath her cool reserve, and the square cut of her jaw that gave such character to her face. She was tall and slender, willowy, a romantic would have said. Her rounded breasts and narrow waist were all that could have been desired, and her creamy white skin was unmarred by the freckles that seemed to plague so

19

many redheads. She was amused by the thought that someone might want to run off with a poor poet's daughter, and told Mister Tinsley so.

"Aha," he grumbled again. "A man would have to be a fool not to see what a prize you are. Why, if I were younger and didn't have a wife, those dandyish bucks wouldn't stand a chance."

"Now, Horace," his wife smiled indulgently. "You know it was all I could do to get you to the altar."

"Hmph!" he snorted, but there was a twinkle in his eye.

Morgana could see his mind was set in a stubborn pattern as usual, so she decided not to agitate him with further argument. But she still had not solved the dilemma of how she was to support herself. Her mother had no relatives that she knew of, and her father had severed all relations with his own, so she was at a loss as to how to continue. And then the letter came.

It was from her grandfather, a man she had never seen. He was the same stubborn old Irishman who'd become enraged when his youngest son became a poet, and further angered when that same son had run off with the young Englishwoman, her mother, instead of marrying an Irish girl of good breeding. He was the guardian who had turned his back on her father and cut him off without a penny. Morgana wasn't even aware that the old man knew she existed. But it seemed, somehow, that he did, for the letter was correctly addressed to her and contained quite explicit instructions. It read in part, "I find it difficult to believe that you will be able to support yourself under the circumstances. I have, therefore, arranged passage for you on the *Portsmouth*, which will be bound for Ireland within a few weeks. The enclosed money is for your travelling expenses. I shall expect your arrival soon." There was more, but the remainder was simply a stiff, formal apology about her father's death and a curt statement to the effect that she would find Ireland more to her liking than the dirty, crowded city of London. It was signed, "Fergus McShane, Duke of Shanetara."

Her first impulse had been to send the money back, to tell her grandfather that she had managed very well without him for twenty-one years and that she could continue to do so. However, since she was unable to obtain a job, Morgana soon doubted the wisdom of this course of action. Besides, she was curious. Her father had seldom mentioned Shanetara, the family home, and she secretly longed to see it and the man who'd cast her father out. From Connor McShane's few comments on the subject, Morgana had drawn a rather horrifying picture of a stern old man who bent people to his will and broke them if they did not follow his wishes. Her pride ached to reject his presumptuous command; but in the end her curiosity and fear of not finding employment won out, and she prepared herself for the journey ahead. It never occurred to her that it was highly unlikely that her grandfather could have learned of her father's death, nor that the handwriting in the letter was too steady to be that of a man in his eighties.

Morgana gazed around the empty room sadly. She would be sorry to leave this small house, for it was the only world she knew. But tomorrow the *Portsmouth* sailed for Ireland and she would be on it. The prospect both frightened and excited her. At last she would meet the man who'd cut her father off so cruelly, and perhaps she would lay to rest the ghosts of bitterness between them.

Lord Braddington Denby, the Earl of Brisbane, leaned back in his chair wearily. It had been a long night and he'd lost heavily, but then so had everyone else at the card table. Damn Keldara! The man was either an ivory turner or a devil, and since Rian McShane was his friend, Denby finally settled upon the latter explanation. One did not call the Earl of Keldara a cardsharp, even in one's own mind. Still, Keldara had held the bank all evening, Denby's empty pockets could attest to that. He drank the remaining drops of wine from his glass, then placed it on the table. Through the window, he could see the first pale pink streaks of dawn lighting the sky, and he stifled a yawn, wishing the two men at the table would finish their game so he could get to bed. If he didn't get some rest, he'd look positively haggard tomorrow—the rest of the day—he corrected himself hastily, glancing out the window again. He didn't understand how Chalmers and Keldara could still look as fresh as when they'd arrived, except, of course, for the faint lines of strain showing plainly upon Lord Chalmers's fat face as he pushed his remaining notes across the table.

"That does it for me, Keldara," Chalmers smiled sourly, for he had never liked the Earl. "I swear you've had the devil's own luck tonight."

"Nay, Chalmers," his lordship replied as he raked in his winnings. "The luck o' the Irish."

"Speaking of Irish," Sir Anthony Reginald roused himself from a drunken stupor. "I went to a funeral the other day. No, couldn't have been the other day because I was at the balloon ascension then. Must have been a couple of months ago."

The three men waited expectantly.

"Well," said Denby, exasperated. "What does that have to do with the price of tea in China?"

"Price of tea?" Sir Reginald rolled his bloodshot eyes. "Is it going up again? You must be a trifle bosky, Denby. I was speaking of funerals."

"For God's sake, man, what do funerals have to do with Ireland?" Lord Chalmers glared at the youth angrily, wondering why he had even invited himself to this gathering.

"Oh, fellow who died was a poet, from Ireland," Sir Reginald added hurriedly as the others stared at him impatiently. "Byron, Shelley and I went. Thought Keldara might have known the man, that's all."

"My dear boy," the Earl shook his ruffled cuffs back from his hands indolently. "Just because I come from the Emerald Isle doesn't mean I know everyone of my fellow countrymen any more than you know all of the chaps who went to Eton."

"Well, this fellow's name was Connor McShane," Reginald said sullenly. "Thought maybe he was a rela-

22

tive of yours or something. No offense meant, my lord."

It wouldn't do to offend Rian McShane who was a crack shot. Sir Reginald had no intention of ending his rather luxurious life in a duel at dawn.

Keldara studied the blushing youth with feigned disinterest. "I believe you may be right about his being a relative, Anthony, but I've never met the man. You say he's dead?"

Sir Reginald stared at him stupidly. "I just said I attended the funeral, didn't I?" his drunken state overcoming the awe he normally felt in the Earl's presence. "Pity. He left a lovely daughter. She was there, too, at the funeral, I mean. Don't know how she'll get on. Too pretty to be a governess, and 'tis unlikely someone will offer for her. Not much money, I understand. Probably wind up as some man's mistress. Thought about that myself, but something in those strange green eyes of hers stopped me cold. She'd drive the devil himself to drink or I miss my guess."

"Well, 'tis getting late, lads," Rian gathered up his winnings and made ready to go. "Thanks for the evening, Denby," he nodded to their host.

"Anytime, Rian," Lord Brisbane smothered another yawn. "See you at the boxing saloon tomorrow."

The Earl of Keldara walked the short distance to his house in Grosvenor Square in a thoughtful mood. So, Uncle Connor was dead. He suspected it would be a blow to his grandfather to learn that his last surviving son was gone without knowing that the old man had been sorry for casting him out. Hadn't he asked Rian to find out what had happened to his favorite child? Indeed, Rian had made private inquiries and kept his grandfather informed, although the old man refused to let Rian tell Connor, wouldn't even let him speak with his uncle. Rian felt sure grandfather would want Morgana, his cousin, at Shanetara now. Where else could she go? He thought about those green eyes of hers, for he had seen her several times in the past. Aye, she was a beauty all right. What a stir this was going to cause in the household!

The Earl of Keldara was an extremely complex man.

Vain, selfish, and arrogant, he had been raised by his grandfather after the death of his parents. A stern, unbending old man, Fergus McShane had overseen the growth and education of his favorite grandchild with a sharp, determined eye. At ten years of age, the boy had been brought to Shanetara after his father drowned at sea and his brokenhearted mother willed herself to death. Fergus had been greatly taken with the lad, who met his piercing eyes unflinchingly and refused to be cowed by numerous whippings in the passing years. Rian grew unruly and wild without the gentle hand of a female to guide him; and it could be said that Fergus encouraged this to a point, carefully instructing the boy in his own proud beliefs, dwelling particularly on the pride of the McShane name and ancestry, and doing his best to stamp out the gentle, tender side of Rian's personality inherited from his mother. Fergus never fully succeeded in this part of his plan, but Rian had so long suppressed any signs of softness that he usually forgot he had any at all.

When the Duke deemed it time, his grandson was sent to England to Eton for a proper education; and once there Rian fell in with the sons of the cream of English nobility. His good looks and way with the ladies would have made him many friends, but most of these he scorned as spiritless,, foppish creatures. Cards became a passion with him. He was fleeced at first, as most young men are, by various sharps and flats who lured him to gaming houses for no other purpose than to divest him of his money. But he was quick to learn in this school of hard knocks, and since he had a better head for liquor than most of his contemporaries, he soon became one of the most clever gamesters in London, a reputation his devilish good luck did much to enhance.

At eighteen, Rian killed his first man in a duel over a tavern wench, largely because his opponent was even a worse shot than he was. Rian himself was slightly wounded in the engagement, and was so angered at his lack of skill that he spent many hours at Manton's Shooting Gallery, Angelo's Fencing School, and Jackson's Boxing Saloon developing himself into an adversary worthy of any foe.

Two years later, with his usual run of good luck, he found himself master of a rather decrepit vessel won in an all-night game of piquet. He sailed her back to Ireland and disovered the joy of life on the sea. He found nothing more exhilarating than standing at the helm of his ship with the wind blowing high into her sails and the taste of salt spray upon his lips. His grandfather was alarmed at this new venture, recalling the manner of death of Rian's father; and Fergus spent many long hours trying to dissuade his grandson from the sea. Rian's mind was made up, however, and he could be as stubborn as the old man. Fergus McShane never made the same mistake twice. The crotchety head of the wild clan of McShanes realized that if he continued to harass his favorite grandchild about the ship, Rian would be lost to him forever, just as his son, Connor, had been.

The Earl prospered as a sailor and, in time, was able to sell his first vessel and purchase a fleet clipper ship, which he took great pains to have outfitted especially with various forms of armaments. He called her the *Sorceress,* and she became the only mistress he ever loved.

Now, at thirty-two, he was cool, reckless, and accustomed to getting his own way in life. With his handsome face, the mocking charm he'd acquired over the years, and his reputation for being deadly in a duel and a dangerous man to cross, he'd gambled and forced his way into London society. He was generally bored, except on the sea, and the fact that escapades undertaken to relieve such boredom tainted his name with scandal seldom bothered him. He had many enemies and so few friends he could count them on one hand. George Bryan Brummell he liked for his droll humor and Lord Alvanley for his wit. Although both of these men were foppish dandies in the extreme, they opened doors for him. Anyone on Beau Brummell's blacklist was cut immediately by all of society; anyone was accepted who appeared in his good books. Sir Anthony Reginald was a rather puppyish youth, but could be counted on to afford a great deal of amusement with his pranks. And Lord Brisbane was Rian's closest friend. Denby and he had attended Eton together; and while Denby often shook his head over Rian's dangerous escapades, his own reputation was not untarnished. These friends, while few, would back Rian to the death.

Rian asked nothing from any man, however, and used all women who were foolish enough to love him, carelessly, tossing them aside when he had finished with them. He had no wife and wished for none, despising the coy beauties he took to bed as bloodsucking schemers, and disdaining the simpering chits just out of the school-room as being unworthy of his notice. The London dowagers termed him a hard case and a dangerous rake; and matchmaking mamas were doomed to disappointment should they set their daughters' caps for him (which they often did, because he was known to be one of the richest men in London). Rian escaped their clutches one and all, for he valued his lazy, restless freedom; and he had never been in love.

When he reached his house in Grosvenor Square, the Earl sat down at his desk and composed a letter to Morgana, signing his grandfather's name, then wrote a short note to the old man explaining the circumstances and his actions. It never occurred to him that his cousin Morgana might disregard his instructions. He was too accustomed to being obeyed. After that, he poured himself a glass of brandy and climbed the stairs to his bedroom, a wolfish, amused smile on his face at the thought of his grandfather's reaction to this night's work.

The Earl would have been pleased had he been at Shanetara to witness Fergus McShane's reaction to his grandson's letters; for although Rian respected his grandfather, the two men were almost too much alike in their iron wills, and were always trying to best each other. The Duke of Shanetara turned a mottled red and his rage knew no bounds. Had Rian been present, the old man would have been sorely tempted to lay his riding crop about the sides of the Earl's breeches. As it was, he subjected his entire household to an ill-tempered tirade without divulging his reasons. Fergus McShane was, however, able to see the humor of the situation and took great delight in informing them all that they should soon have another mouth to feed. The McShane family must now accept the fact that there was one more relative to be cut in on the old man's fortune. All except Rosamunde viewed Morgana's impending arrival with a sharp sense of dismay. Fergus's daughter was slightly mad and could not be thought to count anyway. The general reaction delighted the Duke, who took a great deal of pleasure in holding the terms of his will over his family's heads, forcing them to jump through whatever hoops he cared to hold.

Fergus McShane was out of place in the nineteenth century. He was a throwback to a time the rest of England would have preferred to forget. He was dismayed that he could not carry out his life in the manner of William McShane, his ancestor who'd built the fortress of Shanetara and kidnapped a bride to grace its long halls. Fergus ruled his domain like a feudal lord and was a notorious pinchpenny. He was filled with bitterness over the deaths of four of his sons and the desertion of his youngest, the fifth son. He thought his daughter a silly twit, and three of his grandsons a pack of fools. Only for Rian and his grandson Colin did the old man maintain any hopes whatsoever; and it was only Rian that he really respected and admired.

The old man longed to see his favorite grandchild married and producing strong, sturdy heirs, but so far Fergus's hopes had been unrealized. He had also wanted Rian to manage the McShane estates, which were vast and many, but his rebellious grandson had declared flatly that these were his cousin Trevor's responsibility and inheritance, not his. Since Fergus thought Trevor a pompous fool, he reluctantly allowed his grandson Patrick to assume the reins of management instead, being only mildly comforted by the belief that Patrick was slightly less a fool than Trevor.

Fergus, however, had never been one to shirk his own duties. Since there was nothing he could do about the impending arrival of his granddaughter, the Duke decided, only out of curiosity, he told himself, that he would meet her. Then he soothed his ruffled feathers by assuring himself that if he did not like her, he would send her packing posthaste! He was too proud to admit, even to himself, that he had suffered greatly over disowning his youngest son; or that he secretly hoped, once his initial rage had subsided, that he might in some way atone for his hasty and regrettable actions.

The docks were a bustle of activity when Morgana arrived to board the *Portsmouth*. Mister and Mistress Tinsley had graciously consented to drive her to the harbor to see her safely off, and Mistress Tinsley was in tears as her husband unloaded Morgana's trunk and made the final arrangements with the ship's captain.

"You will take care, won't you, child?" she patted Morgana's hand worriedly. "I don't like to see you going off like this to a strange place and relatives you've never even met."

"Please don't worry, Susan," Morgana replied reassuringly. "I'm sure I'll be just fine, and I promise to write as soon as I've arrived."

"Now, now, Susan," Mister Tinsley joined them. "I've spoken to the captain and he's given me his personal word of honor that he'll look after our little lass."

"Horace, I can't thank you and Susan enough for all you've done for me," Morgana could feel her own tears beginning to sting her eyes.

"No thanks necessary, lass," the elderly man cleared his throat gruffly. " 'Tis the least we can do for Connor's own dear daughter."

Morgana embraced them both warmly, then ran up the gangplank. She waved to them until the shore faded at last and she could see them no more, then she went below to her small bunk.

Rian waited in his curricle at the wharf and watched as Morgana boarded the *Portsmouth*. The greys fretted nervously, champing at the bit, for they were not used to standing still for any length of time. He hoped his grandfather would not be too angry about what he'd done. Aye, that Morgana was a beauty, he thought again. Though she had those copper locks pulled back severely, she could not disguise the loveliness of her face. He waited until the ship left the harbor, sailing slowly down the Thames toward the open sea before turning the horses homeward. Louis, the Earl's sharp-faced tiger, did not understand why his lordship had sat for such a length of time gazing out over the docks, but he was used to his master's whims and asked no questions.

Once home, Rian went upstairs and opened the sea chest he always kept with him. Inside lay a bolt of cloth that must have been spun for a princess. Vivid green silk interwoven with the finest of gold threads, it shimmered when held to the light like a thousand stars falling into the stormy waters of the ocean. He had intended selling the material to Madame Leroux, who owned one of the more famous dress shops in London, for he knew that the woman would pay a fantastic price for such a bolt of cloth. But now he knew there was only one woman who could ever wear such a startling shade of green. He sighed and dropped the fabric back into the sea chest. Morgana would look lovely in the Chinese silk, he had no doubt of that. He hoped she made it to Ireland safely.

Later, he dressed and called for his curricle again. He was engaged to dine with Lady Cecily Brooksworth, a recent widow and his latest mistress. Of late he'd grown rather weary of Cecily's increasing demands and pouting mouth. She knew a hundred ways of pleasing a man, especially in bed, but Rian was becoming bored with her as he soon did with all of the other women who flew into his arms like bees to a honey pot. His lips curved into a sardonic smile. He had no doubt that Cecily hoped to entice him into marrying her despite the fact that she adamantly claimed she would never wed again. But the

Earl still valued his freedom; many a broken heart and matchmaking mama could attest to that!

Cecily pouted prettily when he told her he was returning to Ireland for a time, but she did not make a dreadful scene as he'd feared she might. Cecily was too clever for that. She said merely that she would miss him and that she hoped someday he would see fit to take her along. She knew he had other women, but she was convinced none pleased or attracted him as she did, and she felt secure in the knowledge that he had danced attendance on her far longer than he had on any other woman. She intended to marry him, and spoiled Cecily Brooksworth had always gotten what she wanted.

Still, she felt rather uneasy when he left her bed before dawn, something he had not done in months. Rian did not tell her it was because he had not dreamed of Cecily's dark hair and eyes, but copper curls and eyes the color of the Emerald Isle. Morgana had began to haunt him even then.

The voyage was not unpleasant, but Morgana soon tired of the swaying motion of the ship and the cramped quarters. They had been at sea for a couple of weeks and she had been sick only the very first few days. The captain had been most courteous, allowing Morgana and the other passengers, who were bound for the States, to go above deck whenever the weather permitted. Salt stung her lips where the sea sprayed lightly upon her face as she stood at the rail, eager to come to her journey's end. How she longed to plant her feet upon solid ground again!

Morgana got her wish some days later when they sighted the coast of Ireland. Her first impression of the land was that it had been aptly named, for at first glance it was as green as an unripened wheat field. The ship docked at the small town of Kilshannon, not far from Dingle in the southwestern part of Ireland. She could see Brandon Hill towering in the distance, though she did not then know its name. The captain told her that ships seldom docked there, but that it was the port nearest her final destination. She walked down the gangplank, for the waters along that particular coastal area were deep enough that it was not necessary for her to be rowed ashore, and watched as her trunk was unloaded, trying to still the nervousness she felt inside. She did not know if anyone would be sent to meet her, for she had made no reply to her grandfather's letter, and she did not know how to proceed. Morgana glanced around the docks anxiously, searching for a familiar face, although she knew no one in Ireland. She supposed it was just something one did unconsciously in a strange place.

The village, although small, was busy. Its docks were lined with warehouses; and there was a general store, a church (which also served as the school), and an inn which housed the local tavern. Several horses and shoddy gigs littered the road, but most people trudged on foot through the mire of the unpaved streets. Evidently it had recently rained. Some people eyed her curiously; but, after all, as the captain had told her, Kilshannon was one of the few ports in this part of Ireland and it was certainly not that unusual for the villagers to see a vessel moored in the harbor. So intent was she on her perusal of the town that Morgana did not notice the man who approached her slowly.

"Lady McShane?"

She turned, startled at the unaccustomed form of address. "Yes?"

"I be Kerr O'Malley. Lord Shanetara sent me to fetch ye."

"How do you do, Mister O'Malley? I'm so glad you've come," Morgana said, extending her hand only to have the outstretched gesture ignored as the man turned abruptly and asked,

"This yer trunk?"

She nodded, slightly puzzled by his behavior, and he dragged the trunk to a nearby landaulet.

"I'm afraid it's rather heavy," she apologized as he struggled with the case, and tried to offer her assistance, but he heaved it in with little trouble. The wiry little man was stronger than he appeared.

The ride was rough and jolting, and Morgana studied the uncommunicative man who sat in front of her, having learned little more than his name and that he'd been employed by her grandfather for many years. His weathered face was one of those which shows no time. He could have been forty or seventy, but his hands on the reins were steady and his eyes keen and clear.

"Is it far?" Morgana asked, hesitantly breaking the silence.

"There be Shanetara now," he answered, indicating the direction with an uplifted hand.

The great house loomed above them, dark and foreboding upon the rocky crags overlooking the ocean. It was quite old and sprawling; the original house, enlarged by wings that had been added through the years, was now a mass of strangely mixed architectural styles. The front was lined with long, narrow casement windows, which seemed to peer out at her like eyes behind the slits of a mask. Several towers rose from the places where the massive eaves joined, and a balcony ran all the way around the building. Great trees overhung parts of the roof, adding their shade to the long, dark shadows Shanetara cast over the land in the morning sun. For a moment, Morgana felt as though they had reached out to embrace her and she shivered as she felt an icy tingle run up her spine.

"It's very impressive," she said almost defiantly.

"Aye," Kerr O'Malley was suddenly talkative. " 'Tis been the home o' generations o' McShanes, and a proud and stubborn lot they are. Ain't a one o' them ever fergot its heritage nor left its shadows till yer father did."

He stopped abruptly, as though he had said too much; and Morgana finished the remainder of her journey uncomfortably aware of his disapproving silence and the stubborn set of his jaw. So that was the reason for his lack of communication. He blamed her father for a youthful, impulsive action which had split the family. It seemed that in place of her father she was to bear the brunt of Mister O'Malley's displeasure. If his attitude was any indication of the way her grandfather felt, Morgana was sure she would be unwelcome at the great, looming house, and shuddered again, wishing she had not come.

The landaulet rumbled to a halt in front of the heavy wooden doors of Shanetara. Kerr O'Malley helped Morgana alight, then turned his attention toward her trunk. This time, she did not make the mistake of offering him her assistance. He planted the case on the doorstep and rapped sharply on the brass knocker. She heard the patter of light footsteps within; then the door was flung open wide by a pleasantly plump woman whose roundness belied the lightness of her feet.

"Faith and begorra!" the woman exclaimed, her cherubic face beaming cheerfully. "If ye ain't the spitting image o' yer father. Come in, me lady. We've been expecting ye. Did ye have a good journey? I guess ye'll be wanting to see yer room and freshen up a bit right away," she rambled on brightly, seeming to expect no answer. "Kerr O'Malley, ye take that trunk up to Lady McShane's room this minute. What's come o'er ye, man, standing there like one o' yer old horses kicked ye in the head?" She turned to Morgana with a sigh. "Sure and I tell ye, sometimes I think that man o' mine ain't got a lick o' sense!"

"Mister O'Malley is your husband?" Morgana asked as she watched the elderly man haul the heavy burden up a long curving flight of stairs.

"Aye, and a fine one he is, too, in spite o' his faults. But don't ye 'Mistress O'Malley' me, now. Sure and ye kin call me Mollie, same as the lads."

"The lads?" Morgana asked, absolutely amazed by this woman who was the last person she would have expected to find at Shanetara.

"Why, aye, me lady. Yer cousins, all five o' them, and a handsome lot if'n I do say so meself. Course, Lord Trevor's married. His wife is a frail little thing," Mollie sniffed. "Not at all like ye," her sharp, but friendly eyes took in every detail of Morgana's appearance. "Ye'll be meeting them all later, I expect, except fer Lord Rian, o' course. His ship ain't due fer some time yet."

Morgana tried to grasp all of this quickly. It seemed that she, who had almost always been alone, suddenly possessed an immense family. The visions she'd had of residing at Shanetara with an embittered old man gave way to dreams of a large happy household filled with noisy children and gay laughter. Perhaps it would not be as bad as she'd imagined.

"Are there other relatives?" she questioned, not wanting to pry, but eager to learn more about this house.

"There's yer aunt, o' course. She's anxious to see ye. Connor was her favorite brother, ye know."

No, Morgana didn't know, but she wasn't going to tell Mollie that. Evidently the woman thought her father had told her all about Shanetara, and, for some reason, Morgana didn't want Mollie to know he had seldom spoken about his childhood home and that she knew almost nothing of that period of his life.

"Well," Mollie puffed as they completed the long climb up the stairs. "Here we be."

Morgana's rooms were lovely in forest green and gold. There was a small sitting room and a larger bedroom dominated by a massive canopy bed. Her trunk stood in the center of the circular walls.

"Why, we must be in the tower," she mused aloud, remembering the tall garrets she'd seen rising up from the wings of the house.

"Aye, yer grandfather chose these rooms himself fer ye. I expect he'll send fer ye when he's ready. If'n ye need anything else, just ring," Mollie indicated the bell rope. "I'll send up some tea in a bit."

She stood there for a moment, as though inviting Morgana to confide in her, but the girl kept still. Morgana's almost solitary life had made her naturally reticent; and Mollie, for all her friendly interest, was still a stranger. Morgana had no wish to be chattered about among the servants, though it was doubtless inevitable, and so maintained her reserve.

"Thank you, Mistress—uh—Mollie, you've been most kind."

"Well, 'tis the least I kin do," the woman offered

34

grudgingly when she saw Morgana did not mean to pursue the conversation.

Morgana moved across to the window when Mollie left. It looked out upon rocky crags which stretched into the purple moors and marshlands, and finally the grey sea. It was a coldly cruel and savage scene, though beautiful in a strange, wild way. She wondered why her grandfather had chosen this room for her. If he thought he would intimidate her, he would soon learn that she was Connor McShane's daughter and that she could be as cold and hard as those rocky crags when necessary.

She set about unpacking her trunk and hanging her clothes in the large closet, the space making her few dresses appear even more meager. She put her father's books on the small night table and laid her mother's brush and comb upon the dresser. Splashing some of the water from the small pitcher into the basin, she washed her face and hands, then let her hair down, brushed it, and wound it back into the bun she wore at the nape of her neck. After that, there didn't seem to be anything else for her to do, so she walked back to the window, lost in her thoughts.

A quiet tap at the door interrupted her silent musing. She opened it to admit a slight girl with short dark hair and the biggest, bluest eyes Morgana had ever seen. The girl dropped a small curtsey.

"I'm Bridget, me lady. I've brought yer tea."

The girl set the tray down and poured a cup for Morgana, surveying her with unveiled curiosity.

"Did ye have a pleasant trip, me lady?"

"Why, yes, thank you, I did," Morgana sipped the hot brew.

"That's good," the girl smiled. "Lord Rian says that sometimes the sea is rather choppy and apt to make unaccustomed travellers sick. I'm glad ye suffered none o' that discomfert!"

"No, after a brief, initial illness, I remained perfectly healthy much to the disgust of a stout Methodist woman who was on her way to America to join her husband," Morgana warmed to the impish grin, some of her reserve receding. "Conveniently, she became ill the first day out and I was spared the necessity of listening to her rather strong religious convictions. I'm sure she thought my soul was a lost cause," Morgana was surprised to find herself laughing slightly. She'd scarcely smiled since her father's death.

"Aye, some o' those people do have queer beliefs," Bridget nodded knowingly, for she herself was a Catholic.

Morgana could tell Bridget was yearning to ask her all sorts of questions, but was trying very hard to refrain. Bridget was about her own age, and Morgana had had few friends in London, so it was rather a novelty for her to be able to converse with a contemporary.

"Have you worked here long?" she asked.

"Just about a year, me lady."

"How do you like Shanetara, Bridget?"

" 'Tis a lovely old place, me lady, and me job ain't hard. Mistress O'Malley makes this house run like clockwork."

"I can imagine. She seems like a most capable woman," Morgana replied, remembering Mollie's sharp eyes.

"Aye, that she is," Bridget agreed. "I'm so glad ye've come, me lady," she exclaimed in a sudden burst of confidence. "We thought at first ye might refuse yer grandfather's invitation."

"It was hardly an invitation, Bridget. More like a command, I'd say. However, that is neither here nor there. After my father died, I was unable to support myself, so here I am. I really had little choice in the matter."

"Well, I don't know about that, me lady. Sure and there must have been many men who would have jumped at the chance to marry someone as beautiful as ye. But I'm glad ye decided to come to Ireland instead. Kyla, the other maid, was sure ye'd be very prim and proper, and would most likely look down yer nose at us, being the poor Irish lasses that we are. No, I told her, ye mark me words, Lady McShane will be as fine a lady as anyone could hope fer, not like Lady Lindsey Joyce, who I used to work fer over at Letterick. I'm so happy I was right," she clapped her hands together gaily.

"I'm glad you're pleased, Bridget," Morgana told her, choosing to overlook this rather artless speech and much amused by the girl's almost childlike attitude. She was sure Bridget probably believed in leprechauns as well.

"Oh!" Bridget's hand flew to her mouth. "I'm supposed to take ye up to see yer grandfather right away, as soon as ye've finished yer tea," she conceded. "I clean fergot, I've been so busy talking. Mistress O'Malley is ferever saying me tongue runs away with me. Oh, dear. I do hope the old man won't take a pet. He kin be such a tartar sometimes, begging yer pardon, me lady."

"I don't find that at all surprising," Morgana responded dryly, remembering the commanding tone of the letter she'd received, and ignoring Bridget's out-of-place criticism of her relative. The girl was, after all, very young. Morgana turned and followed her down the long hall.

She didn't see her grandfather immediately. The draperies were closed and the room was in darkness, so it took her eyes a moment to adjust to the lack of light. She was startled when a gruff voice bellowed, "Well, don't just stand there, lass! Come in so I can take a look at you!"

Morgana followed the sound of his words to the large four-poster bed in the middle of the room. She moved closer. The man propped up among the pillows looked like an older version of her father. He had the same clear eyes, but his face was lined with years of struggle and bitterness. His bushy white brows were drawn together fiercely as he watched her.

"So," he spoke after completing his careful perusal of her. "You're Morgana McShane."

"Yes," she replied, returning his gaze steadily, although she found the piercing stare rather disconcerting, and waited for him to speak again.

Had she known him better, Morgana would have seen by the odd smile which quirked at the corners of his downturned lips that he was pleased by her appearance. But as she did not know him and the smile was fleeting, she could only assume that he was amused by her shabby dress and reduced circumstances; and she stiffened her spine slightly with perverse pride. This pleased the old man even more. He was reminded suddenly of another McShane, his grandson Rian, who had met his eyes so unflinchingly and stiffened his own spine as well.

"Hmph!" the old man spoke. "I'd not claim you as kin if I'd had my way," he snorted. "Your father left this house of his own free will. What makes you think we should welcome his daughter back into it?"

"I thought nothing of the sort," Morgana answered calmly, keeping her eyes on his levelly, wondering if the old man was trying to bait her, and beginning to feel most uncomfortable in his presence. "It was you who sent for me, if I recall correctly."

"Aye, well that may be. Sure and I can't have a McShane begging in the streets like some common wench. But mind, that doesn't mean I have to like you!"

Morgana clutched the sides of her gown to keep her hands from trembling. He was horrid! More horrid than she'd even imagined. How could she live here? Hot, angry words rose to her lips, but she suppressed them, saying coldly, "I don't really care whether you like me or not. If you don't want me here, all you have to do is send me back to London." She was at once secretly hopeful and yet mortified at the same time at the thought. She would have to go to work in one of those awful factories. She saw herself turning into one of the scarecrows who scavenged among the garbage pails, their wracking coughs the result of working conditions in the dirty London factories.

"Who said anything about sending you back?" Fergus McShane snapped. "You just got here. I can't afford to be throwing money away on your whims! Faith! You'll stay put until I decide what to do with you, lass, do you hear? I won't have you thwarting me the way your father did!"

"Is that why you brought me here, to get even with

38

my father?" Morgana's voice chilled to ice, and she did not know that her eyes were flashing with sparks of anger. "I shan't give you the pleasure of that opportunity. I'm afraid we have both made a mistake and I shall be leaving as soon as possible."

To her amazement, her grandfather cackled wryly. "Touché, I'm glad to see you're not a spineless thing like Fionna. 'Tis good to know you've inherited the Mc-Shanes's Irish temper at least, even if it is hidden beneath the coldness of your English blood. Whist! I can't abide milktoasts!"

"Fionna?" Morgana asked lamely, thrown off guard by this sudden change in tactics.

"Trevor's wife, a drab, colorless lass if I ever did see one. You'll meet her tonight at dinner. I think you'll agree with my summation of her character."

Morgana stood there stupidly for a moment, feeling as though she had burned her bridges behind her without really understanding how it had happened. Then her grandfather spurred her to action by saying, "Well, run along now, lass. Don't stand there like you've lost your wits!"

"Certainly not!" she retorted dryly, and left the room without another word, glad to escape his piercing eyes and sharp voice.

The bell for dinner had rung and Morgana was a little late because she hadn't realized what it was at first. She'd considered having a tray sent up to her room, using fatigue from her journey as an excuse, but something told her that her grandfather would immediately see this for the cowardice it was, and she was not going to let him have the pleasure of thinking he'd bested her in their earlier encounter. She would go to dinner and show him the stuff of which Connor McShane's daughter was made!

She heard voices as she descended the winding staircase, but they broke off abruptly when she entered the room. Her grandfather barked, "You're late!" and proceeded to introduce her.

Her cousin Trevor seemed rather stiff-necked and

pompous. Morgana judged him to be about forty years of age. He was the main heir to the estate, being the oldest son of grandfather's eldest son, and would become the Duke of Shanetara upon her grandfather's death. Currently, he was Earl of Shaughnessy, another one of the McShane estates. Though his waistline was thickening and his hairline receding, he was still fairly good-looking. For the time being, Trevor was content to play politics, maintaining a seat in the House at Dublin. He had, on several occasions, he informed her, enjoyed the honor of conversing with Wolfe Tone, Henry Grattan, and no less than William Pitt himself.

His wife, Fionna, Morgana was surprised to find, was a young girl about half Trevor's age. She appeared to be a poor mousey woman with little to say or recommend her, but then Trevor rarely let her utter a word. Her looks were plain, to say the least, and because of her nondescript character, it was easy to forget she was present.

Trevor's brother, Gerald, was slightly younger, a big, brawny man, thirty-six years old, obviously Irish, and somewhat drunk as well. Morgana was soon to learn that it was his usual condition. He had been a lieutenant in the British army stationed in Spain during the Peninsular War, but had been sent home when a gunshot wound left him lame in one leg. He'd been drinking ever since, and relied on a small pension and the goodwill of his brother and grandfather for support.

Morgana liked her cousin Patrick immediately. His manner was so engaging and fun-loving that she soon felt more at ease, especially when he winked at her and made a face as if to tell her he knew exactly how she felt. Patrick was twenty-seven, and not as tall as Trevor or Gerald, but nicely built. His clothes were well tailored, and although not as dignified as Trevor's nor as expensive, they were infinitely better than the sloppy garb Gerald wore. He was Viscount of Blackwood, an estate in England he had inherited as the only surviving male on his mother's side of the family. It earned him a modest income, since much of the estate was tied up in an entail, but he preferred to live at Shanetara, for he loved Ireland even though he owned no property there.

Morgana really didn't observe much about Colin. Perhaps it was because he sat so quietly, almost broodingly. She noted only that he was younger than she, only nineteen, and had one of those beautiful faces that, in a man, can only be described as poetic. His skin was light and shown off to advantage by his unruly black locks, and his deep brown eyes were fringed with dark lashes that contrasted sharply against his paleness. Colin, she would learn, had virtually no expectations and was, like her, totally dependent on their grandfather for his livelihood. He would probably have to go into the ministry, a prospect that dismayed him. He would much rather have gone into the military like Gerald; but his grandfather doted on him and, after Gerald's crippling injury, had refused to allow him to enlist.

Her Aunt Rosamunde, however, caught and held Morgana's attention, for she was the first one actually to approach her with affection, hugging her and murmuring that she hoped they would soon become friends. Morgana grasped her hand tightly, fighting back the tears which stung her eyes, for her aunt so closely resembled her late father. Rosamunde must have been beautiful in her youth, and was still handsome in her sixties, although the fading red hair was streaked with grey and the white skin lined with fine wrinkles. She was very delicate and graceful, and each move she made had been carefully studied for its effect. Morgana could imagine her sitting before a mirror, practicing, in her younger days.

As Morgana had been told earlier by Mollie, the entire family was not present. Her cousin Rian, whom she gathered was a sea captain, was missing.

"Not that it's his only enterprise," Trevor dutifully informed her. "He's also the Earl of Keldara, a title he obtained in the most disgusting fashion imaginable. He actually won it gambling! Can you believe that? This poor fellow wagered everything he had and lost, so King George ordered him to turn over his estates and title to

41

Rian to pay off the debt. There was a horrible scandal because the former Earl committed suicide upon losing his fortune. Rian's a heartless devil!"

"That will be enough, Trevor!" grandfather reprimanded him sharply. "No, Morgana, the dear lad's ship hasn't put into port yet, but we expect him to show up soon. 'Tis a shame he missed your arrival, but I know he would extend his warmest greetings to you were he here."

Morgana thanked her grandfather, feeling oddly ill at ease at the sudden mocking smile which had crossed his lips at the mention of Rian, and wondered privately how much of Trevor's stiff prattle she would be able to endure.

Bridget happened to pass by in the hall at just that moment and Morgana saw the girl's eyes widen with surprise as Patrick winked at her broadly. Morgana happened to catch his attention a minute later, and he grinned ruefully when he realized that she'd seen what he'd done.

The family did not hesitate to pummel Morgana unmercifully with all kinds of questions. They seemed to be flying at her from all directions, but Morgana tried to answer as many as she could, wondering if she would ever get a chance to eat her dinner.

"Yes, I do know how to ride, Gerald, but I've never been hunting. I'm sure it's a capital sport, but I don't think I want to learn, thank you. I don't enjoy seeing things killed."

"Oh, come now, cousin," he chided. "Surely they have fox hunting in London, or at least at some of the surrounding estates."

"Yes, I imagine they do, but I was never in a position to mix with the Ton, so I've lived a relatively quiet life."

"Your father was a poet, wasn't he, cousin?" This from Colin, who'd been fairly silent up until now.

"We do not discuss Morgana's father in this house, young man," grandfather broke in angrily.

"I believe that's a rather unrealistic idea, grandfather, in light of the fact that Morgana is here now, and that Uncle Connor has recently passed away. I find it ridiculous to think that you would continue to harbor a grudge against a dead man. I would like to hear Morgana's answer, if she cares to reply."

"Of course I'll answer you, Colin," Morgana spoke hurriedly, anxious to defend her father before her grandfather had a chance to retort. "My father was a very fine poet, although not extremely well known in England. We always felt that the success of Percy Shelley and Lord Byron overhadowed my father's own chances at popularity."

"Hmph!" Fergus McShane snorted. "Your father was a complete failure. Now I don't want to hear another word about him. If we are to get along in this house, I won't have his name mentioned again, and that's that!" the old man snapped heatedly. "And as for you," he turned to Colin. "You're a disobedient whelp. I'll thank you to have a little more respect for your elders, especially when I'm your only means of support. I'll hear your apology now, or I'll not give you the advance on your next quarter's allowance which you asked me for this morning."

Colin trembled and pouted angrily at this public dressing down, but he did manage to choke out an apology. After that, everyone at the table felt a little uncomfortable and they were all relieved when Rosamunde gave the signal for the women to retire, leaving the gentlemen to their port.

"Dear, dear Connor's child," she said when they'd gathered around the fire in the salon, for although it was spring, the weather still turned chilly in the evenings. "I'm so glad you've come. I'm sorry about father's behavior. He won't hear Connor's name mentioned, you know, since the scandal, so we mustn't upset him. But I was truly sorry to learn of my brother's death, child. He was always my favorite in the family. I did so hope that I would see him once again, but, alas, it was not to be," she paused dramatically, and Morgana began to see that her aunt was slightly unhinged in a vague, dreamy sort of way. "I fear I wasn't a very good sister to him, being the

43

coward that I am. I did so want to write, but father wouldn't hear of it after Connor threw his lands over in that fashion to become a poet. But, come, we must speak of more pleasant subjects." She patted the sofa beside her. "Sit here, dear, and let me look at you. My hair was that color once. Ah, 'tis sadness itself, growing old," she laughed ruefully. "Why, when I was young . . ."

The general atmosphere brightened considerably upon the arrival of the men, but Morgana could not help but guess that she had been the topic of a somewhat lively discussion over their port. Grandfather stumped over to a lovely inlaid chessboard and began arranging the black and white marble pieces for a game. Trevor went to sit opposite the old man, but Fergus waved him away.

"Nay, Trevor. I'm in no mood for your unimaginative attempts at battle tonight. I would have a more stimulating adversary, if you please. Do you know the game, lass?" he asked, turning to Morgana.

"Why, yes," she replied, for she had often played in the evenings with her father. "But I fear I would hardly provide you with an interesting match. Surely one of my cousins can give you a better game."

"Nonsense!" he rapped his cane sharply upon the floor. "Colin takes too long to make his moves and—"

"I'm only trying to make them correctly, grandfather," the youth interrupted defensively.

"Don't interrupt your elders, lad," the old man chided him. "Gerald plays heedlessly and Patrick hasn't had his mind on the game lately. Come, lass, surely you're not afraid of losing," he coaxed slyly.

"Of course not," she spoke, stung by the thought, and rose to take the place opposite him. "I shall do my best to win."

They settled down to the business of opening moves, Morgana having chosen the black men. The rest of the family talked softly in the background so as not to distract their attention. Two hours later, Morgana found herself checkmated.

"A game well played, lass, but not good enough to

44

win," Fergus concluded. "Sure and 'tis amazing how much you can learn about someone over a game of chess. You haven't yet learned how to sacrifice for gain. If you'd traded your queen for mine, you would have had the advantage, since I had only one rook to your two. It would be interesting, indeed, to know what else lies beneath your outward calm," his eyes seemed to burn right through her. "I should like to see you play Rian, lass," the old man cackled as though pleased by the notion.

Morgana chose to ignore his remarks upon her personality. "I concede the fact that you are a better strategist, and I perhaps play hastily, with no thought to sacrifice; but I am quick to learn, and someday I shall win," she ended.

"We shall see," he challenged her softly, but she was aware that it would not be only a chessboard over which they battled. He had been testing her. His mind was keen, even if he was slightly eccentric. She would have to stay alert and on her guard until she discovered what it was that he wanted from her.

She lay in bed that night, sleep escaping her, reviewing what she had learned of the household. Trevor and Fionna did not live at Shanetara, but close by at Shaughnessy Bay, Trevor's estate. There was also Kilshannon Hall, the Dower House, where Rosamunde could have lived had she so desired. Evidently she preferred to endure grandfather's continual harassment rather than spend her days in solitude. Patrick and Colin stayed at Shanetara, as did Gerald, Fergus not having seen fit to bestow any estates upon them; but Gerald spent most of his nights at the inn in Kilshannon, dallying with the local barmaids. There were no children here and neither laughter nor love. Her future with the family did not offer a cheering prospect, but as she finally drifted into an uneasy sleep, Morgana wondered if perhaps Rian, the sea captain, the gambler, the Earl of Keldara, would be different from the others.

Chapter Two

Morgana's days soon settled into a pattern. She was free to come and go as she pleased, as she had no particular chores since the house was well staffed; and for the first time in her life she found herself with time hanging heavy on her hands. She used these hours to explore her new surroundings and to become better acquainted with her relatives. Rosamunde and she soon became fast friends, although she often found her aunt's dramatics a little trying; and she learned quickly, as she'd promised him, how to fend off her grandfather's occasional verbal digs. Patrick proved to be invaluable in helping her adjust to Ireland. He was always eager to take her out in the landaulet, to act as her guide over the rugged land, and to drive her into town should she so desire. Trevor, also, stiffly offered to perform these duties, but Morgana found she could not tolerate his stuffy pompousness for very long.

Ireland was a beautiful country, with its wild mountainous crags and grassy marshes. Lough Donareen was not far from Shanetara and she could see it often during the day, its still surface reflecting the blue of the sky like a mirror. Once Patrick drove Morgana over to Shaughnessy, the small scattering of huts near Shaughnessy Bay where most of her grandfather's tenants lived. There was only one main road along which the shoddy shacks straggled pathetically. Their inhabitants, dirty and unkempt, watched listlessly from doorways.

"I wanted you to see a typical Irish town," Patrick told her on the way back. "Kilshannon and Dingle are havens compared to most of the villages around."

"But why doesn't grandfather do something for these people?" Morgana asked. "Surely he could help them."

"Faith, Morgana! Have you not seen what a pinchpenny he is? He cares for no one but himself, with the possible exceptions of Colin and Rian. Aye, Rian is the only one of us who knows how to handle the old man. He does the best he can with grandfather, but even that isn't enough, what with England down our throats and those damn Napoleonic Wars going on, not to mention our own United Irishmen and other radical, underground organizations. The Catholics are fighting for freedom and the tenants want to own the land they farm, but grandfather has some crazy idea of being a feudal lord and refuses to part with even an inch of soil! Why, although he inherited our fathers' titles upon their deaths, he refuses to give Colin and me even a complementary consideration, although he grudgingly allowed Trevor to assume his title. The old man owns every piece of land as far as your eye can see," Patrick lifted his hand in a sweeping gesture.

"Besides, under the law, Catholics cannot inherit property," he continued. "We are all Anglicans, you know. The tenants have no hopes, no dreams, they merely exist. They live for the meager sustenance they draw from the potato patches they farm on Shanetara soil."

"But, Patrick," she asked. "Don't you wish Ireland were free of English rule?"

"Of course I do, but 'tis treason to talk about it. Besides, King George will never agree to it as long as he lives. He refused even to listen to Pitt's suggestions about improving conditions here. At night, the men go into Kilshannon and drink poteen. They discuss freedom and everything else under the sun. Then disagreements break out and there are faction fights."

"What are those?"

"Fights between the clans. Generally, 'tis the Kennedys and the O'Haras. They hang together, these families. If a Kennedy takes an O'Hara woman, then a debt is owed and must be paid; otherwise the pride of the family name is at stake. Usually, there's a killing. More than one poor Irishman has fled to the States to avoid being hanged for murder."

"Why, that's horrible," Morgana said. "Isn't anything done about it?"

"Grandfather usually acts as the mediator and judge, and the clans try to abide by his decision; but sometimes tempers run hot and high, and then there's trouble."

Morgana shivered under the sun. "Are we safe to ride out like this? What if some of them attacked us?"

He looked at her and laughed, but then realized that she was actually serious and apologized. "There's no need for you to be afraid, cousin. There isn't an Irishman in the county who would lay a hand on you. He'd be dead before nightfall."

After that, Morgana never worried much about it and even took to walking, for she had no horse, out along the moors and beaches by herself. Once she went back to Shaughnessy with a basket of fruit and cold meats, which she'd asked the cook to prepare, and attempted to distribute it to some of the more needy families she saw. But they eyed her with hostility, and politely, but coolly, informed her that none of them accepted charity. One of them, Brendan O'Hara, made several scathing remarks to her and Morgana stumbled out of the village, clutching her basket tightly, almost in tears. Later that evening, Bridget crept up to her room and knocked softly on the door.

"Yes, Bridget, what is it?"

"I heard what happened today, me lady, in Shaughnessy, I mean. I came to apologize fer me kin. I know ye meant well, but ye see, me lady, 'tis a matter o' pride. 'Twould have made them feel, well, inferior, if'n they had accepted yer charity. I just didn't want ye to think that we're ungrateful fer yer offer, but, ye see how 'tis, don't ye, me lady?" She looked at Morgana pleadingly, wanting her ladyship to understand. Then she begged Morgana to forgive her if her ladyship thought she was speaking out of turn. "I'm only trying to explain," Bridget ended.

"Yes, I understand," Morgana told her. "And I'm sorry if I have insulted any of your kinsmen. I hope you will make my apologies to them, for as you say, I meant well, but I am a stranger to this land and ignorant of its customs. I shall do better in the future."

Bridget nodded. "And, me lady," she added on her way out. "Me brother said to tell ye he's sorry if'n he hurt yer feelings this afternoon."

"Your brother?"

"Aye, Brendan O'Hara, me lady."

"Ah yes, I remember him, but I did not know he was your brother, Bridget. Please tell him it was of no importance."

"Aye, me lady."

Morgana never made that mistake again. She did attempt to avoid Shaughnessy after that, but if she happened to pass by, she was treated courteously, so she began to think that perhaps the villagers did not hold a grudge against her after all. She supposed her family heard about the incident, but none of them ever mentioned it to her.

A few days later at dinner, however, she did have occasion to come under the critical eye of Fergus Mc-Shane. As she had only one black dress and was still in mourning, she had been washing it out each evening to wear again the next day. She was embarrassed that she had just the one dress, but, rather ironically like the Kennedys and the O'Haras, her pride would not allow her to ask her grandfather for money for new clothes. That evening he said somewhat sarcastically, "Morgana, if that is your favorite dress. I'm disappointed in your taste. I have seen you in nothing else since you arrived."

The table immediately fell silent and her family looked at her with varying degrees of pity and obvious embarrassment for her sake in their eyes. Colin avoided looking at her at all.

"I'm sorry," Morgana managed to say calmly. "But I'm still in mourning for my father."

"Well, 'tis high time you stopped!" he snapped. "Rosamunde, take the lass into Dingle tomorrow and see that the dressmaker sews her some decent apparel."

"I cannot afford—" Morgana began, only to be quickly interrupted.

"Whist! Sure and I'll not have any granddaughter of mine running around in such tattered garments," he thundered at Morgana, rapping his cane on the floor as he always did when he became agitated, unaware that he had, for the first time, openly acknowledged her as his granddaughter. "Faith! You're living under my roof, so I might as well support you in the same manner as I support all of the rest of your shiftless cousins," he growled, glaring at them as well as her.

So the next day Patrick drove Rosamunde and Morgana into Dingle. At the dressmaker's shop Morgana was measured and pinned, materials were brought out for her inspection, fabrics were chosen or discarded, and colors matched with care. Although Morgana lingered longingly over several pretty fabrics in bright colors, she refused to accept more than the dull browns, greys, and beiges she had been accustomed to wearing.

"But I am a spinster," she laughed when her aunt protested. "And I must look the part."

Rosamunde found that she could not budge her niece from this tiresome stance and so soon gave up trying.

Mistress Casey showed them several sketches of designs from which to choose. "Naturally, I'm sure these aren't nearly so fine as what ye were accustomed to in London," the woman spoke worriedly. "But I'll do me best to make ye look fashionable, and ye won't find a better seamstress, not even in Dublin."

Even Rosamunde decided to order a few gowns. "Now we'd better have hats, and gloves, and chemises, too," she insisted. "And, darling, you'll definitely need some kid shoes and riding boots. Cost is no object, Mistress Casey, and if you can have these finished in three weeks, there will be an extra bonus for you."

"Aunt," Morgana whispered. "What are you doing? Grandfather will be furious."

"Let him; this is one time I'm going to stand my ground," Rosamunde declared, a martial gleam in her eye. "After the way he treated poor Connor, he ought to do something for you."

"Three weeks!" Mistress Casey cried. Morgana could see the seamstress mentally adding up the number of her relatives available to help her. "Aye," she finally conceded. "I believe that kin be arranged."

"Good," Rosamunde said. "Come along, child."

By the time they were ready to go home, Morgana was thoroughly exhausted but secretly pleased that she had not allowed Rosamunde to persuade her into purchasing the colorful gowns. She wanted to accept as little charity from her grandfather as possible, and knew instinctively that he would frown on frivolous clothes, being the miserly wretch that he was. She was right.

"I hope you didn't buy out the store, lass, for all of the time you spent in town today," he grumbled upon their return.

"Now, father," Rosamunde interceded. " 'Twas your idea for Morgana to have some new clothes. Besides, I think you'll be very pleased with what we ordered."

"I'd better be," he snapped and thankfully left it at that.

Morgana tried very hard to make friends with Fionna, but the girl was so browbeaten that Morgana scarcely made any headway in that direction. Sometimes she took the landaulet and drove over to Shaughnessy Bay to visit.

Fionna seemed not to mind her coming; indeed, Morgana felt the girl often looked forward to it, but Fionna was a very timid woman. Morgana discovered that she was Lord Andrew Joyce's daughter, of Letterick, the neighboring estate where Bridget had previously been employed. She had one sister, Lindsey, but they were not very close. Evidently the family had fallen on hard times, being out of favor with the King, and Trevor's proposal had come at a highly opportune moment. Morgana guessed correctly that Fionna was overshadowed and cowed by him, but the girl had been far more afraid of her father's wrath had she refused to marry Trevor. It seemed that he had made a very handsome settlement on the family in return for Fionna's hand in marriage. They had been wed barely three years.

"Lindsey received a proposal, too," Fionna told her softly. "From Sean Devlin over at Devlin's Way, but she would have none of him. She is stronger than I. She yelled at father and swore up and down there was only one man in Ireland for her, and then she told father he could rot in debtors' prison before she would lift a hand to save him by marrying a man she couldn't stand. I guess I'm just a weak person," Fionna continued quietly. "But I never was happy at home and Trevor's offer was like a godsend. At least he treats me well," she sighed, and Morgana bit her tongue to keep from voicing her own opinion on this subject. "I don't think Lindsey will ever be happy. She won't rest until she gets her way," Fionna went on. "She's mad for your cousin Rian, and I know he'll never marry her."

Trevor came in then and they had no opportunity to speak further, so Morgana left, her curiosity unsated. She wondered again what he was like, this cousin she had yet to meet, that he could turn a girl's head so that she defied her own father and faced financial ruin because of it. He was grandfather's favorite grandson, the family claimed; a gambler and rakehell, Trevor declared; and yet he had tried to improve the condtions of the tenants, Patrick had told her. A man with many faces, she thought.

Morgana generally left Shaughnessy Bay whenever Trevor appeared. He was always so stiff and formal, and she knew he frowned on her unconventional ways, although she did not herself consider them so. He had been rather shocked and mortified upon discovering that she careered all over the countryside whenever she chose without even a groom or maid to accompany her, but she had never had such in London and saw no reason to change. Morgana heard Trevor one evening attempting to counsel grandfather on the subject.

"Nonsense!" the old man rapped his cane on the floor in response to Trevor's reprimand. "Morgana is a capable lass, and every man in the county knows he would have to answer to me if she were harmed. She's perfectly safe, and you're a fool!"

"I'm warning you, grandfather, no good will come of this," Trevor replied, insulted, and promptly left the house.

Fionna, of course, was never even allowed to venture into the gardens without someone hanging on her apron strings. Morgana was privately delighted over her grandfather's attitude, for she felt that it would have hampered her freedom greatly to be constantly trailed by a groom or maid.

Once on one of her jaunts on the moors, she came upon Colin stretched upon the grass, reading a book of poetry.

"Am I disturbing you?" she asked hesitantly, not wishing to disrupt his solitude.

"Not at all, cousin," he replied politely.

"I see you're reading Lord Byron's latest verse."

"Yes, 'tis very well done, don't you agree?"

"His original works are, but I have not yet read his new book."

"I would be glad to lend it to you, cousin, when I have finished."

"Thank you, Colin."

They sat together for a long time discussing various authors with whom they were both familiar. Colin had a subtle and unusual mind. He was adept at outlining themes and hidden meanings that Morgana, who was more romantic, sometimes overlooked.

He showed her some of the poems he'd written and she was disturbed to find them brutal, cruel, and twisted. She revealed nothing of her reaction to Colin, as he was obviously very proud of his work. When Morgana left him a short time afterwards, he was deeply engrossed in Lord Byron's book of verse.

"Morgana," Rosamunde called from the balcony as she approached the house. "Come upstairs, child, your dresses have arrived. Kerr picked them up this afternoon."

The girl hurried inside, eager to try them on, and soon the room was strewn with hats, shoes, gloves, chemises, and gowns.

"Oh, aunt," she cried. "They're all so lovely."

"Look. Didn't this make up beautifully?" Rosamunde exclaimed, holding up a dress of beige linen.

Morgana's reply was cut off when the door was flung open rudely and her grandfather came stumping inside.

"Hmph!" he growled. "Nothing but a lot of money wasted on this tomfoolery. Put on that riding habit, lass, and come out into the yard."

Rosamunde, clucking her head over her father's behavior, helped Morgana into the dark green habit, and watched as her niece pulled on the high black boots. Twenty minutes later Morgana was outside as Fergus McShane had demanded.

"Took your time," he snapped as she came up beside him. He stopped her intended reply with an uplifted hand. "Never mind, I don't want to hear the excuse I'm sure you're about to offer." He cleared his throat and seemed to stumble on his words. "Patrick brought to my attention the fact that you have either been walking or taking the landaulet wherever it is you go on these expeditions of yours. As your cousins, even that milktoast," he said, referring to Fionna, "have mounts, I decided that it was only proper that you have one as well."

Morgana watched in amazement as a lovely roan mare was led up before her.

"I have therefore procured this hunter for you. Treat her with respect and see that she's adequately cared for."

"Grandfather! She's beautiful. I don't know what to say," Morgana was so overcome, she missed the sudden pleased smile the old man wore at her words; and she tried hard to suppress the impulse she had to hug him.

"Then say nothing," Fergus McShane grumbled. "Faith, I find that persons who don't know what to say are generally better off if they keep their mouths shut!"

He turned and stalked back into the house, but after the stable boy helped her mount, Morgana was sure she saw him at his window, watching her ride off into the distance. She smiled, a little smugly, and waved, and was amply rewarded when the curtain dropped sharply back into place. The old man really had a softer heart than he cared to admit.

Like an unfettered hawk, Morgana flew over the moors, delighted to be in the saddle again. The wind soon whipped her hair from its neat roll and it tumbled down her back, flying wildly out behind her. She breathed deeply. Oh, the joys of riding freely! She laughed aloud and rubbed her face on the mare's long mane, nearly the color of her own cascading mass of curls, and surmised correctly that this was the reason her grandfather had chosen this particular horse. Morgana named the mare "Copper Lady," and soon Shanetara and the surrounding countryside found them a familiar sight.

"Aye," the Kennedys and the O'Haras would shake their heads when she passed. "She's got the devil in her fer sure. One kin tell the McShane blood runs thick in her veins. Sure and she's as wild as any o' them. Whist! Only a witch could ride that mare!"

Morgana found out later that Copper Lady had had several owners, all of whom had traded her off because their wives or daughters could not control the tempestuous mount. She'd last belonged to Lindsey Joyce, who hadn't even been able to get into the saddle.

How her grandfather had known that she would be able to handle the mare was a mystery to Morgana. It was as though they had been made for each other, for the horse never acted viciously toward her and she had no trouble at all controlling her. Sometimes, some of the villagers would make the sign of the cross when she rode by, sure that she was the witch they called her and hoping to ward off evil spirits. But none of them ever harmed her. She could ride where she chose, for in this part of Ireland the McShanes were respected and feared; and their word was law. There was not a soul around who dared offend her, because her grandfather's wrath was legend.

One day not long after she had received Copper Lady, Morgana had gone for an especially long ride and reluctantly turned the horse's head homeward. Her cheeks were flushed with excitement and her green eyes glowed with the same emerald color of her riding habit. Her copper curls tumbled in long disarray down her back. It would soon be dark and it would take a long time to make herself presentable for dinner, she thought. There was always a price to be paid for one's pleasures. She dug her heels in lightly on the mare's flanks and galloped into the yard, nearly colliding with the tall dark stranger who stood there. He grasped the reins, and succeeded in halting the horse and preventing the accident.

Morgana looked down from the saddle into eyes as green as her own. But these eyes were dark and wintery, not emerald; they glittered, but did not sparkle. Their black lashes were spiky and the sooty brows were thick and unruly. In a face that had been bronzed by the sun a sensual, knowing mouth and an aristocratic nose marked this man a McShane. His square jaw was jutting, determined. His shaggy hair was black, the ebon color of nightfall as it washes out over the depths of the Irish Sea. He was built lithely, but powerfully, with muscles hard from years of climbing the riggings on his ship and which rippled sinuously when he moved. He wore tight brown breeches, and the shine on his high-topped boots would have disgraced no valet. His waistcoat was well tailored, his silk scarf carefully tied, but he was no dandy. His casual hunting jacket dispelled any such notion. He was a dashing cavalier come to life from the gilt-edged pages of a poem; and when their eyes met and locked, Morgana felt as though she were drowning, so pulled was she into the dark depths of those green pools. A strange mesmerism seemed to take hold of her; and she thought suddenly, wildly, he has come . . . for better or worse, he has come. She had no doubt that the man before her was Rian McShane.

Rian caught his breath. She was lovely, even more so than he'd remembered; and he felt a wild urge to pull her from the saddle and claim her as his own, but he did not. A surge of excitement raced through his loins as his glance took in the wind-whipped mass of copper hair, the emerald eyes, and the poppy-colored mouth parted softly in surprise. In that moment, he wanted her and knew it, as he always knew upon the first meeting with a woman; and he knew, too, that in his own time and own way, he would have her.

"Well," he drawled lazily, arrogantly. "You must be Cousin Morgana, the wench who's caused such a stir in this household."

"I am," she answered, trying to get a grip on her emotions. After all, she'd hardly expected such an insolent greeting. "And you must be Rian."

He laughed softly. "Aye. Did you know that when you're angry, the flecks in your lovely green eyes float to the surface like the golden sand rushing in with the tide?"

Morgana gasped slightly and did not know what to say. The words were velvet, but somehow when he said them they seemed mocking, and the way he raked her with his dark crude glance made her feel as though she'd been stripped naked under his gaze. She tried to loose his grip upon the reins, but he would not let go. Instead, he reached up and, placing his hands around her waist, swung her down from the saddle.

"I prefer to be looked up to," he noted the change in their positions, for, though she was tall, her head barely reached his broad shoulders.

"If you will loose me, I will take my horse around to the stables."

"Nonsense. What do you think grandfather has those stable lads for? Jim!" he called sharply and the small boy came running forward. "Take Lady McShane's mare around back and see that she's rubbed down and well fed. She looks as though she's been ridden hard." Then he turned back to Morgana. "Come, I'll walk you into the house."

She was puzzled and thrown off guard by this sudden shift in attitudes. It was the same trick her grandfather used. Rian learned well, then, it seemed. He released her at the foot of the stairs.

"A penny for your thoughts, cousin."

"I—I was wondering what kind of man you are," Morgana stammered truthfully.

"One who gets what he wants," Rian gazed down at her. "Remember that." Then he strode off without another word.

His words held both warning and promise, and she trembled with foreboding as she hurried upstairs to the quiet sanctuary of her room.

Chapter Three

Morgana dressed carefully for dinner that evening, but the buttons on her gown were too much for her quivering fingers to manage and she finally had to summon Bridget for assistance. At last, however, she felt ready and smiled at her reflection in the mirror, well pleased with the results. The rich beige brocade of her gown emphasized the flaming red of her hair and the golden glints in her green eyes. Silently she blessed her grandfather for the clothes he had so grudgingly purchased. Being well dressed gave her confidence, and she was in need of all the assurance she could muster.

She had tried unsuccessfully to shake off the strange nervous feeling that had possessed her at the sight of Rian. She was drawn to him in a manner she could not explain, and understood now why Lindsey Joyce had defied her father for him. The man was damnably attractive!

Her stomach churned nervously as she walked into the dining room and took her place between Patrick and

Colin. Trevor and Fionna had joined them for dinner, and Morgana found unfortunately that Rian was seated directly across from her. At another time, another place, she would have been relieved since it was considered impolite to talk across the table, but she'd learned very quickly that the McShanes ignored this rule of society, and indeed any others which did not suit their fancies. But she did not, after all, have very much to say that evening, as Rian was the center of attention, and she was able to study him intently without seeming rude.

The rest of the family plied him with questions about his latest voyage. Rian had been to the Orient and had many interesting tales to tell of his travels there. As Morgana watched him covertly while he talked, she discovered that he was well polished, but with an easy, careless grace that at times bordered on the insulting; and she had the distinct impression that he was laughing at them all. There was an arrogance about his manner as he surveyed them lazily and drawled his words with an accent that smacked of London's high society. The Irish brogue, so pronounced in Gerald, tinged Rian's conversation only when he used it for effect.

Morgana suspected that he was a man of many moods and many faces, and she did not let his careless manner deceive her. He was like one of the Bengal tigers he spoke of seeing in India, languishing indolently in the sun, but ready to uncoil and spring upon his prey when necessary. Yes, out of all of her cousins, this man would be the most dangerous to cross. She would have to be wary of him or she would find herself caught by the easy charm that captivated everyone in his presence whether they liked it or not.

The men did not dawdle over port that evening but joined the ladies almost immediately. They sat in a circle and watched as Kerr O'Malley brought Rian's sea chest in and set it before him. Rian lifted the lid, teasingly obscuring its contents from view as long as possible. He'd told them at dinner that he had brought back something for each one of the family and now he obviously relished the anticipation they felt. He had bright, delicately painted fans for Rosamunde and Fionna, a beautifully carved cane for grandfather, ornate snuff boxes for Trevor and Patrick, a book of haiku for Colin, and a monstrous idol statue for Gerald.

"But you've not given Morgana a gift, Rian," Rosamunde reprimanded him mildly.

"Now, aunt," Morgana spoke politely. "Cousin Rian had no way of knowing that I would be here. I'm not upset that I have no present."

Rian's eyes met hers and a mocking smile curved his lips. "How do you know that I've nothing for you, cousin? You must never be sure about anything concerning me."

With that, he delved into the sea chest once more and pulled out a bolt of silk material that shimmered in the light, reflecting a thousand shades of green and gold, like the sea when the sun plays upon its surface. Morgana gasped as he pulled her from the chair by the fire and draped the glittering folds around her. A tingle ran up her spine at his touch.

" 'Tis said this material is woven by mermaids who entice sea captains to their deaths among the rocky crags by singing sweet love songs. Dare you wear it, cousin?" he murmured softly.

"It's lovely, Rian." She looked coolly into his eyes, although her heart beat rapidly. "I shall wear it with pleasure."

Morgana removed his hands from her waist and folded the yards of cloth carefully as Rosamunde spoke delightedly, "What a beautiful gift, Rian. Only Morgana could wear that particular shade of green. But how could you have known?"

Rian's only answer lay in the mocking half-smile that curved his lips again.

After that evening, Rian treated Morgana politely whenever they had occasion to meet, but he did not seek her out, which for some reason piqued her. Though she found him arrogant and insulting, she was intrigued by him and was for the first time in her life at a loss as to understand her conflicting emotions.

From Bridget, she discovered that he often rode out over the estate and made suggestions to grandfather as to how it could be more efficiently managed. Then he and Fergus, along with Patrick and sometimes Trevor, would be closeted for hours discussing the family's various business interests. Sometimes Rian rode over to Letterick to see Fionna's sister, Lindsey Joyce. At night, he was often Gerald's rowdy drinking companion at the local inn in Kilshannon. She heard rumors of brawls and dalliance, of gambling and card games and enormous wagers. Patrick told her once that Rian could drill the center out of a playing card at fifty paces and was deadly with a rapier.

Morgana felt lonely, but did not know why, since she had almost always been alone and it had rarely bothered her before. She took to riding farther away from Shanetara in an attempt to escape the shadows that threatened to engulf her. The sea called to her and she would often return with the mist clinging to her hair and the taste of salt upon her lips. She grieved for her father and felt lost in this strange land.

Fergus McShane had sharp eyes and a keen sense of intuition, however. Although he refused to admit it, he had grown inordinately fond of his granddaughter and it bothered him to see her so morose. She needed diversion, he decided, and announced one night at dinner that he intended to give a masquerade ball.

"Surely you're jesting, grandfather," Trevor exclaimed in astonishment.

"I think it's a splendid idea, father," Rosamunde clapped her hands together enraptured. "Just imagine, a house full of people and gaiety once more. Why, we haven't had a party since Connor—" At grandfather's stern stare, she broke off abruptly.

"What's your game, old man? Why the devil do you suddenly want to open up the house after twenty years?" Rian surveyed him casually.

"It has occurred to me that Morgana knows no one here in Ireland outside of this family who is of the same social standing as she. I will not have her hobnobbing with the local village men. This ball will introduce her to Irish society and give her an opportunity to meet some gentlemen of her own class. It's time she began to think of her future. She will perhaps find an eligible bachelor to take her in hand, although her frank manners will probably run most of these bored fops away. But I won't have her turning into a bluestocking, or becoming a histrionic old maid like Rosy."

"And whose fault is that?" Rosamunde snapped, ready to do battle, but Morgana broke in hurriedly, more concerned with her own future than her aunt's past.

"How dare you attempt to put me on such display? Good heavens! I won't be treated like a slave on the block with a parade of men coming to barter or buy. I'm already a spinster, grandfather, whether you like it or not, too old to be married off like a piece of unwanted merchandise," she said in mock anger, although her lips twitched with humor.

"Well, lass, what do you intend to do with yourself? A woman's place is at home with a husband and children." Grandfather was not amused by her attitude.

"That's not true," Morgana continued, ignoring the rising color in his face. "It's obvious you've never read Mary Wollstonecraft's book, *Vindication of the Rights of Women.* You men would keep us ignorant, weak and timid to reinforce your assumptions of male superiority. We are governed and yet we have no vote as to how we are to be ruled. Why, only yesterday I decided that I should go with Trevor the next time he makes a trip to Dublin, so that I can speak upon this very issue at the House."

The entire family gasped, all except for Rian, who laughed outright and clapped the much surprised and mortified Trevor on the back rudely.

"Hmph!" grandfather snorted, able to see at last that his granddaughter was bamming him shamelessly. "A lot of nonsense if you ask me. I have no heirs, lass, except for this parcel of ungrateful disappointments, and I want to see my great-grandchildren before I die. None of you is married, except for Trevor, and Fionna has produced no offspring, nor does she look capable of the task!"

Goaded to a rare showing of defiance at this, Fionna burst into tears and fled from the room. Trevor tossed his napkin down on his plate angrily, giving Morgana a nasty glance as if to say he did not appreciate her humor either.

"That was a beastly thing to say, grandfather," he clipped his words stiffly and also left the room, calling to his distraught wife. "Fionna, pet, don't cry."

"I'm giving a masquerade ball," Fergus McShane shouted, "and you will all attend!" Then he stumped angrily out of the room, quelling a strong desire to box his granddaughter's ears for her impertinence!

After he'd gone, Morgana laughed again, much pleased that she had finally gotten the best of the old man. To her surprise, Rian joined in her laughter. He toasted her silently with his glass, and she thought for a moment that there was approval and more than a flickering interest upon his face.

But before she had time to reflect upon this, Gerald staggered drunkenly from his chair and asked if something was amiss, in his stupor, apparently not having heard a word and so frustrated Rosamunde that she rapped his knuckles with a butter knife. He roared indignantly at this treatment and pointed an accusing finger at Morgana.

" 'Tis all her fault. Faith! There's been nothing but trouble since she came here. The villagers are right, she's a red-haired witch!"

"How dare you call me a witch?" Morgana retorted, "Your uncouth and brutish manners are only surpassed by your superstitious stupidity!"

At that, he became enraged and picked up a lamb chop, which he threw across the room at her. Morgana had the presence of mind to duck and it whacked Patrick aside the head. Normally easygoing, he reached his limit of endurance at this point, jumped up, and punched

Gerald in the nose. Gerald swayed, then sank to the floor unconscious.

"By God, that was a wisty castor, Patrick," Rian crowed. "I didn't know you had it in you."

Morgana could not help herself; she laughed again, much to the indignation of Rosamunde, who had been chattering to herself in the corner ever since she had chastised her nephew with the butter knife.

"Why didn't you tell me the knife was dirty?" she asked Morgana, her mouth pursed up ridiculously. "I would have cleaned it first. 'Tis unkind of you to laugh at my breach of manners."

Morgana helped her aunt to the door, much afraid that if she didn't get away from the disastrous scene, she would subside into uncontrollable giggles, a state which was most unlike her.

"Well, that ought to give the servants something to gossip about for a month," Rosamunde shook her head unbelievingly when Morgana had ushered her out of the room. "I can't imagine what's gotten into this family. You all acted like blithering idiots," she muttered, conveniently forgetting her own unbecoming conduct.

Morgana decided it was best not to mention it, having had enough trouble for one evening, and hurried away to her room, lest she fall into another fit of laughter.

Chapter Four

Grandfather was unable to get up in the morning and by noon he had worked himself into a frenzy.

"Rosamunde," he bellowed from his bed. "Get that poor excuse for a doctor out here."

"Aye, father," she said, and wrote a note to be sent around to Doctor Kelsey.

The rest of the family ate breakfast in silence, Gerald sporting a slightly swollen nose and Patrick a somewhat shamefaced, hangdog look. Morgana excused herself as quickly as possible and sought sanctuary in one of the morning rooms which particularly found favor with her, being very light and airy, and done in brighter colors than the somber hues which hung over the greater part of the house. Colin had lent her his book of Lord Byron's verse as he had promised, and she curled up on a chaise longue, eager to lose herself in the romantic passages.

She was rudely interrupted over an hour later by the clanking of the brass knocker at the front door. It was repeated several times and she was puzzled as to why no one had answered. No doubt Stepplewhite, the stiff-necked butler, was down in the wine cellar again. Morgana waited a few moments, then finally went and opened the door herself.

A tall man with laughing blue eyes, red-blond hair, and a rather awkward manner stood in the doorway.

You must be Lady Morgana," he guessed. "The villagers have mentioned you often. I'm Michael Kelsey, the doctor. Your grandfather sent for me."

"Of course. Won't you come in, Doctor?"

He stepped inside and said, "I know my way up, thank you. Your grandfather's had another one of his fits, I expect. He'll give himself apoplexy one of these days if he's not careful. He's quite a remarkable old fellow really. Actually in fine shape, considering his age. He'll probably outlive us all. I really think he just calls me to get some attention on these occasions," Michael Kelsey confided pleasantly. "I'm fresh bait, someone else to harass. Well, don't let me keep you. I'll just pop upstairs and take a look in on the old man."

Morgana watched Dr. Kelsey climb the stairs and felt warmed by his kindness. Obviously, he knew her grandfather well. She decided that she would like to know him better, so she waited around until he came downstairs.

"May I walk you outside, Doctor?" she asked. "I'd like to know if my grandfather's going to be all right."

"I would feel honored," he smiled. "Aye, it was just as I thought. Nothing to worry about. He'll be fine as soon as he calms down and gets some rest. You just pamper him a little and see that nothing else happens to upset him. I gather there was some sort of an argument over a masquerade ball last night."

Morgana flushed slightly. "Yes, there was. Grandfather seems to think I need a husband and the ball is his way of introducing me into society."

"Well, a lass as bonnie as you shouldn't have any trouble managing that," he replied.

"The trouble is that I don't want to get married."

"Perhaps you will meet someone who will change

your mind about that." He laughed at her discomfiture at the suggestion.

"Yes, there's always that chance,"- she finally conceded.

They were interrupted abruptly by the arrival of Rian. He came riding up on the huge black stallion that, Morgana had been told, even sailed on his ship wherever he went.

"Hello, Michael," he drawled. "Is something wrong?"

"No, my lord. Just another one of your grandfather's spells. You're looking well. How goes the life on the sea?"

"Just fine. My ship got in a month ago and I'm having some work done on her."

"Oh, getting ready to set sail again?"

"I don't know," Rian said and glanced over in Morgana's direction for the first time since the conversation had started. "You never know from which direction the wind will blow."

"Aye," the doctor answered, apparently catching something Morgana had missed. " 'Tis time I did some thinking along those lines myself. Well, I'd best be getting back to town."

Morgana extended her hand graciously. "It was a pleasure meeting you, Doctor. Please come back again soon, even if no one at Shanetara is ailing."

"I might just do that, Lady Morgana." He smiled at her and took her hand, holding it a bit longer than was necessary before climbing into his buggy. "Good day, Lady Morgana, my lord."

Rian studied her quizzically after Michael Kelsey had gone. Morgana blushed under his intense stare, for she had the impression that he knew what she looked like without any clothes. She started to speak, then thought better of it, turning her back on him, all of last night's laughing kinship disappearing completely.

Despite her opposition to the subject, Morgana found herself becoming rather excited over the prospect of a masquerade ball after all. Rooms were opened up that hadn't been used in years. Mollie O'Malley and her bevy of housemaids ripped the covers off the shrouded furniture and polished until the dust flew. The air was freshened with lavender, and an atmosphere of gaiety transformed the household.

It had been decided that each one of the family would go as a McShane ancestor, so one morning Morgana strolled up to the portrait gallery to choose her subject. She was fascinated by the pictures, for she knew little of her Irish ancestry. She paused before a rather hard, rugged-looking fellow who greatly resembled Rian.

"That's a many times great-grandfather McShane, the man who built Shanetara." A voice prompted from behind her. "He was a pirate."

"Rian!" she exclaimed. She had not heard his approach.

"That McShane was a seaman, just as I am, only he spent his days plundering other vessels and neighboring villages. That was his wife." Rian pointed to a beautiful young woman with a flowing mass of red hair. "Now you know where you get these flaming tresses." He stroked her hair lightly.

Morgana again felt that odd little shiver run up her spine, and moved away lest he should guess it. "What was her name?" she asked quietly as she stared up into the lilting green eyes and the inviting mouth, the color of poppies in bloom. Her dress was green, also, and matched her eyes perfectly, reflecting the skill of the artist more than the actual coloring, Morgana thought.

"Katy, Katy McShane. She was the daughter of an enemy warlord. William, the pirate, sailed up the northern coast of Ireland one day and kidnapped her as an act of revenge against her father. Stole her from the very castle of which I am now Earl."

"How awful." Morgana shuddered slightly. "What she must have suffered!"

"Oh, I don't know. McShane was a handsome devil. I imagine he knew how to keep her happy."

"I still think it's dreadful," she retorted.

"Why?"

"Well, to be wrenched from your home like that by a pirate, forced into marriage with a man you didn't love, ravished—" her voice faltered as she realized how explicit, and unladylike, her choice of words had been.

Rian moved closer to her, his green eyes glittering mockingly. "And just what would you know of being ravished," he asked, his mouth twitching slightly.

"Noth—nothing," she stammered, trying to regain her composure. "I just assumed it would be a horrible experience. Please, let's talk about something else."

"But I find this topic highly interesting," he said, placing his arms on either side of her so that she was backed up against the wall between them. "I'll wager this is the first time you've ever discussed rape with a man."

"You must know that it is," she replied icily, seeking to escape from his pinioning arms. The conversation was not going at all as she wished.

"You might, in time, come to love such a man, just as Katy McShane did," Rian spoke softly, the odd smile still playing about the corners of his lips.

"That seems rather unlikely," Morgana said dryly.

"Ah well," he sighed, moving away. "There's something to be said for the old ways after all, I guess. Katy accepted it as a fact of life and soon came to love William because she understood how much he desired her and what he had risked to obtain her. Nowadays, women are either bloodsucking schemers or simpering chits!"

"Is that what you think of us?" Morgana's mouth quirked humorously.

"Forgive me, madam," he bowed mockingly. "Present company excepted, of course."

"What happened to Katy McShane?" she spoke hastily in an attempt to divert the conversation from herself.

"Oh, William's ship went down, just off the coast of Kilshannon, and it is said she went crazy in the end and flung herself from the balconies of Shanetara to the deadly crags below." He continued, almost whispering. "They say when the moon is high and the sea raging, William's ghost ship sails the ocean and that you can hear Katy

73

calling to him, crying softly before she touches him again in death. Of course, it might only be the plaintive sighing of the wind, but the villagers swear 'tis Katy McShane, mourning for her lover."

Morgana shivered involuntarily; and Rian, seeing her eyes grow large, laughed. The spell was broken.

"If you decide to appear as Katy McShane, let me know and I'll loan you the emeralds she's wearing in that picture. They belonged to my mother," he told her.

Then he walked away, leaving her alone in the long hall, his footsteps echoing.

Invitations to the ball had been sent out and the news that Shanetara was opening its doors again after twenty long years spread quickly through the county. The guests from far and wide began arriving early in the day. The Devlins, the Gallaghers, the Joyces, and the O'Briens came. Even Henry Grattan came from Dublin upon grandfather's request.

Morgana kept to her room, since Fergus had asked that she make no appearance before the ball. She stood before her mirror, waiting, feeling as though she were indeed Katy McShane. Her dress, an exact replica of the one in the portrait, was a vibrant green satin edged with fine lace. Her hair was down, as was Katy's in the picture, and Morgana fidgeted nervously as Bridget attempted to pin the small green bows into her copper curls. When Morgana again glanced into the mirror, the reflection which stared back at her was the face of a stranger, and she scarcely recognized herself. Why, she almost looked pretty! Who would have thought that a penniless poet's daughter would be attending a ball in her own honor decked out in a frock that even a queen might have coveted? She wondered if everything would fade away at midnight, if Shanetara would turn out to be nothing more than a haunting dream, if she would awaken to find herself in her own bed at her father's small house.

Finally, it was time for Morgana to make her appearance. She lacked only the emerald necklace which

Rian had promised to loan her for the evening. She thanked Bridget warmly for her help, then picked up her mask and fan. Gathering up the folds of her skirt, she found her way down the winding hall to her cousin's room. Morgana hadn't seen him since the rather disturbing conversation in the portrait gallery, and she drew a deep breath before rapping gently on the door. There was no answer.

"Rian," she called and knocked a little louder.

This time the door opened and he stood in the entranceway, handsomely attired in the pirate garb worn by William, Katy's abductor.

"Are you ready to be kidnapped, madam?" he drawled insolently.

"Not in the least," she replied coolly, determined not to let him rouse her out of her composure again. "I might have known you would have chosen that particular ancestor to portray."

"But of course. Can you think of anyone else more suited to the role?"

"I came for the emeralds," she spoke, ignoring his question. "You said I might wear them."

"Ah yes. I should have guessed it was not my charming self which brought you so boldly to my room. Come in and I'll get them."

"Oh, Rian! They're magnificent," she gasped as he pulled the emeralds from a casket on the dresser top. "Are you sure it's all right for me to wear them? What if they get lost or stolen? I'll feel terrible. Perhaps I shouldn't take them."

"Nonsense. I'm sure you'll take excellent care of them." He brushed aside her protests with a wave of his hand. "Turn around and I'll put them on for you."

His hands felt warm against her skin as he fastened the clasp and she felt again the now-familiar tingle of excitement run up her spine at his touch. He handed her the matching earrings and she put them on, tossing her hair back to show them off as she studied the effect in the mirror.

"Hello, Katy," she whispered to the strange reflection, so unlike herself, and did not know that she had spoken aloud until she caught Rian's eye in the glass.

For once, he did not smile mockingly as she'd feared he might, and she again had the curious feeling that he understood her and her thoughts.

"Come on," he said. "I'll escort you downstairs."

They tied on their masks and walked toward the lights and laughter of the ballroom.

"You're late!" grandfather reprimanded them gruffly when they reached the bottom of the stairs, although he had planned Morgana's grand entrance. "You're always late." He told Rian huffily to be sure and introduce her to everyone.

"Mind that you don't try and keep her to yourself."

"Don't worry. I'm certain none of these bucks present would give me that opportunity," Rian grinned in reply.

"Will—will Doctor Kelsey be here?" Morgana stumbled on the words as they moved away, wondering if she would see that kind face again.

She could have melted into the floor when Rian gazed down at her through the slits of his black mask, his green eyes gleaming mockingly, and said dryly, "I scarcely think Michael Kelsey is the kind of man grandfather had in mind when he suggested you meet some eligible bachelors. The doctor is a man of trade, a commoner."

"Well, you're nothing but a ship's captain," she retorted, angry at herself for having asked the question in the first place, and for allowing Rian's earlier consideration fool her into thinking he was anything other than an arrogant, demanding man.

"That is another matter entirely. I am a lord and nobleman. Ships are merely an amusing pastime for me. I am not forced to make my living from them."

Morgana could think of nothing to say after that and wished violently that he would go away, but she found herself strangely provoked and dismayed when he introduced her to several young men and then disappeared.

As the hours passed, she grew weary of the noise, the laughter, and the lights, and Rosamunde's incessant, "Morgana, darling, have you met...?" Morgana knew her aunt meant well, but she was beginning to feel like little more than a china doll. She danced until she thought her feet could dance no more, and flirted lightly (being inexperienced at the game), and smiled until her face felt frozen with the attempt. She knew that spinster or no, she would have had none of these men present tonight. They were faceless figures, all finely attired, not as well as the men she'd seen ride down the cobblestone street in front of her house in London, but nevertheless fashionable by Ireland's standards. They all murmured polite nothings and trivial compliments in her ears, boring her with their simple chatter. They did not laugh at her witty remarks nor understand her more serious comments. One astonished young man responded, "See here, you're not a bluestocking, are you?" after she'd asked his opinion on the political state of affairs in Ireland.

No, were she to choose a man, Morgana knew that she would pick one who knew more of the world than just the realms of Ireland; a man well versed and well read in the arts; a man with a wit as keen as her own, who met her eyes in silent understanding when no one else could comprehend her feelings; a man who sometimes knew her thoughts better than she liked. Rian crept, unbidden, into her mind. He was travelled, polished, intelligent; and although he often laughed at her, she felt he at least understood the workings of her mind.

She saw him dancing with Lindsey Joyce and remembered the rumors she'd heard about them. Lindsey had darker hair than Fionna, and sleek brown eyes that flashed with coquetry. It hadn't taken Morgana long to see why Fionna felt so overshadowed by her sister. Lindsey Joyce obviously knew just what she wanted and exactly how to go about getting it.

"Boring as hell, isn't it, cousin?"

Morgana turned, "Colin?"

"Aye, 'tis I and none other. These dreadful masks are terribly hot, aren't they?"

"Quite," she replied, glad to find someone who wasn't a total stranger to her.

"I would ask you to dance, cousin, but I'm sure your programme is already filled and I'm not a very good dancer anyway. In fact, I'm totally at a loss in the so-called Haut Ton. It often makes grandfather very angry with me."

"Now, Colin, I'm sure it can't be as bad as all that," she attempted to console him lightly.

"But it is. I don't like hunting or cards or anything a gentleman born and bred properly should do. I'd rather write poetry, like your father, but I find myself lacking the courage to face poverty as he did. If grandfather would only let me go into the military, I know I could distinguish myself and find a patron for my poems."

Morgana had no chance to reply, for just then Sean Devlin came up to claim her hand for the waltz the musicians were beginning to play. A pleasant fellow, if a trifle dandyish, he was guiding her toward the dance floor when Rian broke in upon them.

"Sorry, old pal, but I believe this dance is mine. You won't take offense, I hope. Lindsey is dying for some champagne."

"Not at all, Rian," Sean spoke courteously. "Your cousin is charming. I'll see that Lady Lindsey gets her champagne." He turned to Morgana, "The next dance, perhaps, Lady Morgana, if you're not already engaged."

She smiled graciously, glad that he'd overlooked Rian's arrogant cutting in, for Sean's name was plainly on her card. "I'd be delighted, my lord," she promised, seeing that the next dance was Patrick's and sure that he would understand. "That wasn't very nice, Rian," she spoke when Sean had gone.

"Sean and I are old friends. I assure you he didn't mind in the least."

"How do you know? He finds me charming, even if you do not," she was piqued that Rian should insinuate she was not worth arguing over a dance.

"Oh, but I do, cousin. I wanted passionately to

78

dance with you, and your card was filled. I had no choice but to break in upon a man who already had his name upon your list. Why, had he taken offense, I might have faced a duel at dawn. Would you have wept for me, Morgana, and the risk I took to hold you within my arms this evening?" he mocked her lazily.

Morgana bit her lip. "I grow weary of your sarcastic remarks, cousin," she suddenly decided to play the game his way, and deliberately trod on his foot. "I beg your pardon, cousin," she exclaimed in mock dismay. "Did I step on your toe?"

He threw back his head and laughed, causing everyone to stare at them in wonder, for Rian actually seemed to be enjoying himself. The bored look he generally wore at parties had disappeared, and he held Morgana tighter in his arms.

"There, I knew that sooner or later I'd manage to break through that icy veneer of yours. Laugh, Morgana. 'Tis a world worth laughing at," he told her, and she felt that he was half serious. "No one expects you to behave like a governess, you know."

Did she really act like a governess, she wondered. She felt stung and disillusioned. Morgana looked up in dismay into Rian's face, handsome and mocking. She blushed at his knowing smile and her eyelids lowered against his gaze.

They finished the rest of the waltz in silence, and Rian did not dance with her again that evening. She took little pleasure in the fact that she'd made a success of the ball, although grandfather was looking particularly delighted. But had Morgana known then the reasons for Fergus's sly smile, she would have been highly alarmed. As he had watched Morgana and Rian dancing together, an outrageous idea had occurred to him, and the more he thought about it, the more determined the old man became to see it through. The fact that it would please neither of his grandchildren bothered him not at all; for it was in that moment that Fergus McShane decided that Rian should marry Morgana.

Rian needed a wife. This talk of being wed to the sea was just nonsense. A man had to settle down sooner or later, and what better bride for his stubborn grandson than Morgana, a wench as stubborn in her own way, with a wit as sharp as Rian's? The old man cackled in delight, rubbing his hands together gleefully as he decided how he would make the matter come about. It would be no easy task, since both Rian and Morgana would oppose it should they discover the plan; but they would produce fine heirs to carry on the wild clan of McShanes, Fergus had no doubt of that! To hell with Rian's freedom and Morgana's spinsterhood! He, Fergus, would put an end to both of these highly regrettable states, and his grandchildren would thank him for it, once they had reconciled themselves to the idea.

The old man was so tickled over his scheme that he discarded his cane for a moment in order to dance a jig with the Viscountess of Laughlin, who was as surprised as everyone else at the Duke's action.

Morgana watched her grandfather cutting a caper with as much amazement as the rest of the crowd, then was drawn from the sight as Lindsey Joyce came up beside her.

" 'Tis a pleasure to meet you, Lady McShane," Lindsey drawled. "I've heard so much about you. It seems you are a paragon of virtues," she spoke with a sweet hostility that Morgana instantly reciprocated. "Sure and they tell me you can even ride that devilish mare I used to have. You must be as tough as a man. I declare, I'm so delicate, I could hardly hold the reins. Traipsing all over the countryside must have made you a lot stronger than you look," she fluttered her eyelashes.

"Let's just say I'm not the milktoast type," Morgana said with more assurance than she felt, borrowing her grandfather's insulting word.

"My, my, aren't those the McShane emeralds?" Lindsey tried a new tack.

"Yes, they are."

"I thought they belonged to Rian. Whatever did you have to do to get them out of him?"

"Perhaps I just know how to manage him better than you," Morgana replied, suddenly weary, and yet pleased that she could aim her barbs as well as Lindsey.

Then she walked off, seething inside. She felt an overwhelming desire to get away from the crowd, and slipped out into the garden where it was cool. She pressed her head against the trunk of a tree, an immense feeling of relief coming over her. No wonder her father had left the world into which he'd been born! High society snobs were really nothing more than commoners, masked, as they were this evening, with titles and thinly veiled insults. The same desires and hatreds were still present. Morgana felt desperately that she needed a friend in this strange land, a confidant as her father had once been, someone who was neither a McShane, nor one of their foppish acquaintances. She thought of Michael Kelsey. She wanted to see him again, regardless of what Rian said about the man. She felt instinctively that the doctor was a kind fellow, a man who could be trusted. He was a healer of the body, might he not also be a healer of the mind as well? Perhaps if she talked with him she would feel better. She decided abruptly that she would ride into Kilshannon in the morning and seek him out, for she felt that, in spite of her open invitation, he would be hesitant about coming to Shanetara unless someone were sick. Yes, that was what she needed, to talk to someone, to let everything that had been building up inside of her for months now out. Why, she felt better already!

"Are you hiding from someone, or did you make an assignation with one of those smitten fools inside?"

Morgana whirled around, startled. Rian was leaning up against a tree, that lazy smile gracing his face.

"I don't think that's any of your business!" she snapped, suddenly angry at him, too. He disturbed her and mocked her; the cad, she thought irrationally.

"So, you really are a tigress," he drawled. "And at last have your claws showing? Are you going to scratch me? I think not," he suddenly seized her wrists.

"Tell me, my lord," she mocked as nastily as he. "If

81

I scratched you, would your blood run blue, or would it be as red as every other common man's?"

Rian's nostrils flared slightly and his face was white around his tightened mouth. Morgana could see she'd made him angry, but by this time she didn't care. She wanted to hurt him, to get even with him and his damned arrogance.

"Don't push too hard, Morgana," he warned softly through clenched teeth, some inkling of what was in her mind dawning on him slowly.

He drew her up next to him, as somewhere off in the distance a clock chimed midnight.

"The witching hour," he spoke quietly, his eyes wintergreen with hardness. "Shall I remove your mask and see if you really are the sorceress the villagers claim?" Before she could reply, he untied the strings and pulled the mask from her face. "Aye," he muttered. "You could cast a spell over a man with those eyes of yours." He ran his hand over her throat and down her shoulder, pulling one sleeve down to expose the whiteness of her flesh.

Morgana stared at him, mesmerized, then recovering her senses, tried to yank away, causing his fingers to tighten at the sudden movement, making her flinch.

"I shall have a bruise there in the morning," she whispered, her anger draining away at the light in his eyes, the pulse at the hollow of her throat beating rapidly.

"Then look at it and know which of us is the stronger."

"I shall wear a low-cut dress and tell everyone it is you who put this mark upon me," she taunted with a false bravado as she trembled in his rough grasp.

"Aye," he laughed softly. "Tell them all that I have placed my brand upon you and see if any man in Ireland dares challenge me for the right."

Morgana gasped and fled from him, shaking with sudden fear, and feeling his mocking eyes upon her all the way.

Chapter Five

Morgana did indeed have a purplish bruise on her shoulder in the morning, but she did not carry out her threat to show it to the world. She dressed instead in a high-necked gown, trying not to dwell on Rian's actions of last night. Her head ached horribly and she stifled a yawn as she went downstairs to breakfast. When Rian grinned with amusement at her attire, Morgana gave him one cold glance, then pointedly ignored him. She didn't understand the rules of a game he was initiating and she vowed silently not to play.

Apparently most of the overnight guests were unaccustomed to the early hours kept at Shanetara, for there was no one but the family present at breakfast. Gerald, sober for once, was lamenting his loss of a sizable sum of money at the card tables, which had been set up at the ball for those jaded young men who did not care for dancing.

"I tell you, grandfather, Rian's a devil. No one could

win against him last night. He held the bank most of the evening."

"Come now, Gerry," Rian broke in. "I'm a devil and poor Morgana's a witch. Next thing you know, Patrick will be a sorcerer's apprentice. You'll have to come up with a more logical explanation than that. Admit it, cousin, I'm just a better cardplayer than you."

"I'll admit nothing of the sort, Rian. Why, even Sean Devlin said you were a demon in disguise, and he's the most sensible man I know."

"Perhaps that's because he also lost a great deal of money last night," Patrick's eyes twinkled. "And so did Johnnie Gallagher and Max O'Brien, if I'm not mistaken."

"How do you do it, cousin?" Colin asked curiously. "Do you have some sort of system devised, or do you rely solely on chance?"

"Sure and I'm a demon in disguise," Rian joked, much to Colin's annoyance.

"Faith. I see I shall be unable to get a straight answer out of you," he said disgustedly.

"Never tell anyone how to win at cards or with women, Colin. Nine times out of ten they'll not take your advice anyway and will end up despising you for succeeding where they've failed," Rian counselled him.

"Enough of this card talk," Fergus declared. "I want to hear how Morgana enjoyed the evening and if any of the young men she met caught her fancy. Well?" he looked at her, already certain of her answer.

He was privately delighted and sure now that his plan was the right one, for Rian's grinning glance at Morgana had not escaped his notice, nor had the manner in which his granddaughter was doing her best to ignore the rascal. So much the better! If they were already attracted to one another, his work would be that much easier.

"I found the ball very pleasant indeed," Morgana replied calmly. "But there was no one present who particularly interested me. As I told you before, grandfather,

I'm not thinking of getting married. I'm no longer in the marriage mart," she pointed out practically.

"Damn it all, lass!" he swore. "I'll not have another spinster on my hands, or a governess to a parcel of brats, if that's what you're thinking. Never mind," he cackled secretly. "I'll find something to do with you."

Morgana felt a little uneasy after that remark and wondered what the old man was going to dream up this time. But she determined not to let it ruin her day, and after breakfast she hurried upstairs to change into her riding habit.

"Jim." She found the stable boy. "Would you please saddle Copper Lady for me. If anyone asks," she told him when he'd led the mare out and helped her mount. "Say I've gone into Kilshannon for the day. I've some business there."

It was a beautiful day. The sun turned the lough into a sheet of blue glass and the mountainous crags looked less menacing than they often did at night when the blackness of the sky made them seem like angry monsters lurking in the shadows.

Kilshannon was a busy little village, although the larger town of Dingle was nearby, for it was closer to Shanetara and many of grandfather's tenants went there for supplies. Morgana walked Copper Lady through the twisting streets, ignoring the glances she often received from passersby, until she found Doctor Kelsey's tiny office.

"Lady McShane," he said, coming forward at the sound of the bell which chimed when she opened the door. "What a pleasant surprise. You can go home now, Max," he turned to a small boy. "Tell your mother that cut is doing fine. Now, what can I do for you?" he asked when the child had left the office. "No one at Shanetara ailing, I hope?"

"No, nothing really," she somehow didn't know how to say what was in her mind. "I guess I'm just feeling homesick. Have you a cure for that, Doctor?"

"Look," his eyes softened in understanding. "Why

don't we go for a drive and you can tell me all about it, if you want to."

"You're very kind, Doctor Kelsey, but I couldn't take you away from your practice."

"Nothing to it," he said. "I'm not very busy today anyway."

"Very well," she agreed somewhat shyly.

Morgana left Copper Lady in a small leanto by his office and they rode out together in his buggy until they came upon a lovely grassy spot on the moor.

"Shall we stop here and walk for a bit, Lady Morgana?" he asked.

"Please, just Morgana," she said impulsively. "Lady Morgana sounds so formal."

"Only if you agree to call me Michael," he laughed.

"Agreed; this is a fine place to stop."

Michael helped her down from the buggy, his hands strong about her waist.

"Tell me about yourself, Michael," she spoke, casting about for something to say.

"There really isn't much to tell. I was born in Kilshannon twenty-eight years ago. My father was one of your grandfather's tenants, and my mother worked in the great house, as the villagers call Shanetara. I was lucky enough and bright enough to be accepted into the University at Dublin. My father was injured in a farming accident at Shanetara and your grandfather paid my schooling expenses as compensation for his injuries. The Duke was very decent about it really. Unfortunately, there was no doctor here in Kilshannon at the time and the one from Dingle couldn't get away. My father died shortly afterwards. That's why I decided to go into medicine. When I'd completed my studies, I came back here and set up practice."

Morgana digested this piece of information thoughtfully, then said, "My father would have envied you, Michael, for the work you're doing here. Another man would have turned his back on these poverty-stricken tenants and headed for the King's court in London. You'll not get rich here, I'm afraid."

"No, but I feel useful, which is more than I could have done in London. These people need me and I'm glad to be of help to them."

"And your mother?"

"Dead, too, God rest her soul. There was an epidemic. So many people died needlessly, some of your cousins' parents among them. We just didn't know what to do for them."

"I didn't know," Morgana said softly. "None of my cousins has talked of the past. How horrible! Perhaps they have their reasons for acting as they sometimes do. Trevor's so stiff and dutiful, and Gerald's an alcoholic. Colin sits brooding silently most of the time, and spends his days reading or writing poetry. Rian is—well—he's strange. Patrick seems to be the only normal one in the bunch."

"Aye, Trevor and Gerald lost their parents then. It was terrible, the bodies stretched out along the streets, their bellies swollen and their tongues black and thickened with thirst from the fever. God knows we did what we could, but it wasn't enough. The stench was enough to make men retch and women fainted at the sights."

"How awful," Morgana reiterated lamely.

"Rian's father had been killed earlier at sea. His mother never recovered from the shock and died three weeks later of a broken heart. They were fortunate in a way to have missed the disease. Patrick's parents survived the plague, but were killed about a year later when their carriage overturned on the way back from Letterick one evening. Colin's father was shot in a duel. His mother, poor young lass, left the babe on the doorstep of Shanetara and disappeared. No one ever heard from her again."

"And my father ran off with my mother, an Englishwoman. No wonder grandfather seems so bitter at times."

"I don't think he cast your father out because your mother was English, Morgana. Patrick's mother was, too. That's how he inherited his title. I think your grandfather was really angry because your father refused to come back to Ireland to live."

"And my aunt, Rosamunde, why did she never marry, Michael?"

"I don't really know. There was some talk about a scandal involving her and one of the grooms at Shanetara. The local lads say she was in love with him and wanted to marry him, but your grandfather wouldn't hear of it. They say the man was only after her money and I guess they were right, because your grandfather bought him off with a bribe. The fellow left Shanetara and they say your aunt never looked at another man after that. I'm sure you've noticed how she tends to dwell in the past at times, muttering to herself at others. She's been a little out of touch with reality ever since it happened, although she's quite sane most of the time."

"Thank you, Michael," Morgana spoke sincerely. "Perhaps this will help me understand my family better."

It was getting late, so they drove back to Kilshannon. Morgana led Copper Lady out of the leanto and Michael helped her mount.

"I hope you don't mind me taking up your day," she told him.

"No, I don't mind," he smiled. "Please come again whenever you feel like it."

Morgana looked down at him warmly. "I shall."

And there was between them the unspoken, but nevertheless understood, promise of friendship to come. She didn't wait for his reply, but turned her mare's head and found the road home to Shanetara.

Morgana lay in bed that evening, unable to sleep. Finally, she decided to go down to the library to get grandfather's copy of Jane Austen's first novel. She slipped on her wrapper and tiptoed downstairs so as not to waken the rest of the house. Morgana set the lamp on a table and studied the rows in front of her, looking for the book. Grandfather certainly had a fine collection. She'd read many of them since her coming. Suddenly, she stopped short. There, tucked away on an obscure part of a bottom shelf she hadn't seen before, were all of her father's books of poems. She lifted one from its resting place, holding it lovingly. So, the old man had been unable to harden his heart against her father as much as he would have liked.

"Well, well, the bluestocking has crept down to find a book. I would have thought you'd have read them all by now."

Morgana gasped and turned to face Rian. His shirt was open to the waist, revealing the dark mat of hair across his chest, and he held a glass of whiskey in one hand. She drew her robe around her tighter, still clutching her father's book.

"What do you want?" she tried to ask calmly.

"Nothing. I saw the light and came to see who was prowling in my grandfather's library in the dead of night."

"Well, now you've seen. Let me pass, please."

He made no effort to move out of her way.

"Rian, you're blocking the aisle. Will you let me through, please?"

He moved toward her instead, pinning her up against one of the bookshelves.

"You saw Michael Kelsey in town today, didn't you?"

"I don't know what business it is of yours if I did or not."

"I told you to keep away from him," Rian swore at her.

"And what if you did? I'm no concern of yours," she repeated.

"No, Mag?" he used her father's nickname for her as a child, the curiously twisted, alphabetically wrong name she hadn't thought of or been called in years. "But you'd like to be, wouldn't you?"

"I don't know what you're talking about, Rian," she said coldly.

"This," he ran his hand over the curve of her jaw, then tilted her face up to his own.

"Rian, don't," she pleaded softly, understanding his intent then and feeling suddenly frightened by it.

He ignored her, tossing the glass of whiskey against the wall, where it shattered into a million pieces, the amber liquid dripping slowly down the oak panelling. His eyes darkened deeply before his mouth came down over hers, gently in the beginning, then harder, more demanding as his tongue parted her lips, exploring the inner softness of her mouth. She held herself stiffly against him, for she had been touched by no man, but Rian was well experienced. He knew instinctively that he was the first to taste of her innocence, and the thought pleased him. His hands moved within her robe, drawing her up next to the length of his hard, muscular body as he continued his slow onslaught, his mouth slashing across her cheek, down her throat to her breasts.

"Please," Morgana whispered, not understanding the fires that stirred within her at his touch.

She whimpered softly, not even aware that she'd made the sound, and weakened against him, her father's book falling, forgotten, to the floor. That was the response he was seeking, for he drew away, his eyes searching her face; and he made no further move to stop her when she turned and ran from the room.

Chapter Six

Morgana received many invitations in the weeks following the masquerade ball, so she had little time to reflect on Rian's behavior toward her that evening in the library. Occasionally, she would look up to catch him watching her, and she would feel a slow flush steal across her cheeks. But they had no further run-ins. She was too busy. There were card parties at Devlin's Way where they played whist and silver loo until the small hours of the morning, and Johnnie Gallagher held several fox hunts at Laughlin Hall. Morgana rode the course, but refused to be in on the kill, considering it cruel. Rian was present, of course, upon these occasions, but she usually asked Patrick or Colin to act as her escort if none other was available. And gradually, her grief and loneliness began to heal, and much of her natural reserve and somberness to fade.

Her relationship with Michael Kelsey deepened to one of almost sisterly affection; and she rode into town often to see him. Once, she took a picnic lunch.

"How would you like to escape from these bottles of medicine and rolls of bandages for a while?" she enticed him cheerfully.

"Well, now, what did you have in mind?" His eyes twinkled responsively as he wiped his hands on a towel.

"I intend," she began, setting the picnic basket down on a table, "to take you out into the country and stuff you full of all sorts of things which I'm sure your medical mind will heartily disapprove of, bread and cheese, smoked ham, a bottle of wine I filched from grandfather's cellar, and apple pie."

"My medical mind, as you called it, tells me those things are fattening and intoxicating to boot, but my stomach has ruled this day. Lead the way, madam. I shall be delighted to join you."

As always, Morgana left Copper Lady in the leanto, and they took Michael's buggy to the grassy place on the moor she had come to think of as theirs. She laid the spread upon the ground and unpacked, chatting happily all the while.

They talked and laughed, and he cut slabs of the ham and cheese and fed them to her with chunks of the good, rich bread. They drank the wine, getting slightly tipsy, and polished off the apple pie. Morgana looked at Michael and sighed. She felt warm and flushed all over, a feeling she attributed to the wine. She rolled over in the grass, gazing up at the white puffy clouds in the sky.

"Did you ever want to touch a cloud, Michael? Don't they look like they're just the softest things in the world? I feel like I could just reach up and sink my hand down into one. Don't you?"

"Aye," he spoke gently.

Morgana turned then, and gazed into his eyes, as blue as the sky above her. "I'm glad I've found a friend," she said simply.

He was touched, and pressed her hand briefly before they climbed into the buggy.

On Friday, a very dapper, businesslike man drove up to Shanetara in a well-turned-out rig. He did not speak to anyone when he entered the house, but was ushered quickly and quietly upstairs to grandfather's room by Bridget, who kept peeping at him curiously. Shortly afterwards, Trevor and Fionna arrived.

"My God, I saw Angus O'Donnell headed this way," Trevor hurried into the sitting room. "Is grandfather dead?"

"Don't count your chickens before they hatch, dear boy," Rian drawled. "The old man is as fit as a fiddle."

"Then what is O'Donnell doing here?"

"Your guess is as good as mine," Rian spoke again. "But I'll wager my hat that grandfather is changing his will."

"Well, that's what I suspected when I saw O'Donnell," Patrick chimed in.

"My God!" Trevor swore again. "We'll all be done out of our inheritance money, I know it. I knew when Morgana came here the old man would change his will! 'Tis all her fault!"

"I don't know what you're worried about," Colin said peevishly. "You make a good living and the old man has to leave you Shanetara. I'm the one who really needs the money, and Morgana is as poor as a churchmouse, too!"

"Nonsense!" Trevor expostulated.

The man in question came downstairs just then and they had no time for further discussion. Trevor hurried outside and collared the man, trying unsuccessfully to find out what had happened, but Mister O'Donnell was as close-mouthed as a priest, simply shaking his head and driving away, leaving them all unsatisfied and slightly put out at his behavior.

"Well, isn't he the queer one?" Gerald asked of no one in particular. "I just hope the old man left me enough to buy liquor for the rest of my life."

"How disgusting," Colin flicked an imaginary piece of lint from his cuff.

"Don't use that tone to me, you insolent pup," Gerald warned. "I'd just as soon cuff you as look at you."

"Silence! Both of you," Trevor snapped nervously. "There's no telling what that crazy fool has done to his will."

"Well, I imagine we'll have to wait until dinner to find out," Rian said logically, and left the room, his cousins still quarrelling furiously behind him.

Morgana knew none of this, however. She had taken her cloak and gone for a walk, long before her grandfather's lawyer's arrival, and was not there when the dapper man departed either. The air was cool outside and smelt damp, as though it were going to rain. She walked idly toward Brandon Hill, lost in her thoughts. The girl was so engrossed that she never heard the sound of hoofbeats coming up behind her.

"And where are you going, my lovely witch?" Rian gazed down at her from his black stallion.

"Away from you," she snapped, and walked faster.

" 'Tis useless," he laughed. "You'll never outrun Lucifer."

" 'Lucifer,' what a name for a horse," she shrugged indifferently.

To her surprise, he halted the stallion and sat there watching her hurry on. She did not know it, but Rian often watched her on the moors and had seen her several times with Michael Kelsey. He did not know their relationship, and so suspected they were lovers. It angered him that she sought the common doctor's kisses so eagerly and scorned his own. He had wanted her merely to amuse himself during his stay in Ireland, having grown jaded with Lindsey Joyce; but since Morgana had fled from him, and now steadfastly ignored him, his desire had become more than just a passing fancy. Rian's interest was aroused, for he loved a challenge and chase, having been led on so few; and he was determined to win. The Earl had the advantage, for he knew enough of her past situation to guess how she must feel. Her cool dignity was affronted by his insolence, and yet her mind was drawn to one more clever than her own; and the tumultuous stirrings of her body were new and frightening to one who'd had little experience with men.

Her lips, when he'd kissed her, had been soft and trembling; and she'd not known how to cope with, or even to recognize, her own desires. Aye, it was indeed a challenge worthy of a jaded man; and Rian had no doubt that sooner or later he would wear down her resistance, and she would be his.

The fact that she was his cousin, cast into a strange land with strange relatives, impoverished, troubled his conscience not at all. He meant to make use of her penniless, dependent circumstances. Rian's lips curled arrogantly. What woman had ever refused fine clothes and jewels? He was rich. He would set her up handsomely as his mistress; and when he had tired of her, he would give her a nice little estate with a modest income.

Suddenly he grinned and whipped Lucifer up. Several minutes later Morgana was startled by the sound of rapidly approaching hoofbeats. She turned just in time for Rian to pull her up in the saddle in front of him.

"You fool!" she gasped. "You might have killed me!"

"I think not," he breathed in her ear.

"Put me down this instant," Morgana tried to sound authoritative, knowing he would do exactly as he pleased.

He paid no heed, as usual, but ran his hand under her cloak, pulling her up against his chest. It began to rain lightly, and Morgana was sure he could feel her heart pounding rapidly in her breast. He loosed the reins, letting Lucifer wander at will, and grasped her face, turning it so that his mouth came down roughly, bruising her tender lips. Morgana moaned softly under his kiss, hating him for touching her, yet feeling an exciting fire flicker through her body at his caress. She weakened against him, her head upon his shoulder as, at last, she responded to his desires. When he had taken his fill, Rian released her. Then he reined Lucifer in, turning the horse toward Shanetara, feeling Morgana trembling against him.

"You are despicable," she said at last, humiliated at her own wanton conduct.

"Come now, Mag," he eyed her lazily. "Don't try to

pretend you didn't enjoy it. I felt you respond to my kiss."

"You beast," she was almost in tears with shame. "If you ever touch me again, I swear I'll tell grandfather. He'd be furious with you," she warned.

"For you, madam, I would brave the old man's wrath."

Morgana said nothing more as they approached the stables. Rian helped her dismount, his hands around her waist tightly and longer than necessary, before they walked, untouching, back to the house.

That evening grandfather seemed in particularly good spirits, but Morgana thought he appeared a little more sly and smug than usual, and it made her feel slightly uneasy. She could scarcely eat anyway with Rian sitting across the table watching her mockingly. She tried to avoid his meaningful glances, but it was becoming increasingly difficult.

Everyone was, of course, filled with curiosity about Angus O'Donnell's visit, but no one was brave enough to question Fergus over dinner, so Morgana still remained in ignorance of the matter. Fergus waited until he had the men alone, over port, before he dropped his bombshell.

"I'm sure you're all wondering why Angus was here today," he cleared his throat. "I might as well tell you, I've changed my will."

"I knew it," Trevor groaned.

"As you all know," he continued, ignoring Trevor's outburst. "Morgana believes herself a spinster and too old to marry. Well, 'tis my thinking that she isn't; and I've decided I would like to see her wed to one of you. I have, therefore, arranged to leave my entire fortune to the man who succeeds in bringing her to the altar—" he was interrupted by gasps of outrage and surprise. "Hear me out," he raised one hand, staying their comments, "provided that she marry one of you before my death. I'm sure this is ample incentive for all of you, for the wench is not uncomely. And none of you, not even you, Rian," he gave his grandson a piercing stare, "has a fortune which equals mine."

He ended this little speech, much convinced that he had sufficiently played upon their greed to make the game interesting; and certain that Rian would come up the winner, since his grandson could not bear to lose a challenge.

His grandsons sat there dumbly for a moment, not sure they'd heard him correctly, until Trevor burst out, "Why, that's preposterous! The very idea is grossly unfair, especially to me, since I'm already married."

"I must say, it does seem rather out of balance, grandfather, cutting the rest of us out this way," Patrick voiced his opinion.

"How do you expect me to live?" Colin cried. "I can barely make ends meet on my allowance as it is!"

"I expect you to stop dawdling away your hours on that trash you read, and doubtless write, and take an interest in becoming a minister."

"Poetry isn't trash, it's culture. I don't want to be a damn priest!" Colin swore at the old man defiantly.

"Aye, and how's a man to buy a decent drink?" Gerald chimed in, adding fuel to the fire.

"Seems to me you've already had more than your share," Fergus suggested dryly. "Never thought I'd live to see a McShane no more than a drunken sot!"

"May I ask what you intend to do with your money if the lady in question chooses not to wed one of us?" Rian spoke for the first time, greatly displeased by this sudden turn of events.

"You always were sharper than the rest of them," grandfather cackled delightedly. "In such an event, I've left instructions for an orphanage to be built as a memorial to me. It will be known as the 'Fergus McShane Home for Poor Children.' The fortune will be used for its construction and the remainder will go into a trust fund for its upkeep."

"You've become senile in your old age," Trevor

insisted loudly amidst Gerald's guffaws of laughter. "Such a thing would never be upheld in court."

"Angus O'Donnell drew it up. Are you saying you're a better lawyer than he is?" Fergus gave him a piercing glance.

Trevor had no answer to this, and in the momentary silence the old man continued. "One other thing. Morgana is not to know of this will. She has the McShane stubbornness," he noted, not without pride. "And will flout the scheme if she gets wind of it. Any one of you who discloses its contents to her will be banished from Shanetara and cut off without a penny. Is that clear?"

They all nodded, still somewhat stunned by his unexpected announcement.

"Good," he spoke sharply. "She is to be courted with all respect due a lady and your cousin," he suddenly glanced meaningfully at Rian, as if he'd guessed his grandson's rakish intentions. "And you will, all of you, I presume," he smiled dryly. "Keep in mind the stakes of this game."

He turned to Trevor. "Trevor, you mentioned earlier that this scheme is unfair to you, and so it is. Nevertheless, you will still inherit Shanetara under any circumstances, and its income is nothing to be sneered at. Besides, if Gerald succeeds in marrying the wench," he snorted as though this were highly unlikely. "I have no doubt that he will share his good fortune with you, since you have taken care of him all of these years."

"Admit it," Rian said coldly before Trevor had a chance to reply. "This is something you've dreamed up to make up for all of the years of poverty she had to suffer because of you. She'll not have any of us because of her damned pride. You're growing soft and sentimental in your old age." Rian was dismayed at this sudden aspect in his grandfather and now his own plans had been thrown into disarray.

"If I am," the Duke answered wryly. "It's certainly not your concern. There comes a time in every man's life when he realizes that he must give back something for all of the things he's taken out of it. Remember that, and you'll be a better man for it."

Fergus closed his eyes tiredly then, feeling that, at last, he had done all he could.

Chapter Seven

On Saturday, Morgana met Michael as usual, and they passed a pleasant afternoon picking wild flowers. But her gaiety ended when she she was returning home to Shanetara. She ran into Brendan O'Hara. Morgana had not seen the man since that fateful day several months ago when she'd attempted to take the villagers at Shaughnessy a basket of fruit; when she, new in Ireland and ignorant of its ways, had so deeply insulted his pride, stinging him into driving her from town with his cold, cruel comments. Now he blocked her path, studying her coolly with deep blue eyes, the color of his sister Bridget's. Brendan raked her insultingly with those eyes. How he would have liked to bed the red-haired witch, but even she was not worth the penalty of death, and the McShanes had wicked tempers. Suddenly Moragna knew without a doubt that he'd seen her with Michael, had probably been watching them for some time now. God, would the man keep his mouth shut? The McShanes would put an end to her friendship with the doctor, if they knew.

"You're blocking my way, Mister O'Hara," she returned his cool stare.

"Am I now, Lady Morgana?"

The man was insolent and not be trusted. It dawned on her then that she was totally alone, without a groom or a maid to accompany her. Now she wished fervently for one as she looked down at the bold Brendan, and staid Trevor's admonishments came back to haunt her. She whipped up her mare and, surprisingly, he moved out of her path. She rode by, unmolested, except for the cool blue eyes that raked her as she travelled down the road.

Several weeks later Morgana became aware that the attitudes of her cousins toward her had undergone some distinctly profound changes since her arrival. She first noticed it when Gerald, dressed in exceptionally nice attire, approached her one morning and asked if she wanted to drive over to Dingle with him.

"I thought perhaps you might like to do some shopping. The stores there are much better supplied than the few we have in Kilshannon, and I would appreciate your company," he said.

Morgana sniffed suspiciously for the smell of liquor, but could discern no trace of alcohol on his breath. It occurred to her that she hadn't seen Gerald really drunk for several evenings now, so she drove to Dingle with him. He chatted companionably the entire distance, even to the point of apologizing for calling her a red-haired witch.

"Even though I still find you bewitching," he glanced at her from under half-closed eyelids.

Why, he's trying to flirt with me, she thought. Gerald, who had not paid her the slightest heed since her arrival, with the exception of that one evening at dinner when things had gotten out of control after grandfather's announcement of his intention to host a masquerade ball. Morgana looked at her big, brawny cousin and blushed.

"You're quite pretty when you go all pink like that. I've noticed it for quite some time now."

His remark only served to make her face redder.

Gerald stared even harder as Morgana became uncomfortably aware of a strong undercurrent of unspoken thoughts between them. Then, because he wasn't watching the road, they hit a nasty bump and Morgana was flung against his chest. Gerald put his beefy arm around her.

"Steady there, lass. Wouldn't want you to fall out and get hurt. No, sir. That wouldn't do at all."

He clucked to the horses as she tactfully disengaged herself. They did, after all, pass a pleasant day. Gerald took her shopping, being extremely patient while Morgana browsed through bolts of cloth. He bought some lovely green ribands for her hair. When they returned home, Morgana thanked him for a pleasant afternoon and thought nothing more about the matter. However, his attentions to her rapidly increased until they reached the point of being overwhelming and confusing. The men in her family noted her discomfiture with varying degrees of amusement and suspicion, while she unsuccessfully tried to discover the reason for the change of heart Gerald was apparently experiencing.

When she rode over to see Fionna one morning, she was jolted into a rude, even more confusing, awakening about Gerald's intentions. Morgana spied her young cousin-in-in-law in the garden and dismounted, planning to call aloud to the girl, when she was stopped by the sound of raised voices coming through the large bay window at the back of the house. It appeared that Gerald and Trevor were having a heated argument. Morgana edged nearer, not consciously eavesdropping, but nevertheless soon becoming engrossed in the conversation.

"You're going too fast," she heard Trevor say.

"And I say I'll soon have the little vixen wrapped around my finger," Gerald countered smugly.

"Damn it all, Gerry! She's a lot smarter than you give her credit for. You've got to go easy, pamper her, make her see you're more than just a brawny dolt."

" 'Brawny dolt,' is it? Let me tell you something, big brother. If it weren't for me, you wouldn't even have a stake in this hand."

"I realize that, you fool. Can't you see I'm only trying to help you? If you scare her off before you've gotten her to the altar, we'll never get our hands on the old man's money."

Morgana backed away then, her face flushed with anger, not wanting to hear any more, for she was sure they had been talking about her. What did it mean? What money? Then it hit her. The dowry, of course. The dowry grandfather had promised her, should she wed. Why, the very idea was absurd! Surely Gerald wouldn't go to such lengths just to get his hands on what must certainly be a paltry sum of money, knowing her grandfather's pennypinching ways. The thought was so ridiculous, she shoved it out of her head. But thereafter, she developed an icy aloofness toward Gerald, unfailingly polite, but reserved. The harder he tried to please her, to seek her favor, the more coldly she treated him, until the poor oaf was wracked with confusion, and the rest of her cousins overjoyed!

One evening, Morgana was sitting in her bedroom, brushing her hair, when Bridget came in to pour the water for her mistress's nightly bath. Morgana spoke to the girl briefly, then returned to her silent task, so it was some time before she noticed the tears slipping quietly down Bridget's cheeks.

"Why, Bridget," she jumped up, immediately concerned, "my dear, whatever is the matter? Surely you've no cause for tears."

"Oh, me lady," Bridget moaned softly. "I'm so ashamed. I kin't be telling a decent lady like yerself me troubles."

"Of course you can. Aren't we good friends? Of course we are, and that's what friends are for. Now tell me what's bothering you."

"Oh, me lady," Bridget moaned softly. "I'm going to have a baby."

Of all the confidences the girl might have offered, this remark was the last thing Morgana would have expected. Bridget was such a sweet girl, Morgana was stunned.

"Are you sure?"

Bridget nodded miserably.

"Bridget, look at me. Do you know who the father is?"

The maid cast her frightened eyes downward once more. "Aye," she whispered almost inaudibly. "But I kin't tell, me lady, really I kin't."

"But you must, Bridget," Morgana coaxed softly. "This man must be made to right the wrong he has done you. Surely you can see that."

"He kin't, me lady."

"Why not? Have you told him about the child? Has he refused to wed you? Good God! He's not already married, is he?"

"No," she murmured.

"Then he must be made to pay," Morgana concluded stoically, for she could not believe other than that the innocent girl before her had been callously seduced and tossed aside. "Do you love him, Bridget?" she asked on a kinder note.

"Aye," the maid agreed. "I love him more than me life. That is why I kinnot bring this shame upon him. He—he's not of my class."

Something inside Morgana flickered and blazed into anger at the girl's words, perhaps something left over of the child who had smarted under the hateful remarks of the girls at the seminary; and she set her jaw, determined that the maid should not suffer.

"Such thinking is foolish, Bridget. We are all of us human beings, no better, no worse than our fellow mankind. Does this man love you in return?"

"I think so, otherwise I would never have—" she broke into sobs again. "Oh, me lady, what am I going to do?"

"First of all, you must tell me his name. Trust me," Morgana encouraged the weeping girl.

"It's—it's yer cousin Patrick," the maid finally said reluctantly.

Morgana drew her breath in sharply. Of course. She remembered Patrick's wink at the girl the first night

Morgana had arrived in Shanetara. How had they managed to keep their affair a secret this long?

"Sit right here," Morgana ordered. "Until I return."

"Where—where are you going?" Bridget cried nervously.

"To get Patrick."

"No, no, me lady, ye mustn't!"

"Of course I must. Don't be silly, Bridget! My cousin is a man of honor. If he loves you, he will accept you as you are, regardless of this social snobbery."

After making sure that the maid was not going to flee out the door, Morgana hurried down the hall to Patrick's room.

"Cousin," she knocked on the door. "May I come in?"

He seemed rather surprised to see her, which was only natural, but that was nothing compared to the glance of mortification she received when she requested that he come to her room at once.

"Morgana, what is the meaning of this? Surely you know how improper this is."

"I don't care," she told him. "I can't explain it right now. You must come with me," she tugged on his sleeve, intending to haul him away by physical force if necessary.

Bridget's startled and frightened blue eyes surveyed them from across the room when they entered, then the girl began to cry miserably again.

"Bridget," Patrick crossed to her side. "What's going on here?"

"She's with child, Patrick," Morgana blurted out bluntly.

"My God!"

"I'm sorry, Paddy, I'm so ashamed," the maid moaned quietly.

"Patrick, do you love her?" Morgana faced her cousin squarely.

"Hell, yes!" he swore. "Sorry, girls, it's just that—my God—what are we going to do?"

"You're going to get married, naturally, like any other young couple in love," Morgana spoke calmly.

"But grandfather will never agree to this, he'll cut me out of his will for sure—" Patrick began, then broke off abruptly.

"What are you, a man or a mouse?" Morgana questioned dryly. "Do you want Bridget, or don't you?"

"Of course I do," Patrick took the girl's hands in his. "I love you," he told the anxious lass. "You're right, Morgana," he turned to his cousin, throwing caution to the wind. "I've got to stand up for myself in this matter. We'll get a special license and be married tomorrow, though how the devil I'm going to get one of those things is beyond me. I never had any reason to associate with bishops and the like, except at church, of course. And I'm sure the priest in Dingle will be much too terrified of grandfather's wrath to give me one."

This was something Morgana hadn't considered. Bridget bit her lip.

"It'll never work, Paddy. What'll we live on? I'll be ruining yer life ferever."

"Nonsense!" Patrick spoke sharply, making Morgana aware that her easygoing cousin could possess the McShane temper and backbone when he chose. "I don't want to hear any more talk like that out of you! We'll manage somehow. I still have my mother's estate in England."

"Rian!" Morgana snapped her fingers together suddenly, meeting their curious stares. "Rian will know how to get a license. I'll go and get him."

"Oh, no," Bridget cried. "He'll tell yer grandfather fer sure."

"No, he won't," Morgana decided, not sure why this was the case.

"How the devil do you know what he's likely to do?" Patrick snorted.

"I just know. Wait here."

And once again, Morgana hurried down the hall to a cousin's bedroom.

"Rian," she began when he'd come to the door. "I need your help. Will you come down to my room, please."

Unlike Patrick, Rian did not ask a lot of questions, but cocked a quizzical eyebrow in her direction and drawled lazily, "I hope you intend to make it worth my while."

This remark she chose to ignore and received a low laugh for her pains.

"You are well aware that the old man will hit the roof when he finds out," Rian said slowly when he'd heard the entire story.

"Of course we are," Patrick was a trifle impatient. "We've already thought about that, but it can't be helped."

"You're determined to go through with this then, Patrick?"

"Aye, Bridget and I love each other, and now, with the child on the way, I can't just throw her out and let her starve."

"Nay, I guess not. I've got a friend who's a bishop. He'll give me the license, I'm sure. I'll ride over tonight and get it. I just hope you can convince that priest in Dingle to marry you once I've got the permit. I suppose Morgana and I can go with you tomorrow as witnesses and vouch that the old man's given his consent, even though you don't legally need it. I know everyone around is afraid of the old buzzard."

"Oh, would ye do that fer us?" Bridget asked breathlessly.

"Certainly," Rian conceded. "Wouldn't we, Mag?"

"In for a penny, in for a pound," she answered fatefully.

They left the anxious but happy lovers to their hopes and fears, while Rian and Morgana walked back to his room, plotting and planning like partners in crime. She helped him into his jacket and greatcoat with its many capes.

"I should be back before dawn," he told her.

"I'll see that Bridget and Patrick are ready to go in

the morning. Thank you for doing this, Rian," she murmured softly, only to bite her tongue when he mocked her thanks a moment later.

"Don't worry. I'll be sure and exact a price for my services," he drawled and strode out into the blackness of night.

A very anxious bride and a slightly defiant groom were married in Dingle the next morning, but married they were by a nervous priest who'd only half believed their fervent assurances that the wedding had grandfather's blessing and consent. Fortunately, Rian could be most charming and persuasive when he chose and a small bribe, for the church of course, did much to help matters. After the brief ceremony had ended, Morgana suddenly realized the full import of what she'd instigated, and the thought of her grandfather's ire began to make her knees knock with fright, though she was determined to stick to her guns.

"Having second thoughts, Mag?" Rian probed amusedly. "Don't worry. I'll be there to back you up."

"For once, I am truly grateful for your support," she admitted grudgingly.

Wrath is not an adequate word to describe what Fergus McShane displayed when he was told about the marriage. To give him credit, Patrick faced the old man unflinchingly, and Bridget, though tears filled her eyes, stood her ground as well. Morgana thought wryly that at least grandfather would not be able to label Patrick's wife a milktoast.

"Married! Married!" grandfather yelled, the veins popping out on his forehead as he rapped his cane angrily and violently upon the floor. "How could you do this, you ungrateful brat? And you," he turned to Bridget. "You sly minx, ingratiating yourself into my household. I trusted you to be a loyal servant and this is how you repay me! By God, Patrick! I shall cut you out of my will at once."

"You've already done that, grandfather," Patrick reminded him calmly, then almost bit off his tongue.

"Then I'll cut off your funds and banish you from this house, do you hear?" the old man was too agitated to notice the slip, as was everyone else present. "Pack your things immediately and get out of my sight, both of you!"

"As you wish, grandfather. Come, Bridget."

"Aren't you being a little hasty?" Rian asked. "It seems to me you've gone this route once before and suffered for it."

"Don't you bring that up, you ungrateful cur, aiding and abetting them the way you've done. And you, Morgana. I took you in when no one else would have you. I've nourished a snake to my breast. Just look at all the trouble you've caused!" he shouted.

"If Patrick goes, I'm leaving, too," Morgana said quietly. "I cannot live in a house which harbors a petty hypocrite."

"I've been thinking about setting sail again. Now might just be the best time to do it," Rian shrugged his shoulders indifferently.

"Hmph! Think I'm wrong, do you? Intending to punish me, both of you, aren't you." He was slightly pleased to see they had banded together in this. "Well, I won't have it, do you hear? Faith! That girl is nothing more than a common housemaid," the old man snorted.

"Which does not alter the fact that she's carrying Patrick's child, your great-grandchild," Rian reminded him sternly, for they had thought it best to explain the reason for this hasty and unseemly marriage.

"My great-grandchild, indeed. We have no assurance that her child is Patrick's."

"The child is mine, my lord," Patrick spoke, trying to control his obvious anger as he came into the room with his bags. "And you will show my wife due respect by never repeating that remark again. I am to blame, if anyone. I love Bridget and have taken advantage of her and used her unforgivably because I was not man enough to face your wrath and marry her in the first place. I hope she will find it in her heart to forgive my weakness and accept the steps I have taken to correct the matter." He turned to Rian. "I'm taking Bridget to the inn in Kilshannon. I'd appreciate it if you would see that the rest of my things are sent over in the morning."

"Be happy to, cousin. Mind if I kiss the bride before you leave?"

"Not at all."

Rian leaned forward and planted a cousinly kiss upon the girl's cheek. "Welcome to the family, my dear, such as it is. I hope you won't judge us too harshly."

"No, me lord," she whispered gratefully as Morgana, too, hugged the brave lass and wished the couple well.

There was silence in the room as they listened to the sound of the buggy wheels drift away into the dusk of the settling twilight. Finally Morgana got to her feet again.

"I'd best go upstairs and begin packing. Kerr can drive me into town in the morning. I'll take the rest of Patrick's things with me then," she told Rian.

They were halted by the sound of grandfather's cane clattering to the floor as the old man put his hands to his throat and made a dreadful choking noise, his face turning a ghastly shade of blue.

"Grandfather!" Morgana cried, running to his side. Rian was already loosening the old man's cravat. "Rosamunde, get Michael." Morgana was unconscious of the fact that she'd called the doctor by his first name until she caught Rian's quick, searching gaze, but he said nothing, returning his attention to grandfather.

"Let's get him on the sofa," he said.

They worked in silence, trying to make the old man as comfortable as possible. In due time, Michael arrived, sparing a slight, reassuring glance for Morgana before he turned his attention to Fergus McShane. They hovered anxiously in the background until he began to pack his complicated-looking instruments away in the little black bag he always carried.

"Well, Michael." Rian was the first to speak. "What's wrong with my grandfather?"

"He's suffered a slight stroke, nothing serious, I hope, but he must be made to rest. Keep him absolutely quiet, no excitement. His physical condition is fairly good, but these things worsen with time, and especially for a man his age. Another upset like this could kill him. I suggest you try to keep him in bed for as long as possible."

"Is he going to be all right, Doctor Kelsey?" Morgana flushed slightly at the use of his professional title, for he was now Michael to her, her dear and trusted friend; and she was annoyed at having to maintain this false pretense in front of her family when she wanted to cling to him for comfort and tell them all of her fondness for this quiet man.

"I believe so, Lady Morgana." He was equally polite. "However, there may be some minor paralysis, it's just too early to tell."

She walked him out to his buggy, and he gave her hand a gentle squeeze to comfort her before he drove away.

Chapter Eight

In the end, Patrick was not banished from Shanetara after
all, for the old man was very weak for several days and,
in fact, never fully recovered his former vigor; and since
Patrick had acted as grandfather's overseer for some
time, he could not now be spared from this duty, as no
one else knew how to run the estate. Rian had been away
too many years at sea; Trevor had been at law school
during those years when he might have learned, and had
spent too much time in Dublin at the Parliament since;
and Gerald and Colin had never even expressed an interest in the management of the stately house. Patrick, with
his intense love of the good, rich earth and his decision to
remain in Ireland, although he had an estate in England,
had unknowingly acquired a place in the old man's heart;
so although grandfather could not find it in himself to
forgive Patrick openly for what he still believed was a
disastrous marriage, he did permit the young couple to
move into Kilshannon Hall, the Dower House Rosamunde
had never used.

Privately, the McShanes thought Patrick a fool for settling for a common housemaid when he might have acquired a fortune, and began to lay bets on the outcome of the battle for Morgana's hand. Rian and Colin were now the only two left in the running since she had made it quite plain that she would have nothing to do with Gerald.

Patrick rode over every day to maintain the smooth and orderly progression of management, and little by little he and Bridget edged their way into a safe niche within the family circle.

Rian was very good about riding over to Kilshannon Hall with Morgana every day to help Bridget move furniture and clean until the place shone like new. When he was able to get away from the heavy demands of management, Patrick joined them, and he and Rian kept the girls laughing with their tales and jokes of youth, growing closer than they had been since childhood. Morgana began to discover a lighter side of Rian's character that she found strangely disturbing. Sometimes Fionna joined them as well, and Morgana was delighted to find that the girl did not hold Bridget in contempt, but welcomed her into their family with a certain becoming shyness. When the work was finished for the day, they would retire to Shanetara, talking and laughing together while they stitched delicate, embroidered clothes for the coming child. In fact, the entire family unknowingly and gradually acquired a more normal atmosphere with the acceptance of their onetime housemaid. Morgana looked across the room and smiled at Bridget, content with the change she had wrought.

But, as always, the peace at Shanetara was not to last. One Saturday Morgana was returning home from her afternoon visit with Michael, preoccupied with thoughts of the small child he'd told her about whose infected hand he was trying to cure; she came upon Brendan O'Hara, Bridget's brother. The man was angry, but worse than that, he felt that his pride had been irretrievably insulted.

"Once again, you are blocking my path, Mister

O'Hara," Morgana managed to say calmly, but this time he made no effort to move out of her way.

"Ye think yer pretty smart, don't ye?" he sneered. "Fixing Bridget up real quicklike while I was in Ulster." Ulster? Morgana didn't even know he'd been gone. "Well, let me tell ye something, Miss Grand Lady o' the Great House, ye've made the O'Haras the laughing stock o' this county."

"I fail to understand what you're so angry about, Mister O'Hara," Morgana tried to keep her nervousness from showing. "Your sister has made a very fine marriage to a man she loves."

"She's married too good fer herself and pregnant, too." Morgana jumped. "Ha! Thought I didn't know about that, did ye? Well, I paid a little visit to me sister early this morning. The whole county thinks she's nothing but a seducing little tramp with a scheming mind. I've heard them talking. 'The O'Haras think they're better than the rest o' us, lads.' Oh, yes," he stared coldly. "That's what they're saying all right. Well, don't think we'll be asking any favors o' the high and mighty McShanes!"

"No such thought had entered my head, Mister O'Hara."

"Huh! Think ye're such a fine lady, don't ye? Well, ye ain't. I've seen ye with Michael Kelsey, the poor besotted fool." Morgana gasped. Why, the man thought she and Michael were lovers! "Ye aiming to trade places with Bridget?" he continued. "Or are ye just amusing yerself? Why don't ye pick a real man, a man who knows how to handle a wench like ye?" He reached up and yanked her from the saddle.

Morgana was really frightened now as she stared into those cold blue eyes.

"Aye, I could teach ye a thing or two," Brendan wrapped his hand in her hair and twisted her face up to his. "Yer sorry cousin seduced me sister. She was an innocent maid till he began trifling with her. Now she's out o' her depth. She don't know how to get on with rich

115

folks like ye. I'll bet yer grandfather is none too happy about it either, is he? And 'tis one less person bringing in the money to help support our family," he went on without waiting for a reply.

"I hardly think Bridget would allow you all to starve," Morgana managed to say dryly.

"Ye think we'd take anything off o' her now? We don't accept charity, Lady Morgana," he said sarcastically. "Even from our own kin, or don't ye remember? I believe I deserve something for the loss o' me sister, don't ye?"

"What did you have in mind, Mister O'Hara? I'm sure my grandfather would arrange something."

"I'll bet he would, but that's not what I want," he leered at her. "I want yer family to suffer as much as mine has, tit fer tat, so to speak. Do ye understand?"

Morgana understood all too well when his brutal mouth closed over hers cruelly. She struggled ineffectively against him as his hand caught the neckline of her gown and ripped the bodice down. She screamed horribly as he threw her to the ground and planted one leg on either side of her body, towering over her with a satisfied smile of anticipation on his face. Morgana moaned as he licked his lips and gave a low laugh at her distress. His hand reached for his belt buckle, then he crumpled down upon her. She cried out, for she knew she could not fight him off, but something was wrong. He wasn't moving. And then there was blood, blood everywhere, warm and red, pouring out over her torn dress, and soaking into the ground beside her. She screamed again, hysterically this time. She couldn't stop herself. The screams turned to choked sobs and tears ran down her face like rain as she stared into the sightless, cold, accusing blue eyes of Brendan O'Hara. He'd been shot through the back! She could feel the gaping hole as she tried to push him off her body. God! She'd never even heard the sound of a gun. Then someone was shouting, "Mag! Mag!" and Rian was there, pulling Brendan's body from her own. He knelt beside her, and in her confusion she beat upon his chest, still screaming and sobbing until he shook her, then slapped her hard across the face. She gasped with shock at the stinging blow.

"I'm sorry, Mag, but I couldn't think of anything else to make you stop," Rian told her gently when she'd quieted down. "Are you all right?"

"I—I think so," she felt numb all over.

"Good." He turned his attention to the dead man. "I guess we'd better ride back to the house and send someone out to bring Brendan's body in."

"Oh, God," Morgana moaned. "Poor Bridget. It's all my fault."

"Shut up! You couldn't help what happened. I don't know what possessed Brendan to attack you anyway. He knew better."

Morgana looked at the body and it occurred to her for the first time that Rian had killed a man.

"He wanted to get even with us, because of Bridget."

Rian helped her to her feet and lifted her up into Lucifer's saddle since Copper Lady had run away from the disastrous scene, then mounted behind her, his arm holding her close. She closed her eyes and laid her head back against his shoulder, feeling strangely comforted. Rian had killed a man rather than see her raped. She did not think to question his reasons or his motives for being in this particular area of the moors. She was never to know that he had followed her with the sole intention of putting an end to what he thought was her affair with Michael Kelsey.

Brendan O'Hara's wake lasted three days. The McShanes did not attend the funeral, although Bridget and Patrick went and were shunned openly by the O'Haras. Grandfather had been told as quietly and briefly as possible what had happened; and Rian sent Trevor unceremoniously packing when he stopped by to gloat over them all for ignoring his warnings. Morgana was thankful that Bridget did not hold a grudge against her for the tragic occurrence; and everything soon settled back into place—with two exceptions: She was forbidden to ride out again without a groom trailing her, which put a halt to her meetings with Michael; and she developed a respect for Rian which she had previously lacked, although she refused to like him any better.

Chapter Nine

The days were growing shorter and cooler with the approach of winter, so Morgana's meetings with Michael could not have continued as before in any event, but she missed her friend, for now she had no one to talk to. She found herself spending more time with Rian. It was an odd, mocking relationship; and every time she told herself she disliked him, she would turn and find him grinning at her, which for some reason made it hard for her to remain angry at him for long. Besides, Colin was too brooding and Rosamunde too vaguely dazed most of the time to carry on a witty conversation.

In preparation for a small party she planned for New Year's Eve, Morgana pulled the bottom drawer of her bureau open and lifted out the material Rian had given her upon his homecoming. She would have Mistress Casey make up something special with it for the party, something Oriental perhaps. It was, after all, Chinese silk. Rian would know what she wanted. Morgana gathered up the shimmering folds of cloth and went to seek him out.

"Ah, want something Chinese, do you?" he said when she described what she had in mind and, taking a thick pad, he began sketching. After a time, he said, "This is the kind of gown the ladies wear in China."

Morgana gasped when she saw the picture, for he had drawn a long, flowing robe with huge bell sleeves, innocent enough, but it was slit up the sides, Oriental fashion, almost to the thighs. She could tell that, if made properly, the cut of the gown and the material would cling to her, revealing every line of her figure when she walked. It was outrageous, unthinkable, but he goaded her into it with his next remark.

"What's the matter? Too daring for you, Mag?" he asked insolently.

"Not at all," she met his challenge coolly. She would not let him get the best of her again. "It shall be made exactly as you have drawn."

Morgana left the room. Oh, just once she'd like to make that infuriating man grovel at her feet, she thought heatedly! Rian, on the other hand, was thinking how fetching she would look in the slightly shocking dress, and how shocked everyone would be at her appearance. Lindsey Joyce would positively choke with jealousy. He chuckled at the thought. It certainly promised to be one hell of a New Year's Eve party! That green-eyed cousin of his was always stirring up havoc; not that he hadn't encouraged her, Rian grinned. Then he thought of Michael Kelsey and his fingers tightened on the glass of whiskey he was holding. That upstart doctor! Mag was seeing him secretly, and Rian felt sure she fancied herself in love with him. He should ride into town and put a stop to it, but then Mag was bound to find out and react with fury. Were they really lovers? No, surely not. Michael had too many strong religious convictions for that to be the case. A man of his morals would find the thought of intimacy before marriage rather shocking and mildly distasteful. Poor fool. Mag must be making Michael's life hell right now. He was too much of a gentleman to marry her and subject her to a life of poverty and ridicule, and not cad enough to carry on a quiet affair with the wench. God! What a hopelessly weakminded fool, Rian thought again. Thank heavens he had no scruples where women were concerned. Was it only yesterday that he'd taken Lindsey Joyce and used her until she had clawed little furrows in his back and begged him not to stop? Aye, she amused him, but she did not evoke in him the all-consuming desire he had begun to feel at the merest touch of Morgana's hand. The wench was driving him crazy as well. He remembered that day when he'd kissed her, and the sweet taste of her trembling lips beneath his flaming mouth. He wanted her and meant to have her on his own terms, whatever the cost; and despite his grandfather's stupid will. Hadn't he killed a man for her? Confidently, arrogantly, he dismissed Michael Kelsey from his mind.

The Chinese silk was made almost exactly as Rian had drawn it, some of Morgana's common sense returning at the last moment. Mistress Casey had been appalled, so Morgana had allowed her to alter its construction somewhat, lessening the length of the slits up the sides. Now she stood arrayed in its glittering folds. She drew in her breath sharply. It was magnificent! Rian had been right, as usual. Still, the dress was rather shocking; its design came from another world; it did not belong in her grandfather's ballroom, but in a bamboo bath with geisha girls and painted fans. Nevertheless, she was determined to wear it. She wore no jewels to detract from the gown and had piled her hair high upon her head, Oriental fashion. In the end, she decided she might as well be hanged for a sheep as a lamb, and she painted her face, lightly, artistically to slant her emerald eyes. At last she was ready. She picked up the delicate Chinese fan Rian had produced at the last minute from his seemingly bottomless seachest of treasures, and walked toward the ballroom.

Rian met her at the bottom of the stairs. "I must admit, Mag, I didn't think you had it in you," he whispered, an appreciative gleam in his eye.

"Well, now you know differently," she arched one

eyebrow smugly, though the hand she offered him was trembling slightly as he led her inside.

The dress caused an instant sensation, and for a moment Morgana didn't think she would be able to endure the raised quizzing-glasses and the buzzing whispers. But Rian was with her, laughing at whatever she said, and acting as though her attire was totally conventional. To her surprise she carried it off in style, at least until Lindsey Joyce approached them.

"Well, well, is this what they're wearing in the Chinese bordellos?" Lindsey stared at Morgana's gown with ill-concealed displeasure.

"Lindsey!" Rian spoke sharply.

"Darling, I was simply commenting upon the obvious," she cocked her head at him speculatively.

"You're being insulting," he took her arm. "I can see that I need to teach you some manners."

Morgana watched them walk away and felt something akin to jealousy prick her soul. How could Rian tolerate the woman? He almost seemed amused by the little cat. Morgana absently accepted Colin's invitation to dance.

Rian was displeased when he saw Morgana with Colin, her head bent forward to catch something he was whispering in her ear. The insolent pup! No doubt Colin hoped to entice Morgana into marrying him. Rian's lips curled into a sneer. Well, if all his plans went as he hoped, Morgana would be his before the evening was out, much to young Colin's surprise! In a black mood, he poured himself a glass of whiskey and sought the gaming tables.

"Oh, damn. I beg your pardon, cousin. I've stepped upon your gown," Colin confessed contritely. "I told you I didn't know how to dance well."

"It's only a small tear. I can mend it quite easily, if you'll excuse me."

Morgana slipped away from the noise of the party and crept upstairs to find a needle and thread. She finished sewing up the slight rent, but instead of returning, she decided to slip outside for a while, and took the back stairs down, heedless of the light rain that was beginning to fall. She walked along the beach for a time, enjoying the cool night air, then reluctantly decided that she really should return to the party, but glad of the short breather.

"I see you're an indifferent hostess, Mag. Was the party not up to your expectations?"

Morgana whirled to face Rian, his jacket gone, cravat undone, and shirt open to the waist. "You! What are you doing here?"

"I saw you slip away and decided to join you. Tsk, tsk. What an errant lass you are. Grandfather will be greatly displeased."

"Why, you're drunk," Morgana said disgustedly as he staggered toward her.

"So I am," he conceded, grabbing her arm.

"Let go, you muddle-headed fool," she spoke coldly, sorry now that she had come out for the fresh air.

"Be still!" he replied curtly. "I've come to make you a proposition. Damn, I want you," he muttered, and she found the flame of desire in his eyes oddly disturbing and yet somewhat exciting as well. "I've wanted you since the first time I saw you. Well, not exactly," he amended drunkenly. "The first time I saw you, you were only about seven years old; and whatever else I may be, I am not a cradle robber."

Morgana frowned, confused. What in the world was he talking about? How could he have seen her when she'd been just a child? Then she dismissed it as drunken babble.

"Aye, I want you, my dear, and I mean to have you," he continued, his eyes narrowing.

Why, Morgana thought suddenly, the arrogant Rian McShane is actually offering for my hand. A proposition, he'd said. She smiled triumphantly, sure that she had won the game they played between them.

"I've no wish to marry you, Rian," she said coolly.

"Marry! Marry!" he threw back his head and laughed. "By God, that's rich! I'm married to the sea, my girl. I was asking you to become my mistress."

If he had slapped her face, Morgana could not have been more shocked or stunned.

"Your mistress?" she cried.

"Oh, come now, Mag," he sobered suddenly, pressing hot, searing kisses upon her hands and wrists. "Don't play the affronted governess with me. You know that you want me just as much as I want you."

"You're mad!" Morgana tried to yank away from him. "I've never given you cause to speak to me like this."

"Of course you have. I've seen you watching me, wondering what it would be like to go to bed with me. All women have such thoughts," he went on, ignoring her gasp of outrage. "You needn't be ashamed of it. I'll set you up in your own house, a townhouse, in London. You'd like that, wouldn't you, my girl? I'll buy you fancy clothes and jewels. What do you say, madam?"

"Let go of me!" she screamed, afraid that her head would burst if she had to listen to any more of his talk.

"Goddamn you!" his face was suddenly nasty, very nasty indeed. "It's Michael Kelsey, isn't it? By God, I'll get rid of that meddling leech! I'll ride him out of town on a rail if it's the last thing I do! You think you're in love with him, don't you?" he shook her roughly.

"Don't be ridiculous. Michael and I are just friends."

For a moment, Rian almost believed her. Then his eyes narrowed and he sneered, "Who are you trying to fool? I've seen you with him. By God, you'll forget him soon enough. I'll make you forget him!"

They grappled in the sand as he forced his mouth down on hers, hard, his tongue teasing, exciting, between her lips. In spite of herself, Morgana felt her head spin dizzily and she thought she must swoon if his strong arms had not supported her.

"You see," he whispered huskily in her ear. "You do want me, love."

"No, it's not true! It's not true," she gasped, but even now her mind was filled with doubts. Had she encouraged him? Oh, she had! She had! She'd kissed him; and she knew in her heart that she'd responded to him, to something physical and animal in him that even now she scarcely recognized. Had she driven him to this? "Oh, God," she moaned softly as his hands swept down to her breasts.

She twisted in his arms, fighting him desperately now, for he was crazy drunk and she did not know what he might do to her. They fell upon the beach, and Morgana scooped up a handful of sand, flinging it violently into his eyes. He released her immediately, clawing angrily at his face, swearing like the drunken sailor he was; and she ran from him blindly, wildly, like a startled fawn. She did not look back, not even when she heard him yell, "I'll have you yet, witch!" and then laugh mockingly, drunkenly, once more.

Shivering violently, Morgana ran into the house and upstairs to her room. She smoothed her disarrayed hair and gown, trying to calm herself down. The fool. The conceited fool! Was this the game he'd been playing? His mistress! The word pounded in her head like a hammer, and it was some time before she realized there was someone knocking on the door. Cautiously, she opened it a crack, fearing it might be Rian, but it was only Colin.

"Did you get it fixed all right, Morgana?"

"What?"

"The tear, I'm so sorry. Is it mended?"

"Yes, oh—yes—" she smiled hesitantly, some of her composure returning. "It was only a small one, just as I thought."

"Good. Cousin, I—I want to talk to you," Colin seemed to stumble on his words as she waited expectantly. "I—I'd like to make you a sporting proposition."

"Proposition," she almost screamed.

"No, no, it's not what you're thinking," he realized his mistake and plunged on hurriedly. "I thought you might consider marrying me. Oh, I know that you don't love me any more than I love you, but we have many interests in common, especially poetry, and I don't think it really matters that you're a couple of years older than I am, do you?" He continued without waiting for a reply. "I've done a lot of thinking about this recently, and I believe it's the answer to both our situations. With the money—uh—with your dowry, I can buy a commission in the army. You'd be free to travel, to do pretty much as you pleased, then; and I'd look the other way as far as affairs go, providing you kept them discreet. We wouldn't have to be—uh—intimate right away, though naturally I'd want heirs in the future. Please say yes, Morgana. I promise you won't be sorry," he ended rather breathlessly.

Morgana looked at him rather stunned for a moment, not being able to absorb the impact of an illicit proposition and a proposal of marriage in one night! It had never occurred to her that Colin might propose, especially in this fashion, and she was rather taken aback at first. Then slowly, she decided it really wasn't a bad idea. He wasn't bad-looking, she could manage him easily enough, and it would be the greatest insult imaginable to Rian, the arrogant, mocking Rian. She could just imagine the look on his face now! And so, hastily, and in a fit of pique, Morgana told Colin she would marry him.

"You won't regret it, Morgana," he grasped her hand fervently. "When shall we set the date?"

"Oh, as soon as possible, don't you think?" she spoke coolly, now that her mind was made up.

"Oh, I knew we'd deal famously together," Colin crowed. "I'll get a special license and we can be married in two weeks, is that enough time?"

"Fine, just fine," Morgana replied, her voice hard as she thought of Rian's face again, and wondering why she was suddenly starting to regret her hasty decision. But she could think of no way to retract the impetuous words in light of Colin's pleasure, and so allowed him to kiss her hand feverishly before they went back to the party.

"Colin," she said when they'd reached the door of the ballroom. "Let's wait until tomorrow to announce our wedding, please. All these people—and—and such a fuss—"

"Of course, you're right. Always so thoughtful and intelligent," he smiled. He would have done anything for her in that moment, so gloating and secure he felt at getting his hands on grandfather's fortune. "Whatever you'd like, my dear."

Morgana never knew how she made it through the rest of the evening. The smile she wore felt frozen on her face and she stared at her guests without really seeing them. She clung to Colin's side the remainder of the night, giving Rian the cut-direct when he sought to speak to her. He scowled furiously, realizing he had only himself to blame; and all three of them, for their own reasons, thought it had, indeed, been one hell of a New Year's Eve.

Chapter Ten

Fergus McShane was angry, more angry than he'd ever been in his life, for all of his well-laid plans seemed to have suddenly gone awry. There was Rian, standing about with a black scowl upon his face, biting off the head of anyone who dared talk to him. There was Morgana, floating in a frozen daze, trying to pretend that she was happy. And there was Colin, preening like a cat who'd swallowed a canary! Fergus could have roared with vexation, but it was too late now, for the wedding was today. Today! He groaned at the thought. A parcel of fools indeed. He would never have believed that Rian and Morgana could have behaved so stupidly, although he did not know the reason for the breach between them. Colin had secured a special license; Rosamunde had posted a notice at the church; Mistress Casey had made the wedding dress, and he, Fergus, was to give the bride away.

He straightened his cravat, grumbling to himself in the silence, for everyone else was already at the church, waiting for the ceremony to begin. All, except Colin, who had stayed behind to drive his grandfather. Colin! Suddenly, the old man cackled to himself slyly. Too late? It was never too late! With another outlandish scheme brewing in his ancient brain, he crept silently down the hall to Colin's room. His grandson was inside, humming triumphantly under his breath. Colin did not hear his grandfather, did not see the old man reach inside the door and remove the key from its lock. In triumph greater than Colin's, Fergus McShane turned the key from the outside, laughed shortly, and stumped gleefully away from his grandson's room.

Driving himself to the church, he did not look back at the empty house, where even now Colin must be trying desperately to escape from his locked room. The Duke chortled at the thought. That was one groom destined to miss his own wedding!

"Grandfather," Morgana hurried out of the small alcove in the church. "Where's Colin?"

"Don't know, lass. Isn't he here? I couldn't find him and thought he must have come on ahead," the old man lied without a trace of conscience.

"No, he hasn't arrived," she glanced about worriedly.

"Well, don't trouble yourself over it, lass. There's still plenty of time left yet."

They walked inside to the little alcove where all Irish brides for generations had waited to take their long walk up the aisle of the church. From a small chink in the wall, Morgana could see that the pews were filled with the McShane acquaintances, and was surprised at the number present as she had sent out no invitations. Evidently the posted notice and word of mouth had been sufficient. Rian, who ironically was to be best man, and Patrick were standing at the altar rail opposite Bridget and Fionna, Morgana's attendants. Many of those present were knelt in prayer, but the McShanes simply stood, waiting.

They waited, and waited, and waited. For fully half an hour, they waited; and all the while Colin tried furiously to break down his door, but the solid oak frame refused to budge. He even contemplated jumping out of the window, but realized that he would doubtless only break his neck. When he sought to retrieve the key, still in the lock on the outside of the dor, it fell out into the hall beyond his reach. Then he pounded on the walls and screamed, but to no avail. There was no one at Shanetara to hear him.

At last Morgana turned to her grandfather. "He isn't coming," she said dully. "He isn't coming. Something must have happened to him."

Fergus McShane caught her arm in a grasp of steel, nodding to the organist to begin the march as he propelled his horrified granddaughter toward the center aisle. Everyone present rose expectantly.

"What are you doing?" Morgana whispered frantically. "There can be no ceremony without a groom. Stop! Stop this instant, I say!"

"You shall have a groom, my dear," Fergus spoke out of the side of his mouth, nodding and smiling to the guests as they passed. "Have no fear."

Slowly, decorously, he guided her toward the altar rail where the priest and the McShanes stood. Fergus forced the confused and quaking Morgana to her final destination, and then calmly took Rián's arm in the same grip of iron, speaking so softly and rapidly that not even Morgana, who stood by his side, could hear him.

"Colin isn't coming," the old man said flatly. "I've locked him in his room. You'll have to take his place. Don't say a word! I know you want the wench. 'Tis been written all over your face for the past two weeks. Sure and 'tis high time you took a wife anyway, and you'll find none better than our own wild stock. She's comely and healthy, Rian, and will bear you fine sons. The pride of the McShane name is at stake here today," grandfather continued as his grandson stood there before him in stunned and angry silence at having been out maneuvered. "Colin's not the man for her, and I never intended him to be. You're the man she needs, and you're a fool if you can't see it," the old man gave him a piercing stare. "I want you to marry the wench."

Rian gazed down at him, his green eyes narrowed

with hardness. "You certainly seem to have had this all planned," he said dryly. "I'm of no mind to lose my freedom."

"Your freedom. Bah!" Fergus snorted. "You shall lose more than that if you don't wed the lass and now, I promise you. I can make life difficult for you, Rian, very difficult indeed; and don't you forget it!"

Without another word, Rian took Morgana's hand, longing to beat his grandfather senseless for having trapped him in such a manner. And Trevor, ever mindful of his duty and manners, having some dull inkling of what was happening, moved up so quietly and unobtrusively to even out the attendants that the entire episode, which had taken only a few minutes, appeared like the most natural occurrence in the world.

But those few minutes had seemed like hours to Morgana, whose hand felt cold in Rian's; and she could scarce credit what was happening, feeling only a dull, immense relief that she was not to be left at the altar before all these people. She did not stop to think of what would happen after the wedding was over. An aching memory from her past haunted her. She had been a child then, at the seminary, waiting for her father to come speak to her English class about his poems. How proud she'd been, certain that none of the other girls had a father as famous as hers, and determined that this would make them like her! She'd waited and waited, but the appointment had slipped from her absentminded father's thoughts, and he hadn't come.

"He's not coming! He's not coming!"

She could still hear those horrible girls chanting that refrain over and over, laughing at her, taunting her. She looked up into Rian's hard face.

"You'll marry me?" she asked in a whisper.

"What makes you think I still want you?" he snarled quietly, cruelly, as Fergus stepped away from the couple, having done his duty by placing Morgana's hand in Rian's.

Her head reeled. They would laugh at her. Everyone would laugh at her! She couldn't bear it!

"Please," she implored softly, biting her lip.

He gazed at her mockingly, appraising her as though she had been a slave. Aye, he did want her, damn her! And he knew now that he would have her no other way. He would take her to wife then, by God; and both she and grandfather would regret this day's work!

Was ever there a stranger wedding? Morgana's face was as pale as her gown, the gown turned out by a frenzied Mistress Casey in only three days. No, not a gown, Morgana suddenly thought wildly, a shroud, a shroud of the palest cream, trimmed with lace and thousands of tiny seed pearls. Her voice trembled as she repeated her vows, but Rian's was steady and clear; and then he was kissing her, angrily, possessively, as the priest blessed them. Her lips felt scorched under his searing mouth and she shook in his arms as she was struck suddenly by the full import of what she had done. She was married! Married to Rian McShane, a man who mocked her and had sought to make her his mistress; and in that moment she despised him. God, what had she done? What had she done? He could do anything he liked to her now, and she would be powerless to prevent it. He must have guessed her thoughts, for he smiled at her grimly, a tight, hateful grin that didn't quite reach his eyes as he walked her out of the church.

"Congratulations, Rian," Sean Devlin approached them after they'd somehow made it outside. "I must say you gave us quite a turn in there, though. I thought Morgana was to marry Colin."

"Colin?" Rian raised one eyebrow coolly. "Rosamunde must have made a mistake on the notice. You know she's a trifle mad," he lowered his voice conspiratorily.

Morgana blushed as the disastrous moment passed off quite easily under Rian's level explanation. So, at least he did not mean to tell anyone the truth of their marriage. She could be grateful for that!

After the congratulations had finally ended, Morgana sat quietly beside Rian in the carriage back to Shanetara, the carriage that should have been for her and

Colin. Colin! What had really happened to him? She twisted the heavy gold ring on her finger pulled hastily from Rian's fourth finger to mark her as his possession. She glanced up at his stormy face, wondering what he was thinking, this strange, arrogant man who was now her husband. He felt her gaze upon him and looked down into her emerald eyes, eyes flecked with gold and fear; and the poppy mouth for which he had hungered. She was his now, for good; he could do with her as he pleased. The thought made him conscious of his power over her, and he put his arm around her casually, feeling her flinch at his touch. He swore mockingly under his breath.

"You're my wife," he spoke coldly. "Regardless of the circumstances, you're my wife."

"No," she whispered. "I don't want you—I—"

Before she could finish, he yanked her to him, his eyes glittering like steel. "You wanted me enough to marry me back there." He shook her slightly. "And now that I've been forced to sacrifice my freedom for you, I don't ever intend to let you go."

"Forced? How?"

He laughed. "Grandfather locked Colin in his room; and told me that if I didn't marry you, he would make life hell for me."

"No. I don't believe it. No one could make you do anything you didn't want to, Rian. You must have had some other reaon for doing this."

His crude glance stripped her naked. "I think you know that," he said softly.

She tried to draw away from him, but he forced his mouth down on hers, hard, pressing her close to his chest. She could feel the marriage license rustling in his pocket, the special, blank license which the priest had filled in with their names. Oh, if only she and Colin had waited, had posted the banns, this could never have happened! She moaned softly under his lips.

"Let me go, please," she whispered when he'd released her.

His only reply was to rest his hand gently, but threateningly, against her white throat.

"You're mine," he taunted.

Morgana shuddered with fear as once more he claimed her mouth, roughly, hungrily.

Colin heard them come in, and renewed his pounding upon the bedroom door with a vigor born of rage and frustration.

"Let me out of here! Let me out of here, I say!"

"Why, 'tis Lord Colin," Mollie spoke disbelievingly as she bustled inside, as confused by the sudden turn of events as everyone else.

She hurried upstairs, saw the problem immediately, and picked the key up off the floor, turning it in the lock to free the irate youth.

"Sure and who would have done such a thing, me lord?" she questioned with surprise as Colin burst past her, shoving her roughly in his haste.

"You! You locked me in," he advanced angrily on grandfather when he'd reached the bottom of the stairs. "But why? I won her fair and square. You've ruined my wedding day and no doubt made Morgana the laughingstock of the county. Everyone will think I deserted her at the altar! How could you, grandfather? Morgana," he turned to the girl, still standing by Rian's side, much overcome by the day's events. "We'll be married tomorrow, I promise you," he vowed, grasping her arms fervently.

"Take your hands off my wife," Rian drawled in the sudden silence.

"Your wife! Your wife! No, she can't be!"

"Oh? But she is, dear boy, thanks to grandfather," Rian replied.

"By God, Rian, you'll pay for this. You planned this together, you and grandfather, so that you could get your hands on the old man's money! You always were his favorite, but, by God, you'll pay!" Colin swore, shaking his fist at his cousin and grandfather.

"Money? What money?" Morgana found her tongue at last, gazing at them all with searching suspicion.

"Grandfather changed his will," Colin turned to her again, heedless of his words. "He left all of his money to the one of us who could get you to the altar first; and I would have had it all!" Colin screamed.

Morgana's head spun dizzily and for a moment she thought she would faint. Her face went white and then she blushed furiously as she stared at Rian.

"Is it true? Is it?" she asked.

"Aye, lass," Fergus spoke gruffly. " 'Tis true, but I meant it for the best."

Money! Rian had married her for money; and she had thought—what had she thought—that he wanted her, even loved her? She could have laughed and cried at the same time. He didn't want her; all he wanted was the old man's money. Without another word, she turned and ran from them all, slamming her bedroom door and locking it with fingers that trembled with shock and dismay. Downstairs, the quarrelling continued until finally, after the slamming of more doors, the house was strangely, eerily silent.

Morgana did not go down for dinner, and sent away untouched the tray Mollie had prepared.

"Poor little bairn," Mollie muttered as she took the unwanted meal away. "Poor little bairn, sure and 'twas a sad, confusing wedding day. No wonder the child refuses to eat."

In the servants' quarters, the staff gathered around the table for the evening meal to discuss the strange turn of events and shake their heads with pity for the poor Lady McShane, betrothed to one man and suddenly married to another; for all of them knew that Rosamunde had made no mistake in the wedding notice.

Darkness settled. The household retired for the night, only one of them, Fergus McShane, pleased with the day's events. The old man felt sure Rian and Morgana would come around eventually. 'Twas only a matter of time.

Morgana took off her wedding dress, washed her

face, and let down her hair, brushing the copper locks mechanically as she stared, unseeing, into the mirror. She put on the negligee that was to have been for Colin, and got into bed. But she soon found that she could not sleep, and so rose again, pacing the room restlessly. What she needed was a drink, a good, stiff glass of Irish whiskey to calm her torn nerves and bring its delightful numbness to her body. Was there ever such a horrible day? At last, she opened her door.

"Is this what you want?"

Rian stood in the hall in a black dressing robe bound loosely at the waist, open at the top to reveal his strong chest covered with thick black hair. He was holding a glass of whiskey in one hand. Quickly, Morgana tried to shut the door, but he pushed it aside easily.

"Go on, take it," he said. "I've heard you pacing about in here like a caged tigress. 'Tis what you want, I know. Damn! I don't care if you drink, my dear."

She took the glass, drawing her wrapper about her tighter as she reached for it, flinching as he laughed lowly, mockingly.

"A hell of a wedding day, was it not?" he asked.

"Rian, please, let's be sensible about this. Neither one of us wants this marriage," Morgana said as she downed the whiskey. "You can keep the money you won by marrying me. Just keep away from me."

"But I want all I'm entitled to receive as the man who married you. And this is our wedding night, my lady, or have you forgotten?" he laughed jeeringly.

She backed away from him until she was up against a wall and there was nowhere else for her to go.

"I shall scream if you touch me," she whispered.

"I can stop your screams with kisses," he spoke softly, drawing her to him, feeling the rising heat in his loins like a fire. She was his, and he wanted her . . .

Morgana fought him. God, how she fought him; but she was no match for his steely strength and determination. He picked her up, flinging her over his shoulder violently as he carried her to his own room and then dropped her onto his bed. She tried to rise, but he forced her down again, his rough hands tearing at her filmy gown. She cried out as the nightdress fell away, and he clamped one hand on her mouth angrily.

"Be quiet," he snarled. "Or do you want grandfather to know how well his little plan is working out?" he jeered.

"Don't, please don't," she pleaded with him. "I don't want you to touch me!"

"Then why is your heart pounding so violently?" he laughed huskily in the darkness.

She shuddered as Rian's hard, demanding lips came down on hers, his tongue ravaging the inner sweetness of her mouth, and his hands exploring every line, every curve of flesh that no man had touched. He nibbled her ears and stroked her hair while she writhed beneath him, moaning softly as he set her aflame with his burning kisses and experienced hands. She begged him, pleaded with him to stop, but to no avail. He leaned the weight of his body on hers, the muscles rippling in his arms and back. She made a gentle, incoherent cry and tried to free herself, but he caught her hands easily and held them as his mouth travelled downward to her breasts, moist upon them, tracing wet swirls upon them, teasing the nipples into hard, flushed peaks. Then his hand moved over her belly, between her thighs, pulling at soft curls and stroking gently, rhythmically.

"Oh, God, Rian, no," she whispered, half sobbing.

"Hush, sweet," his breath was hot against her flesh.

He drew his knees up, then, and parted her thighs. She cried out in anguish before he covered her mouth with his once more, and waited for his assault, her young, lithe body betraying her, a burning ache spreading through it like fire. Sweat glistened in the firelight as he mounted her, penetrating her slowly in one clean, upward thrust. His pacing was gentle, even, as he put his hands under her back, arching her hips to receive his motions. She whimpered softly down in her throat as he laid fiery kisses on her hair and face. Without even realizing that she did so, Morgana put her arms around his neck, drawing him to her. Rian whispered in her ear words she'd never heard before, panted her name, then finally drove homeward deeply within her as his desires overcame him, shuddered, and was still.

"You green-eyed witch," he said as he stroked her tear-stained face, kissing her tenderly now while he cradled her in his arms like a child.

"You hurt me," she sobbed.

"That's because there is always pain with first love."

"Love!" she gave a strangled cry and stared at his wintergreen eyes in the darkness, the hatred in her own splintering like shards. "I hate you, Rian McShane," she breathed. "And I swear upon my father's grave that you shall rue this day you wed and raped me!"

He laughed softly in the blackness as he rolled over and forced himself upon her again.

Chapter Eleven

Morgana awoke the next morning with a feeling that something was different about the day. She felt a gentle tug and turned to find Rian's arm around her, his hand wrapped in her hair. Of course, she was married now. It seemed strange to wake up with this man beside her. She studied him curiously in the dawning light, noting the peaceful rise and fall of his chest as he lay sleeping. Was this the same man who'd caused such exciting sensations in her body last night. He was handsome; she had to admit that. His body had been bronzed by the sun. His strong muscles rippled as he moved in his sleep, reminding her of the feel of them as he had lain atop her last night, and she blushed at the thought. He had taken her, and in the end she had responded to him!

Gingerly, she pulled her copper curls from his grasp, not wanting to awaken him. Then she slipped out of bed, dressed, and went out to the stables. It was early, so there was no one about to saddle her mare, but she felt like riding, so she coaxed a bridle on Copper Lady and mounted the horse astride and bareback as she had long ago when she was first learning to ride; and then she set off toward the beach to sort out her thoughts.

Two things seemed evident. She was married to Rian and had lain with him. And secondly, grandfather seemed to have planned that it should be so. If Rian wed her for the money, and did not really want her, why then had he forced himself on her last night? It didn't make sense. She shivered as she thought of lying in his arms and how her traitorous body had responded. He would take her and use her again whenever it pleased him; she had no doubt of that, and she felt frightened at the thought. He had touched something inside her which she did not recognize and had no desire to face.

Rian turned, reached out a hand to draw his wife up next to him and grasped the empty air. With a start, he opened his eyes. She was gone. Damn the wench! Where could she be this early in the morning? Quickly he slid out of bed and threw on his clothes. He checked her room first (her old room, he told himself angrily, intending to have Mollie move Morgana's things into his own room as soon as possible), but it was empty. He did not find her downstairs either. Finally, with grim determination, he checked the stables. Sure enough, Copper Lady was missing.

"Jim!" he climbed up into the loft and shook the lad awake roughly. "When did her ladyship leave here?"

"Her ladyship?" the boy repeated stupidly, rubbing the sleep from his eyes. "Why, there's been no one here but me, me lord."

"Nonsense. My wife's horse is missing. You must have saddled it for her."

"I've saddled no horse, me lord," the lad told Rian truthfully.

"But I tell you her mare is gone." He yanked the boy to his feet. "She couldn't have lifted that saddle by herself."

They went downstairs, where Jim pointed out that Morgana's saddle was still in the stable. However, he had no explanation for the missing horse, and he was afraid his lordship was becoming very angry.

"Saddle Lucifer, and be quick about it," Rian ordered.

Once outside, he picked up the mare's small hoofprints. They led toward the sea, making him somewhat anxious. Surely Morgana wouldn't do anything foolish. He thought about last night. She hadn't wanted him, but he'd forced himself upon her. Perhaps she's angry, or at the end of her endurance, he thought grimly, and dug his heels into Lucifer's sides cruelly. He could see Copper Lady's tracks clearly now as he galloped over the moor. At last, he spied her figure in the distance. At another time the sight of his wife riding her horse bareback would have amused him, but he was worried and used his anger to cover his concern. Furious now, he rode toward her, ire written plainly on his face.

Morgana heard the soft thud of hoofbeats in the sand, turned and saw her husband's rapidly approaching figure. Why, he looks angry, she thought, and felt a sudden quiver of fright run through her. Slowly, Rian came abreast of Copper Lady.

"What in the hell do you think you're doing?" he stormed.

"Riding," she managed to reply nervously.

"At this hour of the morning, without a saddle, without a groom? I ought to beat you for this."

She cringed at his angry tone, expecting him to hit her any minute. "I'm sorry, Rian. I felt like riding and there was no one around, so I came out by myself. I've often ridden like this in the past."

"You were instructed not to go anywhere without a groom to accompany you. Suppose one of the O'Haras had seen you and decided to finish what Brendan started?"

"I'm sorry," she said again. "I just didn't think."

"That's your entire trouble," he told her coldly. "You don't think, unless it's some manner of deviltry to stir up the countryside. Get off that horse."

143

Good Lord, was he going to make her walk home? No, he grabbed Copper Lady's reins and tied them onto Lucifer's saddle, then, his face stony, lifted Morgana up in front of him. She wanted to placate him, but couldn't think of anything to say that might lessen his black mood. His arm was like steel around her, and when she began to apologize once more, he tightened his grip against her, shutting off her breath.

He left the horses to Jim's care without a word, causing that young man to feel much relief at being spared one of his lordship's dressing downs. Then Rian ushered Morgana up the back stairs of Shanetara in that same dreadful silence. When they reached his bedroom, he closed the door firmly behind them.

"You are never, ever to do that again, or I shall beat you within an inch of your life. Do I make myself clear?" he asked harshly.

She nodded her head, not trusting herself to speak. He glanced at her contrite face and suddenly felt a little less angry. What a way to start out a marriage.

"Morgana, come here," he said softly.

She looked at him suspiciously, wondering at this sudden change, but nevertheless did as he asked, afraid that he had decided to beat her after all, but knowing he would doubtless catch her if she tried to run away. Rian pulled her up next to him.

"Put your arms around my neck."

Morgana thought she surely could not have heard right. How dare he attempt to woo her after threatening her life? She lifted one slender hand to slap him, but he caught it deftly, twisting it around her back just tight enough to make her flinch.

"One day you'll learn that I master those things I possess, Mag," he mocked arrogantly, then brought his mouth down on hers, kissing her slowly, deeply, the last bit of the morning's rage draining out of him as he tasted her honeyed lips. With passion-darkened eyes, he pulled her to the bed.

Morgana stirred, flustered, as the maid knocked on the door. She was sure that by this time the entire

144

household must be aware of her presence in Rian's bedroom. God, if only she hadn't opened her door to get a drink last night! She attempted to remove herself from Rian's arms, but he held her tightly, merely drawing the sheet up to cover their nakedness before telling the maid to come in.

"We'd like a breakfast tray sent up also, Kyla," he informed the girl when she'd finished opening the curtains and banking up the fire. "I think my grandfather will excuse us just this once," Rian looked at Morgana insolently.

She blushed, wishing the maid would hurry up and leave. The girl was staring at her rather slyly and knowingly.

"She knows," Morgana snapped angrily when the maid had finally shut the door behind her, aware of how she must have appeared, her hair tangled and her shoulders bare above the sheet. "She'll tell all of the servants you were making love to me this morning."

"So?" Rian cocked one eyebrow toward her coolly. "You are my wife."

Morgana could think of nothing to say after that, and bit her lip helplessly as he pressed her down among the pillows again, taking her roughly this time, without any foreplay.

Later that day, Rian suggested they ride into Kilshannon so that he might see how the work was progressing on his ship. Morgana found this a capital idea since she was vastly curious about the vessel. She'd seen it moored in the harbor, but had never been aboard. Besides, she wanted to get away from the curious stares of the family and grandfather's sly cackling. The old man had been delighted when Rian told Mollie to move Morgana's things into his own room. Morgana had protested the idea, but Rian had been adamant.

"You married me for better or worse, witch," he laughed at her. "And now that I've tasted your charms, I don't intend for us to have separate bedrooms."

This time Copper Lady was properly saddled, and

what better escort could Morgana have than her husband? They covered the road into town quickly, leaving the horses tied up at the docks while they climbed on board.

It was a magnificent ship. Morgana thought she had never seen one so beautiful. Called the *Sorceress*, her lines were gracefully curved, her main mast proud and tall as her sails billowed gently in the wind. Rian introduced her to his first mate, Mister Harrison, who could not conceal his surprise at being told she was Rian's wife.

"Shame on ye, Cap'n, for not letting us know. Why, the boys and me would've prepared a celebration, and only yesterday, was it? Course, seeing the lady, I kin understand your hurry. She certainly is a beauty, if ye don't mind me saying so, Lady Keldara," he turned to Morgana respectfully.

It felt so strange to be addressed as Lady Keldara.

"Not at all, Mister Harrison," she assured him.

He and Rian conferred at some length about the progress on the ship while Morgana inspected the deck of the vessel interestedly, trying to ignore the curious stares of Rian's men. At last her husband joined her, offering to show her the rest of the ship.

On their way home Lindsey Joyce almost collided with them, sawing at her horse's mouth when it reared up nervously at the near accident.

"Rian McShane, you lousy scum. How could you marry that—that red-haired witch, especially when my back was turned? You knew I was going to Dublin to visit my aunt. Now I come back and find this," she screamed. "I was a virgin when first you took me. You've ruined my name and left me like some common trollop. I won't have it, do you hear?" her eyes flashed. "I intend to tell the entire county what a contemptible scoundrel you are!"

Morgana felt sick to her stomach. Lindsey Joyce! She and Rian had been lovers! Morgana saw the lines in her husband's face tighten whitely around his mouth.

"What you tell the county is your business, Lind-

146

sey," his words were clipped with rage. "But you were no virgin in our first encounter. You dissembled nicely that night, but it didn't fool me. I'm willing to bet Sean Devlin and Johnnie Gallagher have both tasted your charms, and probably quite a few others I couldn't even begin to name. You'll only be hurting yourself by the scandal. My reputation has been established for some time now. I'm warning you, however," he continued softly, "that if you spread any false rumors or hateful remarks concerning my wife, I shall personally break your pretty neck."

"But, Rian," Lindsey wailed.

Morgana didn't stay around to hear the rest. Feeling very ill, she whipped Copper Lady up and rode wildly toward Shanetara. She never even heard Rian hoarsely calling her name.

When she got home, Morgana flung herself upon the bed, burying her head in the pillows and sobbing as though her heart would break. She didn't think she could bear it. Lindsey Joyce was nothing but a malicious little tramp. How could Rian have taken her to bed? Morgana didn't stop to ask herself why she even cared whom Rian saw or slept with. She only knew that she hated him with a passion. She would have Mollie move her things back into her old room immediately. Angrily, she began yanking her dresses out of the armoire.

"Just what do you think you're doing?" Rian burst into the room without knocking.

"Moving back into my own room," Morgana replied shortly, not caring if he beat her for her insolence.

"You're doing nothing of the kind," Rian snatched a gown out of her hands. "Put those back and be quick about it."

"I will not!"

"I'm warning you, Mag," he advanced toward her slowly.

She backed away from him. "I won't have you touching me again. Go on over to Letterick, to your little tart," she cried. "I'm going back to England as soon as I can find a ship to take me."

"What do you think you'll do there?"

147

"My mother must have had relatives. I'll find out who they are and throw myself on their mercy. They surely can't be any worse than you and grandfather!" she spat.

"Lower your voice," he threatened. "I won't have you upsetting the old man."

"Why? Because he might change his will and you wouldn't get the money you married me for?"

He grabbed her and shook her until she thought the teeth would rattle right out of her head.

"Shut up! You don't know what you're saying. Now get this mess cleaned up. There isn't any place you could go that I wouldn't find you."

With that, he marched out of the room, slamming the door behind him. Shaking all over, Morgana slowly picked up her clothes. He was right, of course. There wasn't anywhere she could hide that he wouldn't discover sooner or later. She would never get away from him, not as long as she lived!

That night, when Rian approached her, Morgana fought against him wildly, screaming hysterically until he clamped his hand over her mouth, nearly suffocating her in the attempt. He was not gentle with her that evening, treating her instead with a cruel arrogance. She loathed him for it, and when it was over, she tore herself from his arms, crawling as far away from him as she could without falling off the bed. He laughed huskily at her anger.

"When you get cold, love, you'll seek the warmth of my arms willingly," his voice was silky in her ear.

Her days grew endless, and the nights even longer. Rian became even more arrogant and withdrawn; and she would often look up from some piece of embroidery to catch him watching her speculatively, like a lazy tiger. If she commented on his behavior, he would turn on her with taunting remarks as he sought to crumble her defenses against him. He took her nightly, though she fought him passionately and cried out her hatred of him till he became tired of her sharp tongue and shut her mouth angrily with his searing kisses. He rode her as he

148

would a wild filly, with a tight rein and a whip. There were nights when she dreamed of every excuse she could think of to remain downstairs long after everyone else had retired, and nights when she hurried upstairs immediately after dinner to get away from him, then sat for hours, nervously awaiting the moment when he would walk through the bedroom door to claim his rights.

Rian stripped away the vestiges of her childhood, forcing her to face the passionate woman she was becoming in his arms; and she despised him for it. It was as though he had recognized something wild and savage in her, and sought to free it from its cage of cool reserve; and he changed her, God, how he changed her. He laughed at her and mocked her, forcing her to develop a temper to match his own, a mind that cut as quickly and sharply as his, and a stubborn will that rivalled the best of the McShanes.

They were like fencers, except that he was stronger than she; and time and time again he lunged toward her for the final thrust, only to turn away at the last moment, allowing her to see that he merely toyed with her mockingly and could finish the duel whenever he chose. She felt weary from being constantly on guard, from parrying his clever thrusts only to have the blade knocked from her hand as his mouth came down on hers with flaming desire before he possessed her completely.

Once, when she'd pushed him too far, he'd slapped her as he'd so often promised her he would, flinging her to the floor and satisfying himself there, not even bothering to remove all of her clothes or allowing her the small comfort of their bed only a few feet away. And once he sank his teeth into her shoulder, making her beg for mercy before his bite turned into a kiss as he drove home within her.

In quieter moments, Rian reflected upon his cruel behavior, wondering why he tormented them both; then he would glance at her scornful face and his stung pride at being rejected would harden his purpose. So he drove himself and his wife almost beyond endurance, hoping to break her spirit, hoping to force her into admitting she desired him as he so desired her; and when she bent without breaking, he realized that while for the first time in his life he had met his match in a woman, she was one who did not want him. It was indeed a severe blow to his pride and manhood. So he watched her and waited, hoping to see some sign of tenderness or caring in her face for him; and when none surfaced, he laughed at her and mocked her, using his only power, his physical possession of her, to force some kind of response from her.

Morgana stirred and yawned sleepily, stretching like a lithe little cat in the big bed. Rian, knowing that his wife would slip out of bed in the mornings while he slept, had taken to waking the minute she moved. Now he tightened his arm around her, pulling her warm body up next to his. She made no attempt at resistance, having learned that to do so was to invite him to use force; and he smiled, amused as she lay pressed against him afraid to move. He kissed her lingeringly on the lips, felt them part softly in response, a response he knew she hated him for more than anything else.

"Good morning, love."

"Good morning," Morgana whispered.

He felt the familiar desire rise within his body and resolved to take her gently if he could. He laid his hand upon her breast, but before he could begin there was a loud knocking on the door.

"Who is it?" he called sharply, annoyed by the interruption.

"Kyla, me lord. Lord Patrick says to come quickly. Me lady's having her baby."

"Christ," Rian swore under his breath. "Tell Patrick we'll be there as soon as possible."

He glanced at Morgana and sighed, knowing that she was secretly relieved at having been spared his advances. He couldn't resist kissing her just once more, however, his tongue shooting deeply into her mouth before he rose reluctantly from the bed.

"Later, sweet," he promised softly and was rewarded by her faint blush.

When he had dressed and gone, Morgana raised

herself from the bed, feeling again the slight dizziness that had bothered her for the last two weeks. She hadn't wanted to tell Rian about the odd feelings, for fear that he would think she was only dreaming up some excuse to ride into town and see Michael. Now, not only did her head swim most unpleasantly, but she was desperately ill, barely making it to the chamber pot before sudden spasms of retching seized her. When the spell was over, she wiped her mouth tiredly with a wet rag, a horrible suspicion beginning to take hold of her. Then she, too, dressed and went downstairs.

Kerr was outside hitching up the big carriage and grumbling under his breath.

"What's the matter, Kerr?" Morgana asked, coming up beside Rian.

"Me lady, Lord Shanetara says no grandchild of his is going to be born in the Dower House and he's insisting that we bring Lady Bridget to Shanetara immediately."

"Why, that's insane," Morgana snapped. "Bridget might have her child in the carriage."

"We don't know when she went into labor," Rian said thoughtfully. "There might be time to move her."

"Rian, don't do it. She's probably in terrible pain and the ride might kill her."

"Nonsense. She's a strong lass and it's not that far. Better get a move on, Kerr," he turned to the old man. "There's no point in us riding over there, then," he said when the grumbling Kerr had driven away. "Go inside and tell Mollie to get everything ready. I'll run into town and get Doctor Kelsey."

Morgana's face softened at the mention of her friend and Rian saw it. He grabbed her jaw with his fingers, tilting her head up.

"Just remember to which one of us you belong," he warned before walking to the stables.

"Don't be silly!" Morgana spoke more sharply than she'd intended, fearing he might still harbor plans to drive the doctor out of town as he'd once promised. "Michael and I are just friends."

Rian laughed softly, knowing now that there had

been no affair between Morgana and Michael. There had been no other men before him, for Morgana had been a frightened virgin when he'd taken her. And he knew, too, that she did not love the doctor as once he irrationally believed. Still, he couldn't resist taunting her simply because of his jealous, possessive nature. Better to frighten the wench a little than have her cuckold him behind his back!

Bridget was brought to Shanetara, for her pains had only just begun, and she, like grandfather, felt that the child should be born in the great house. Soon she was installed in her husband's old room and Mollie was bustling about, a wide grin upon her ruddy countenance.

Morgana squeezed Bridget's hand briefly, then left the room as Mollie suggested. She found the rest of the family in the main salon, Trevor and Fionna having already driven over from Shaughnessy Bay.

"How is she?" Patrick asked anxiously.

"Fine. Mollie says it will be quite awhile before the child comes."

"Stop worrying, Patrick," grandfather spoke gruffly. "Bridget's a strong, healthy lass. 'Twill be easy enough for her." Then he looked at Rian and Morgana slyly. "You'd best tell your cousins to get to work, Patrick, so that your bairn will have some company," he cackled, knowing full well how matters stood between the two grandchildren he'd forced into marriage. But Fergus was a wise old fox and he knew that where there was violent hatred and passion, there was also the beginning of something else more lasting than either. It was only a matter of time before Rian and Morgana would realize it, too, the proud, stubborn fools!

Rian said nothing, but looked at his wife thoughtfully, and Morgana blushed under his intense gaze, wondering if he had guessed that she might be pregnant.

"Doctor Kelsey's here," Trevor broke into everyone's thoughts abruptly.

Rian saw Morgana start longingly toward the door and felt another quick stab of jealousy. Silently he put out a restraining arm and pulled her toward him.

"The doctor doesn't need your help," he snarled in her ear.

Morgana started to respond, then bit back the sharp retort. This was not the time or the place for quarrelling. Besides, Rian was right. She knew nothing about delivering a child.

It was after midnight when they finally heard the small, unhappy wail of the babe. Morgana had long since fallen asleep on the sofa, her head on Rian's shoulder, and Mollie had not had the heart to awaken her. Now the girl woke fitfully at the sound. Patrick was already heading anxiously toward the stairs when she caught him.

"Wait here," Morgana said. "Bridget might not be ready for you to see her yet."

He nodded and allowed her to go upstairs while he hovered nervously below. Morgana entered the room quietly. Bridget's face was quite red from the exertion, but she was smiling.

"Oh, Morgana," she breathed. " 'Tis a girl."

"She's lovely, Bridget," Morgana pulled the soft blanket away to peek at the child's tiny, wrinkled face.

"Aye," Mollie spoke proudly. "She's about the prettiest little McShane I ever saw."

"May I take her downstairs? Patrick is becoming quite difficult to restrain," Morgana laughed ruefully, suddenly meeting Michael's searching eyes.

Bridget seemed slightly unwilling to part with the child, but upon the doctor's suggestion that she needed some rest, she relinquished the small bundle after extracting Morgana's solemn promise that the babe would be returned when all had been given a chance to see her.

"And, Morgana," Bridget called as she was leaving the room. "I've named the child Maureen, after yer—your grandmother." Tired as she was, Bridget did not forget to correct her speech, something she had undertaken so that Patrick would not feel ashamed of her in the presence of society, although he had never claimed that such was the case.

Morgana nodded in understanding. It was Bridget's

way of trying to please the irascible old man who'd shunned the young couple after their marriage. Michael walked her to the door. When they were outside in the hall, he turned to her.

"Morgana, I've been so worried about you," he whispered so as not to let their conversation reach Bridget's room. "Are you well? Are you happy? Your marriage, it was so sudden and unexpected."

"I know," Morgana spoke softly, too. "I'm sorry I haven't been able to see you lately. I've missed talking to you; and I guess I'm as well as can be expected. Please, Michael, I must get downstairs or Rian will come up after me. He's quite—quite possessive," she stammered.

He nodded in understanding. "Morgana, if you should ever be unhappy or in need, remember me."

"Thank you," she said gratefully. "You were ever a good friend, Michael."

"Patrick, you're the proud father of a baby girl," Morgana spoke as soon as she'd reached the salon, handing her cousin the tiny infant.

"She's so small," Patrick gazed at the bundle wonderingly.

"All babies are small." Rian looked over his cousin's shoulder at the child.

"She's called Maureen," Morgana informed them all quietly.

"Maureen," Fergus spoke thoughtfully, his dead wife's face floating before him briefly. "I like that."

Morgana could tell the old man was genuinely pleased and was glad for Bridget's sake.

"Is Bridget all right?" Patrick asked, turning his attention from the babe in his arms.

"She couldn't be better. All she needs is a little rest. Why don't you take Maureen upstairs to her now," Morgana suggested, and watched as he made his way carefully up the steps, awkward about carrying the child.

"I think we could all probably use some rest," Rian declared, catching hold of his wife's hand. "I recommend that we call it a night."

Once inside the sanctuary of their room, Rian closed

the door and poured himself a drink from the whiskey decanter upon the dresser.

"God, I hope it doesn't take you that long to have a baby." He dropped tiredly into a chair.

Morgana placed her hand over her womb unconsciously at his words.

"You know, then," she said.

"What?" his head jerked up sharply at that as he studied her searchingly, suddenly noting her gesture.

"I—I think I'm with child."

"Are—are you sure, Morgana? You've not been ill."

"Aye, I was sick this morning, and have not felt good for the past few weeks. I didn't want to tell you for fear that you would think I merely wished to see Michael," she explained hesitantly.

"I see," he spoke slowly, wondering if she hated the child she carried, his child. He was half drunk, for they had been drinking practically all day, but Rian carried his liquor well. "Come here," he commanded softly.

Morgana advanced across the room slowly and dropped to her knees on the floor before him. He reached out one hand, wrapping it in the flowing mass of copper curls, twisting her face up to his so that he could plant his lips upon her own, lingeringly, savoring the sweetness of her mouth. He set the glass down upon a table, then unfastened the buttons down the front of her dress so that he could slip his hand inside to fondle her swelling breasts. Aye, she belonged to him, and seeing her tonight with Patrick's child had stirred something inside of him, something even more strongly felt now that he knew she was carrying his own babe. Aye, grandfather had been right. She would give him fine sons and a man needed heirs, proud sons to carry on his name.

Morgana moaned gently at his touch and he drew in his breath sharply, feeling the quickening in his loins like a searing flame. He reached for the glass of whiskey again, accidentally spilling some of the amber liquid upon her. It trickled down over one bare breast, feeling cool against her burning flesh. He lowered his mouth to that soft place, his tongue tracing patterns of tiny swirls as he licked the whiskey from her satin skin, teeth nibbling gently on her hardened nipple.

"Hold me," he whispered huskily and Morgana complied, shaking at the strange sensations he was causing in her body, this father of her unborn babe.

He pulled her up onto the chaise longue beside him, removing her clothes and divesting himself of his garments. This time he deliberately poured the remaining contents of the glass over her body, his mouth upon the already moist curls to catch the whiskey which slipped down between her thighs. He heard her speak his name brokenly as, in spite of herself, she drew his head closer as his tongue probed deeper within her, then traced its way back up to her mouth so that she could taste the slightly salty scent mingled with liquor that clung to his lips before she felt his hard maleness inside of her.

Morgana sighed as, sometime later, his sweet release came, feeling the slight sense of frustration she always knew when he aroused her in this manner, as though there was something more, something which she couldn't quite find before his lovemaking ended. Slowly awakening beneath Rian's experienced hands and lips, Morgana couldn't know that it was only a matter of time until she would feel the answer she was instinctively seeking.

Chapter Twelve

Maureen proved to be a delightful child, seldom cross or fretful. Her eyes were big and blue like Bridget's, but anyone could see that her hair was going to be a brilliant copper, "like Cousin Morgana's," Bridget laughed. Even grandfather seemed to have forgotten his earlier rejection of Bridget and could often be found sitting in the large salon with her child in his arms. Bridget was not one to remain bedridden for long, and soon she was up and about.

One rainy afternoon they were all sitting in the salon playing whist when Rian, bored by the game, suggested they all go down to the cellars and explore the dungeons.

"There are dungeons in this house?" Morgana asked, rather horrified at the thought.

"Oh, yes," Colin reported excitedly. "There are all kinds of catacombs down there, too. Some of them wind out into the caverns in the rocks along the sea. In the old days, they were used by the pirates to get in and out of the house without being seen. 'Tis said several poor relatives became lost in them and were never heard from again."

Morgana did not want to go, but in the end everyone else laughed at her and said it would be capital sport, so they lit several torches and proceeded to the cellars, Morgana lagging reluctantly behind them.

It was dark and eerie, even with the torches, and the steep steps were wet with slime. Morgana guessed that the sea must trickle through the caves and under the house in some fashion to cause the formation of green moss she saw clinging to the crevices. There was a hollow, ringing echo when anyone spoke, even though for some reason they all talked in whispers. They wound carefully through the passageways, Morgana holding tightly to her husband's hand. She thought that he looked even more rugged and unusually barbaric in the flickering torchlight. Aye, two hundred years ago, he would have roamed the seas looting and plundering his enemies. Even now the blood of their savage ancestors coursed freely through his veins. She herself had seen it the night he'd attacked her on the beach. Morgana shivered at the thought.

"Afraid, Mag?" he mocked her softly. "You aren't usually wont to cling to me in this fashion."

She refused to answer him and he laughed softly, his green eyes surveying her frightened face insolently, hungrily, in the flickering light.

The dungeons were dank and clammy, and the heavy, wooden doors creaked and groaned on their rusted iron hinges. Rats scurried from the light of the torches, chattering angrily at having their havens invaded. Heavy iron chains hung from some of the walls, and old instruments of torture stood in some of the rooms. Rian told Morgana the names of many of them: the eye-gouger and branding iron, a spine roller, thumbscrews, and a forehead tourniquet. He explained how some prisoners had been bound on the rack with ropes that were gradually tightened around the limbs so that the body was slowly stretched out. The two methods generally reserved for the most stubborn prisoners were the worst of all, strappado and squassation, the latter an extremely cruel version of the first. Heavy weights were attached to the feet of the prisoner as he hung with his hands bound behind his back and was jerked at the end of a rope. Rian told her that squassation completely dislocated the hands, feet, elbows, limbs, and shoulders of its victims, and that sometimes the victims had been disemboweled while still hanging there alive.

"God," she cried out. "I don't want to hear any more of it."

Rian saw that she really did look rather pale and so he didn't tease her anymore about it. Morgana, for the most part, actually did feel quite ill and wanted nothing more than to return to the safety of the salon. Her shoes and the hem of her gown were wet from the damp, stone floors, and the muscles in her legs ached from walking. She was staring at an iron boot that Colin had tried to put on when she noticed for the first time that the others were no longer in the cell. She thought she heard them talking farther down the catacomb and promptly hurried after them. But her one torch did not give enough light, and she took a wrong turn somewhere in the blackness, stirring up a horde of bats in the process. With shrill shrieks, they flapped toward her in the darkness, their ratlike faces menacing as they came at her, beating their skeletal wings furiously. One struck her in the head, and Morgana gave a frightened cry, every tale she'd ever heard about vampires and bats coming back to haunt her. She turned, dropping the torch, and ran blindly, falling through the first open door she found, watching with horror as it suddenly slammed shut behind her. She clawed at it frantically, but it refused to budge. She screamed and screamed, till at last, exhausted, she realized that no one could possibly hear her cries through the heavy wood, and she sank, sobbing, to the cold floor.

Morgana didn't know how long she sat huddled there, the damp stones wetting her dress, chilling her to the bone. She had no way to tell. Her sobs choked in her throat, remembering Colin's tales of how many persons had been lost and died in the catacombs, and she wondered fearfully if the same fate was in store for her. She could hear the scurrying of rats in the blackness, and she pulled herself as close as possible to the door, drawing in her hands and feet as one brushed across her shoe. At last, she dozed fitfully.

She awakened with a start. God, how long had she been asleep and what had awakened her? She strained to hear in the chilling quiet and finally believed she heard voices, or was it only her pitiful imagination again? She didn't care. She rose and pounded on the door again tiredly, screaming for help. It was no use. Her imagination must have been playing tricks on her again. Would she go insane before starving, she wondered? Was her mind already showing signs of wandering, of going mad? Then she heard a scraping, a moaning of hinges, and the door swung open, casting the shadow of her husband upon the walls in the flickering torchlight.

"Rian," she said, before she fainted into his arms.

Morgana's eyes fluttered open slowly, the smelling salts Rian held under her nose finally taking effect. For one horrifying moment, she thought she was still in the dank dungeon, but then she realized with immense relief that she was on the sofa in the large salon.

"My God, Mag," Rian's worried face bent over her. "Why did you go wandering off like that? We might never have found you."

"I didn't," she sobbed. "I turned around and none of you were there. I was trying to find you when these horrible bats flew at me," she felt the wound upon her face where one of them had struck her.

"I thought you were right behind me, Morgana," Colin said. "I'm sorry."

"Are you all right?" Rian asked.

"I think so," she winced as he applied an unguent to the cut on her forehead.

"You're lucky we even found you," Patrick told her morbidly. "If Rian hadn't discovered the torch you dropped, we would never have known which passageway to search."

"That's enough, Patrick," Rian's voice was rather sharp. "Morgana's had enough for one day."

He lifted her up in his arms and carried her upstairs to their room, ordering Kyla to send up a dinner tray, as they would not be joining the family for supper. Morgana ate very little and, for once, Rian did not attempt to make love to her, seeming content instead to hold her in his arms tenderly. She sobbed on his chest quietly for a while, while he tried to calm her with soft, soothing words, treating her as though she had been a small child frightened by a nightmare.

Morgana didn't know how long she slept in his arms before she was awakened by the sound of someone crying outside the room. Puzzled, she rose from bed and pulled on her wrapper. She opened the French doors quietly, not wanting to awaken Rian, who still slept peacefully. The moon was full and a mist had settled over the moors, casting elongated shadows in the blackness. The weeping seemed to be coming from the balcony, and she walked slowly toward the sound, for the balconies at Shanetara wound around the entire house. Morgana's breath caught in her throat when she spied the ethereal figure of a woman with long, red hair gazing out to sea crying as though her heart were breaking. She seemed to float as she walked, her pale, white gown swirling in the mist like a shroud. Morgana recognized her at once from the portrait. The unworldly figure was Katy McShane. Morgana glanced out over the ocean and saw the hazy, silver outline of a ship there in the gloom, a ghost ship; she shivered, remembering Rian's tale. She was so close to the woman now, Morgana could almost put out one hand and touch her. The gentle spectre turned, her luminous eyes bright with tears as she gazed at Morgana's startled face. Then she moved toward the edge of the balcony once more.

"William. I'm coming, William," her voice was hushed like the music of the lute she'd once played.

Then, slowly, her silvery ghost faded into the mist. Morgana looked out to sea and saw the ship disappear from the coast, leaving only the pale moonlight shimmering upon the waters.

"Morgana, what are you doing out here?" her husband spoke from behind her.

"Rian. I saw her, Rian."

"Saw who?"

"Katy McShane and the ghost ship."

Softly he quoted in the darkness:

There, in a moment we may plunge our years
In fatal penitence, and in the blight
Of our own soul turn all our blood to tears,
And color things to come with hues of Night;
The race of life becomes a hopeless flight
To those that walk in darkness: on the sea
The boldest steer but where their ports invite;
But there are wanderers o'er Eternity
Whose bark drives on and on, and anchor'd ne'er
    shall be.

"Why, Rian," Morgana turned in surprise. "I didn't know you'd read Lord Byron."

"Come inside, Mag," he took her arm quietly. " 'Tis late and you'll catch your death of cold."

Morgana lay awake for some time, reflecting on this new aspect of her husband. How could he be so cruel one moment, and quote the most beautiful poetry the next, understanding perfectly the mood created by the lovely ghost? Gazing at him in the moonlight, Morgana had felt the music of his words play upon the strings of her heart. Was she falling in love with Rian?

In the morning, she decided the ghost must have cast a spell on her, for Rian was his usual arrogant self, bruising her lips hungrily as he made love to her, showing no signs of the gentle understanding he'd displayed during the night. Morgana told him she hated him, and he laughed at her insolently, causing her to stick out her tongue at him. This made him laugh even harder and he ripped the sheets away from her and began tickling her unmercifully. She gasped and managed to grab one of the pillows, with which she gave him a resounding slap on the head. Rian immediately grabbed the other one and they were soon in the midst of a horrendous pillow fight. Rian's pillow burst open at the seams and soon the entire bedroom was covered with feathers, much to the annoyance of Kyla, who had to clean up the mess and was heard later grumbling about her employers' pranks.

One morning Morgana decided to ride over to Kilshannon Hall to visit Bridget and see little Maureen. She was in a good mood and sang as she rode along, giving Copper Lady free rein as she laughed with Ben, the groom. It was this, perhaps, that saved her life. The mare stumbled in a rabbit hole, causing her unwitting rider to be thrown from the saddle. At that precise moment a shot rang out, the bullet gouging a huge hole in the leather of Morgana's sidesaddle. Were it not for the fall, she would surely have been killed. Shakily, she picked herself up off the ground and glanced up into the hills, searching for some sign of a hunter. She heard Ben call out that there were people below and then ask if she were all right. She nodded, trembling, while he helped her up on his horse, Copper Lady having run hellbent from fright toward Shanetara.

Rian was in the yard with the mare when they arrived.

"What in the hell is going on?" he demanded.

By this time, Morgana was practically in tears. "Someone tried to kill me. Just look at my saddle, it's ruined," she wailed illogically.

"I'll get you another one." Rian tried to calm her hysterical fears. " 'Twas probably only a poacher, Mag. I'll have Ben investigate."

The groom searched the countryside and questioned the tenants, but was able to report nothing. No one had seen any sign of a hunter that morning. Morgana decided that Rian was probably right, that she was just letting her imagination run away with her, for certainly nobody she knew would want to hurt her.

Her body was changing, taking on a rounded fullness as the child grew inside her. She was now almost four months pregnant and it was starting to show. She didn't realize it, though, until one evening when Bridget asked, "When is the child due, Morgana?" She and Rian decided it was time to tell the family.

Grandfather was overjoyed when he heard the news and insisted on having a small celebration. Patrick clapped Rian on the back gaily, saying, "What took you so long, cousin?" causing Morgana to blush with mortification. Rian gave her an amused glance, but one she could have sworn was filled with tenderness in that moment, and she hoped he was pleased about the babe.

In the general uproar, no one noticed that Colin did not extend his congratulations to the couple, but slunk off as soon as possible. He resented Morgana more each day for marrying Rian and causing him to lose out on his grandfather's will. He did not know that Fergus had never intended on cutting the rest of the family out of his will, and that it had been but a ruse to try and force Rian into wedding the girl. After the marriage, Fergus had sent a note to Mister O'Donnell, his attorney, instructing the lawyer to destroy the latest document. Unfortunately, he forgot to inform his family that he had done this.

That evening as Rian and Morgana were starting down for dinner, she remembered that she'd forgotten to close the French doors on the balcony. Since the sky threatened rain, she decided that she really ought to go back and close them.

"You go ahead, Rian," Morgana told him. "It will take me only a minute."

The hallway seemed darker than usual when Morgana came out of the bedroom, and uneasily she hurried toward the stairs. She had just put one foot on the top step when a hand thrust sharply between her shoulder blades, and she found herself falling downward, over and over again. The last thing she remembered was Rian's face bending over her before the blackness swirled up to engulf her.

Chapter Thirteen

Rian's face was stricken as he lifted his unconscious wife up from the foot of the stairs and hoarsely called for help. He carried her up to the bedroom and laid her upon the bed. Thank God, he saw that she was still breathing. There seemed to be blood everywhere. He pulled off her clothes and saw why, but he spared only a moment's concern for the lost child.

"Mollie, get me some linens and hot water," he yelled, working feverishly, for Morgana's face was deathly pale and her breathing extremely shallow.

Bridget and Fionna came to help him and together they bathed Morgana's cold body and cleaned the cuts on her face and shoulders where she'd struck the stairs going down.

Patrick had ridden for the doctor and Michael Kelsey almost broke his neck to get to Shanetara, so distraught was he at the news. That was nothing compared to the shock he received when he hurried into the bedroom and Rian pulled a sheet over his wife, shouting at him to get out.

"My God, man, I'm a doctor," he pushed Rian aside, forgetting for the moment the difference in their ranks.

Michael sent Bridget and Fionna out of the room, and impervious to Rian's anger, he yanked the sheet from Morgana's body and began to examine her. He worked quickly and quietly.

"She's lost the child," he glanced at Rian's anxious face.

The two men studied each other in the silence, conflicting emotions showing upon each of their countenances.

"I—I'm sorry, Michael," Rian tried to regain his composure. "I shouldn't have acted the way I did. 'Tis just that, once, I thought you and Morgana were lovers. I know now it wasn't true—but—God! Is she going to be all right?"

Michael Kelsey studied the dark Earl quietly, guessed what it had cost the proud man to make the apology, and nodded briefly in understanding.

"I was and am still but her friend, my lord." He glanced at Morgana's white face again. "We've got to pack her in ice or she's going to bleed to death. Do you—love her, my lord?" he asked hesitantly.

"Love? I don't think I know the meaning of the word," Rian spoke bitterly with sudden insight before he went to get the ice.

Morgana lay unconscious for over a week and during that time Rian remained by her side, allowing no one but himself to nurse her. He grew gaunt with worry, unkempt from lack of sleep. The rest of the family tiptoed in his presence, for his concern had made him half mad and they were all afraid of the rage and torment they saw in his eyes. Grandfather grieved openly for the lost child and Morgana's precarious state of health. He sat often in her old room, mumbling to himself.

Rian blamed himself bitterly and dwelled on the

times he'd forced himself upon his wife and how she'd hated him for it. Silently he vowed to himself that if she recovered, he would take her away from Ireland, would introduce her to society, buy her pretty dresses, and make her laugh again. But if someone had asked the proud, arrogant Earl why he wanted to do these things, he still would not have known or admitted the answer. He only knew that if she died, he would never forgive himself.

"Morgana Shelley McShane, did you spill ink on my desk?"

"Nay, father."

"Sure and 'tis a sin to tell a lie, child."

The child gazed at the dark stain, watched fascinated as it turned into a crimson tide of blood on the ground beside her. She screamed.

"Lie still, you must rest."

"He's going to rape me. Somebody help me, please."

"Who?"

"Brendan, no, Rian."

"I'm here, lie still."

"He doesn't want me."

"Who?"

"Rian."

"I'm here, Mag, try to rest."

The child watched the stain grow larger, until it was as big and black as the Irish Sea. The water felt cold against her naked skin. She screamed again, frightened, as the devil rose up from the honey-colored sand, beckoned to her, then put his hands upon her breasts.

" 'Tis a sin, child."

"No, I don't want to go to hell. He forced me. Don't take my baby."

"Swallow."

"Morgana, with the copper curls, thinks she's better than the other girls."

Her schoolmates formed a ring around the child. They laughed.

"He isn't coming."

She cried. The tears were gently kissed away. By father? No, father was dead. Who, then? A teardrop splashed upon her breast and turned into whiskey as it drifted down her flesh.

"Let me go. You're drunk."

She gazed into wintergreen eyes that twisted into Chinese silk.

"No one else could wear that color, but how could you have known?"

A pirate stood before her. He laughed mockingly before his hands tore at the fragile material, bruising the creamy whiteness of her shoulder.

"The witching hour."

"She's a red-haired witch."

"No!"

"Lie still."

" 'Tis a sin, child."

The pirate was a devil again, chasing her on a big black horse. She couldn't run. Her legs wouldn't move. She licked her lips.

"Swallow."

It felt cool upon her forehead. A shot rang out. He was falling. No, she was falling, falling, falling . . .

She could see the silver ship in the grey mist. The woman was crying, her white gown flowing like a shroud.

"William. I'm coming, William."

"But there are wanderers o'er Eternity/Whose bark drives on and on, and anchor'd ne'er shall be."

The woman faded into the night. God, it was so dark. Her dress was damp. It was cold upon the stone floor. She could hear the rats as they scurried across the floor. Their feet spread, grew into skeletal wings. They flew at her, shrieking. She dropped her torch. Then she was lying on the rack. They were stretching her limbs, harder, harder. She could feel the thumbscrews piercing her flesh.

"Confess, you're a witch."

"No."

"Your father is dead, child."

They lowered the casket into the ground. She could hear the thud upon the coffin as the chunks of dirt were shovelled in. She was in black, no, it was a creamy white dress with thousands of tiny seed pearls.

"You'll marry me?"

"What makes you think I still want you?"

There was a heavy gold band on her finger. No, it was a chain. She was chained to a cold stone wall. It was dark. Wait, someone had brought a light. She set the lamp on the table. There were no walls, only shelves and shelves of books. It was a library.

"Who robs my grandfather's library?"

The glass of whiskey shattered into a thousand pieces. The book. She dropped her father's book. It was on the floor. She was on the floor, in front of the fire. The glass was cutting into her flesh. No, it was bits of sand. She flung the pebbles at the demon. He was clawing tiny furrows in her back that ran with blood. She could feel it wet and sticky between her thighs. She screamed.

"Rian!"

Morgana opened her eyes slowly, trying to remember where she was. The room was in great disorder, clothes and wet towels thrown upon the floor; and it was dark, the curtains tightly closed. The emerald bits of glass in her face focused confusedly on the unshaven man in the chair near her bed. Of course, she was in her room at Shanetara and the bearded stranger was her husband, Rian.

She wondered why Kyla hadn't been in to tidy up. She must get this mess cleaned up right away. She tried to move, but found she felt stiff and sore, then recalled that she'd had an accident, fallen down the stairs. No, not fallen, had been pushed by someone; her befuddled mind was beginning to clear. But why would anyone want to harm her? She glanced at Rian again, dozing fitfully in the chair. Was he sorry he'd married her? Was Lindsey Joyce proving to be too much of a temptation to resist?

Had he decided that her death was the only release from this mockery of a marriage? He moved so quietly, like a panther. He could have fired that shot out on the moors. And it was he who had suggested exploring the dungeons. Had that door really slammed shut by itself? And how had he known where to look for her? Could a torch have told him that? And when she was lying at the bottom of the stairs, how had he gotten there so quickly? Had he been the one who'd pushed her?

Morgana thought about how Rian had laughed at her fears and called her foolish. Had it all been just a ruse so that she wouldn't suspect him? She tried to recall the expression on his face as he'd bent over her at the bottom of the stairs, but the image was dimmed by the feeling of moisture rushing through her. God, no, she implored silently, but was sure in her mind that she'd lost the child, his child, a child she hadn't known whether or not she'd even wanted. Her belly felt flat again. Was there nothing to be had from marriage with this mocking devil of a man?

Rian awoke with a start, feeling his wife's glazed eyes upon him. For a moment, he thought she was still delirious, but then he saw that they were only misted over with tears.

"I've lost the baby, haven't I?" she asked softly.

He took her hands in his. "There'll be other children, Mag."

"Nay! I don't want another child. Not from you, not ever. I want a divorce," she breathed bitterly. "I want out of this mockery of a marriage. I want to get away, to forget that I ever came here or saw you!"

"Hush, Mag. You're overwrought from the accident and the shock of losing the child."

"Accident!" she fairly screamed now. "That was no accident. Someone deliberately pushed me down those stairs."

Rian gazed at her speculatively for a moment, then said, "We'll discuss this later, when you're feeling better. I'll take you away from here, if you like. But understand

172

this, Morgana. You're my wife and under no circumstances will I ever agree to a divorce."

Morgana turned her face into the pillow, sobbing brokenly. The beast! The devil! She hated him; and she was convinced that he was trying to kill her.

BOOK TWO

A Tall White Sail

Chapter Fourteen

The Atlantic Ocean, 1813

Two weeks later, as he had promised, Rian took Morgana away from Shanetara. They set sail for England, Rian explaining to the rest of the family that he felt that Morgana needed a change of scenery. Morgana was glad to be leaving the shadows of Shanetara, and the fact that Rian was to accompany her only faintly marred the sudden, wild freedom she experienced at leaving the great house behind. Since she could find no reason in her mind for him wanting to destroy their child, her suspicion that Rian had tried to kill her gradually evaporated. She watched the green coast of Ireland fade into the distance and did not know it would be over four years before she saw it again.

Morgana savored the kindness of Rian's crew and gradually she began to lose her pinched, worried look. Rian was strangely subdued, but he, too, felt the change in atmosphere and the thin, anxious expression he'd acquired when nursing his wife began to fade as he found himself once more master of his ship and fate.

Still, he made no move to touch his wife, and Morgana took comfort in the fact that he left her alone, not even sharing the big, warm bed which had taken the place of the narrow bunk in his cabin. He slept instead on the small sofa near his desk, although his feet hung over the end and he was often thrown to the floor when the ship swayed. She was afraid to suggest he move to the bed lest he take it as an invitation to resume his husbandly duties.

So they managed to stumble along in an unspoken truce for a while. Rian showed her how to read the charts which he often studied at night and how to tell direction by the stars, although he used the sextant she'd seen the first time she'd been on board. They played chess in the evenings, and sometimes, at his suggestion, she read aloud from her father's books of poetry. Still, it was an uneasy, wary arrangement, and Rian found it increasingly difficult to woo his wife without winning her. The ache in his loins grew deeper as he watched her undress every night and slide into bed alone.

Morgana watched his restraint with puzzled fear, wondering why he did not rape her as he had before. She would have liked to tease him, to taunt him subtly with her charms, but was afraid of driving him too far. She often strolled about the deck in the morning if the weather was clear, watching him work. She was, however, forbidden to explore the remainder of the ship, as Rian said he did not want to hang any of his crew for violating her person, "Though you would doubtless find it a welcome change from my beastly attentions," he mocked, and she stormed back to the cabin, convinced that she hated him all over again.

One morning she went upon deck only to find the sky darkened with a greyish cast and the wind rising. She saw Rian's tall figure at the helm and approached him hesitantly.

"Is it going to storm, Rian?"

"Looks like it. You'd best go to the cabin and stay there. These sudden squalls can be very dangerous."

She sighed, disappointed, for these walks were her sole entertainment and she hated to forego her pleasure, but she returned to the cabin as bid. Lacking the stabilizing weight of a cargo, by midafternoon, the ship tossed and heaved upon the rapidly shifting waves like a leaf on the wind. Morgana could hear the nervous whinnying of Lucifer and Copper Lady from below the decks as they pawed anxiously in their stalls.

Suddenly, the wind howled and torrents of raindrops shattered down from the swirling clouds. Morgana cringed as a clap of thunder roared and a blast of lightning lit the sky. A jolt of the ship sent her spinning across the cabin, the oranges on the table spilling out and rolling over the floor like children's toys. She grasped the bedpost for support and wondered what Rian was doing outside. She was absolutely terrified of storms, and could barely see through the porthole as the rain pounded maddeningly. God, what if Rian were up on the topmast or something? No, she tried to calm her fears; he was sure to be at the helm. But suppose he wasn't. What if he got washed overboard? What would she do, where would she go?

Morgana shivered again as the thunder rang out like God's hammer on an anvil. She was afraid and wanted desperately for her husband to come to the cabin and laugh away her fears with his mocking smile. She waited until she could stand it no longer, then grabbed her cloak and flung herself to the door.

The wind almost knocked her off her feet once she managed to get outside and the rain beat down upon her unmercifully, blinding her eyes with its fury. She flattened herself against the wall and slowly inched her way forward. Yes, there Rian was. Morgana could barely make out his tall, dark figure, struggling with the wheel as he shouted orders to his scrambling sailors. She left the small safety of the wall and staggered across the deck toward him. The wind whipped her cloak wildly about her lithe body and a sudden shift in motion sent her reeling toward the edge of the ship. She fell, grabbing a coil of rope tied to one of the masts, but the rocking of the ship was too strong for her to hang onto the heavy strands and she found herself slipping to the starboard side.

She screamed, "Rian!" the wind tearing the words from her mouth, and then he was pulling her to him, picking her up in his arms as he lurched unsteadily to the cabin. He kicked the door shut with a slam louder than the thunder which had so terrified her only moments before. They were both drenched and chilled to the bone, but Morgana shivered only from the cold wrath she saw upon her husband's face.

"You little fool," he hissed. "We might both have been killed. Didn't I tell you to stay in the cabin?" he shook her angrily despite her chattering teeth and the fear he saw in her eyes.

"I was frightened of the storm," she was crying now.

Rian stared at his wife as she dropped her wet cloak upon the floor, her soaking gown clinging to her like ivy on a wall, revealing every curve of the body he had gone without for almost two months. An overwhelming desire spread through him like wildfire. Damn her to hell and back! She hated him with a passion and had caused him more trouble than she was worth. By God, she was going to pay. He was tired of her foolish whims and fancies. The fury of fighting the storm sought release, and Rian yanked her to him, forgetting his ship, the storm, and everything else as his mouth swooped down upon hers like a hungry hawk. Morgana fought him like a crazy woman, her fear giving her strength she didn't even know she posesssed as he lit into her. She pulled away from his arms, clawing him and screaming hysterically.

"You bitch!" he swore. "I'm going to teach you a lesson you'll never forget, and from now on when I give you an order, you're going to follow it, or I'll beat you within an inch of your life."

"You—animal," she panted. "You'll never own me, I swear it."

He slapped her brutally, then cast away his garments. She tried to run, but he caught her in a cruel caress, his demon laughter ringing in her ears as he ripped the sodden gown from her flesh. The ship heaved and rolled upon the cloudy seas, sending them both tumbling into the huge poster bed. He covered her mouth with kisses, forcing his tongue between her parted lips, pillaging the softness inside. Morgana fought for air while his hands moved on her breasts, taunting them, cupping their creamy roundness till they swelled with the passion he knew he aroused in her, in spite of her hatred, and he felt her pink nipples harden in response. Rian opend her thighs with a swift movement of one knee and dropped one hand down to that sweet inner flesh he would soon possess, touching softly, gently, till she flushed with excitement, her eyes closing as she gave a low cry of surrender. He mounted her then; and Morgana couldn't have said whether the ship or her husband rocked her so violently yet with tender fury that awakened her body's wildest desires. She felt a quivering delight spread through her until she finally exploded against him in pleasure and pain, like the fierce waves crashing against the hull of the ship, over and over again until at last the tide ebbed and she lay still beneath him, raindrop tears streaking her cheeks.

"Rian, oh, Rian," she moaned softly. "I didn't know it could be like this."

And he knew that at last she had experienced the full, far-reaching depth of her womanhood. He smiled triumphantly, satisfied at last, and slept.

As the first pale streaks of dawn lit the sky, Rian turned and reached for his wife, and once again they recaptured the ecstasy they had known the night just past. When it was over, he left her sleeping and went on deck to inspect the damage done to his ship. One of the masts had been snapped in half by the gusty wind, but that was all. He could wait until they reached London to repair it.

He thought about last night. Would it make any difference in his wife's feelings for him, he wondered?

Well, one thing was sure, it would probably be the last time she disobeyed his orders again. Damn it! Why couldn't the wench realize that he was thinking of her safety? His mind lingered on the sweet curve of her lips and the sight of her nakedness on the bed before he took her. Lord, he was worse than a rutting stag when it came to making love to her. What in the hell was the matter with him anyway—daring, dashing Rian McShane who'd always taken what he wanted and parted without another thought? When it came to his green-eyed wife, he felt like a callow youth. What was it about her that drove him to the brink of madness?

Morgana, stretching languidly in the bed and yawning, was wondering how she could possibly have responded so passionately to a man she hated, a man who abused her, used her to his own satisfaction, and then went about his daily chores as though nothing had happened. And how would he act when he came in? Would he spare some small crumb of compassion for her, or be his usual demanding, arrogant self? He used his physical strength to his advantage whenever she started to get the best of him. Would she ever win? Did she even really want to win? If she were honest with herself, Morgana had to admit she was not sure.

Rian did not come in until dinner time. Morgana had dressed carefully in one of her most becoming green gowns and sat trying to read, anxiously awaiting the moment when he would walk through the door. She didn't know whether to run to him or let him come to her. Finally, she compromised by crossing the small room partway and inquiring about the state of the ship.

"Just some slight damage, that's all, nothing too serious."

"That's good," she replied.

"You look very fetching this evening, my lady, beautiful enough for a ball. Will you dance, madam?"

"But there's no music," she replied.

Without another word Rian turned and left the cabin. When he returned, the soft, harmonious melody of a guitar filled the air.

"Ask and you shall receive, my lady," Rian said, taking her in his arms.

"But, Rian, where is the music coming from?"

"Jeb, one of the hands, is playing just for us outside the door."

They whirled in silence to the romantic tune, Rian's arms tightening around her waist as they danced. Morgana laid her head upon his chest and, as he gazed down at her, he could see the thick, bristly lashes which fringed those enormous emerald eyes, and the square tilt of her jaw. With a frown, he noticed that there was a slight purplish bruise upon it from where he'd struck her. He shouldn't have marred her lovely skin, but hell, what was a man supposed to do with such a headstrong woman? He glanced down to the curve of her rounded breasts which rose and fell rapidly as he breathed softly in her ear, "Sweet, I think we'd better eat now if you want to eat at all."

"Whatever you say, Rian," Morgana spoke demurely, her eyes downcast, but Rian was not deceived by her manner. Even now, she was probably just itching for a chance to get even with him. He would have to be on his guard!

Chapter Fifteen

London was a hub of activity as they sailed up the Thames to its docks. Morgana, standing on the deck of the *Sorceress,* did not realize how much she had missed it until she saw the city again in its full splendor. How glad she was that Rian had brought her here. They landed and she ran down the gangplank eagerly, whirling about and hugging herself with delight, not caring that passersby were staring at her as though she had gone quite mad. Rian, watching her from the helm, smiled to himself. She was such a strange mixture of half-woman, half-child. He barked orders to the crew and saw that the ship was safely moored in the harbor before he joined his wife on the ground. Mister Harrison was promptly dispatched to his lordship's stables to fetch the Earl's matched greys and carriage. While they waited for his return, Rian and Morgana sought refreshment in a nearby inn. When they had finished their light repast, Harrison came in to announce that his lordship's curricle awaited.

"Lord, guv'nor," a short, wiry man hollered from

the team's heads as they walked toward the vehicle. "I was beginning to think that bloody green isle 'ad swallowed ye up."

"No such thing, Louis. Now do try to behave in the presence of my lady, or she will think you're no better than a common footpad," the Earl eyed his tiger fondly.

"Footpad! Why, guv'nor," the little man looked hurt. " 'Ow kin ye say sech a thing 'bout me?"

"I say it quite easily, Louis, since on several occasions you have robbed my friends quite blind. I hope you haven't forked so much as a guinea while I was away."

"M'lord," Louis appeared highly mortified. "I've done no sech thing."

"Well, see that you don't," Rian turned to his wife. "Morgana, allow me to present my tiger, Louis. You must keep a tight hold on your reticule whenever he's around. Louis, this is my wife, Lady Keldara."

"Lord, guv'nor, ye done got married and didn't tell yer poor tiger nary a word, and sech a purty lass, too. No wonder ye snatched 'er up so quicklike," he touched his cap respectfully and gave Morgana an impish grin.

She smiled in spite of herself. "Does he really steal things, Rian?"

"Unfortunately, yes, but he's always sorry afterwards and blurts out the entire story before we're even home. You've no idea of the number of my friends' watches, fobs, and seals I've had to replace."

Rian gave the horses the office to start, and Louis, having long been in the Earl's service, let go the wheelers and made a hasty scramble for his perch.

"Don't ye believe 'im, m'lady. I wouldn't take so much as a tuppence from ye."

"You'd better not, Louis," Rian warned him lazily. "Or you'll have to look somewhere else for employment."

Louis sniffed. "Lord Chalmers was asking me t'other day if I'd go to work for 'im."

Rian laughed. "That sour-faced, old pudding. You'd best go to Lord Brisbane. He has a much smarter set of horses and very well kept stables. I'll give you a recommendation if you like."

Louis turned his reproachful eyes on the Earl. "Lord, guv'nor, ye'd not be turning me out on the streets now."

"Certainly not, Louis. Now do be still or I'll turn you over to the Bow Street Runners for your petty thievery instead."

Evidently Louis knew when he'd tried his lordship's patience far enough, for he made not another sound.

"Well, sweet," Rian maneuvered the curricle gracefully through the crowded streets. "Would you like to go directly home? I fear the house will be all sixes and sevens on such short notice of our arrival."

"I didn't know you had a house in London."

"There are quite a lot of things you don't know about me," he responded rather dryly.

"If you don't mind," she glanced at him timidly. "I'd like to go for a drive in Hyde Park."

"Your wish is my command." He gave her an insolent look.

They were soon spinning gaily through the park, Morgana drinking in the sights with fond remembrance, quite unashamed of her rather dishevelled appearance and the fact that she was not at all dressed for driving. A perch-phaeton swept by them and she gazed at it longingly, exclaiming, "Oh, Rian, I do wish I had a rig like that."

"Don't say rig, Mag. It doesn't sound at all ladylike." He reprimanded her in much the same tone of voice he'd used with Louis earlier. "Do you know how to drive a team?"

"Of course. Father never neglected that portion of my education."

"Well, let us see if you know what you're talking about," he pulled the curricle to a halt.

"You mean I'm to drive, now?" she asked in amazement.

"Why not? Are you afraid?"

"Certainly not!" she spoke indignantly and moved to exchange places with him.

"Blimey, guv'nor, ye'll not be letting a female drive

us?" Louis appeared rather alarmed. "What will me competitors be thinking, a tiger be'ind a gentry-mort with the reins? What 'bout me reputation?"

"Disregard it, Louis," his lordship replied.

Louis puffed up like a balloon, but made no further comment as Morgana flicked the whip, pointing her leaders and driving them well up to their bits. They trotted briskly around Hyde Park, unaware of the stir they seemed to be causing.

"Good God, Denby," Sir Anthony Reginald grasped his companion's arm hastily as the curricle rounded the promenade. "It's Keldara."

"Wonder when he got back?" Denby was busy flirting with Miss Winwood, a saucy brunette whose chaperon had lagged behind to examine the roses.

"For God's sake, man!" Anthony was exasperated. "He's got a redhead driving his curricle, and a real minx, too, or I miss my guess."

Lord Brisbane was sufficiently impressed by this bit of information to glance up at the oncoming vehicle. He gave a low whistle at the sight which was rapidly approaching. "Keldara must be moonstruck, Anthony. I do believe you're right."

"That female looks devilishly familiar," Sir Reginald was trying to recall where he had seen that face. "I've got it, Brad. That's the poet's daughter. The one whose funeral I attended. Remember? I told you about it one night over cards."

"So you did," Denby agreed. "But what in the hell is she doing in Keldara's curricle, much less handling the ribbons on those greys?"

They were so overcome by curiosity that they flagged the curricle down and Morgana pulled obediently to a stop.

"Brad, Anthony," Rian acknowledged his cronies with an amused smile, for he could see they were plainly bursting at the seams to know what was going on.

"Rian, old boy, when did you return? I swear, 'tis been quite dull without you." Denby ogled Morgana quite openly, causing a much mortified Miss Winwood to remark her chaperone's absence with a sniff, claiming she must go and find that young woman posthaste! Anthony stood, obviously transfixed by Morgana's beauty, impervious to his lordship's frown.

"Only this morning," Rian responded. "Morgana, my dear, allow me to present Lord Braddington Denby and Sir Anthony Reginald. Gentlemen, this is my wife."

If the sky had fallen, two men could not have been more amazed. Morgana watched silently as their mouths dropped open in dumbfounded shock.

"Your wife, did you say? A pleasure to make your acquaintance, Lady Keldara. You can't imagine how many hearts this news is going to break. Every matchmaking mama in town has set her daughter's cap at this devil for years," Denby announced delightedly.

"But how came this, Rian?" Anthony was plainly confused at the sudden turn of events.

"Lady Keldara is my cousin, dear boy," Rian surveyed him lazily. "We met at my grandfather's estate in Ireland. You might say she was *willed* into falling into my arms," he said with a wicked glance at Morgana, who feared for a moment that he was going to tell them the truth about their marriage. However, it appeared that he was only teasing her, for after accepting an invitation to Lord Brisbane's card party the following week, he declared firmly that they must be going and took the reins from his wife's hands, leaving his friends to digest the unexpected news of his wedding.

"You may have your perch-phaeton, sweet. Haverill's will probably have just the thing," Rian announced when they were out of sight. "And I'll go to Tattersall's to see about getting a suitable team for you to drive."

Even Louis broke down and admitted that she did a bang-up job of handling the ribbons, a sincere compliment Rian told her, making Morgana feel quite pleased with herself as they pulled up in front of the Earl's elegant townhouse in Grosvenor Square.

As Rian had predicted, all was in a highly confused, disordered state, although his well-trained servants did their best to make the couple comfortable. The staff was curious about his lordship's bride, but none were surprised because their long years in the Earl's service had taught them to expect anything and everything from that devilish rake. Morgana's appearance only confirmed their beliefs that his lordship knew a good thing when he saw it; and Bagley, the butler, proudly presented her with a hastily bought bouquet of flowers from the entire staff. She made a pretty speech, slightly overwhelmed by their kindness, then went upstairs to unpack while Rian sent for Mister Wright, his man of business and abruptly demanded to know where Chilham, his valet, was.

Chilham, he was informed, was upstairs taking a survey of the damage to his lordship's garments and clucking his tongue over the sad appearance of the Earl's highjack boots. Chilham could not endure the rigors of the sea and flatly refused to sail anywhere with Rian, leaving his lordship to fend for himself whenever he was out of the country; and each time upon Rian's return, the state of his clothing made Chilham almost as ill as the motion of the waves. With a look of great disgust, the valet began to scrape the mud from the Earl's boots and requested one of the chambermaids to fetch a bottle of champagne to restore to them the famous shine that made all of Rian's dandyish friends so covetous and envious of Chilham's services.

Not wishing to place a further burden on his staff, Rian, after seeing Mister Wright and informing that astounded young man to place an advertisement in the *Morning Gazette* announcing the Earl's marriage, escorted Morgana to the Piazza, where they dined on deviled crabmeat, stuffed peppers, and hummingbird tongues, and were obviously the talk of the town. Morgana was forced to endure the flirtatious ogling of many young bucks and the murderous stares and pouting faces of the women. News travelled fast, it seemed.

"Goodness," she whispered to her husband. "You didn't tell me that half of London was just aching to get their hooks into you. Which one of these ladies present is likely to go berserk and stab me in the back?"

Rian threw back his head and laughed, causing many to remark upon the obvious delight the Earl was taking in the sensation he had caused. One raven-haired beauty in particular was quite put out. Her name, Morgana learned later, was Lady Cecily Brooksworth, and she had, until now, been the favorite at Watier's, Brooks's, and White's, where bets had been placed as to which lovely lady was most apt to snare the elusive Lord Keldara. Cecily was furious at having been made a laughingstock, for she had been Rian's mistress for some time in London and had held high hopes of snagging him. To see him show up with a bewitching bride on his arm was almost more than she could bear. Her fingers itched to claw those lovely emerald eyes and pull those copper curls, but she was smart enough to realize that Rian would be most angry if she made a scene. Resolving irately to get even with him later, she told her escort, the Vicomte de Blanchefleur, that she was suffering from a splitting headache and must return home at once. The Vicomte, Phillipe du Lac, was immediately concerned and called for her carriage. Cecily ignored the smirks of amusement the more vicious females directed toward her, pretended she hadn't seen Rian, and pointedly disregarded Lady Jersey's loud statement that the Earl of Keldara had given more than one pack of hounds the slip and that she'd always known he was a sly fox.

The next morning Rian announced that he had some business to attend to, told Morgana that she might refurnish the house any way she chose, and that she could call on Lord Brisbane to help her if she so desired, his taste being considered to be almost as exquisite as that of Beau Brummell. After ascertaining that Rian would return later to dine with her, Morgana requested Bagley to send a note around to Lord Brisbane, then dressed herself, for Chilham had not yet procured her an abigail. Mistress Cadwalder, the housekeeper, was pleased to find that the new bride did not intend to make any changes in the manner in which the household was being run; and Mistress Northbridge, the cook, fairly beamed when Morgana instructed her that she was to continue preparing whatever meals most pleased his lordship.

Lord Brisbane soon arrived, delighted to accompany the Earl's bride, and much gratified by the confidence his friend had displayed in him by placing his wife in his care. Brad, as he begged Morgana to call him, did indeed possess a great deal of knowledge concerning all matters of the Ton and had no hesitation in escorting his young charge to some of the finest shops in London. He guided her with an unerring hand in the selection of wallpaper, furniture, and beautiful Dresden china knickknacks for her drawing room. She was horrified at the cost, but when she made mention of this to Denby, he merely laughed and said that Rian could afford it.

This puzzled her, for Morgana did not understand where Rian's money came from, nor could she imagine their tightfisted grandfather agreeing to the upkeep of a townhouse in London. She felt very confused, for she had understood all of her cousins' inheritances to be tied up in entails and trust funds until the death of their grandfather, and that none was as large a fortune as the one the old man had destined for her husband in his will. She supposed, of course, that Rian garnered some income from his estate in Ireland and his ship, but she hadn't thought it was a great deal of money. Perplexed, she asked Denby about it.

"I don't know," he shrugged off her question airily. "I believe he has holdings in the East India Company, and he won the townhouse at hazard. Devilish fine card-player and man with the dice Rian is. I've seen him win and lose fortunes at the gaming tables."

This satisfied her completely, for she knew gambling was not a steady way of providing one's earnings and assumed that Rian had no doubt married her to stave off a string of creditors with his expected monetary gains from grandfather's will. Besides, as Denby patiently explained to her, if one couldn't pay one's debts, one simply ordered more and promised payment at a later date. That usually satisfied most creditors, especially since it was considered in bad taste to dun a member of the Ton. Some persons, Denby told her, borrowed money from Howard and Gibbs, but he conceded, " 'Tis very bad business to get mixed up with those vultures." He'd seen more than one good fellow go bankrupt from their exorbitant interest rates.

They soon tired of shopping, however, and returned home to find Rian waiting. As it was almost time for supper, Morgana naturally invited Lord Brisbane to dine, and the three of them passed a very pleasant evening, Brad filling them in on the latest London gossip.

In the weeks that followed, Rian took Morgana dancing at Vauxhall Gardens, and procured her a box at Drury Lane. He took her to see the wild beasts at the Royal Exchange and even consented to shopping with her at the Pantheon Bazaar. She found that he was well versed in the history of England when they visited the Tower of London, and that he liked music and had seen both Mozart and Beethoven perform.

There were mornings when he dragged her out of bed and tickled her unmercifully, and nights when he wrapped her long red hair around his throat and whispered his desire for her. They dined in the very best places, gambled until the wee hours of the morning, and went riding in Hyde Park.

Rian introduced her at Holland House, the social pinnacle of the Whigs where she met Lord Brougham, Louis Phillipe, Duc d'Orléans, Talleyrand, Prince Metternich, Madame de Staël, and Thomas Moore. She renewed her acquaintance with Henry Grattan there, and was pleased beyond belief when her husband introduced her to Lord George Byron, who often frequented its rooms. There, Morgana mingled with George, Prince Regent, and Lady Jersey, one of the patronesses of Almack's. Rian discussed the background of current politics, informing her that the Whigs, in power for almost fifty years, had lost much control to the Tories under William Pitt.

Morgana saw many sides to her husband and began to realize that there were depths to his character she had yet to fathom. She discovered that he was a Corinthian and a Libertine. In fact, she learned everything about him, except what he really was.

She received many invitations and when Rian could not accompany her, Lord Brisbane or Sir Reginald proved willing to act as her escort. She felt awkward at first, but Anthony assured her that it was not considered at all strange for a married woman to acquire a string of cicisbeos to take her out when her husband proved unavailable. There were many young dandies willing to hang on her arm, but Morgana preferred Denby and Reginald to any others; Denby because he gave her no reason to believe that he was interested in her other than as his best friend's wife, and Reginald because he belonged to a rather fast and exciting set.

Indeed, she and Rian seemed to be getting along famously until Lord Brisbane held another one of his card parties to which invitations were most cherished. There Morgana had the misfortune to meet Lady Cecily Brooksworth. Cecily smiled sweetly as Lord Brisbane approached her with the handsome couple and congratulated them on their happiness; but Morgana who had by this time heard the rumors about Cecily and her husband, could take no joy in the meeting, and begged Brad to show her his collection of jade. Cecily knew Denby hated her and was taking no pains to hide his merriment at her discomfiture. She longed to hit him with a poker, for she felt it was he who had prevented her from gaining the Earl's hand in marriage, and she was glad when he acquiesced to the bride's demand and left her alone with Rian.

"You cad," she hissed to the Earl when Denby had departed with Morgana. "How dare you come back here with a bride on your arm?"

"Jealous, Cecily?" Rian raised an inquiring eyebrow, for he wanted no scene like the one in Ireland with Lindsey Joyce. He was quite tired of catty females and was hard put to understand how he could have chosen to bed them in the first place. "But it was you who said

194

marriage was highly boring and placed such great restraints upon one's freedom."

Cecily bit her lip, for she had indeed spoken those very words, but with the hope that her disinterest would entice him up the very path she pretended to deplore. Never one to admit defeat, however, she countered brightly.

"So I did, darling. It must be terribly dull for you. Such a shocking color of hair, too, in these days when it's so fashionable to be dark." She patted her own black hair securely. "What a trap you must have fallen into. However do you stand it?"

"Oh, I manage," he answered languidly. "All cats look grey in the dark."

Cecily gasped audibly at his crude insult.

Rian laughed unpleasantly and said, "Don't worry, my dear. A wealthy widow with your obvious charms shouldn't have too much trouble finding a husband, if you really want one."

He saw his wife at the gaming tables, blushing merrily at some remark made by Anthony and felt a momentary pang of the same jealousy Cecily was experiencing. Morgana was his wife, by God, and he didn't like the way Anthony was bending over her. He strolled over to find that she had lost all of her money and had cast her emerald earrings onto the table in lieu of cash. With a deft movement, he retrieved them and placed a handful of pound notes in their place.

"I have money, my dear. There's no need to barter away your jewelry."

Morgana, jealous of her husband's attention to the lovely widow and unaware of the words which had passed between them, was suddenly overcome with a desire to strike out at this man who possessed her. Moreover, the champagne had quite gone to her head, and she said sarcastically, "Do you really? Aren't you cashing in on your expectancies a trifle early. I thought grandfather was still alive when we left. Oh, and by the way, is that one of your infamous broken hearts, or should I say tarts?"

He leaned down and breathed in her ear, "If anyone had heard those remarks, I would have killed you. Now get your cloak. We're going home before you make a complete fool of yourself. Lady Jersey and Princess Esterházy are both here and they will refuse to give you vouchers for Almack's if you continue to behave in this lowbred manner."

He made their excuses and they left, neither quite understanding how they had come to quarrel again. Fortunately, no one else noticed anything amiss, and as Lord Brisbane claimed that if he had a wife as pretty as Morgana, he'd hurry home, too, everyone assumed that Rian just wanted to be alone with his bride.

The silence in the carriage was deafening. Morgana's head felt as though a million drums were beating inside and she longed for the comfort of her bed. Rian sat beside her, an icy, grim look on his face which boded ill for her upon their return. He waited until they had reached the sanctity of the bedroom before he turned on her.

"I want to know the reason for your unseemly behavior this evening," he shook her roughly.

"My behavior?" she cried. "You coax the smiles of such as Cecily Brooksworth and reprove me for my actions when others who have no interest in the money you hope to get for marrying me find me charming."

Rian stared at her disbelievingly. He could not for the life of him understand why she kept referring to grandfather's will in every argument. Did the wench think him a pauper? His eyes narrowed. Perhaps it was best. But he was amused by her comments about Cecily, for his wife would not have been jealous had she not felt some emotion for him. He turned away from her with pretended disinterest.

"Why, Morgana, I do believe you're jealous."

"Jealous? Of that milk-faced cow?" she pouted angrily. "My earnest desire is that you run away with the wench and leave me alone."

He swore at her then, but she remained stubborn

and refused to apologize even when he stripped the garments from her body and pressed her down upon the bed to take his pleasure of her.

Morgana did, after all, receive vouchers for Almack's and begged Rian to take her there at once, paying no attention to his claims that it was an accursed dull place. She was disappointed, however, to find that he was right, for dancing was the main diversion of the evening and nothing stronger than orgeat and spice cakes was served. However, as this was where she met Beau Brummell, she was not entirely put out. The exquisite dandy of society immediately found favor in her eyes because of his sense of humor and the knowledge that were it not for his impertinent absurdities, he would probably have left no mark in history at all. He did as he pleased and made everyone else feel gauche if they refused to follow his examples, thereby imposing his eccentricities on the Ton and laughing as, like sheep, they hurried to follow.

Rian had kept his promise and gotten her a perchphaeton and a pair of chestnut horses, and soon it was not an uncommon sight for Morgana to be seen tooling about Hyde Park in the mornings with Rian's tiger, Louis, standing proudly behind her. It did much to improve his standing with his colleagues, for none of them could even boast a lady who handled the ribbons, with the exception of Letty Lade, who was considered to be a most shameless and vulgar piece of baggage, and even she did not drive as well as Morgana. She took great delight in teasing poor Louis unmercifully about it, reminding him of his actions when first she'd driven him.

Rian watched his wife climb the ladder of success with some amusement, wondering and waiting for the time she would become jaded and bored with the frippery, and games, and like so many others, look for more intriguing ways to occupy her mind. He took possession of her nightly, as always, and watched carefully to see that she took no lover from her many cicisbeos, for he surmised that behind her mask of gay frivolity she still hated him with a passion and would seize the first opportunity to even the score.

Several evenings later Rian, intending to keep an assignation at Cribb's Parlour with some of his cronies, was astounded when his wife appeared in the most becoming gown of gold crepe which set off her figure to great advantage and caused the gold flecks in her eyes to swim to the surface in a manner he most admired. She frowned at him and reminded him that no one was admitted to Almack's in pantaloons, then told him that even if Lady Jersey thought him a sly fox, she was not apt to relax the Assembly's stern rules for him.

"Almack's?" he questioned disbelievingly. "But I am engaged at Cribb's Parlour."

"Rian, you cannot have forgotten that we're to meet Brad and Miss Winwood this evening. I distinctly promised Anne's mother that I would act as the girl's chaperone tonight, and it would certainly be in poor taste to offend Lady Winwood."

He clapped his hand to his forehead. "Christ! Can't Brad find someone else to chaperone that young female? Why, the chit's barely out of the schoolroom. I cannot miss this game tonight, I tell you. There will be some extremely heavy wagers, or I miss my guess."

"Anne Winwood is a delightful girl and if you'd pay more attention, you'd know that Brad is intending to offer for her. Anne is the first woman he's paid any attention to since his wife's death some years ago."

"Do you mean to tell me Brad is going to marry that chit?" Rian could not credit this piece of information. "Why, Lady Winwood will never consent to the match. She's had her eye on the Duke of Hawthorne for some time now."

"Well, Anne doesn't like him. She told me so the other day, and I can hardly blame her. The Duke must be seventy if he's a day," Morgana sniffed. "However, if you do not mean to escort me, I shall send a note around to Anthony in hopes that he is not already engaged also."

She flounced out of the room, leaving her husband

to curse mightily about the whims of females. In a rather sour mood, he called for his curricle and slammed out of the house.

To his great displeasure, Rian discovered that he could take no joy in the game at Cribb's Parlour, for his mind kept dwelling on the thought of Sir Anthony Reginald escorting his wife to Almack's. It roused his jealousy that she would have the young baron escort her, and the picture of the two couples laughing and dancing together at the Assembly kept crossing his thoughts most unpleasantly. Moreover, since he could not keep his mind on the game, Rian lost several wagers through his inattention, and after tossing off a stiff glass of whiskey, he threw in his cards and left the table, causing his friends to remark that the devil himself could not have been in a worse mood that evening.

He was halfway to Almack's when he remembered that he was still in pantaloons and his wife's sarcastic words about the rules at the Assembly came back to haunt him. With a snarl, he yanked the greys about toward Grosvenor Square, calling impatiently for Chilham upon entering the house. He changed into his knee breeches at once and ruined no less than seven cravats in his attempt to hurry. However, his haste did him no good, for he arrived at the Assembly rooms at precisely twelve minutes after the hour, and not even the Duke of Wellington could gain admittance after eleven o'clock. Not one bit of his cursing or pleading did him any good, although Willis, who presided over the club, took great pains to be sympathetic with his lordship, having once had his ears boxed by a very irate, young blueblood.

Rian returned home in an even more foul mood, which the whiskey he soon consumed did nothing to alleviate. It became even worse when Bagley announced the arrival of Beau Brummell and Lord Alvanley.

George Bryan (Beau) Brummell and Lords Alvanley, Mildmay, and Pierrepoint composed what was known in polite circles as the Unique Four. They were the Bow Window Set, those haughty dandies who refused even to wave at their most intimate friends passing by in the street, if they were seated in the window of their favorite club. True, Rian belonged to the set, but he had many other interests besides fashion.

Now he surveyed his friends with a chagrined frown. "Well, what is it, George? Have you discovered some new tailor that you must come pounding upon my door at this late hour?"

"My dear boy," Beau flicked an imaginary piece of lint from his sleeve. "Whatever is the matter? Do not tell me you have been gaming again."

"We merely wished to discover whether or not you desire to go shooting at Manton's Gallery with us tomorrow," Lord Alvanley sniffed, much put out at his crony's attitude.

"Surely you do not mean to shoot, Beau?" Rian roused himself with an effort.

The King of Fashion gazed at him from half-closed eyes. "Certainly not; however, I have agreed to partake of a light breakfast, provided Alvanley does not wish to go hunting afterwards. Such a tiresome sport. It always muddies one's boots," he glanced down at his shining Hessians proudly.

"Aye, 'twill no doubt do me good," Rian told them sourly.

Alvanley gave him a look of concern. "I say, old boy, you're in poor spirits this evening. 'Tis not like you to be so glum. I saw your lovely wife at Almack's with Miss Winwood, a most charming young girl. Lady Keldara was taking quite pains with her. Denby and Reginald were there, too," he continued.

"That is precisely the reason I'm in such a foul mood," Rian spoke again. "Really, what gives Anthony the right to escort my wife to the Assembly?"

"Nothing wrong with that, Keldara," Beau hastened to assure him. "He behaved with the utmost propriety, I promise you."

"That may be," Rian stared at them, frowning. "Nevertheless, I should have taken her there myself. My evening has been quite ruined."

His two friends did their best to cheer him up and

after having consumed the better part of the Earl's brandy, soon took their leave, their arms companionably entwined.

Morgana arrived home to find her husband at least somewhat cheered and told him she was sorry to learn that the game had not gone nearly as well as he'd hoped. He noted her bright eyes and flushed cheeks with displeasure and resolved that the young baron would not have another chance to hang on his wife's arm like a moonstruck schoolboy. With passion-darkened eyes, he pulled her to him and parted her lips hungrily.

Morgana stepped out from the lending library, having satisfied herself with Lord Byron's latest edition, and was much delighted to see Sir Anthony Reginald making his way toward her.

"Anthony," she hailed him gaily. "Can I take you up?"

"My pleasure, Morgana, but only as far as the corner. I'm due at Jackson's Boxing Saloon and I'm afraid I'm already somewhat late."

"Ugh!" she exclaimed as he assisted her into the barouche, for Rian had insisted that she have something besides the shocking high perch-phaeton in her stables, and barouches were, as he put it, all the crack. "Why must you engage in such a silly sport? Rian is forever frequenting that place, speaking of being quite handy with his fives and drawing someone's cork."

"Morgana," Anthony laughed ruefully. "Whatever will you say next? It's very wrong of Rian to teach you such cant."

"Oh, Tony, don't be such a prig. You'll start sounding like dear, old Brad, who is forever telling me what I must and must not say or do; besides, Beau says he finds me quite refreshing, a welcome change from those simpering milktoasts who gather at Almack's to prey upon all the bachelors in town. Tell me, how have you managed to avoid their avaricious clutches?"

"Ah, 'tis only because you already have a husband, my lady," he cast his eyes upon her boldly and was rewarded by her blush. "But enough of this. Do you go to the masked ball at Ranleigh next week?"

"Alas, no. My lord claims 'tis naught but a public romp and not the proper thing at all."

"I say." He flicked a piece of lint from his ruffled cuffs. "Rian has gotten devilishly straightlaced recently. He never used to be such a dull dog."

"Well, perhaps he fears I shall do some horrible thing. Why, only last week he came home just in time to prevent me from going to the Peerless Pool," she sighed disappointedly.

"Oh, no, surely you jest."

"No, but I did not know it was Bad Ton to be seen there. I was very sheltered as a child and am sadly ignorant in the ways of society."

"Well, perhaps we can manage a way for you to go to Ranleigh. It really won't be that bad since everyone shall be masked," he said as he disembarked from the carriage, for they had reached the end of the street. "I'll try to think of something," he promised as he released her hand.

"Oh, do, Tony. It would be such fun," she agreed longingly.

He bowed, then made his way through the crowd, pretending not to hear when she called out for him to be careful that he didn't get levelled a facer, although, if she could only have seen, an amused smile lurked about the corners of his mouth.

By one of those odd freaks of chance, Rian's man of business, Mister Wright, called upon them within the next few days and advised the Earl that there were some pressing affairs at his lordship's country manor in Sussex that he felt Rian really should deal with personally. When the man had gone, Rian told Morgana to get her bags packed, for despite it being the height of the season, he guessed they would have to make a trip to the country.

"But, Rian," she wailed. "You can't have forgotten Lady Jersey's soirée tomorrow. It would be extremely rude of me to cry off at this late date and I can't possibly cancel all my other engagements in time."

"Damn," he swore. " 'Tis a pity it was she who gave you vouchers for Almack's. Well, you go and express my regrets, for I must go to Mandrake Downs to settle these matters with the tenants. I'll try not to be gone too long."

Rian, however, underestimated the time it was going to take him to hear so many grievances from the men who farmed his estate and raised his sheep, for he was engaged in many business ventures. He did not intend to find himself at last with ruin staring him in the face and naught but his title to sustain him as so many bluebloods of the day did. In addition, he was angered to discover that his overseer had taken advantage of Rian's long absences from the manor to line his pockets with much of the estate's profits. And so it chanced that what Rian had thought to be a matter of a few days soon stretched into more than a fortnight, and his defiant wife was able to inform Sir Reginald that she would be more than delighted to go to Ranleigh with him.

The evening started off innocently enough, the crowd being no more rowdy than some she had seen at many of the card parties she'd attended, and so Morgana was able to calm her anxiety at what Rian would do if he discovered she had disobeyed his orders. Surely there was no harm in a simple masquerade. She looked quite fetching with her burnished gold domino buttoned up to conceal her dress and a matching gold mask on her face. She'd affixed a small black patch to the corner of her mouth which twitched enchantingly each time she smiled at the adoring Anthony.

They drank and danced, laughing with merriment each time an unfortunate maid was caught and unmasked by a gallant pursuer, Morgana taking great care to see that such a fate did not befall her and Anthony dutifully defending her from some of the bolder young rakes. She surveyed the crowd rather mistily, the wine beginning to have its usual dizzying effect, then suddenly giggled quite tipsily, exclaiming, "Oh, look, Tony, isn't that Denby and Miss Winwood?"

He glanced in the direction in which she pointed,

then said, "I do believe you're right. I'd know that wig of Brad's anywhere."

"Oh, Tony," Morgana tittered again. "What a lark. You really must run and unmask Miss Winwood. I'll lay you a monkey Denby will expire on the spot."

"Done," he accepted the challenge rather breathlessly, for the sight of dear old Denby's face sent them both into gales of laughter, then he bounded over the edge of the box to catch the unsuspecting couple.

Morgana watched until she lost sight of him in the crowd, then turned to find a tall dark figure next to her in the box. For a moment, her heart leaped to her throat, for she thought it was Rian, but then she realized that the intruder was much too pale and slender to be her husband.

"Well, what have we here?" he spoke, and she thought she detected a slight French accent. Her suspicions were confirmed when he continued, "Come, ma chère, let us see what beauty lurks beneath your mask."

"Sir, you are annoying me. I must ask you to leave at once," Morgana was chagrined to find her speech was beginning to sound slurred.

"Tsk, tsk. Ma jeune fille has perhaps partaken of too much wine, eh? Bien, she will not be able to run so fast when I try to catch her," he moved closer.

"Non, monsieur," she was pleased to find her schoolgirl French lessons coming to mind. "Je suis engagée."

"Qu'est-ce qu'il y a, ma chère? I saw votre ami leave. He will not be back for a while. We have plenty of time." He made a sudden move, seizing her around the waist so she could not escape, then deftly unfastened the strings of her mask. "Mon Dieu, you are lovely."

Without warning, he bent his head and placed his mouth upon her own. Morgana ought to have swooned, but instead she found his kiss subtly exciting, gently teasing; she felt as though she were drowning. With a sharp cry, she realized the wine had gone to her head and yanked away from the masked stranger, running wildly from the box through the raucous crowd. With great relief she caught sight of Anthony across the room and managed to reach his side.

"Morgana, it was Brad and Miss Winwood. I do wish you could have seen their faces. Why, what's wrong? You're all out of breath."

"Someone was chasing me." She managed a weak laugh, not wanting to tell him the entire truth of the matter. " 'Tis of no consequence. I got away, but I would like to go home now, if you don't mind."

"Of course not," his face showed concern. There would be hell to pay if the Earl found out about this. " 'Tis my fault, I should never have left you alone in the box."

"No, no. It's quite all right, I'm fine. Tell me, was Denby properly horrified?"

Fortunately, Rian did not learn of Morgana's little escapade to Ranleigh, for Lord Brisbane and Miss Winwood were much too embarrassed to mention the matter, and Sir Reginald felt it would be in his best interests of survival to remain silent regarding that issue; so Morgana was able to say without fear of contradiction when his lordship mentioned that she had seemed somewhat subdued since his return that things had been a trifle flat without him. Rian eyed her suspiciously for a moment, but said nothing, leaving Morgana much relieved.

The fates are often mysterious, however, and what chances a small incident can sometimes lead to the most extraordinary turn of events, as Morgana was soon to discover. It so happened that Lady Brooksworth had decided to hold a small dinner party in hopes of showing Rian that she was not mourning his loss and to make him jealous of her string of admirers. Morgana had no desire to attend, but realized that to make excuses would only give the young widow a great deal of satisfaction, so she found herself seated next to a decidedly senile old man in Cecily's rather tasteless drawing room, and feeling most uncomfortable.

The widow had gone to some trouble to maneuver her rival into conversation with Lord Bromley, who was not only eccentric, but stone deaf as well, and was now taking a tremendous amount of pleasure in the young bride's obvious annoyance. She was just about to engage the attention of the Earl of Keldara when another cavalier was announced.

"Phillipe! Mon cher, how good of you to come," she cried delightedly, casting a quick glance at Rian to see if he'd noticed her handsome beau, thereby missing Morgana's horrified gasp. It was the bold Frenchman who'd accosted her at Ranleigh. "Your attention, everyone, I want you to meet a very dear friend of mine, Phillipe du Lac, Vicomte de Blanchefleur," Cecily hung onto his arm as she finished the introductions.

To Morgana's immense relief, the Frenchman merely murmured something polite as he bowed low over her hand, and gave no sign of recognition. Not until dinner, when she found herself unfortunately placed by his side and Rian next to the sly widow at the other end of the table, did he make it known to Morgana that he had recognized her instantly.

"For, my lovely masquerader, how could I forget the sweet taste of those honeyed lips." He eyed her with pleasure.

She implored him to be silent, casting a fearful glance at her husband, but Rian was too busy laughing at some remark made by Cecily to take any notice of her.

"Ah, you are worried about your husband, ma chère. But see, he has eyes only for the charming widow. He is not a man to make a jealous scene, n'est-ce pas?"

Phillipe did, however, confine their conversation to other matters, explaining to Morgana that he was a French emigré, fleeing the forces of Napoleon because of his aristocratic blood, and that he'd barely escaped with his life.

"Now I have nothing. My home, my lands, and title, all are vanished. That monster has taken everything. But come, we must talk of more pleasant matters. My thoughts have lingered long on your lovely face since that night at Ranleigh. I have hungered often in the wee hours of the morning for your mouth, ma cheri." He noted with pleasure her rising color. "When can I see you again?"

"It is impossible, monsieur. Please, speak of this to no one. My husband is very possessive. He would kill me if he knew I'd been to Ranleigh."

"You have a saying here in England, I believe. Where there is a will, there is a way. I will find a way, ma petite."

Morgana did not encourage his bold advances and, regardless of Cecily's triumphant smile, told Rian immediately after dinner that she had a headache and had to go home at once. He was only too glad to leave the young widow's grasping hands and insinuations, for he was beginning to find her boring in the extreme, and he complied easily with Morgana's urgent request.

The Frenchman called upon her the next morning, but Morgana sent word down that she was ill and he went away without leaving his card, much annoyed by her refusal to admit him. He felt frustrated, but his conceit knew no bounds and he felt that she was just being coy.

Phillipe really was destitute, and had come to England with no other desire than to find and marry a rich woman. He was convinced that once he had enough money he could return to France and recapture his lands and title. He had been on the verge of proposing to Lady Cecily Brooksworth, for she was quite wealthy and her antics in bed amused him. He had told the truth, however, when he spoke to Morgana of his desire for her, for she had indeed haunted his dreams since that night at Ranleigh, and now he was determined to have her. No woman had ever refused the Vicomte de Blanchefleur, and he would not accept it now.

He was determined and persistent, but his manners were faultless and Morgana was forced to be polite to him lest Rian learn about her escapade at Ranleigh; and Phillipe finally managed to inch his way into a niche among her devoted string of cicisbeos.

Chapter Sixteen

"Phillipe," Morgana turned to him in the drawing room. "You really must try to control yourself. If you persist in these advances, I will have no other choice but to send you away. I was a fool to ever let you into my life to begin with."

"But, ma chère, 'tis only your breathless beauty that makes me so bold," he murmured, trying to conceal his impatience.

It had been over two months since the party at Cecily's and Phillipe was fast running out of what little money he had been able to save or win at gambling. Worse still, his creditors were dunning him, threatening to have him thrown into Newgate Prison if he didn't pay. Moreover, he had tried honorably to win Morgana's love and had failed. Either she was just using him, which his ego refused to accept, or she was frightened of her husband, for she had told her flatly that Rian would never grant her a divorce.

"But, ma petite, if you tell him you want a divorce

and that you are in love with another man, he will not want you, I assure you," he tried again, exasperated.

"No, he would kill me. You don't know him as I do, Phillipe. He——" No, she could not tell this man how she came to marry her husband. He would only become more determined for her to divorce Rian. Instead she said, "Please go. He will be home soon and I am very tired."

Phillipe had sense enough to realize that to continue would only make her more stubborn, so angrily he gathered his gloves and walking stick and left.

Morgana sat for a very long time after he'd gone, searching her mind. Phillipe du Lac loved her, she felt sure of that. And although he was not as handsome as Rian, he was still a very good-looking man. He would treat her well, with all of the affection and devotion she could ever want. Except for Rian. Rian would never let her go. He didn't love her, but he wanted her, wanted her in that same carnal way he'd desired Cecily Brooksworth and Lindsey Joyce. He hated her, used her, abused her, and mocked her, but she belonged to him and he kept those things which he possessed. Still, he'd been gone much of late, occupied with politics and gambling he said, but Morgana felt convinced he was frequenting the whorehouses, seeking arms more welcoming than hers. Maybe he had tired of her. Perhaps he would let her go.

That night, she broached the subject hesitantly.

"Rian, I want to talk to you. Do you mean to go out this evening?"

"Not if you desire my company, sweet," he grinned insolently.

"You must know that I do not," she replied coldly. "Any more than you seem to desire mine of late."

"Why, Morgana, I didn't realize you'd been pining for my charms."

"Don't delude yourself, my lord." She was fast losing control of herself and the conversation. "I loathe your touch."

Angrily he yanked her around to face him. "Is that why you always melt in the end, why your knees turn to jelly when I kiss you, and you whimper like a wounded

animal when I drive your body to the stars and back?"
He shook her.

Morgana was mortified. It was bad enough that he
knew the effect his lovemaking had upon her, but to
discuss it openly made her want to die of shame.

"You, you arouse nothing in me," she lied as she
tried to free herself.

"Ha! Don't lie to me, you green-eyed witch. Shall I
prove it to you?" he twisted her jaw up cruelly.

"No, don't touch me," she breathed, frightened of
the anger she saw in his eyes. "I want out of this marriage. I hate you."

His green eyes darkened, bored into her intensely.
"Do you, my love, or is it merely that you crave the arms
of someone else? Young du Lac, perhaps?"

She gasped with fear and the color flooded her face
like fire. Dear God, how could he know? Was he spying
on her or simply guessing? Or was he really the devil his
friends claimed he was?

"Oh, yes, I have my ways," he laughed tauntingly.
"I know the Frenchman has been chasing you like a
lovesick schoolboy. Is he more to your taste, a penniless
gold-digger? Tell me, Mag, have you let him make love to
you, have you?"

"No," she managed to speak finally.

"Forget him, sweet, I'm warning you." His voice was
soft, but Morgana was not deceived. "I'll never let you
go." He ran his hand down her throat, tightening it
momentarily before releasing her and slamming out of the
house.

She sank to the floor, sobbing like a child.

Rian did not have to search long before he found du
Lac at one of the more notorious gaming houses, frequented by sharps and flats, ivoryturners, or, to put it
more bluntly, card cheats.

"Evening, du Lac," he dropped a hand casually on
the younger man's shoulder. "How goes the play?"

"The fates have smiled upon me tonight, my Lord."
Phillipe glanced up at the Earl warily.

"Mind if I join you?"

"Not at all. It will be a pleasure, Lord Keldara," du Lac spoke smugly.

It would indeed be a pleasure of no mean delight to fleece the man who kept him from the one woman he desired above all else, and perhaps when he was done, he would fleece his lordship of his wife as well.

But Rian was an extremely fine cardplayer and he set the Frenchman up like a partridge on a carving table, losing heavily at first until only he and Phillipe remained at the table. The Earl studied the cards, and it didn't take him very long to break the code on their backs. The diamond pattern was so slightly and subtly different on each card that only an expert or someone who was examining them purposefully would have noticed they were marked. Then, quite determinedly, Rian began to win.

"It seems your luck has changed for the better, my lord," Phillipe remarked sourly.

Very soon there was a pile of IOU's placed in a neat stack before Rian's glass of whiskey. "Well, du Lac," he said softly. " 'Tis getting late and my wife awaits me. I'd like to settle these debts before I go."

"But, my lord, I cannot possibly pay such a sum tonight. It is ungentlemanly of you to ask. You must give me time to redeem my vowels. I promise you I shall do so as soon as possible," Phillipe was horrified.

"I am ungentlemanly, Phillipe," Rian smiled slowly, cruelly, in a way that sent shivers up du Lac's spine. "But you are a card cheat. Nay, do not raise your voice, fool. If anyone else discovers it, you will be ruined and Madame Frampstead will be forced to send for the Bow Street Runners, which she despises doing as it gives her gaming house a bad name. Tsk, tsk, du Lac. I really thought you were a much smarter man. It will do you no good to pull that little pistol you have concealed. You see, I already have my own trained upon you. Don't make me use it, such a nasty sight, wouldn't you agree?" Rian gathered up the vowels. "I'll just take these with me, never know when they might come in handy, especially if you continue to woo my wife with your ardent proclamations of love. Oh, yes," he laughed unpleasantly at the

Frenchman's startled glance. "I know all about it. I'm very good at keeping track of those things I possess. You really are a fool, du Lac. No wonder Napoleon has slaughtered you French like sheep. Take care that you do not wind up with a fate worse than the guillotine. I'm not that merciful."

With that, the Earl disappeared silently into the night.

Morgana was downstairs drinking when Rian came in. It was the only thing she'd found that could, for a time, make her forget that devil incarnate she called her husband. She jumped, startled, when the door banged shut, for she had not expected him back so early.

"What are you doing home?" she staggered to her feet.

"Drowning your sorrows, sweet? Really, I know a much better way."

All his pent-up anger against the Frenchman and his wife broke loose and Rian grabbed for her like a wildman. Besotted as she was, Morgana was quicker, and like a flash she had put the sofa between them. They circled warily, like a tiger and fawn until she dashed toward the door and headed up the stairs. If only she could get to the safety of her room, perhaps she could lock him out. On the fourth step, she tripped, sliding backwards until she lay sprawled before him on the floor.

"Get up," he spat coldly.

"No."

With a muttered oath, he heaved her over his shoulder and proceeded up the stairs, pausing only to kick the bedroom door shut behind him before he tossed her onto the bed. Every inch of flesh burned where he touched her, softly, longingly, even lovingly, as he laid his lips upon her breasts and belly. Against her will Morgana cried out as the familiar ache spread like flame through her loins.

"Your body says you want me, love," his hand was between her thighs. "What do you say?"

"I hate you," she panted, but even she could not believe those unconvincingly spoken words.

He laughed. "Do you, sweet?"

"No," she moaned, surrendering even before he thrust upwards within her, closing her eyes as he took her to the edge of heaven and back.

The Earl of Keldara was prompted in the morning by another visit from Mister Wright to decide to close the townhouse and retreat to his country manor, Mandrake Downs. Since the London season was almost ended, Morgana made no objection to this plan of action. She had felt sure that he would find some way to prevent her seeing Phillipe; and besides, it would be good to get away from the city's activity for a time. In spite of herself, she had to admit that she missed the country life she had become accustomed to in Ireland.

"But, Rian," she said over the breakfast table. "I cannot understand why this estate is causing you so much trouble."

" 'Tis in Sussex, love," he buttered a muffin casually. "And many of the men there are smugglers. It seems that the dragoons have been making inquiries again. If they arrest my men, I won't have anyone to work the land or tend the sheep."

"You have sheep?" she giggled at the thought.

" 'Tis a very profitable business, sweet."

"And smuggling, is it profitable, too?"

Rian surveyed her intently for a moment. "I have no need to engage in that sort of endeavor."

Two weeks later Morgana found herself bouncing along inside of the huge coach Rian had purchased for such trips with Penney, the young woman finally procured to act as Morgana's abigail, and Chilham. Louis and two other coachmen also accompanied them, for the Earl had no wish to be waylaid by the highwaymen who plagued the country roads.

"Oh, surely they would not harm us, Rian," said Morgana, somewhat frightened at the prospect.

Rian's green eyes met her own, travelled over the copper curls and creamy skin, and for a moment pictured her in the arms of those common robbers. He shuddered at the thought and added another coachman to the entourage, his caution causing poor Penney to wail that they would all be murdered afore they reached their destination.

"Don't worry, Penney," Morgana soothed her. "His lordship would not allow anything to happen to us."

The trip to Mandrake Downs passed without incident and everyone was glad to alight from the coach for the last time, for even though it was well sprung, it was not entirely comfortable on the rougher roads over which they'd journeyed.

Behind them they had left a very irate Phillipe du Lac, half-crazed with his desire for Morgana and desire for revenge upon the Earl of Keldara. Phillipe's rage increased at finding the Earl's townhouse closed and the knocker off the door. He surmised correctly that his lordship wished to get Morgana away from him as quickly as possible, and this did nothing to abate his anger. He saw no other choice but to proceed to re-establish himself in the favor of Lady Cecily Brooksworth.

When he called upon Lady Brooksworth, he was pleased to find her willing to see him again. Although she was somewhat reluctant to reinstate him as a suitor, they found they had much in common. They were both eager to vent their anger upon the McShanes.

"I tell you, Cecily," Phillipe said morosely, "I cannot understand your passion for Rian McShane. The man's a monster."

"He has the lure of the unattainable, I guess. His witch of a wife attracts you for the same reason, dear boy. How I'd like to see her humbled, the proud hussy." Suddenly Cecily was struck by a thought. "Phillipe," she inquired, "when you found the house closed, did you think to check the harbor to see if Rian's ship was still there?"

"Non. Why do you ask?"

"Well, if Rian's ship is still in port, they've surely gone to Mandrake Downs, his country estate in Sussex."

"What good does that do me? I know no one there."

"Oh, but you do, Phillipe. My dear, departed husband, Lord Brooksworth, left me a wonderful little cottage not far from Rian's land. I believe it's high time you and I got some of that fresh country air. London can be rather stifling this time of year."

Therefore, it changed that a portly little innkeeper along the road from London to Sussex had, within a matter of a few days, not one, but two well-bred couples pass the night at his tavern.

Morgana was absolutely amazed by Mandrake Downs. It was as though she had stepped into another time, another place. Rian kept most of his treasures there and the manor was like an Oriental palace with its woven rugs, Ming vases, and Chinese dragons. There were ornate jade carvings, ivory statues, and tiger skins, as well as African spears and shields. A strange, exotic atmosphere hung over the entire house, and a pungent, spicy fragrance dominated the rooms. Rian told her that it was the incense that he often burned in the evenings. She was especially fascinated by a carved box which he said was a Chinese puzzle box. It had many latches that, when opened, revealed more boxes within boxes. She would sit for hours testing the tiny latches and opening box after box, only to make a mistake and be confounded by one small lock. It frustrated her, but she determined to find the key, while Rian laughed at her unrelenting efforts and told her that even he had never been able to reach the center box.

"What do you suppose is in it?" she asked him one evening.

"The old Chinese woman I bought it from said that it contained the key to happiness," Rian spoke softly. "She said that whoever reached the final box would know the secret to everlasting love."

"I wonder what it is," Morgana eyed him curiously.

"I guess you'll have to open the box to find out," he replied, stroking her hair quietly.

In the evenings they spent together, trying to solve the puzzle, Morgana and Rian grew closer than they had been in the past, sharing with bated breath the quiet pleasure of being totally alone together for the first time in their marriage, discovering like lovers hidden facets of each other's character. Both were highly annoyed at finding that Phillipe and Cecily had followed them to Sussex. At a hunting party held by a close neighbor, Squire Johnston, the first social engagement the McShanes had accepted since coming to Mandrake Downs, Cecily openly chased Rian as he maneuvered Lucifer over the tricky course and Phillipe caused Morgana no end of dismay by riding so close to Copper Lady that the mare missed a jump, thereby toppling her fair rider into a pond.

"You fool," Morgana spat at him as he helped her out of the water. "It was madness for you to come here. Rian has told me what passed between you at Madame Frampstead's gaming house. He will ruin you."

"It will be worth it if you will but say you love me, ma chère." Du Lac proffered a handkerchief in an attempt to dry her off. "I'm so sorry about your mare throwing you."

"Well, she would not have done so had you not ridden so close. Now please go away and leave me alone. I must get out of these wet clothes."

Phillipe watched her ride away, a burning hatred for Lord Keldara blazing inside of him; and he vowed silently to get rid of his adversary by any possible means. It was several weeks later that fate afforded him the opportunity.

Squire Johnston, pleased at having so many of the Ton virtually camped on his doorstep and urged on by his wife's none too subtle reminders that they had three daughters to marry off, had consented to stage a private cockfight between two of his best roosters in order to become better acquainted with some of the more eligible youngbloods. Word of the event was bound to leak out, helped by his loose tongue, and by late afternoon on the day of the fight, his lower pasture was filled with horses, curricles, and the like. Wagers were being placed; latecomers were trying to find spots; and the Squire was right in the thick of things, missing no opportunity to shake a

217

young viscount's hand or clap a handsome baron on the shoulder.

Rian had managed to wedge his curricle in somehow and was betting heavily on the rust-colored cock. He was not at all amused when Baron Linton, whose estate marched with his, suddenly broke off the negotiations, exclaiming, "Good Lord, would you look at that!"

The Earl turned in time to see Lady Brooksworth, parasol and all, being helped out of her barouche by the Frenchman. "A cockfight is no place for a woman," he snarled harshly. "Let's get on with it, Ned."

The cocks were evenly matched and the Squire had reluctantly agreed to let them fight to the death. Their spurs glistened as the two roosters circled and jabbed ferociously, urged on by the pungent odor of blood which soon spurted, matting their proud feathers. Not a soul, including Rian, noticed Phillipe when he slipped up behind the Earl's curricle with a stout branch and finally succeeded in loosening one of the rear wheels.

Twenty minutes later the fight was beginning to tell. The grey was cut badly and now sought only to escape the deadly thrust of the rust's bloodied spurs. It was therefore to the great dismay of those onlookers who had bet on the red rooster that, with a clap of thunder, a quick summer storm descended. Local farmers and nobility alike dashed for their vehicles before they sank into what would soon become a large field of mud, Squire Johnston pausing only momentarily to retrieve his prize cocks, somewhat relieved that he was to lose neither that day. Rian whipped the curricle around, intent on getting out of the crowd as quickly as possible and narrowly missed hitting Lady Cecily, who implored him to drive her home as she had lost Phillipe in the midst of the frantic rush and could not handle her team in the storm.

"Didn't I warn you not to buy Bixby's bays?" he yelled angrily, seeing no choice but to take her up.

She made no reply to this ill-timed remark, being too busy trying to shield herself from the pouring rain with her sodden, ineffectual parasol.

218

The Earl, notorious for his fast driving anyway, now flicked his whip grimly, pushing his horses to a dangerous pace, especially in the blinding rain. Under normal circumstances, he would have seen the folly of this, but Cecily had made him furious, and he was not thinking clearly. Her whining pleas for him to slow down only infuriated him more and even Louis, hanging on for dear life in the back, could not reason with him. As they were rounding a rather sharp turn in the road, the wheel Phillipe had loosened shot free of its axle and sent the curricle shattering down into a ditch. Rian tried desperately to control the frightened horses, but the wet leather reins slipped in his hands and he could do nothing to stop the terrible accident. For one brief moment, his eyes focused on Cecily's horrified face, then all was blackness.

Louis picked himself up gingerly. His head ached and from the pain in his side, he knew his ribs were cracked. He didn't know what time it was, but the rain had stopped falling and night was upon him like a black cat. He staggered blindly toward the curricle, for he had been thrown clear, and as his eyes began to focus, he saw that it had gone farther down the hill and was almost hidden among the trees. He reached it painfully. Cecily was still inside the gig. He spoke to her, but received no answer save the rustling of the wind. Her flimsy parasol and her pretty neck were broken. He looked for the Earl, but could not find his master anywhere, and finally gave up the search, the dim recesses of his mind telling him that he would not locate his lordship in the darkness. With a broken cry, he began the long trudge to Mandrake Downs.

Morgana listened to the distraught tale the tiger unfolded quietly. She had longed to be rid of her husband, but never like this. Then she began to sob in great silent gasps. The tears pencilled her cheeks with light streaks, but not once could she manage one painful cry.

With the first light of day, Louis was gone, taking with him as many men as he could muster. They searched the entire area, but found no trace of the Earl's body. The Sussex farmers concluded that he had tumbled into the creek which wound down through the countryside and had been drowned, his body washing out into the English Channel. It was not until they lifted poor Cecily's lifeless form out of the curricle that Louis spied the marks around the rear axle and began to be suspicious about the wheel coming off. He said nothing, but he knew the Earl had many enemies, and he silently determined to keep his daylights open and to discover whether any of them had wished his lordship dead.

Cecily was taken up to London to be buried and Morgana did not travel north to attend the funeral. She stayed instead at Mandrake Downs, drugged most of the time with the laudanum the doctor had given her for her nerves. She grew pitifully thin and her eyes were red-rimmed with constant weeping; indeed she seemed almost mad with grief. The neighbors pitied her, for they did not know it was guilt that was eating away the edges of her sanity, for she found she could take no joy in the release Rian's death had provided her. Mandrake Downs was like a tomb. She allowed no curtains to be opened and the house was shrouded in darkness. She refused to see any of the many visitors who came to pay their respects, and when Chilham timidly approached her about burial arrangements, she told him tonelessly not to make any since one could not have a funeral without a body.

"He may not be dead at all, Chilham," she spoke in a voice that sent shivers up the valet's spine and caused him to tell Penney that their mistress had surely gone mad.

She sat in the darkness for hours on end playing with the Chinese box, trying to solve the secret of the puzzle. When she could not, she would fling it aside, crying, Rian's face coming back to haunt her with his words; and she felt somehow that she would never know what lay within the maze. Her body cried out in the night for the pressure of his upon her and the ache between her thighs would not be eased. She could not sleep and took to walking about the house in the dead of night, whispering to the ornate Chinese faces that mocked her from the walls.

The servants became so frightened about her behavior that when Phillipe called again for the twenty-third time in as many days, they admitted him into her presence. He was so shocked by her appearance that, for a moment, he could not speak, but he recovered himself masterfully and went at once to her side.

"Mon Dieu, ma chère, why would you not see me sooner? You are but a shadow of yourself."

Her glassy eyes stared at him sightlessly. "Why have you come, Phillipe?"

"Morgana." He suddenly had sense enough to realize she was hopelessly drugged. "I have come to take care of you, my love. You must let me help you upstairs."

"Rian will be very angry. You must go away at once."

"Rian is dead, ma fille. You remember," he moved carefully so as not to frighten her, "he was killed in the carriage accident."

"Yes, I remember now," she said slowly. "My head aches so and I keep getting things all muddled. I want to lie down."

"You shall, my love," he helped her to her feet and led her to the stairs.

Her bedroom was in darkness. Phillipe looked at her slowly, desire building inside as he lit the candles one by one until a hundred blazed, filling the room with flickering light, casting eerie shadows on the wall. She was his now. He had killed for her and he meant to have her. Morgana made no sound as he approached her. Indeed, she had already fallen into a deep, drugged sleep when he removed her gown and triumphantly made her his.

For one brief moment, Morgana could hear the carriages rumbling over the cobblestone streets in front of the small house in which she lived with her father, and the merchants hawking their wares farther down the block. Then she turned, the memory receding as she saw the dark head next to hers on the pillow and realized that she was in the huge four-poster bed at Shanetara with the man who was now her husband. She sighed and gazed into the brown eyes which had opened abruptly, suddenly aware that she was awake. Memories of the past few weeks flooded through her mind. No, she was not in Ireland and the man beside her was not Rian. She broke away from Phillipe's startled grasp with a broken cry.

"How did you get here? My God, what have you done?"

"Hush, ma chère. 'Tis all over now and I am here to take care of you. I love you and I will never let anyone hurt you again," he crooned soothingly. "Come, ma fille, we'll have a lifetime together now. Last night was just the beginning." He had her in his arms again, instinctively laying soft, wet kisses on her throat and hair.

Slowly, he twisted his body until it lay upon her own, then gently she felt him enter her. He was very tender, seeming to know that Rian had been hard, savage with her. He did his best, his hands in all the right places, but she did not feel that burning ache rush through her like wildfire, nor did he drive her to the edge of a cliff and send her falling over and over again. In fact, Morgana felt nothing. She might as well have been a marble statue so cold was her flesh where Phillipe touched it. He withdrew quietly after satisfying himself, understanding that he must give her time to adjust, and wisely said nothing.

Morgana realized from her abigail's absence that the entire household must be aware of Phillipe's presence in her bedroom. She allowed him to kiss her once more before rising to fetch a wrapper and ring for the maid. She was aware that his eyes followed her every move, but she felt no desire to blush until he spoke fondly that she was indeed the most beautiful woman he had ever seen. "For you would tempt the devil himself, ma chère," he said earnestly, prompting her to remark coldly that she had.

And so easily, perhaps without a second thought, and certainly almost without even trying, Phillipe became

Morgana's lover. She preferred not to dwell on the idea, for she knew she would never again be the gay, laughing child who ran to kiss her father upon hearing his footsteps in the hallway. Brendan O'Hara had laid his filthy hands upon her, mentally degrading her and dragging her down into the mud, down to his carnal level of animal desire. Rian had abused her, tearing away the fragile veils of her childhood and forcing her to face the reality of the passionate women she was. What then mattered one man more?

The days passed slowly, Morgana seemingly immune to the gossip which filled the countryside and Louis's sharp, outspoken reminder that her husband was not yet cold in his grave. The nights passed slowly also, as endless as the many candles Phillipe lit and watched gutter in their sockets as he continued his gentle onslaught upon her body and senses. Sometimes his obsession with the flickering bits of lights troubled her, for at times she would gaze into his eyes and know that he looked at her, but saw something or someone else instead.

She did not even try to begin to understand him; he was so foreign to her nature. He did not mock her or force her to defend herself against rapier remarks as Rian had done. He had no use for poetry beyond a few pretty phrases he'd picked up with the intention of flattering some foolish maid; and if they quarrelled, he turned stonily silent, withdrawing into his solitude until a decent interval had passed, after which time he would continue as though nothing was amiss.

Morgana found to her surprise that she missed Rian's insolent grin and his unbearable arrogance and often discovered herself comparing Phillipe's boyish handsomeness to her husband's hard, masculine looks. She had longed to banish the Earl from her life, and yet now that he was gone, she perversely wished him back.

Phillipe sensed her disquiet and realized he must take her away from all things which haunted her memory and walked within the shadows of her past. He had several connections along the coast, and with much of

Morgana's money was able to arrange for them to leave England and to be smuggled into France.

Morgana was cold and wet as she sat in the tiny boat with her lover and watched the coast of England grow smaller and smaller until it faded into the mist.

Chapter Seventeen

The Earl of Keldara was not dead. He had indeed fallen into the creek, as Louis surmised, and would probably have drowned had it not been for a forked branch slamming into his back so that his head remained above water as the current propelled him swiftly downstream. He came to rest in a most unlordly position, face down in the muddy slime which lurked along the banks of the brook. It was there that a country wench named Bess, who had disobeyed her mother's severe warnings that she was not to bathe unclothed in the creek again, had chanced upon him.

Thus when Rian felt the first dull twinges of pain which signalled his return to consciousness, he found himself not in the depths of hell as he'd fully expected, but in a wonderfully soft featherbed.

"So, yer awake at last. I was beginning to think ye planned to sleep forever."

Rian jumped, startled to find that he was not alone in the room. His eyes focused uncertainly on a not unpretty maid with wide blue eyes and honey-brown tresses. She was young, he realized dimly, but a hard life had left its marks.

"Where am I?"

"Ye be in a small shack on me ma's land. We 'ave a little inn farther on, the Blue Boar, per'aps ye've 'eard o' it?"

"Nay." He closed his eyes wearily, for his head ached like the devil, and missed the flash of disappointment on the girl's hopeful face.

"What be yer name?" the lass' curiosity far outweighed her concern for Rian's obvious pain.

He opened his eyes, staring at her dumbly, because for the life of him, he couldn't remember. He spied his highjack boots, caked with mud in the corner, felt dimly that someone would be angry about the state they were in, and said the first thing that came into his mind, "Jack."

"Well, Jack, are ye 'ungry?"

He nodded. "How long have I been here?"

"Oh, 'bout nigh on three weeks now, I guess. I've been coming every day and sometimes at night if I could slip out without me ma catching me. She'd skin me alive if she knew what I was 'bout."

From somewhere the girl managed to produce some thick bread and slabs of cheese. Rian wolfed it down lustily. Three weeks. He'd been unconscious for three weeks, and before that? He could not remember, and it pained his head to try.

"What's your name?" he asked finally, brushing the crumbs from his mouth.

"Elizabeth. Named after a queen, I was. But most folks call me Bess. Say, ye don't look like nobody from around 'ere. Leastways yer clothes weren't rough like most folks I know. They was soft, real fine linen. Ye some kind o' gentleman?"

"How do you know I didn't steal them?" he managed a wicked grin, because for all he knew, he might have.

"Gentleman Jack, a 'ighwayman," Bess giggled at

the thought. How exciting if it were true. Then her face changed abruptly. "Who's Morgana?"

The ghost of a red-haired, green-eyed witch flicked through his mind briefly, then was gone as quickly as the morning mist. "Why do you ask?" he questioned roughly.

"No reason," Bess shrugged her shoulders indifferently. "Except that ye called 'er name whilst ye was unconscious."

"Did I?" He closed his eyes again and was silent once more.

It was four more days before Rian was able to get out of bed, and even then his head ached terribly, and he lost his balance at first when he tried to stand. Bess had told him of how she'd found him on the banks of the creek and had dragged him to the shack, but she knew no more than he how he came to be there. Now he stood and stared at his reflection in the mirror and saw only a stranger, Gentlemen Jack, as Bess had taken to calling him. He was frightfully unkempt, and unruly ebon locks, a moustache and a beard covered his face. An ugly wound slashed across his left cheek. It had been acquired recently he judged from the scab which encrusted it. It would leave a scar he would carry the rest of his life. Bess had washed and mended his clothes and he put them on, wondering again who he really was. At the moment, it didn't matter. He had to live and he could not continue to depend on Bess's charity.

"Ach, Jack," he heard her come in. "Ye should not be up and 'bout," she clucked over him like a mother hen. "Ye've been much too ill."

"Bess," he ignored her admonishment. "Do you think you could get me a pistol and a rapier?"

"Lord, Jack, 'twill not be easy, but I'll try," she answered, for she thought him the most handsome man she'd ever seen. Even the scar on his face could not detract from his dark good looks. She fancied herself in love with him already and would have done anything to gain his affection.

That night, armed with the weapons Bess had stolen

from a guest at her mother's inn, Rian began the first of many robberies as Gentleman Jack, the bandit who was to terrorize the Sussex countryside for months to come. Bess waited breathlessly in the small shack until he returned, terrified that he would be killed, but excited at the most thrilling adventure of her unhappy life.

"Here," he tossed a purse of gold coins in her lap when he came in. "Go into town tomorrow and buy me a better horse. That one you borrowed is almost blind."

"I'm sorry, Jack, but 'twas the best I could do. Tim, the ostler, was afraid to let me 'ave one at all. They 'ang ye for 'orse-thieving."

"They also hang you for highway robbery," he laughed insolently. "And for God's sake get yourself a decent dress. I grow weary of seeing you in rags."

"Do ye mean it, Jack?" she asked excitedly. "Am I really to 'ave a new gown?"

He eyed her speculatively. She was pretty enough with her big, blue eyes and her cheeks flushed as they were now. Not savagely beautiful like that witch who haunted his dreams, but comely in a raw, country fashion.

"Sure, lass," he said before he took her, willingly, into his arms.

Bess lay very still lest she awaken the man who slept peacefully beside her. She watched the rise and fall of his chest in the moonlight. She had made love with many men, but never had one satisfied her as he did. Quietly she slipped from the bed and dressed. She would tell ma in the morning that she was leaving home, for she knew she could not bear to be parted from him for even an hour after this night.

"Ye foolish slut," her mother howled when informed of the girl's decision. "Found ye a man, did ye?"

"Aye, ma, and I won't be coming back 'ere no more."

"That's the thanks I get for raising ye all these years. Ye know well I can't run this place without ye."

Bess turned away abruptly. "Ye don't need me 'ere, ma. Ye'll be glad when I'm gone for 'twill be one less mouth for ye to feed and one less body to clothe. 'Ere," she held out one of the gold coins. " 'Tis payment enough for all ye've done."·

She watched her mother bite into the sovereign greedily to be sure it was real, then slammed the door shut behind her. Bess's mother never even heard her go, so intent was she on the piece of gold her daughter had given her.

Bess walked the short road to town and bought not one, but two horses, taking great pains not to be cheated, and was amply rewarded for her efforts by the blacksmith saying she surely drove a hard bargain. He was curious as to where she'd gotten the gold, but she tossed her head and told him it was none of his damn business. She mounted the smaller mare, leading the stallion behind her. Then she went to the dress shop and bought the prettiest gown that fit. Her last stop was to purchase some food and wine, then she headed back to the shack where Jack waited.

"I've left 'ome," she told him shyly. "So we mustn't stay 'ere any longer. 'Twill not be safe any'ow, for the smugglers know o' it and sometimes use it when they've nowhere else to go."

Rian listened silently. He'd been planning to leave the shack anyway, but being saddled with a wench was something he hadn't bargained for. Still, he felt it would be wrong of him to leave her, for she had surely saved his life.

In the end, he decided to take her with him. After searching for several days, they leased a tiny house from a farmer who took no interest at all in his tenants as long as they paid their rent. Rian continued his life of crime, always alone. He refused to let Bess accompany him on his expeditions although she pleaded dreadfully with him to take her; and with each holdup, he became even more daring. He got a perverse thrill out of stopping the coaches of the nobility and shouting, "Stand and deliver!" to their occupants as he relieved them of their fat purses, watches, fobs, and seals. He delighted in divesting the women of their fancy jewelry, for, to him, each one wore the face of the green-eyed witch who haunted his dreams. Morgana, Bess had said he'd called her; and he avenged himself on her lovely spectre every time he frightened some poor maid into a swoon. After each robbery, he returned home to make love to the smitten Bess, who laughed gaily and clapped her hands as he kissed her and regaled her with some new tale of how he'd managed to outwit the dragoon guards again.

Rian often wondered who he was and where he came from, but he could not remember and soon became frustrated with the attempt. Vague, shadowy images sometimes floated into his head, but none so clear as the force of Morgana. He tossed restlessly in his sleep at night, seeing a tall, white sail on a handsome ship, so real that he could almost feel the spray of the sea upon his face. Fragments of pictures taunted him, only to slip away like grains of sand through an hourglass. He saw the green-eyed witch clothed in glittering folds of Chinese silk, laughing, crying, as he wrapped her long red hair about his throat, her poppy-colored lips pouting, her bristly, black lashes starring her slanting eyes. He woke up in a cold sweat with an ache in his loins which even the compliant Bess could not ease, and wondered again who the spectre was and why she haunted him so.

Lord Chalmers did not care to be travelling at night, especially in Sussex where the countryside was agog with tales of a bold, handsome highwayman known as Gentleman Jack. No, his lordship would not be sorry to reach his destination, and the sooner, the better. Still, Chalmers was astute enough to realize that he was running an even greater risk at his journey's end. Trafficking with smugglers was a hanging offense. Not only that, the smugglers were a motley crew, cunning and dangerous; and he could never be certain that one would not put a knife into his back, given the opportunity. He paid them well, and the goods he received in return brought him an even higher margin of profit on the black market. French silks and brandy were especially profitable. Nevertheless, Chalmers decided that this would be his last trip. He had banked a fortune over the past few years and had no further need to consort with common criminals whose demands for payment were rapidly increasing and who were becoming more threatening with each visit. Lord Chalmers shifted his sizable bulk into a more comfortable position in the carriage and drifted into a doze.

Rian eyed the oncoming coach with considerable interest. The crest emblazoned on its panels bespoke nobility and a fat pigeon waiting to be plucked within. With a mocking smile, he drew his pistols, positioned himself in the middle of the road, and shouted the now familiar order.

Lord Chalmers snorted, wheezed, and awoke with a start. Good God! His coach was being attacked! Why weren't his grooms putting up any resistance? He'd sack them in the morning for this! He dare not put his head out of the window to see what was going on. Perhaps if he crouched down onto the floor, he would go unnoticed. With that thought in mind, his lordship heaved his blubbery self down in between the seats as the coach springs creaked ominously under his weight. Alas, it did no good, for the door was rudely flung open and the barrel of a deadly-looking pistol shoved at his nose.

" 'And over the gewgaws, tubby, and be quick 'bout it," Rian said in the lingo he'd picked up from Bess, who had been born in a poor part of London and had moved to Sussex only a few years ago.

Chalmers stared at the scarred face and cold eyes, and decided not to argue with the man. He began pulling the rings from his fat fingers with as much haste as possible, silently cursing his cowardly grooms and the arrogant highwayman.

"I'll take that, too, mate," Rian indicated the heavy purse at Lord Chalmer's waist.

"Now see here," his lordship was mortified. How was he to pay for the smuggled merchandise? Those cutthroats would not hesitate to kill him if they thought they'd been double-crossed. "I've already given you my jewelry. Surely you can do without my purse. I've some considerable debts to pay this evening."

" 'Ave ye now? Well, 'tain't me problem, tubby. Besides, 'twill do ye good to be rid o' some o' that weight," Rian grinned at him insolently, poking his lordship's fat belly with the barrel of his pistol.

Lord Chalmers had no wish to be murdered, especially for a few pieces of gold, and he handed over his purse without another word of protest, but groaned inwardly, for now he would surely have to return to London without the booty he'd travelled so far to obtain. He marked the highwayman's face well, intending to report the incident as soon as possible. There was something naggingly familiar about those hard, cold eyes. He shivered in spite of himself. 'Tis the devil and no gentleman at all, he thought frantically, much relieved when the robber thanked him for his hospitality and rode off into the night. His lordship wiped the sweat from his face, then told his hirelings sourly just what he thought of their protection, and directed them to turn the coach around at once.

Rian directed his horse homeward. The gold and jewelry he'd obtained eliminated the need for another robbery this night. With a silent smirk, he thought about the fat old goat hunched between the seats of the coach, his arse poked up into the air like the tail of an ostrich. Lord, how Bess would laugh when he told her. He did not have time to reflect further on her gaiety, however, for the sound of hoofbeats warned him of approaching danger. With a muttered oath, he kicked his horse into a gallop. Damn those dragoons! They came closer to catching him with every raid. He'd have to be more careful. He forced the stallion off the road and into the trees, heedless of the branches which slapped at his face. He bent his head low into the horse's mane, riding like the devil now. He could hear the guards shouting as they joined in the chase, barking orders to each other. A shot rang out and then another. With a start, Rian felt the bite of a bullet sting his shoulder and realized the last shot had winged him. He pressed on, unmindful of the blood which soon soaked his coat, and the pain in his arm. He was quick and clever, and he'd come to know the countryside well over the past few months. He twisted and maneuvered, backtracking and hiding, snaking his way through the night until he could hear them no longer. Then, a little out of breath and weary with pain, he rode on to the small house he shared with Bess.

"Ach, Jack," she cried upon seeing him. "Ye're 'urt. Let me 'elp ye."

"Nay, lass, 'tis naught but a scratch," he protested, but allowed her to minister his wound.

It was, as he'd claimed, slight, but the amount of blood made it appear worse than it was, and Bess nearly fainted at the sight.

"Lord, Jack, ye've got to stop this now," she said, truly frightened, for what would she do if he were killed? "We've enough money saved to buy us a farm and settle down like decent folks."

Her statement annoyed Rian, for of late Bess had begun to speak more and more of getting married and raising a family. It plagued him to hear her talk of it and with a mind toward diverting her attention, he began to describe the portly Lord Chalmers. Soon she was laughing conspiratorily, as he'd known she would, all thoughts but his daring driven from her mind.

Perhaps Rian would never have remembered who he was had not a strange twist of events befallen him. Lord Brisbane, having failed to win Lady Winwood's consent to marry her daughter, Anne, had become so distraught as to ask his beloved to elope with him. She readily agreed, being entirely devoted to him and petrified that her domineering mother would force her to wed the odious Lord Hawthorne. Although Anne was not of legal age, Brisbane had assured her that her mother would not annul the match, once made, as to do so would cause a horrendous scandal and besides, he himself was no poor catch. With this thought in mind, the two had determined to travel to Sussex where Brisbane had a friend who was a bishop and could be counted on to perform the ceremony.

As fate would have it, Rian held them up. Lord Brisbane was so afraid the highwayman would steal his special license to be married that he did not even recognize his best friend. In truth, much to Rian's fortune, or misfortune, it was doubtful that even Morgana would have recognized the bearded stranger who paraded nightly as Gentleman Jack. Brad drove away, greatly relieved that the scarred man with the mask had let them go without harming his bride-to-be, who was crying hysterically upon his shoulder. Still, Brad's mind was plagued by the highwayman's insolent laugh when Brisbane had informed him indignantly that they were on their way to be wed. There had been something strangely familiar about that, but he shrugged off the thought indifferently as he sought to comfort his dear Anne.

It began to rain before Rian reached the small farmhouse and he never knew afterwards whether it was seeing Brisbane's face or the jolt when his horse slipped and almost fell on the slick road that suddenly made him remember exactly who he was. It all came flooding back, the driving rain, Cecily's last, stricken glance, and the carriage wheel coming off before he was thrown down the hill into the brook.

Bess knew at once that something was wrong when Rian came in the door, but he refused to answer her questions, saying only that he was tired, and with that she had to be content. Rian found himself still wide awake long after the lass had fallen asleep in his arms, reliving the terrible carriage accident. He realized now that he'd been driving entirely too fast, but he knew that fact alone would not have been enough to cause the wheel to come off the curricle. He didn't know how, but he guessed that the Frenchman was somehow to blame. Phillipe had certainly hated him enough to want to kill him. Had he somehow convinced Morgana to go along with the plot? Did she now lie in du Lac's arms even now as Bess lay in his? Damn Morgana! What had become of her?

Morgana was, at that time, on her way to Paris where Phillipe insisted he had many friends who would help them. They had landed in Dieppe and she was not enjoying the long ride. France was filled with cutthroats and thieves, the populace searching out the last of the aristocrats as Napoleon's reign drew to an end, for the New Coalition (consisting of Russia, Prussia, Great Britain, Sweden, and Austria) had defeated the little Emperor at Leipzig and he was fast losing control of his empire. Even now they pursued him to France.

"He was a fool to invade Russia," Phillipe told her as they travelled southward. "We will soon be rid of the monster."

Last year Napoleon had attacked Russia, his only remaining rival on the Continent. He had managed to enter Moscow, the capital city, but after the Moscow fire, was forced to order a retreat. The Russians had attempted to avoid battles, preferring to practice a scorched-earth policy instead, burning all of their land and anything else which might have been of value to the French emperor. Thus, without supplies and lacking winter quarters, Napoleon had no choice but to retreat homeward. The Russians took advantage of his plight and began to harry his army. After the passage of the Berezina River, the Grande Armée was all but annihilated and Napoleon had hastened to Paris to raise a new one. Now, almost a year later, he had suffered another serious defeat.

"He cannot hold out much longer, chère," Phillipe announced with joy.

Paris was no better than Dieppe and Morgana was soon glad that Phillipe had cautioned her against wearing any jewels and had insisted she appear only in her plainest clothes. The Paris she entered might once have been the gay city of romance, but war had left its scars. The ravages of the Bastille and the guillotine would not soon be forgotten. She did not even have to glance at the wooden carts which rumbled slowly toward the graveyards to know that the tumbrils were filled with dead bodies. It was late when Phillipe finally led her through the small, twisting streets to a tiny flat up three flights of stairs. He beat out a signal on the door, and it was cautiously opened.

"Phillipe!" The young woman who'd answered it

was in his arms in a moment, laughing and crying as she clung to him with great affection and amazement.

"Gabriella," he embraced her fondly. "I prayed you would still be here, would still be alive after all this time."

"It has not been easy, mon ami, but come inside and I will tell you. Claude will be delighted to see you again."

"Gabriella," he turned to Morgana standing quietly forgotten in the shadows. "This is Lady Morgana McShane. I hope to persuade her to become my wife."

The young woman approached her slowly, eyes searching for what Morgana did not know, then she kissed her quickly on both cheeks.

"My dear, I am so happy for you both."

They went inside and Gabriella fixed them something to eat. "It's not much, Phillipe, but what we have will always be shared with friends. Come, tell me how it is that you have returned to France."

They talked for hours, Phillipe beginning with the deaths of his parents upon the guillotine. Gabriella and Claude, her husband, had managed to save him from the same fate, and had gotten him safely to the coast and on a boat bound for England; and somehow they had kept quiet and saved themselves as well.

"You are English," the woman turned to Morgana. "You can have no idea of how dreadful it was under the Great Committee. Robespierre was mad. He used the Reign of Terror to attempt the realization of Rousseau's theories. He executed some of the most brilliant men in France: Hébert, Danton, and Desmoulins. We lived in fear. Saint-Just and Couthon, his lieutenants, were just as bad. When Saint-Just demanded the heads of another group of so-called traitors, the Convention at last rallied in self-defense. Robespierre was tried and sentenced to the guillotine, a rather ironic death. We stood in the square and watched the blade fall on the man who was responsible for the deaths of so many of our loved ones. I am not ashamed to say that I was glad."

They sat in silence for a while, remembering, until

Phillipe voiced his intention of reclaiming his lands and title.

"It will not be easy, Phillipe," Gabriella shook her heard slowly. "I don't wish to discourage you, but the time here has been hard. Perhaps it is best to forget and try to make a new life for yourself. I will never again be Comtesse Creux-Gai, who danced with Louis XVI and attended my petite Marie Antoinette. Non, now I am only plain Citizeness St. Ville," Gabriella spoke sadly. "Oui, forget, mon ami."

"Forget, Gabriella? You watched our parents beheaded, and stood beside me and saw ma pauvre Françoise, your sister, burn inside your own home. How can you forget? Françoise was my wife and yet I could not save her. I will never forget it as long as I live."

"You did all that you could, Phillipe. Do not blame yourself for her death. You would have died yourself had we not prevented you from entering the chateau."

Finally, Morgana thought, I know why he has such a morbid fascination for the candles and why he looks at me, but does not see me. Poor Phillipe, he is as crazed with guilt and grief as I.

Their reminiscing was interrupted by the arrival of Claude St. Ville. He was a handsome man who still managed to retain some of his past gaiety. But, like his wife, he had resigned himself to fate.

"We cannot turn back the hands of time, mon ami," he told Phillipe quietly, his eyes saddened by his old friend's proud determination.

He explained to Phillipe that Napoleon had attempted to recall survivors of the Old Nobility as a foil to still the revolutionary Jacobins, but the émigrés scorned him as a parvenu usurper. They denounced his policies, satirized his manners, looks, and speech, and made fun of the Emperor's new aristocracy. Gradually, some of them had returned: the Montmorencys, Montesquious, Sígurs, Gramonts, Noailles, and Turennes, and had received part of their estates back.

"Merde!" Phillipe exclaimed. "So many old friends. How could they do it?"

237

"If you really want to know what's going on, go to Juliette La Récamier's salon. Her enticing beauty and husband's wealth attract many who are not afraid to speak their minds," Claude answered. "Perhaps Mathieu de Montmorency will be able to help you."

They stayed with the St. Villes for several days, during which time Phillipe did visit the notorious Juliette La Récamier. There, he mingled with Generals Bernadotte and Moreau, François René de Chateaubriand, Benjamin Constant de Rebecque, and Madame de Staël, whom Morgana had met at Holland House. She was saddened to learn the outspoken woman had taken to using opium, but was pleased that Madame de Staël had sent her a copy of *De l'Allemagne,* which Phillipe told Morgana was considered to be the woman's greatest masterpiece.

Morgana felt very depressed when they finally took their leave of the St. Villes. The couple had faced so much and lost so much that would never be found again, yet they were brave-hearted, looking ahead instead of dwelling on yesterdays like Phillipe.

He insisted on riding to Ille-et-Vilaine, where his family's estates had been outside of Rennes, and Morgana had no choice but to accompany him. At every inn in which they passed the night, Phillipe and she masqueraded as husband and wife, Phillipe posing as a poor peasant, a guise she realized he must have used a hundred times before. They attracted little interest, dressed as they were, and since Morgana's French was rather limited, Phillipe told people that she had been mute from birth.

"Mon Dieu, if only my wife were so," one little innkeeper had confided to Phillipe before they went to their room.

Strangely enough, the chateau in which Morgana's lover had been born was still standing, but it was obvious that it had been deserted for some time. They approached it cautiously, but when Phillipe saw Guillaume, his old groom, he tossed his cares to the wind and went galloping pell-mell toward the old man.

"Guillaume, Guillaume, it is I, Phillipe," he shouted, a wide grin splitting his face.

"Is it? Is it really you, Monsieur Phillipe?" the wizened fellow's face crinkled with delight and tears. "Why, I thought for sure you were dead all these years."

Guillaume let them into the chateau, seeming to take Phillipe's strange return and Morgana's presence for granted. The house was covered with dust and cobwebs from long disuse, and Morgana did not know how Phillipe could possibly mean them to stay there; but since he obviously did, she set about making his old bedroom and one of the sitting rooms at least inhabitable.

"Ma chère," Phillipe spoke with a satisfied smile when they retired for the evening. "I feel certain I will have these lands restored to me once Napoleon is ousted. Let us stay here for a while and see what happens."

And since she had no reason to return to England, nor Ireland for that matter, Morgana reluctantly agreed. They lived quietly, almost furtively. Phillipe and Guillaume hunted and fished, while she tended a small, neglected vegetable patch. She often looked at her work-roughened hands and wondered how she, the daughter of an Irish baron, the wife of a notorious earl, a woman who had danced at Almack's with Beau Brummell and had her hand kissed by George, Prince Regent, had come to work like a peasant on a desolated French estate. Still, she felt an inner peace she had not known since her father's death and was, for a time, content.

Phillipe continued to be gentle, tender, almost boyish with her, and it was only when the room was ablaze with the many candles and she saw again that strange look in his eyes that she felt vaguely disturbed and out of step with reality.

Rian sat in the shade of the trees and studied Mandrake Downs curiously. Life seemed to be going on as usual, but he saw no sign of Morgana. He narrowed his eyes intently. There was Louis, polishing the wheels of the coach, so she must not have returned to London.

Where then could she be? He considered letting his presence be known, but decided against it. Not until he had discovered the whereabouts of his wife and the Frenchman would he let them know he was still alive. He smiled grimly. What a shock du Lac was going to suffer! He turned the stallion's head and rode slowly toward the local tavern. Perhaps he could gain some news there.

He was in luck, for Baron Linton and Squire Johnston were there, sharing a friendly drink of ale. Rian took a chair in the corner, ignoring the barmaid's bold glance, and tried to glean what information he could from their conversation without appearing overly interested. The Baron and Squire were discussing an upcoming cockfight. For almost an hour, they talked of nothing else and Rian found himself becoming restless and impatient. He cursed silently under his breath and was making ready to go when a remark from Baron Linton halted him.

"To bad about the last cockfight you held, Squire," the Baron was saying. "Devilish bad luck, Keldara getting killed like that."

The Squire shook his head. "Aye, 'tis queer his curricle overturning in that manner. I believe he was a member of the Four Horses Club. Must have been a fine whip. His tiger said the wheel came off the rear axle."

"Aye, the right one. The curricle itself was destroyed. I attended Lady Brooksworth's funeral in London, but Lady Keldara refused to admit me when I went to pay my respects to the late Earl."

"Hard to believe," the Squire shook his head again. "Her running off to France with that emigré. Always thought he was a curst rum one, myself. Poor thing. She must have been mad from grief," the Squire lowered his voice so that Rian had to strain to hear. "The servants said the Countess took to walking the floors at night, talking to the portraits and playing with some kind of a Chinese box."

"You don't say," Baron Linton was suitably impressed.

"Aye, but there, I've never been one to gossip," the

Squire tossed a few coins on the table. "We'll be seeing you Saturday for dinner?"

"Of course, I've something I must discuss with you then."

The Squire smiled. It looked like he was going to get rid of one of his daughters at last.

Rian rode back to the farmhouse thoughtfully. So his wife had gone to France with du Lac. Mad with grief, hell, he snorted to himself. She couldn't wait to be rid of me. And poor Cecily. He'd been tired of her, yes, but he hadn't wished her dead. Well, what to do next? It seemed ridiculous for him to go after them. They could be anywhere in France by now. He would just have to wait. Aye, he would wait and watch Mandrake Downs for some sign of her return and then they would see. In the meantime, Gentleman Jack would continue his life of crime. He'd have to be more careful though. No telling if Lord Chalmers or Denby had recognized him. It seemed highly unlikely, however, and with a grim smile of determination, he dug his heels into the stallion's flanks.

Perhaps Morgana and Phillipe would have continued their dreamlike existence, would never have been discovered, except for the fateful accident. It occurred, oddly enough, because of Phillipe's insistence on those candles. They had been at Blanchefleur for three months, awaiting word that Napoleon was no longer in power. But so far, the little Emperor had succeeded in retaining his hold on the crumbling empire.

Morgana was sitting in front of the mirror, brushing her copper curls when Phillipe entered the bedroom one evening and proceeded with his nightly ritual of lighting the tapers. Then he came to stand behind her, one hand sliding underneath the flimsy material of her dressing gown to caress one creamy breast. With a soft moan, he led her to the bed, placing one of the candlabras on the table next to them. Morgana did not know how long they made love before she suddenly realized that Phillipe, intent on his desire for her, had unthinkingly set the candles too close to the drapes at the window. The curtains, dry and brittle with age and disuse, crackled and caught flame, and suddenly the whole room was ablaze with fire. With a startled cry, she sprang from his arms, pulling her clothes on hurriedly.

"Come on, Phillipe," she shouted above the roar of the fiery timbers. "We've got to get out of here."

"Françoise, Françoise," she heard him whisper hoarsely as he held out his arms to her.

Choking with smoke and fear, she managed to drag him from the room, gathering his clothes in haste. By the time they got downstairs, she knew the entire house was going to burn. They stumbled outside, where a group of onlookers had gathered.

"Please, somebody help me," she cried out in English, in her panic forgetting where she was.

She saw at once how grave a mistake she had made. The French hated the English, and some of them now recognized Phillipe as well. Whispers of "English whore" and "aristocrat" spread through the crowd. With dismay, she realized that these people would not help her and might possibly kill them both.

"Guillaume," she whispered, relieved to find the old man. "You must help us get away and quickly."

Between them, they managed to get one of the horses out of the stable, but had no time to saddle it before the mob of onlookers came pouring after them. Phillipe, his head in his hands, was sobbing Françoise's name over and over hysterically. Morgana suddenly recalled that day upon the moor when Brendan O'Hara had come crumpling down upon her, blood spurting from the bullet hole Rian had put in his back, and Rian's hard slap across her face when she could not stop screaming. With all her strength, she struck Phillipe. The shock seemed to awaken him; and after Guillaume tossed her upon the bareback mount, she was able to pull Phillipe up behind her.

"I can never thank you enough," she told the old man.

"It is not needed, mademoiselle. Please, ride quickly now."

Morgana dug her heels into the horse's sides and galloped wildly down the road into the night. She needed no further urging. She did not know how long they rode, Phillipe clinging tiredly to her waist like a small child. She travelled north, to the coast, determined to find a way to get them back to England. She felt wonderfully free again, in charge of herself and her life as the wind whipped her hair wildly about and tore at the fabric of her dress. Her mind and wits were sharp and clear for the first time in months.

With all of the money she had left and the horse, she succeeded in bribing a young Frenchman to take them back to England. She sat in the small boat, Phillipe's head on her shoulder, and watched the coast of France slowly fade from sight. As she shivered in the spray of the Channel, she cursed Phillipe a thousand times for a fool. The sight of him, weak and self-pitying, sickened her, and she resolved to leave him as soon as possible.

"Phillipe," she faced him calmly in the drawing room of Mandrake Downs. "I'm going back to London and try to start a new life for myself. I realize now that I've only been fooling myself. I can never marry you."

They had been home for over a fortnight, and Morgana had come to dislike him more with every passing day. She felt sorry for him, yes, but she did not want to spend the rest of her life with someone out of pity.

"Morgana, ma chère," he attempted to smile. "We can start again. I promise I will be a better man. I love you."

"I'm sorry, Phillipe, I cannot return your love," she said quietly, but her eyes were like bits of glass. "We might have been killed because of you. Rian would never have lost control like that."

The Frenchman shivered in spite of himself. Perhaps it was true that she was a witch. She bored into his soul with that piercing stare; he didn't like it. He'd seen eyes like that before on the aristocrats who bravely, boldly, appraised the executioner before laying their heads upon the guillotine.

"At least let me ride with you to London," he spoke, intending to change her mind and silently cursing the dead Earl. "You know the entire countryside lives in fear of that dreadful highwayman, Gentleman Jack. They say he wears fine linen clothes and laughs in your face while he robs you. Louis and Joe won't be much protection."

"That's true," she admitted grudgingly, for she had sent the other grooms, Al and Billy, and Chilham and Penney back to London before going to France. "Very well, but you must promise to stop annoying me. My mind is made up."

Dusk was almost upon them when they set out, much to Louis's dismay. "M'lady, 'twould be best to wait till morn," he spoke, alarmed by her behavior, and wondered again if she were mad. "That 'ighwayman gets more daring all the time."

But he could do nothing to stop Morgana. She wanted to leave as quickly as possible and claimed that they still had several hours for travel before halting for the night. She laughed at their warnings about the terrible highwayman and said she would shoot anyone who tried to stop her coach. Nevertheless, she trembled when, after journeying several miles without mishap, she heard a mocking voice order them to stand and deliver.

Rian had recognized the coach at once, for it had his crest emblazoned upon the side, and he knew that his wife and the Frenchman must be inside. It gave him a great deal of pleasure to stop his own vehicle, to see her again after the months she had haunted his dreams.

"I'm sorry about this, Louis," he said softly to the startled tiger before he cracked the younger man over the head with his pistol, then felled the groom, Joe, in the same manner.

"You inside, come out or I'll shoot you," he spoke arrogantly, intending to frighten his wife out of her wits. It was no surprise to him at all when Phillipe stepped down out of the coach.

"Du Lac," Rian breathed harshly.

Phillipe stared at the bearded stranger before him. "I'm afraid you have the advantage. I wasn't aware that I was acquainted with a common robber."

"Better a robber than a murderer, wouldn't you agree?" Rian asked coldly, his mind working furiously. Aye, the two of them had planned it together, for he could see Morgana's frightened face at the window and he assumed her to be worried about Phillipe. "How did you manage to loose the wheel on my curricle?" he snarled without warning.

Phillipe jumped. "Mon Dieu," he whispered. "You are still alive. I can't believe it," he recognized the Earl of Keldara at last.

"Draw your sword, you whoreson coward," Rian's voice was deadly. "I'm going to kill you."

Morgana cowered in the corner of the coach, her eyes fastened upon the drama unfolding before her. They spoke so quietly she could not hear them, but she knew the highwayman could be none other than Gentleman Jack. His clothes were indeed very fine. She saw suddenly that the two men were going to duel and a sob tore from her throat. God, why hadn't she listened to Louis? They would all be killed. Why, Louis and Joe were probably already dead. She felt bad about taunting Phillipe, for she could see that he was determined to save her, to prove himself a man to her under the moonlight this evening. She shuddered to think what would happen to her if he failed to kill the highwayman.

The two men saluted briefly, then began the ritual of feinting and thrusting. The swords flashed, scraping steel on steel as they glittered in the moonlight, wickedly parrying, lunging.

"My wife, du Lac, was she in on this with you?" Rian spoke through clenched teeth.

"Perhaps she did not care for your company," Phillipe managed to say grimly and felt the Earl's blade sear his arm. They did not check, realizing that this was a duel to the death.

Again and again the blades flashed, relentless and

untiring, forte upon forte, foible upon foible. The blood dripped slowly from Phillipe's arm, but he paid no heed. He was breathing heavily now and realized dimly that he was no match for the Earl. Rian was just playing with him. Time and again he lunged, only to turn aside at the last moment, taunting Phillipe with his arrogance. Phillipe attempted to thrust through the Earl's guard, but with no luck. Rian countered rapidly, the muscles rippling in his arms and back, his legs quick to shift his weight against his opponent. He laughed savagely as the sweat poured into Phillipe's eyes, blinding him momentarily. Rian checked, and withdrew, and du Lac knew that once again his life had been spared. The clash of steel echoed in the night, rang, then disengaged again.

Morgana's heart leaped in her throat. She could not swallow and sobbed raggedly each time Phillipe missed a parry. She wondered why the highwayman did not end it. Phillipe used all his strength to beat off the Earl's attack as Rian began to press home, feinting in high carte and thrusting in low tierce as the fight went on, scraping, riposting.

"How did you manage to seduce my wife?" Rian questioned sharply.

"I am a gentleman. I never brag of my conquests," Phillipe panted tiredly.

"You bastard! Take a good look at her because she's the last thing you're ever going to see," Rian jeered at the Frenchman.

Phillipe glanced for one brief moment at Morgana's frightened face in the window of the coach. It was a look that cost him his life, for he lowered his guard and Rian drove three feet of shining steel into his heart.

"Morgana," du Lac gasped, dropping his sword to clasp his wounded breast.

He held out one dying hand to her before he shuddered and lay still.

"Phillipe," she screamed frantically, tearing open the door of the coach to run to his side. "Mon Dieu," she whispered, tears streaming down her cheeks. "Let him be alive. I cannot bear another death upon my soul."

Rian could not stand the sight of his wife crying over the Frenchman's body. With a harsh oath, he yanked her roughly to her feet.

"Let go of me!" she cried out wildly, for she did not know her own husband, and Rian saw no reason to enlighten her.

He dragged her struggling body off the side of the road and flung her down into the grass. Morgana screamed and screamed again as he towered over her like a demon, the scar on his face showing white in the moonlight. He lifted his head and laughed mockingly before he tore the clothes from her flesh and raped her. Morgana whimpered, moaned as she felt his rough hands upon her silken skin. His mouth seared her lips, his tongue pillaging the sweetness inside, then he bit the corner of her mouth savagely, only to cover it with flaming kisses once more. She tasted the blood, bittersweet, from the tiny wound. Her breasts ached, burned, bruised from his touch. She died a thousand deaths when he entered her hard, driving deep into the inner softness of her body. Then, with a rising horror, she felt herself begin to respond, her thighs quivering, shaking, melting into his until her whole body blazed and exploded, and her soul plummeted into a blackness that was neither heaven nor hell, but a chasm where her senses met and fused into one fleeting moment of eternity.

Rian believed for one horrible minute that she was dead, that he'd killed her, frightened her beyond what she could endure. Then he saw with relief that she was still breathing and realized that his wife had experienced le petit mort, the little death. He kissed her swollen lips longingly, then dressed and mounted his horse, riding hard on the road north to London. He hoped fervently that she would not hate him too deeply.

Far and away, Bess waited patiently for her highwayman to return. She waited six days before she took a butcher knife and slashed her wrists.

Chapter Eighteen

Morgana came back to earth slowly, the exquisite pain still lingering between her thighs. She moaned softly and attempted to rise, the dew on the grass wet against her skin. She pulled her clothes into some kind of order and tried to push the thought of what had just happened from her mind. It was hopeless. She could still see that demon towering over her, laughing, and the jagged white scar which ran across his cheek. She would never forget it, not as long as she lived. She would never forget, either, the sensations he'd aroused in her body and how wantonly she'd reponded to his kisses, his caresses. God, she blushed at the very image in her mind! She ached all over from the passionate response he'd forced out of her. With a soft cry, she turned and went to look for the others.

Louis and Joe were not dead, as she'd feared. They'd been knocked unconscious, and both were coming to when she reached the carriage. They rubbed their heads gingerly as they grasped the wheels for support. She could not bring herself to gaze upon Phillipe's poor, lifeless form, the blood caking upon his ruffled, silk shirt.

"Are you boys all right?" she managed to ask calmly.

"I think so, m'lady," Joe mumbled in reply.

"Lord, m'lady," Louis glanced at her, stricken. "I swear that 'tweren't no 'ighwayman. 'Twas the Earl, 'imself, come to life again, it were."

"Don't be ridiculous, Louis," Morgana spoke more sharply than she'd intended. "That blow must have addled your brains."

She turned away numb, not daring to let him see the expression on her face. Gentleman Jack could not be her husband. The idea was preposterous. Even if Rian were still alive, he would not be careering around the countryside posing as a common robber.

"Would you—would you look after Phillipe, please? I'm afraid he's dead," she said hoarsely.

The two men noticed the Frenchman for the first time.

"Looks like the froggie bought it." Louis knelt down by the body. "Duelled with the 'ighwayman, did 'e?"

Morgana nodded wordlessly.

"I'm afraid we'll 'ave to put 'im in the carriage with ye, m'lady, lessen ye jest want to leave 'im 'ere."

"No," her voice sounded strangled. "He has earned more than that."

They travelled the entire night and part of the next day to reach London, for Morgana insisted that they get to the city at once. She could not bear the sight of Phillipe's blind eyes staring at her accusingly as they rumbled down the road. When they would hit a bump, his lifeless body would be thrown against hers, and she would have to prop him back up in a corner of the carriage. At first, it was dreadful, but after several hours, poor Phillipe stiffened in rigor mortis. Now it was an unspeakable horror for her to touch him; and she sat as stiffly cold as he, until the journey's end.

Rian made it back to London in a matter of hours, for he travelled on horseback and could travel faster.

Once he reached his house in Grosvenor Square, he let himself inside without waking the servants and went upstairs to the bedroom he and Morgana had shared. He bathed and shaved himself, then promptly fell into bed, where he slept like a dead man. He was awakened abruptly at dawn by a loud scream and a crashing of glass.

"Oh, me Gawd, don't 'aunt me, please, Lord Keldara. I never done nothing to ye when ye was alive," Penney's teeth chattered.

"For God's sake, Penney," he cursed angrily. "I am not a ghost. Now get that mess cleaned up and get out of here."

"Aye—aye, m'lord," she bent nervously to pick up the pieces of the pitcher she'd dropped, then hurried out of the room as fast as her legs would carry her. "Me Gawd, Bagley," she didn't even apologize for running into the butler. "'Is lordship's alive and upstairs in the master bedroom."

"Really, Miss Simpson, don't be ridiculous. I cannot abide games at this hour of the morning," Bagley eyed her disdainfully, for everyone in London knew that his lordship had been killed in a carriage accident and that her ladyship, poor thing, had gone completely mad with grief and run off with a penniless French aristocrat.

"I ain't fooling ye, sir. 'Tis the Gawd's truth. I swear it," Penney crossed herself hastily.

Bagley was sufficiently impressed by this to send for the valet, Chilham, whom her ladyship had seen fit to retain although he was, as Bagley put it, "an utter ninny."

Chilham was promptly dispatched upstairs to determine whether or not the abigail's preposterous story was indeed true, Bagley considering it beneath his dignity to examine the matter since it was likely only the prattling of a rather scatterbrained maid. He knew that he could rely on Chilham to discover whether or not the Earl was actually upstairs, for even though Chilham was a ninny and a prig besides, he at least had his wits about him and was not, the butler looked down his long nose at Penney, "a foolish young woman."

The valet received some very sharp words and a muddy highjack boot thrown at him for his pains, and was able to report that his lordship was very definitely upstairs, and, he said sourly, very much alive. This bit of information sent the entire household into an uproar and the cook into hysterics, for, there being no one at home, she had spent her time nipping from the Earl's wine cellar instead of attending to the marketing, and claimed frantically that she had nothing to prepare for breakfast. One of the young lads who helped in the kitchen was immediately sent out to fetch some lamb chops and fresh strawberries which his lordship had been known to order for his morning meal.

"And see that yer quick 'bout it or I'll break yer 'ead," the cook rapped the lad's knuckles with her large wooden spoon.

The sight of their lord alive and well, however, was nothing compared to the shock the household received when Morgana tumbled in looking like a cat someone had dragged in out of the rain, and dumped the Frenchman's corpse upon them. Penney immediately fainted dead away at the sight and had to be revived with smelling salts; and even Bagley, who'd seen quite a few nasty things in his day, felt his stomach turn over. Chilham sniffed his nose and pressed his silk handkerchief to his face, saying it was indeed a most unfortunate occurrence.

"I'm sure I don't know what his lordship is going to say about this, Lady Keldara." He could feel one of his migraine headaches coming on.

"Have you gone daft as well, Chilham?" she turned on him with disbelief.

The valet realized with a start that she did not know the Earl was alive and mumbled around stupidly, at a loss for words.

"There, didn't I tell ye 'twas the Earl 'imself what attacked us last night?" Louis eyed his mistress stubbornly, his dirty feet propped up on the drawing room sofa.

"Please remove your feet, if that's what they are," Bagley glanced at Louis's muddy boots disgustedly, "from her ladyship's sofa. I'm sure Lord Keldara did no such thing."

" 'Uh, think yer the foine hoity toity one? Well, ye ain't. I 'appen to know yer father was a chimney sweep." Louis deliberately spit a wad of tobacco in the brass spittoon near Bagley's leg.

"Indeed?" Chilham giggled, pleased to find something he could twit the old stuffed shirt about.

"Really, Lady Keldara, I do not have to tolerate these insults," the butler swelled up like a toad.

"Will you all just be still, and will someone please tell me what on earth is happening here?" Morgana screamed at them.

"I'll be glad to, love."

Silence fell upon the entire room like a tomb as Morgana whirled to face her husband. The beard and the moustache were gone, but the scar, she would never forget that scar. For a moment, the room rocked dizzily and she thought she was going to swoon.

"You!" she spat. "It was you!"

Then she fairly flew across the room, her nails raking into his face before Rian even realized what was happening.

"I hate you, I hate you," she sobbed wildly, screaming and beating upon him with her fists.

He caught her arms roughly, pinioning them behind her back, and said over her shoulders, "I'm afraid Lady Keldara has suffered an extreme shock. Bagley, you and Louis make arrangements for that Frenchman's funeral," he indicated Phillipe's body stretched out on the floor. "I will take care of her ladyship."

He picked up his irate and disbelieving wife and carried her to the bedroom.

"You bastard," she panted after he'd flung her on the bed. "How dare you let me think you were dead while you jaunted around the countryside posing as a notorious highwayman?"

"And you, my sweet wife, could hardly wait to climb into bed with that penniless frog. No, I don't want to hear any of your stupid explanations. I have no doubt that you and he plotted my demise quite carefully. Was it you who pried the wheel on my curricle loose? No, I can see that it was du Lac after all. What a pity, my dear, for you that I am quite alive and your French lover is dead," his voice was soft, mocking.

It sent shivers up her spine. God, had Phillipe really done such a horrible thing?

"I didn't know," she sobbed quietly. "You must believe me. I didn't know."

Rian stared at her stricken face and knew she spoke the truth. Nevertheless, he couldn't forget that she'd lain in the Frenchman's arms, that du Lac's lips had touched her poppy-red mouth, lingered there, savoring that sweetness Rian alone had known, and that her body had found release with another man.

"You bitch," he snarled softly. "Did you enjoy it? Was he a better lover that you turned from me so quickly?"

"No, Rian," she whispered, frightened. "He was nothing. I swear it."

"Don't lie to me," his voice was harsh as he shook her roughly.

Morgana shrank away from his grasp. "Don't touch me," she moaned before he slapped her hard and made her forget that Phillipe had ever shared her bed.

BOOK THREE

No Gentle Love

Chapter Nineteen

London, England, 1814

Morgana stirred. How strange it was to waken with Rian sleeping peacefully beside her again. She studied the scar on his face curiously, wondering how he'd received it. Probably from the carriage accident, she decided. She wanted to hate him for what he'd done to her, but found to her dismay that she could not, for remorse at his death had plagued her conscience sorely. Now that he was back, she discovered joy in his mocking smile and witty remarks. Then anger overwhelmed her again.

The devil with him, she thought. He lets me think him dead, then shows up again without a word of explanation. Jaunting around Sussex like a common robber and nearly frightening me out of my wits. I ought to hate him for attacking me like that and killing poor Phillipe. Had the Frenchman really sabotaged Rian's curricle? She knew in her heart that he had; he had certainly been desperate enough. She glanced at her husband again. Why does he arouse me so easily? He turns his eyes upon me and I quiver and melt inside. I do not love him. Why then does my body burn with flame where he touches it and my lips hunger for his kisses? I am daft with longing for a man I loathe. He takes me so easily, then turns away when he is satisfied as though I were just a toy to ease the ache in his loins. Yet, he watches me. I have seen him when he thinks I do not look, studying me, searching my face for something. What then does he want from me? Sometimes I feel he is about to say what's in his heart and then the moment slips away. And what is it that I seek from him? I do not know even that. She closed her eyes wearily once more.

London appeared to accept the news of the Earl of Keldara's miraculous return from the dead quite calmly. There would probably have been more comment had it not been for the fact that immediately upon Rian's return, the King suffered another one of his fits and the town was buzzing with the rumor that the Prince Regent was going to have to assume the throne at last.

"My dear, have you heard?" Mistress Drummond Burrell remarked to Morgana one evening at Almack's. "They say the old boy's quite gone this time. It looks as though Prinny may be crowned King after all."

However, all the excitement came to nothing as the King recovered again, and the Prince Regent told Morgana over a glass of punch at the Piazza that his hopes were quite cut up. He insisted that she come out to Brighton, where he had decided to redecorate and remodel the Pavillion using an Oriental theme, "For you know I was quite impressed with the decor at Mandrake Downs the last time I was there," he confided, and she promised to visit as soon as possible.

Of course, they could not entirely avoid a scandal; but, to his credit, Rian stood behind his wife like a tiger, and many who sought to satisfy their curiosity about Morgana's escapade with the Frenchman found their questions received with a cold hauteur. As none was brave enough to invite a duel with the Earl of Keldara by challenging his wife's honor point-blank, the wagging tongues soon stilled and the exact truth of the matter remained unknown. Morgana was forced to endure many pointed stares and smirks, however, but since Beau Brummell steadfastly acknowledged her presence in society, making light of the raised eyebrows, no one dared give her the cut direct. For, as the dandy informed Morgana, the entire affair was, "certainly no worse than the furor Prinney caused by setting aside Mistress Fitzherbert and entering into an affair with Lady Jersey."

Rian never mentioned the matter to her again, and Morgana soon found that sometimes she even had difficulty recalling the color of Phillipe's eyes, and she breathed a sigh of relief that her husband did not taunt her unmercifully as she'd feared he would. Indeed, he treated her with a cold scrutiny she found unnerving, and she began to feel that anything would have been better than the silent, calculating looks she was forced to endure.

"Why do you watch me so? 'Tis most unpleasant," she complained wearily.

Rian lowered his eyelids to cover his gaze, screening his thoughts from her as he laughed mockingly. "What's the matter, Mag? 'Tis no secret that I find your beauty pleasing." His eyes raked her boldly now, for she was indeed a delectable sight as she bathed in the ornate tub in their bedroom. She was immersed in bubbles up to her shoulders as she sank lower in the water to avoid his gaze. "May not a husband look upon his wife, sweet?"

" 'Tis most unseemly, for I am no more wife to you than you are husband to me. 'Tis folly to pretend so. Had you controlled your ardor, I would not wear this gold band which binds me to you and marks me as your possession," she snapped. " 'Tis only a symbol that I am your prisoner."

"Ah, sweet," he ran his hands through the curls piled high on top of her head, down the nape of her neck, and along her silken shoulders, caressing gently though she stiffened at his touch. " 'Tis true I took you unfairly, but I was bewitched by your loveliness and you would not come to me of your own accord. I swear no other prisoner has ever known such a gilded cell or more appreciative captor."

"Aye, you keep me in a golden cage, but it was not my beauty which enticed you," Morgana spoke bitterly. "Do not seek to play me for the fool with your glib compliments and flattery. I know it was grandfather's money you sought to gain by marrying me. 'Twill serve you right if the old man changes his mind and his will again. What then will you harvest from the seed you sowed so recklessly?"

"Why, then, I will still have you, love." His hands moved to cup the rosy breasts beneath the bubbles.

He pulled her to him, heedless of the water which soon soaked his ruffled shirt and dripped upon the floor as his lips brushed her temples and throat, fastening upon her mouth with a hunger that could not be denied. His fingers tangled hurtfully in her copper tresses to keep her from turning her face away, sending the hairpins scattering all over the carpet. His lips travelled to her breasts, teeth nibbling gently at the soft flesh and the flushed peaks, before one hand slid down over her belly, stroking gently between her thighs. He kissed her hair and lips again, and the small pulse which now beat rapidly at the hollow of her throat, murmuring low in her ear, his breath hot against her skin until the blood raced through her veins like fire. She whimpered incoherently as he carried her to the bed and cast off his clothes.

"Aye, I will still have you, love," he whispered, huskily before he parted her thighs with his knee and she felt the hard maleness of him pressed within her, sending her senses reeling as his kisses became more demanding, searing, as his body arched against hers until she felt the familiar mounting of pleasure. A thousand suns flared within her, blazing with brightness and flame, as Rian took, possessed, yet gave again and again with deep thrusts that brought her fulfilling rapture.

Afterwards, he retrieved the sponge she had used to bathe herself with and gently wiped away the fine film of sweat which covered her body. The tepid water felt cool against the fire of her flesh; and she gazed at him intently, wondering at his quicksilver moods. Aye, there was more depth to her husband than she had ever dreamed possible. In fact, Morgana was beginning to realize that he had more riches than just the money he so carelessly gambled. At any rate, he was by no means a pauper, and she bit her lip with great consternation as she asked herself for the hundredth time, why then had he married her? The mocking words he had spoken earlier haunted her. I will still have you, love, he had said. In God's name, what did he really want from her?

Several days later, Morgana was delighted to receive a letter from Bridget. She had thought often of her family in Ireland and wondered how they were doing, and she had come to miss her grandfather's wry comments and the angry thud of his cane upon the floor. She opened it up and read the contents eagerly over the breakfast table.

Kilshannon Hall, January 22, 1814

My dearest Morgana—I cannot tell you how much we miss both you and Rian. Even grandfather complains constantly that the house is like a tomb without you. Christmas was just not the same last year.

You would not recognize Maureen, she is growing so. She took her first steps only a few days ago and has learned to say several words. She is such a happy child and Paddy just dotes on her.

I am very glad to be able to tell you that Fionna is at last with child. The babe is due sometime in the summer. Trevor is puffed up like a peacock with delight and his pompousness has become even more unbearable. Gerald is still drinking. I do so wish he could find a wife and settle down.

In case you haven't heard, Lindsey Joyce finally agreed to marry Sean Devlin. They were wed a few

*days before Christmas, but I do not think it can
have suited for already Sean strays from home and
the servants say Lindsey's temper grows worse.*

*I am greatly worried about Colin. He retreats more
and more into himself, brooding and writing. He is
often gone until the small hours of the morning and
refuses to say where he has been. Rosamunde claims
he's joined the Irish rebels, but you know you cannot believe anything she says. Patrick thinks he has
a woman somewhere. Grandfather is sick with anxiety about the boy; and Colin will not listen to words
of advice.*

*Well, 'tis getting late and I must close for now. We
miss you and await your return eagerly. Please write.
All our love.*

Bridget

Morgana passed the letter over to Rian and he read
it with interest.

"If you wish to reply, I will be glad to frank a letter
for you," he told her after brushing the crumbs from his
mouth.

"Yes, I do want to write. May I not say when we
intend to return, Rian? I do not like for them to worry
so."

"Why, Mag, I didn't realize you pined for Ireland. I
have made plans for yet another run to the Orient. We
cannot possibly go back anytime soon," he said.

"To the Orient? Oh, Rian, do you really mean I am
to see all the places where you bought those marvelous
curios?"

"Aye, I intended to tell you later, but now is just as
good a time as any, I guess. I plan to set sail sometime in
the fall.

The excitement of seeing Africa, India, and China
drove all thoughts of home from Morgana's mind; and,
after writing a letter to Bridget, she ran upstairs to begin
planning, although she had, as Rian spoke laughingly, at

least five months to wait. She bombarded her husband with questions of what she was to wear, and the kind of people she would meet, and what kind of weather to expect. He answered patiently and did his best to describe the Orient for her. In the end, he was glad he'd told her, for she now had something with which to occupy her time and she grew more cheerful than she had been in weeks.

A few days later, Rian suggested that they give a small dinner party for Lord Brisbane and his new bride. Morgana thought this was a capital idea, for they had seen relatively few of their friends since returning to London and she did not want them to think she felt guilty or was hiding from the gossip and piercing stares. She sent out invitations and was pleased to have them all accepted.

Spring hung fresh and inviting in the air, and the house was soon filled with the scents of gardenia, cape jessamine, sweet William, and honeysuckle. The evening was fine and clear, although the musky dampness of the night promised a light rain later on. In the house lamps glowed warmly, casting bright halos upon the walls as Morgana descended the staircase. She had chosen this evening a gown of the palest ivory which turned her fair skin to cream and made the red of her hair seem like burnished flame. Her green eyes slanted and danced teasingly as she laid her hand upon her husband's arm and tilted her face up to his for approval. The small pulse beat at the hollow of her throat where two strands of moonlight pearls encircled that slender column. She smelled of lilacs, and the fragrance of her nearness made him curse the oncoming party silently.

"In truth, you are uncommonly beautiful, Morgana," he whispered before lowering his lips to graze hers hungrily for one fleeting moment.

He broke away from her reluctantly as the rumble of carriage wheels over the cobblestones outside warned them of their approaching guests.

The party was, after all, a success. Morgana need not have worried. Only their closest friends had been invited, and none of these was so lacking in good taste as to mention the scandal which in polite circles was second only to the stories of King George III's periodic fits of insanity.

Morgana thought Brisbane's wife, Anne, looked very well indeed. She was a demure girl with dusky curls and just the faintest smattering of freckles across her nose which, she informed Morgana merrily, had worried her mother most unduly. Lady Winwood had used Denmark Lotion, crushed strawberries, mashed cucumbers, and several other less agreeable concoctions to eradicate the offensive spots from her daughter's face, but to no avail.

"However, my lord likes them, so it don't signify in the least," Anne tossed her curls gaily. "Mama was much mortified at our elopment and said she washed her hands of me entirely, for which I was profoundly grateful. You cannot imagine how horrified I was that she would actually succeed in getting that odious Lord Hawthorne to offer for me. Ugh!"

Morgana could sympathize with this sentiment, for she had on several occasions been forced to remove the Duke's gnarled, groping hands from her own person, and the thought of the sweet Anne married to that hideous old man was almost more than she could bear.

"Oh, surely Lady Winwood will come about, Anne. After all, Brad is no mean catch and he obviously dotes on you," Morgana said.

"Aye, he is wondrous dear and takes such great pains with me, for you know I am barely out of the schoolroom and don't know how to get on. I'm afraid I've made some dreadful faux pas. But he just laughs and says I'm a silly chit. 'Tis no doubt true," she giggled gaily. "I know he thinks the world of you and Lord Keldara. He says Rian has pulled him out of more than one scrape during his lifetime."

"And probably he has returned the favor." Morgana studied the two men who were engaged in conversation.

"Oh," Anne clapped her hands together suddenly. "Did I tell you we were held up by that horrible highwayman, Gentleman Jack?"

"No," Morgana began to have a decidedly uneasy feeling.

"Well, we were. 'Twas most unpleasant at the time, although now it only seems rather exciting. We were on our way to be married."

Anne rattled on cheerfully for a time, taking no notice of Morgana's sudden stillness or the concern upon her friend's face. Morgana felt frozen, for surely the law would not look leniently upon highway robbery, even if it was some lord playing a prank. She wondered how many other friends Rian had held up.

Lord Brisbane was, at that time, wondering exactly the same thing. It had not come to him at first, but the more he'd seen Rian, the more convinced he had become that Rian and Gentleman Jack were, indeed, one and the same. The likelihood of there being two men with that particular scar was very slim indeed. He lowered his voice.

"Rian, dear boy, I don't know what prompted you to play such tricks, but there are more than a few in London who were frightened out of their wits by Gentleman Jack, and would remember such a scar. Tread carefully, my friend, lest you wind up at the end of a hangman's rope."

"Aye, Brad, I do not take your warning heedlessly. Such a thing has troubled me for some time. Still, there's naught can prove such an allegation and those who bandy such words about will have me to reckon with. That carriage accident left me without a memory for some time, and though none will believe it, 'tis the truth."

"I believe you, Rian, for, in truth, I thought that even you would not play such a dastardly prank in your right mind. Rest assured that this conversation shall go no farther. I will not even speak to Anne upon the matter, for indeed I fear she was much too distressed to recall your face."

"You were ever a good friend, Brad," Rian clapped the older man on the shoulder. "I will call on you if I have need of your assistance."

"You have it always," Brad spoke earnestly, for he

265

would never forget that Rian had been the one man in London to stand by him when he'd gone more than a little crazy over his first wife's death.

The Earl of Brisbane would never forget going home one evening to find his beloved Sally brutally beaten and slain, and for what reason he knew not. He'd been mad with grief and almost killed himself until Rian had brought him to his senses and made him realize that Sally would not have wished him to end his life in such a manner. Still, he had not glanced at another woman until the pert, freckle-faced Anne, so different from Sally, had claimed his attention and won the heart he'd felt was dead for years.

"She's a fine girl Brad," Rian said, noticing his friend's attention had strayed toward the two women bent in conversation.

"Aye, she's been like a breath of sunshine to me," Brad smiled indulgently, for Anne's sweet, lively face and Morgana's pale, lovely countenance made a pretty picture. "Your wife's haunting beauty is well suited to your devilish grace, Rian. You're a handsome couple."

"Aye," Rian muttered, more than a little jealous of the obvious devotion which showed upon Anne's face when she glanced at her husband. Just once he wished Morgana would look upon him with such favor.

Why is it that I cannot gain her affection? Am I so ugly that she needs feel repulsed by my very gaze? Perhaps the scar has marred my appearance, but she fought me before I was wounded. She struts about baring her rosy breasts and buttocks, and expects me to remain unmoved by the sight. Does she think me less than a man? Does she not realize that the slant of her jaw where it meets her slender throat just aches for kisses? She tempts me like a sorceress when she veils those emerald eyes with her long sooty lashes, and her red mouth curves invitingly. She seeks to cool my ardor with her sharp remarks and cries of hate, but cannot see that so walled a fortress as her heart fairly begs to be stormed. Only in the darkness when I lay my hand upon her throat and take her by force does she whimper her surrender and reveal her need of me. There is always that between us, if nothing else.

Morgana felt her husband's dark gaze upon her and wondered again what thoughts crept through his mind that he watched her so intently, the desire evident in his eyes. 'Tis bad enough that he looks at me thus in private, she thought. Must he needs make his longing plain to everyone else? How dare he leer at me so openly in front of our guests?

With an aim toward distracting his attention, she begged Anne to play for them upon the pianoforte, "For I have heard you perform Bach's Fugue in C Minor beautifully," Morgana assured her.

When finally persuaded to perform, Anne did, indeed, play very well. Her fingers fairly flew over the keys, coaxing the music from the instrument. She slipped easily into one song after another, the haunting melody of "Greensleeves" filling the air. Morgana went to stand beside the pianoforte, for this was one of her favorite songs, regardless of its origin. Softly, she began to sing.

> *I cared for thee when thou wast down,*
> *I served thee with humility;*
> *Thy foot might not once touch the ground,*
> *And yet thou wouldst not love me.*

> *Greensleeves was all my joy,*
> *And Greensleeves was my delight.*
> *Greensleeves was my heart of gold*
> *And who but my lover, Greensleeves.*

Morgana's voice died away, all the aching and longing she held in her heart apparent in the song. To her surprise, everyone applauded and she was brought back to earth with a most unpleasant thud. She cast her eyes upon her husband's face. God, what a terrible song to have sung. What must he be thinking? She attempted to smile at him mockingly as he put his arm around her waist and whispered that she was full of pleasant surprises.

Fortunately, Anne broke the spell by beginning a lively, rollicking tune from *The Rape of Lucrece,* a play by Thomas Heywood. Rian and Brad threw their arms abut each other's shoulders and began to jig as they sang.

Then Rian lifted Morgana from the chair where she'd retreated and pulled her to the center of the circle again. He had a very fine baritone voice as he sang to her.

I took her out and spent my pay,
Mark you well what I say,
I took her out and spent my pay,
And then this maiden just faded away.
I'll go no more a-roving with you, fair maid.
A-roving, a-roving, since roving's been my ruin.
I'll go no more a-roving with you, fair maid.

By this time, all their guests were laughing as Rian made a great show of being a browbeaten husband, and Morgana tried hard to give him a stern look of disapproval. She had not meant her dinner party to turn into a cavorting jest. Even Anne was giggling so hard the tears streamed down her face and she could not finish the song. Beau Brummell so far forgot himself as to slap Sir Anthony Reginald on the back gaily, and was not even troubled when that bemused gentleman accidentally spilled his wine on Beau's new breeches.

The party was the talk of polite circles for weeks to come, leaving all who were not invited feeling dismayed that they had missed what Beau Brummell assertively proclaimed was one of the highlights of the season. The scandal was all but forgotten as those who had attempted to ignore her hurried to seek Morgana's favor.

"Just imagine," Rian laughed as he escorted her upstairs. "At any other time, Beau would have died of shock if someone had spilt wine on his breeches. He must have been foxed, I swear."

"Well, he'll be crying about it, no doubt, in the morning," Morgana remarked, an accurate prediction as Beau's valet later informed Chilham.

The April rains came, leaving the grounds wet and lush and the flowers glistening. Morgana suffered from spring fever and found she was unable to read or embroider patiently, and would often finish a novel with no recollection of its plot, or would take several stitches only to have to unravel them again. She longed to get out of the house, but did not care to drive in Hyde Park in the rain, for it drenched the feathers on her riding hat. She was not sorry, therefore, when the rain stopped and the sun peeked once more from behind the clouds.

One morning she watched Rian cleaning and reloading his duelling pistols across the room, and asked hesitantly if he had quarrelled with someone.

"Nay, love. I am engaged to shoot at Manton's Gallery with Anthony this afternoon."

"Might I come, Rian? I'm so tired of being cooped up in this house and today in the first pleasant day we've had in a fortnight."

"Females don't patronize shooting galleries, sweet. I'm sorry, but I cannot take you. However," he did not miss the disappointment plain upon her face, "if you desire, I will take you out into the country tomorrow and teach you how to shoot."

Morgana heartily approved of this plan and was delighted the next day when Rian kept his promise. He'd bought her a much smaller pistol, his own, he said, being too heavy for her to aim accurately. They took a picnic lunch and drove to a spot just outside of the city limits. Rian set a bunch of empty bottles on a nearby fence, then showed her how to load and prime the tiny weapon. It actually fired two shots without reloading.

He handed it to her warily, saying warningly, "Do not think you shall ever use this on me, love. No," he grabbed her hand. "Don't point the thing at your foot either. You're liable to blow it off. Don't ever aim at anything you don't intend to shoot."

He came up behind her, placing his hands upon her own, showing her how to lift and aim the pistol. Morgana tingled at his touch in spite of herself and could hardly keep her mind on what he was saying.

"Always squeeze the trigger gently. Never jerk it, you're more apt to miss your target if you do so. Now, see how you must sight down the barrel? Line it up with one of those bottles. That's right. Cock the pistol, now pull the trigger."

Morgana tried to squeeze the trigger as he'd told her, but her hand was unaccustomed to the weight of the gun, and she jerked it without meaning to. It went off with a sharp report, the bullet imbedding itself into the trunk of a tree. The kickback sent her reeling into Rian's chest. He steadied her with one hand, trying to keep her from accidentally firing the pistol again with the other.

"Nay, love, you yanked the trigger. You must pull slowly," his lips longed to caress her temples. "Come on, let's try again."

This time, she was prepared for the explosion and the force with which the gun would recoil in her hand. She did as Rian coached and was rewarded by the shattering of glass upon the fence. After a few more times, he let her try by herself and though she only hit three out of the remaining seven bottles, he told her that she had not done badly at all for the first time.

"Can we come again, Rian?" she asked excitedly, her cheeks flushed with the day's exertions.

"Aye, sweet, we'll come whenever you like," he was pleased that she'd enjoyed the day. He only hoped she did not intend to use that deadly little weapon on him.

He did take her shooting again, and he also taught her how to fence, although he usually went to Angelo's for such sport, something of which the servants entirely disapproved.

" 'Tain't seemingly, m'lady," Penney sniffed. "Ye running around in them breeches," for Rian had insisted she could not fence in a gown and had managed to produce some old clothes of his own that had been shut up in a trunk since before he went to Eton. "What will people think?"

"No one sees me save the servants and my husband, Penney. Besides, 'tis fun. Anyway, Rian has blunted the tips of the foils so I cannot get hurt, although I really think he fears that in my ignorance I will injure him."

She pulled on her plumed hat and hurried out into the garden.

"Well, how do I look, my lord?"

Rian smiled, for his pants rode her very tight indeed, outlining her buttocks and the slender legs encased in her knee-high boots. The loose-fitting blouse only served to emphasize the rounded breasts visible through the thin material. She had stuffed her hair up under the hat, which she wore on her head at an extremely rakish angle.

"I don't believe I've ever had an opponent who tried my eyesight so sorely," he said.

Morgana grabbed her foil. "On guard, my lord," she saluted, then launched her attack.

She had learned from previous experience that Rian could beat her by brute force, if necessary, and that the best way to duel with him was to remain quick upon her feet, parrying defensively until she saw him drop his guard. This seldom occurred, however, and he had the advantage anyway in that his arms reached a greater length of distance than hers and he did not have to come so close to score a touch. She feinted well though and sometimes managed to delude him, thereby coming in quickly to make a hit before he had a chance to pull back.

Morgana was beginning to breathe heavily now, while Rian panted only slightly. The foils clashed, and she withdrew, attempting to thrust while disengaging. The maneuver failed and Rian made a direct hit upon her chest, the tip of the blade becoming entangled in the cords which laced the shirt. With an oath, he yanked the blade free, ripping the blouse in the process. Morgana gasped as the material bared her breasts to his gaze. She sought to clutch the fragmented edges together as Rian saw his opportunity and knocked the foil from her hand. He brought the point of his blade to rest upon her throat.

"A game well played, my lady, but I am the victor and must claim the spoils."

"What will you have, my lord?" she attempted to match his light banter.

Rian's eyes narrowed appreciatively. "What is your life worth to you, madam? Loose that cloth and let me see what I bargain for."

"Does my lord seek to attack me with another kind of foil? He knows full well what lies beneath this blouse. Would he wish the servants to know also?" she turned her eyes frantically toward the windows of the house.

"Nay," he tossed away his blade and grabbed her. "I know a place free from prying eyes."

He led her to the gazebo, sheltered from the house by the branches of many trees, and forced her down upon its floor, ignoring her half-hearted attempts at protest. With passion-darkened eyes, he loosed her grasp on the thin material and feasted his gaze upon the display. His mouth sought one hardened nipple greedily as his hands fumbled with her boots and breeches. Soon he had tossed her clothes into a little pile and removed his own.

"Don't fight me, love," he whispered, for she was frantic with worry that someone would see.

He pinioned her arms behind her back, then pulled her knees up over his shoulders, his mouth seeking that soft nest between her thighs, probing that sweet place with his searching, searing tongue. Her hat fell off and her hair tumbled down in disarray, spilling upon the floor and over her breasts. She gave a feral cry as the fever spread where his tongue darted and her release came moments later. He freed her then, and pulled her to him, his breath like dragon's fire against her flesh as his voice purred in her ear.

"Now you do that for me, sweet."

"I can't," she almost sobbed.

"Yes, you can."

272

He wrapped his fingers in the long, copper tresses, kissing her hair, temples, mouth, throat, and breasts with flaming lips before he forced her head down. He groaned with pleasure as her swollen lips closed over his heated pride. When he could stand her gentle touch no longer, he pulled her body upon him, his hands upon her hips, helping her with the motion. She buried her face in his shoulder, moaning softly, as she felt his seed spew forth within her and the ebbing tide flowed through her body once more.

Rian and Lord Brisbane had surely partaken of enough Blue Ruin at Cribb's Parlour this sunny afternoon to have filled the Mediterranean Sea, and were engaged in a wager which Sir Anthony and Lord Alvanley both agreed was likely to be capital sport, but would lead to naught save trouble if carried out in their present inebriated state. However, neither of the two principals could be persuaded that the wager was folly. Both being notorious whips, each had backed himself to graze no less than the wheels of five coaches on the road from London to Brighton. As neither Lord Alvanley nor Sir Reginald desired to ride with Rian or Brad for obvious reasons, they followed in Lord Alvanley's phaeton.

"I swear, Anthony. 'Twill be the devil to pay for this bit of nonsense, and Rian only barely recovered from one curricle accident already." Lord Alvanley frowned upon pranks.

"Aye, but I'm not about to risk my neck trying to stop those two. Why, even Keldara's tiger is half afraid to ride out with his lordship in one of his fits."

"I should think Denby, of all people, would have better sense, and him with a new bride at home, too."

They pulled the phaeton to the side of the road and proceeded to watch events with anxiety. Each of the two men managed to graze three coaches without overturning any, although the occupants were none too happy and shouted epithets at them, one old man even threatening them with a loaded blunderbuss. This did nothing to dim their enthusiasm, however; and in fact, Lord Brisbane dared to increase the amount of the wager as Rian geared up for the next approaching vehicle.

"You're on, Brad," he shouted, then raced cheerfully at the oncoming curricle.

Rian's wheels grazed the coach, but the driver was unable to control his startled team and the curricle overturned into a ditch. Neither its occupant nor its tiger was injured, but both were extremely indignant over having such a foolish prank played upon them. Rian wheeled around to ascertain they were all right and came face to face with a sputtering Lord Chalmers.

"See here, Keldara," his lordship spoke sourly. "What's the meaning of this nasty trick? You might have killed me."

"Sorry, my lord, just a wager between Denby and myself. I hope there's no harm done."

"No, none at all," Lord Chalmers said suddenly, for his eyes were riveted upon the scar on Rian's face and he smiled acidly.

Damned if it hadn't been Keldara who'd robbed him down in Sussex! The man was given to no end of eccentric whims, such as this little escapade! Lord Chalmers drove off, an appropriate revenge beginning to take shape in his fat, bald head.

"I say, wasn't that Chalmers?" Denby drove up.

"Aye, terribly cow-handed, isn't he? Strange, though," Rian's eyes narrowed. "He drove off without so much as a by-your-leave, and I was plainly in error. Odd, his behaving like that. I know he hates me, but he barely even berated me for the trouble I caused."

"Well, perhaps he had no mind to meet with you in a duel," Lord Brisbane was now bored with the endeavor. "At any rate, you've lost our wager and owe me five hundred pounds."

"I wonder," Rian stared at the curricle lumbering on down the road.

Lord Alvanley and Sir Reginald were highly amused, however, for neither of them liked Lord Chalmers either;

and the sight of his roly-poly figure, sputtering indignantly in the ditch, was riotously funny. Pleased to find themselves in such agreement, they turned the phaeton around and headed toward town. There, they repeated the tale at Watier's, making Lord Chalmers the butt of their joke, much to his annoyance; and his lordship resolved to get even with the Earl of Keldara for every slight he'd ever suffered at that arrogant man's hands.

Morgana did not find the incident amusing at all and told Rian it was a wonder he hadn't been killed. He laughed at her annoyance, and said he'd caused no harm.

"Yes, but how could you be out fooling around in those curricles, especially after the last accident you suffered?"

"Ah, but that was through no fault of my own, sweet," he reminded her grimly.

She bit her lip and turned away, not wanting him to see the sudden bright tears which dimmed her eyes. How could she have been so careless as to bring that up again?

They were awakened the next morning by a loud pounding on the door. Morgana hurriedly threw on her wrapper, wondering who it could be at this hour of the morn. She was met halfway down the stairs by a very upset Bagley.

"My lady, it's the King's men. They wish to speak with his lordship."

"Where are they, Bagley?" she was thinking furiously. Surely they could not arrest Rian for overturning a coach. But what if they'd discovered he was Gentleman Jack? He must have time to get away.

"I've put them in the drawing room, my lady."

"I am the Countess of Keldara," she swept into the room, displaying her iciest manner. "What can I do for you, gentlemen? I am not accustomed to being so rudely awakened at this hour of the morning," Morgana surveyed them coldly.

The guards were flustered by her appearance, her hair flowing over her breasts and down her back, the light wrapper doing little to conceal her lithe figure. One of them, a young man with sandy hair and a pleasant countenance, stepped forward and cleared his throat.

"I'm Captain Summersby, my lady. We wish to speak with your husband on matters pertaining to the King's business."

"My husband is abed, where everyone in his right mind is at this early hour. What is it you want?"

"My lady," the young captain was obviously distraught. "Perhaps you had better sit down. I'm afraid this is a particularly delicate and serious situation."

"Do not stand there gaping, Captain," Morgana snapped. "When you are plainly the one who needs the assistance of a chair. Out with it now. What has my husband done that you must come banging on my door so rudely?"

"My lady," Captain Summersby swallowed hard, for he was not used to dealing with presumptuous, outspoken females. "I'm afraid Lord Keldara is under arrest."

"On what charges?" Rian demanded from the doorway. "I swear Lord Chalmers was unhurt when I careened into his curricle yesterday."

"Lord Chalmers? I know nothing of him." The captain quelled under his lordship's piercing stare and began to wish he'd never volunteered for this duty. "You are under arrest for the murder of a British officer and as a suspected leader of the rebellion of the radical United Irishmen in Dublin last November."

"Why, that's preposterous," Morgana snorted. "Rian was nowhere near Ireland seven months ago."

"He will be given a fair chance to prove that, then, my lady, when he stands trial in a court of law. Will you come peaceably, my lord, or must my men take you by force?"

"Take him? Take him where?" Morgana stared in disbelief. Surely this was all some horrible joke.

"I'm sorry, my lady. My orders are to deliver Lord Keldara to Newgate Prison, where he is to remain until his trial." Captain Summersby was beginning to feel extremely sorry for the Earl's lovely wife. What a shock this must have been to her.

"Oh, Rian, no," she wailed, falling into his arms. "How can this this be?"

"Don't worry, love," he kissed the top of her head soothingly, staring at the uniformed officers intently. "I'm sure this is all just some dreadful mistake. It won't take long to get to the bottom of the matter."

Morgana watched, frightened, as the officers led her husband away, his reassuring smile doing little to abate the fear he saw on her face.

After they had gone, she sent a billet around to Lord and Lady Brisbane, desiring that they wait upon her at once. They came immediately, the tone of her missive prompting them to leave their breakfast half eaten.

"My dear Morgana," Anne burst into the room. "Whatever has happened? Are you ill?" her face was white with concern for her friend.

"Oh, Anne," Morgana broke into tears. "The dragoon guards came and arrested Rian this morning."

"What?" Denby asked, amazed. "Not because of that foolish prank we played yesterday? Why, that's ridiculous!"

"No, Brad. 'Tis much more serious than that. They say he's mixed up with those Irish revolutionaries and that he murdered a British officer last November."

"Why, you and I both know last November Rian was—" he broke off at once, a look of consternation upon his face.

"Aye, Brad, and what kind of defense is that? 'Twill most likely get him hung at any rate," Morgana dabbed at her eyes.

Anne glanced at them both. "If you're referring to Rian parading around Sussex as Gentleman Jack, I already know about it," she said quietly.

"You do?" Denby gazed at his wife with surprise. "But you never said a word to me."

"A scar like that is not an easy thing to hide, but 'twas none of my business. I'm sure Rian had his reasons for holding up coaches. He does not seem to me to be an insensible man."

"Oh, Anne, he'd lost his memory. That accident did something to his mind. He couldn't remember who he was, and when he did, he'd already committed those terrible crimes," Morgana began crying again. "What am I going to do?"

"There, there. Crying's not going to help and you're spoiling your pretty face," Anne spoke logically, causing her husband to wonder if he had underestimated her. "Brad will go and speak to Prinny as soon as possible. I'm sure George doesn't mean for one of his best friends to rot in jail. Then we'll try to find out who brought these charges and what kind of witnesses they have against Rian. After that, we'll determine what's best to do."

Chapter Twenty

The dragoon guards escorted Rian to Newgate Prison, treating him courteously, although making him no less aware that he was under arrest. At the heavy iron gates, he was placed in the custody of one of the jailers, who manacled him, then led him by lantern-light through the dank, twisting corridors till they reached what was to be Rian's cell. It was a dark, foul-smelling room. As his eyes grew accustomed to the light, Rian saw the reason. The slop jar obviously had not been emptied for weeks, and the previous occupant had evidently been quite ill, for there were traces of dried vomit on the sides and around the stone floor, as well as other more odious matter.

"Ye're to be kept in solitary," the jailer's teeth showed yellow in the flickering lamplight. "If'n ye don't gimme no trouble, we'll git along jest foine. If'n ye do, jest remember that ye ain't no 'igh 'n mighty lordship in 'ere. Ye're jest one more filthy crim'nal," he cackled unpleasantly before closing the door on its rusty hinges and turning the key in the lock.

Rian flung himself upon the straw pallet which lay on the floor, filthy with dirt and vermin. The manacles chafed at his wrists and the stench turned his stomach. God, how had such a thing happened? Lord Chalmers was sly, but even he could not have trumped up such charges. From what source then did they spring? He thought of Morgana's frightened face. No, she would not have brought such madness against him. She had been tender, almost loving these past few weeks, and her face had been genuinely shocked and concerned. He did not know how long he lay in the darkness, listening to the scurrying of the rats in the cell. He must have dozed, though, for the scraping of a key in the lock brought him to his senses fitfully.

"Awake, are ye?" the jailer studied his new charge with interest. "They tell me ye kilt an officer o' the law, and that ye're one o' them Irish rebels. 'Ere," he held out a bowl of thin gruel warily, for there was something infinitely dangerous about this prisoner's lazy, arrogant grace. " 'Tis likely all ye'll be gitting for a while, lessen ye've relatives who'll see that ye're sent better."

"I have relatives," Rian spoke. "They will see that you're well paid for any services you perform. Do you think something could be done about that chamber pot? I find the odor quite offensive."

"Not quite what yer used to, eh? We empties them on Wednesdays and Sundays, not before."

"Well, Mister—?"

"Crotchetts. Mister Crotchetts be me name."

"In that case, Mister Crotchetts, you can plainly see and smell that this one hasn't been cleaned for over a month and certainly not on Wednesday."

"Aye, an what am I like to git if'n I takes the trouble to empty it now, 'stead o' waiting till Sunday?" Crotchetts glanced at him slyly.

"I've told you before that I have relatives. I'm sure my wife will be happy to reimburse you for any amount of trouble you go to on my behalf."

"Oh, an who might the lil' liedy be, me lord?"

"The Countess of Keldara," Rian spoke softly.

Crotchetts stepped away as though shot. Lord, he'd heard more than one tale of the Earl of Keldara. The man was a Corinthian and Libertine, a notorious gambler and rake, deadly with a pistol and rapier. The jailer would have to be on his guard. There was no telling. This prisoner might throttle him with his bare hands. With those cold green eyes he certainly looked capable of the task. He shoved his stout stick in Rian's direction.

"Ye jest keep over there in that corner whilst I takes this out o' 'ere." He grabbed the wet, sticky jar, then backed out of the cell.

Rian glanced at the thin gruel in the bowl Crotchetts had given him. It looked most unappetizing to say the least and there was a large cockroach swimming in the murky contents. With a snarled oath, he shoved it away. He would have to get word to Morgana to send him some money. Crotchetts came back with the pot, which still reeked, but now at least was empty.

"What's the matter, me lord? Ye don't fancy the menu this evening?" he sneered.

"Hardly. Cockroaches haven't been part of my diet for some time. If you find it a tasty dish, Crotchetts, however, feel free to sup," Rian indicated the wooden bowl.

"Ye takes what ye gits down 'ere, me lord, or ye don't git nothing at all," the guard plucked the offensive bug from the gruel and crushed it between his thumb and finger.

Rian watched as he slurped up the contents of the bowl greedily, licking the last drops out of the dish like a dog before he smacked his lips with delight.

"Ye'd best git some rest. I 'spect they'll be in to question ye in the morn."

Once again, he turned the key in the lock and left Rian in darkness. The Earl of Keldara shivered upon the palet. God, the damp, stone floor was cold, and he had only a moth-eaten blanket for warmth, a far cry from the feather comforters and the heat of Morgana's body at home. Where was she now, his lovely wife? Did she miss him as she lay alone in the huge bed they shared only this morning.

No one came, however, the next day. Only Crotchetts, with his snide comments and thin porridge, entered the cell, and soon Rian began to doubt his faith in his wife. For over a week, he ate practically nothing, growing gaunt and thin, vomiting most of the gruel he managed to consume. He looked worse, covered with lice and filth as he was, than he had when he paraded nightly as Gentleman Jack. Had she forgotten about him, his enticing witch of a wife?

Crotchetts swung the door open. "Git up. There's a liedy to see ye."

Rian stared as Morgana entered the cell and saw the look of horror that passed over her face at his appearance. She turned on the jailer.

"You whoreson coward," she glared at him coldly. "Is this how you've cared for my husband with the money I gave you? Why, you filthy creature. No less than the Prince Regent himself shall hear of your behavior. Fetch me some decent food and clothes immediately, and some brandy. I've no doubt you have some here, your breath fairly reeks of it. Be quick about it," she eyed Crotchetts icily, the hatred on her face sending chills up his spine. "Or yours shall be the corpse swinging from yonder gallows."

Crotchetts scurried to do her bidding, thinking it had been most unwise to keep the wench's money for himself. He had not thought a woman would venture into these dungeons, however. Lord, there would be the devil to pay now.

"Rian," she turned to the stranger before her. "I'm sorry. I did not know he was treating you ill."

"Nay, 'tis not your fault, Morgana," he was relieved that his wife had not deserted him after all. "I should have known the thief was keeping the money."

She moved toward him, but he waved her away.

"Nay, do not touch me, love, for I am filthy with

282

vermin. How is it that you come here? 'Tis no place for a woman."

"I could not rest, worrying that you might be starving in this horrible place, and they would not let Brad or Anthony come. God, how wretched you look, my lord. That little ape had best hurry with the brandy or I shall kill him myself."

So, his wife had been so concerned about him that she'd descended to this hell to see about his welfare. Hope that all was not lost soared in Rian's heart.

"Morgana, love, what's happening outside? Why has there been no one here to question me?"

"I do not know. Brad and Anthony both have talked with Prinny. George says the evidence against you is overwhelming. You are to stand trial in two weeks. Oh, Rian, how can this be? He told me they have witnesses, British soldiers, who are not the type of men to concoct such a story. I fear the Prince Regent believes you guilty," she sobbed.

"Why do you weep for me, Morgana? If they hang me, you will be rid of me for good."

"Nay, Rian. I never wished you dead. There has been too much between us and your ghost would haunt me always."

He had no time to ask her more, for Crotchetts returned bringing food and brandy. Rian drank the fiery liquid, its heat bringing the life back into his body, then fell like a wolf upon the bread, meat, and slabs of cheese.

"Me liedy," Crotchetts whined cunningly. "I beg ye not to be too 'ard on me. I've a wife an kid o' me own to support an 'tis lil' enough pay I receive."

"I pity your family, then," Morgana stared at him unflinchingly. "The stench of you is enough to make me retch."

"Me liedy, I've arranged for 'is lordship to 'ave a bath an shave," Crotchetts was petrified now. "The woman was as much a witch as her husband was a devil. "An for 'is clothes to be brought."

"Very well, then. But I'm warning you, I shall not

hesitate to visit my lord again, and will have your head on a platter if I find him in this condition."

"Aye, me liedy. Thank ye, me liedy."

"And see that these chains are removed and those sores tended. The wounds will fester and putrefy otherwise."

"Aye, Liedy Keldara. All will be as ye say."

"It had better be," Morgana sounded amazingly like her flinty grandfather. "Rian, I must go now. I will do what I can. I know you are innocent of these charges against you."

Rian watched his wife walk away, the determination evident in the squaring of her small shoulders. Aye, she was one hell of a fine woman. Few others would have braved what she had borne this evening. Grudgingly, he acknowledged how lucky he was to have her, and, then, smiled bitterly at the thought that she would probably have pitied even a dog in his condition.

Morgana found it a miserable task to go anywhere without Rian. The minute she entered a room conversation would cease, only to start again abruptly and loudly so that she could not help but guess she had been the previous topic of discussion. She could not bear the pitying glances of the women and the men who frawned upon her thinking she would soon be a rich widow. Almost no one save a few of Rian's closest friends believed him innocent. They all knew that though he had lodgings in London and was received in all the houses, he was not an Englishman, but a full-blooded Irishman. They could not help but feel he had preyed upon them, using them to gain information for the revolutionaries. After all, he was constantly at Holland House with Henry Grattan; yes, and it was his fault that dear Cecily Brooksworth had met such an ill-fated, untimely death. Why, everyone knew the devil himself walked in the shape of Rian McShane. More than one woman had heard her husband speak of the Earl's notorious luck at cards, and a few had lost their lovers to his marksmanship at sunrise duels. Every scheme, every prank, every turn of fate in Rian's past was dredged up and twisted to suit their malicious views of him. Even the fact that his spirited black stallion bore the unholy name of Lucifer and that his ship was called the *Sorceress* was offered as evidence of his being in league with evil.

Dark rings deepened under Morgana's eyes as she passed the nights sleepless with worry and longing for his touch. She often awoke to find herself wrapped in clinging sheets, wet with her own perspiration, and she reached for him in the blackness only to remember that he lay in a hole in Newgate Prison.

The trial was presided over by a stern-faced magistrate in a curly white wig tied at the back of his neck in a queue. He wore a long, somber black robe and peered out over the courtroom from behind a pair of wire-rimmed spectacles. Morgana's heart sank when she saw his grim, thin lips and beak nose, for he did not look like a man who would be lenient with those who broke the law. She had dressed in a solid-colored gown of deep russet, completely devoid of frills, and pulled her hair into a knot on the top of her head, intending to make herself appear extremely dignified. She failed utterly, for the judge could not help but notice the creaminess of her skin in contrast to the reddish-brown material of her dress, and the brilliant green of her eyes which gazed at him thoughtfully from under her bristly, black lashes. He noted with appreciation the square set of her jaw and the slender, aristocratic nose, the cheeks touched with the faintest bloom of color, and the lush, poppy mouth. Aye, Lady Keldara was indeed a fine figure of a woman.

The bailiff ushered Rian in then, and the magistrate had no time to study the woman further. Morgana saw that her husband was garbed fitting to his rank at least, and that Mister Crotchetts had apparently been frightened enough to treat his captor a little better. Rian's eyes searched the room and lingered on his wife as he gave her a reassuring smile.

The court was called to order and the prosecuting barrister, representing His Majesty, King George III of England, began his opening remarks.

Treason. It was an ugly word. Morgana closed her eyes hurtfully at the sound of it. God! What a sensational scandal this trial was causing. It wasn't every day that a member of the House of Lords was charged with such a serious crime. What if they hanged Rian? She looked at her husband's stony face and wondered what he was thinking. Two British officers had already identified him as the man who'd slain their major. Now a third was preparing to enter the witness box. The prosecuting barrister, the Honorable Lloyd Danfield, discreetly shuffled the papers he held in his hand.

"Now, Lieutenant Vickery, will you tell us in your own words, please, exactly what happened on the night of November 12, 1813," Mister Danfield tossed the scrolls upon the table.

In bits and pieces, the entire sordid story came out—how the rebels had sought to invade the Parliamentary House in Dublin, apparently with the intention of assassinating Lord Melford, a visiting British dignitary. The plot had failed, however, the small committee of lords meeting at the House that evening having been given sufficient warning by an unknown informant in time to escape. After attempting to burn the premises, the rebels had fled into the night, hotly pursued by dutiful officers.

"One of the rebels, evidently their leader, managed to fire at us, killing Major Durand in the process. Unfortunately, a thick fog fell upon the land soon afterwards and we were unable to capture any of them," Lieutenant Vickery reported bitterly.

"I'm sure you did your best, Lieutenant," Mister Danfield smiled at the young officer. "Will you please tell us if the man whom you believe to be the leader of the Irish revolutionaries is in this courtroom today."

"Well, it's hard to say," the young officer cleared his throat nervously. "The Earl of Keldara certainly resembles the man I saw, but, begging your pardon, his lordship looks a trifle older than the rebel leader and I don't remember that scar, which would have been hard to miss. However, it was dark, and I may be mistaken."

The courtroom gasped in surprise and Morgana felt her hopes rise. So, there was to be some shadow of doubt cast upon the trial after all. Perhaps Rian would go free. Mister Danfield seemed rather displeased by this confession and, after an icy glance at the young lieutenant, announced that he might step down. The barrister then called two more witnesses, one of whom also refused to confirm the Earl as the man he'd seen.

After that, the Honorable Tyrone Cambridge, Rian's barrister, was allowed to continue with the proceedings. Mister Cambridge had no choice but to put his client on the stand. In sharp contrast to the British officers, Rian appeared almost carelessly relaxed. He answered the questions put to him with easy grace, and Morgana could tell that the magistrate was impressed with her husband's manner. His voice was calm as he explained about the carriage accident, his prolonged recovery, and his subsequent loss of memory. He did not mention, however, his masquerade as Gentleman Jack. Rian's story, although rather hard to believe, was at least credible and the magistrate conceded that he'd heard stranger tales of truth.

The magistrate was, in fact, facing somewhat of a dilemma. He had sentenced many men in his day and prided himself on being a good judge of character. Now, he eyed the Earl intently. Aye, the man was no doubt an arrogant devil, but somehow the magistrate just couldn't see Rian as a rebel leader. Not that he didn't think the Earl could have played such a role, but he couldn't see the man before him bungling such an operation as this had been, or even taking part in such a stupid plan for that matter. Lord Melford would have been an insignificant target at best, his death arousing little interest except for the ire of the British soldiers. Still, his lordship's alibi was farfetched and he himself had admitted to losing his memory. Perhaps he'd committed these crimes in his amnesic state. Three out of the five witnesses had positively identified the Earl as the man they'd seen. At any rate, the hanging of such a prominent member of society was no easy order to give. When in doubt, the magistrate decided, procrastinate.

"I've reached a decision in this matter," the magistrate banged his gavel upon the bench loudly. "I hereby decree that the Earl of Keldara, Rian Alexander McShane, be returned to Newgate Prison for a period of three months, after which time, if no new evidence in this case has come to light, he shall be condemned to hang as a traitor to the Crown of England. God save the King."

Three months! And then to hang! Morgana thought she was going to faint. Rian appeared almost unmoved by the news. His green eyes narrowed intently, but that was all. Morgana had no chance to speak with him before he was hustled away by the guards. With a broken sob, she allowed Lord and Lady Brisbane to take her back to the house.

Rian paced the small cell restlessly, like an animal, as the stub of a candle flickered eerily in the darkness, casting ever-changing shadows on the wall. There was, so far as he had been able to determine, no way to escape from the walls which confined him. There were no windows from which he might have pried the bars, nor could he tunnel through the cold stones which served as the floor. The Earl could perhaps throttle the whining jailer, but the manacles hampered his freedom of movement and, upon being returned to the prison, they had chained his ankles also. Two months. He had been in this filthy hole for two months and still there came no word of his release, no new evidence to change the course of his fate. Yet, he was determined that his neck should not be stretched for a crime of which he was not guilty. His wits had been sharpened by the close confinement and the instinct to survive. He had his own ideas of how the crime of which he was accused had come about, but no way to prove them, caged as he was. Aye, if by some trick of fate he managed to cheat the hangman, he would seek out the cur responsible for this dastardly deed. His senses reeled at the thought. Ah, the reward would be sweet indeed, the payment high for all of the degradation and humiliation he'd been forced to endure. Still, at least Morgana had made certain he was decently fed and clothed, coming often to gaze upon his ravaged countenance. His lips curved in a sardonic smile. She was appalled by him and the naked beast he had become.

Of late, she'd seemed to have grown accustomed to the inevitable fate which awaited him, resigning herself to the end. Did she know how she mocked him? Parading herself before him like an unattainable prize now that he was helpless, the creamy whiteness of her flesh tempting him beyond all endurance, reminding him of his forced celibacy most sharply. The fragrance of her perfume—lilacs, always lilacs—wafting toward his nostrils, the heady scent that permeated his very soul. Aye, she was his, the green-eyed sorceress. Would he ever possess her again?

His mind dwelled upon fond memories, recalling in sharp detail the cold mask with which she hid her shyness, her fears and insecurities. The winsome loveliness of her face, the flame of her copper tresses, the rich emerald of her eyes flecked with gold, the inviting curve of her honeyed mouth. Morgana! The name echoed in his mind hollowly, enticingly, mockingly. Morgana shivering upon the beach, Morgana galloping wildly across the purple moors, Morgana laughing at Almack's, Morgana lying in his arms within the shelter of the gazebo. Always Morgana! Even in death her emerald eyes and poppy mouth would haunt him, tease him, lure him back again and again. She was like a drug to him, a sickness of the mind he could not shake free. He could not lie in peace in some dark grave, his head laid to rest finally beneath a chiselled stone. He would walk to the ends of the earth, a tormented, haunted ghost, forever seeking the warmth of her touch, the shadow of her smile, the trembling of her lips beneath his though it be naught save the icy kiss of death. Aye, she was his and would remain unto him for all the days of eternity.

With a satisfied smile, he closed his eyes and slept.

Lord Chalmers pushed his chair away from the table slowly, a contented smile on his fat, avaricious, gloating face. Events were proceeding even better than he'd planned. The Earl of Keldara was going to swing for a crime he hadn't even committed! How maddening to have a perfect alibi and be unable to produce it. Chalmers licked his lips, smacking them greedily, savoring the flavor of the roasted duck he'd just finished. The picture of the Earl's wife floated into his thoughts and he seized upon it. Aye, if all went well, he should soon bring the wench to heel. The thought of her begging him for mercy, pleading with him to save her husband's life, amused him. Only he could spare that wretch from almost certain death, but his price would be dear. How sweet the taste of revenge. Death on the gallows was not good enough for the Earl. Chalmers wanted that arrogant bastard to suffer, to grovel in the dirt. What better way than to cuckold the man with his own wife? He wanted the Earl to live and know that he, Lord Chalmers, held Lady Keldara within his keeping and used her nightly for his own satisfaction.

"Maria," he called loudly.

Madame Frampstead eyed her gluttonous brother with distaste. "What is it you want, Harry? More food?"

"Nay," he patted his rounded belly and belched contentedly. "I wish you to perform a little mission for me."

"What sort of mission? If it has aught to do with those smugglers, I shall not do it. I've warned you time and again about trafficking with those thieves. It will be the ruination of us yet, my lord."

"Why, Maria," the little eyes, lost in folds of overhanging flab, glared at her evilly. "I did not hear you complain thus when the gold we reaped purchased this bawdy house," he indicated the rooms of the gaming hell with a wave of his hand.

"I did not know 'twas money ill-gained."

"Aye, you knew. Where else could I have secured such a sum? The estate was in debt and like to be sold, wasted away by the drunken sot we called father. I had to save us," he grasped her hand feverishly. "We would have been ruined, disgraced."

"Better that than what we have become," she yanked away from him fearfully.

"You always were a whore at heart, Maria," his shrewd eyes pierced hers cruelly. " 'Tis my good fortune none know of the relationship between us."

"What is it you wish me to do?"

"Merely to deliver a message for me," he shrugged his shoulders indifferently.

"What kind of message, and to whom?"

" 'Tis none of your business. Just do as you're told," he spoke angrily.

"Nay, Harry. I'll not be a party to any more of your wicked schemes. You're lying and evil," she shuddered.

He twisted her arm cruelly. "You will do it, Maria, or I shall cut off the funds that purchase the perfumes and silks of which you're so fond."

"Ha!" she snorted in his face. "Think you, my lord, that I have need of your money now? My gaming house is well frequented and brings in a tidy sum. Do not seek to threaten me with poverty, my lord."

"You are forgetting, Maria, that I possess the deed to this property. I can close this place down anytime I choose. What then will you do, my loving sister? Throw yourself on the mercy of one of those aging fops you're so fond of bedding?"

"Nay, Harry," Madame Frampstead smiled triumphantly. "You are the one who forgets. Do I need to remind you that I am the only person who knows 'twas you who murdered Sally Denby? The Earl of Brisbane would pay well a goodly amount of gold to learn what secret I have harbored all these years."

Lord Chalmers struck her viciously. "Do not tempt me to do the same to you, Maria. 'Twas an accident. You know full well I did not mean to kill the bitch. I loved her," his face puckered up sourly. "I only sought to plead with her, to ask her to run away with me. But she laughed in my face, called me a gross, stupid pig. I could not bear it! Such insults coming from the sweet lips of my beloved. I hit her. I didn't intend to hurt her, but she became hysterical, started screaming for the servants. I had to silence her," Chalmers blubbered. "She fell and hit the bedpost. The blow must have killed her instantly. I saw the blood trickling from her mouth and ears, and I ran. What else could I do?"

"Nothing, Harry. But do not forget 'twas I who helped you that night. How many times did I tell you to leave the bitch alone? She encouraged your advances not and made it plain she wanted naught to do with you."

"No matter. I have found an angel to take her place. Aye, an angel," he muttered. "Beyond all comparison. She will not turn from me as my beloved Sally."

"Eh? What foolish prattling is this, Harry?" Maria Frampstead felt frightened once more.

"Why, 'tis whom you are to deliver the message to. She will come to me, I have no doubt."

"Who, Harry, who is this woman?" she saw the evil lust plain upon her brother's face now.

"Morgana McShane."

"Lord Keldara's wife? You're daft, Harry. What could she possibly see in you? An overgrown hog with spittle drooling from your lips at the very thought of her. I won't do it, I tell you."

"You will, Maria, just as you have always done everything I wished, unless, of course, you desire to take her place in my bed," he leered at his sister wickedly.

"Nay, Harry, not that!" she tried to pull away from him, the years flooding back horridly.

She had been Lady Maria Chalmers then, a comely lass of fourteen. Even then she had sensed something wrong with her lustful brother, had seen his evil, prying eyes gaze with desire upon her budding breasts and rounding buttocks.

One night, when their father had been in a drunken stupor, Harry had come to her room. He laughed at her frightened face. The sour smell of ale reeked on his breath, and his red eyes raked her foully. God, how she'd struggled, but to no avail. At nineteen, he was already a heavy man. He'd stuffed his handkerchief in her mouth to silence her screams and tied her wrists to the bedpost with his cravat. She would never forget his greedy, grasping hands on her breasts, the weight of his pudgy body squirming on top of her as he violated her virginity with his fat, stiff organ.

Maria Framstead hung her head in despair and shame. "Very well, Harry. I shall do whatever you ask."

Chapter Twenty-one

"Come on, Morgana, 'twill do you good to get out of the house," Anthony urged her. "You cannot sit here moping about Rian forever."

"Oh, Tony, 'tis misery to venture out. Everyone stares at me and whispers behind my back when they think I do not see. 'Tis horrid! I cannot bear it," Morgana shuddered.

"Well, they had best not do so in my presence," Anthony declared indignantly. "I swear I'll kill the man who mocks your plight, my dear."

"You're too good to me, Tony," she patted his hand gratefully. "All right, if you think it's best, I shall go with you tonight."

"Good. I'll call for you around seven o'clock. Please try to cheer up. I don't like to see you looking so morose," he tilted her face up to his, longing to plant his lips upon her trembling mouth, to console her sorrow with his devotion.

"I will, Tony, I promise."

"There's a good girl.".

Sir Anthony Reginald was whistling as he left the Earl's house in Grosvenor Square. He could not help himself. He'd fallen head over heels in love with Morgana McShane. Although he did not wish the Earl's untimely demise, it certainly made things look a hell of a lot brighter for him. He held high hopes in his heart that, once a widow, Morgana would be encouraged to look kindly upon his suit. It wouldn't do to press her, however, he must give her time. He knew she was fond of him, and he hoped her feeling of affection would grow into something deeper with passing time.

Morgana took particular pains with her appearance that evening, for she did not want the Ton scoffing at her dress. She wore a gown of gold crepe, which emphasized the honeyed flecks in her eyes. It was cut low to reveal the curve of her rounded breasts and exposed the slender neck and shoulders. With it, she wore a brilliant set of topaz jewels Rian had given her for her birthday. Penney dressed her hair carefully, piling it upon her mistress's head in an array of tiny curls, allowing a few of the stray wisps to caress the nape of Morgana's neck.

After pulling on gloves of gold mesh, Morgana picked up her fan, and allowed Anthony to drape the folds of her glittering wrap about her. She thought she felt him kiss the tresses of her hair lightly, but then decided it must have been her imagination. Surely he would not tease her in such a fashion. He helped her into the barouche and they drove toward the lights and laughter of Drury Lane.

The play that evening was *A Midsummer Night's Dream* by William Shakespeare. Morgana knew the story well. She settled into the box beside Anthony after bidding Lord and Lady Brisbane greetings. However, she soon decided it had not been such a good idea to come to the theater after all when she began to hear some of the lines spoken by the actors.

> Quince: And you should do it too terribly, you would fright the duchess and the ladies,

that they would shriek; and that were enough to hang us all.

All: That would hang us, every mother's son.

Bottom: I grant you, friends, if that you should fright the ladies out of their wits, they would have no more discretion but to hang us; ...

She cracked a wry smile at Anthony and wished fervently that the actors would cease chattering of hangings. She glanced out over the audience for others' reactions and spied a well-dressed woman in the box across from hers. Morgana was surprised to see the woman return her stare, then nod in her direction. Confused, she nodded back, thinking the woman must be an acquaintance of Rian's, for she did not recognize her. Lowering her eyelashes, she studied the woman covertly. Although obviously in her forties, the woman was well preserved. Her dress was of the finest of French silks, a pale rose which set off her blonde hair cunningly, and the jewels she wore, although not outstanding, were handsome enough. A sadness hovered about her otherwise pretty face which Morgana could not comprehend. Nor could she recall ever seeing the woman at Almack's or anywhere else for that matter. She longed to ask Anthony if he knew the woman, but dared not question him while the play was in progress, since he was obviously enthralled by the lovely actress who had the part of Titania, the fairy queen.

"I have forsworn his bed and company," the fairy queen said.

And Oberon, the fairy king, replied, "Tarry, rash wanton: am not I thy lord?"

Morgana could not keep her attention on the actors. She kept returning her gaze to the woman across the room. Why, she does the same to me, Morgana thought as she met the woman's glance with a shock. Perhaps she has heard the dreadful scandal and seeks only to satisfy her curiosity. Still, how rude she is to peruse me so carefully and through her quizzing-glass at that! Morgana turned away abruptly with a toss of her copper curls.

At intermission, she asked Anthony to fetch her a glass of punch and fanned herself most vigorously, her eyes searching for a glimpse of the provoking woman. To her chagrin, Morgana saw that she was no longer in the box. Hmph! No doubt she is in the lobby seeking further information about my most notorious person, Morgana decided, her eyes flashing. Such was the expression of ire upon her face at the thought, that several young bucks, who desired no more than to press their feverish lips upon her hand, concluded that Lady Keldara had the most forbidding appearance imaginable and that her husband should consider himself lucky to be hanged!

She was alone in the box, Brad and Anne having decided to take a short promenade, and was slightly startled when the blonde woman slipped up behind her.

"Lady Keldara?"

"Yes," Morgana favored her with an icy stare.

"You don't know me and my name is of no importance. I have been entrusted to deliver this message into your hands, however. Here," she thrust the missive toward Morgana. "I must go now. 'Twould not do at all for me to be seen in your box."

And just as quietly as she had come, the woman disappeared into the throng within the lobby. Morgana quickly unfolded the billet. Was it perhaps a note from a secret admirer? Her lips curved into a slight smile at the thought. Lord Chalmers, watching her from the shadows, was pleased.

"Very well done, Maria," he smirked contentedly.

"Well done, indeed," she snapped. "I beg you to think again, Harry. It may well be that you've chosen a most dangerous adversary. I do not think this woman will grovel at your feet."

"Silence! I have no desire to listen to your foolish prattling. The lady will do as she's bid. Have no fear of that."

Morgana scanned the contents of the missive, then

298

folded it with trembling hands, the words imprinted on her mind. The letter read:

> *My dear Lady Keldara—I have news which may be of particular interest to you concerning a mutual friend, Gentleman Jack. If you wish to save him from a most unpleasant fate, come to Madame Frampstead's gaming house this Friday evening. Dress plainly and veil yourself. I shall know you.*

It was unsigned and she could not think who might have sent it. And who was the woman who'd been the messenger? Madame Frampstead herself? She glanced toward the box across the theater and saw it was still empty. Like as not, the woman did not intend to return. Morgana concluded that she must keep the appointment. She dare not risk throwing away even the slightest chance at saving her husband's life. Determinedly, she thrust the billet into her reticule.

Only the applause told Morgana that the play had ended. She'd sat through three more acts and hadn't heard a word. Still, she smiled at Anthony's anxious face and told him she'd enjoyed it immensely.

She could not wait to get home, back to the quiet sanctuary of her room to tear open the letter and read through its contents once more, but she allowed none of her frustration to show when Anthony insisted on partaking of a light supper at the Piazza. They dined on buttered lobster and broccoli with Hollandaise sauce, then went dancing at Vauxhall Gardens.

When they reached the house, he came in with her, pouring himself a glass of whiskey from one of the Earl's decanters. Lord, Morgana groaned to herself. It appears that he's planning to stay for a while, she thought, and found herself wishing violently that he would go away.

"Tony, if you don't mind, I'm rather tired," she said.

"Of course you are," he replied soothingly. "Why don't you have a glass of brandy? That'll make you feel better."

Outside of pointedly being rude, there was no way she could ask him to leave and he refused to take the hint when she flung herself on the sofa and yawned widely. The letter was fairly burning a hole in her reticule.

Anthony joined her a moment later. "Morgana, I—I don't know how to tell you this," he stammered, then, flinging all caution to the wind, he bent and kissed her lips.

She drew away from him in shock. "Oh, Anthony! How could you? All this time I thought you were my friend and now you've ruined everything."

"I'm sorry," he was as mortified by his behavior as she. "I couldn't help myself. I don't know what possessed me."

"Oh, this is dreadful," she clasped her hands to her burning cheeks.

"Well, I said I was sorry," he pouted angrily, for after all she was a married woman and had run off with that damn Frenchman besides. Who would have thought she'd act so horrified?

"Leave me, please. And never mention this night to me again," Morgana regained some of her composure.

"You're not angry with me?" he asked anxiously.

"No, now please go away."

Without another word, Sir Reginald slammed out of the house, much relieved that the Earl was locked up in Newgate Prison. Anthony had no doubt that his lordship would not have hesitated to put a bullet through his friend had he found him trifling with his wife.

Morgana dressed herself in a pale, grey gown, one whose purpose was to draw as little attention as possible to its wearer. It had a cape lined with swansdown which buttoned severely up the front all the way to her throat. Only when this was removed could the deeply cut bodice be seen, revealing the tiny hollow between her breasts and the creaminess of her throat and shoulders. She painted her face lightly, for she knew what manner of establishment Madame Frampstead's was, and suspicioned that this would raise less interest than if she appeared with no makeup at all. She was careful to affix a distinctly black patch to the corner of her mouth. It twitched enticingly when she smiled, as she did now, well pleased with the results of her efforts. Then Morgana did something she had never done in her life. She powdered her hair. She found the custom distasteful, but there was nothing to be done for it. Those copper curls would reveal her identity, for she was now a notorious figure in London—the red-haired wife of the Lord of Keldara.

At last, she was ready. With a small sigh of satisfaction and more than a great deal of anxious foreboding, she pulled on her gloves and set out to keep her ill-fated appointment at Madame Frampstead's, wondering whom, indeed, she was to meet there. She was astute enough to call for a hackney, realizing that the crest on her carriage would cause a goodly amount of comment if seen in front of Madame Frampstead's.

The night fog hung low over the city and there was a hint of rain in the air, for the mist was damp and clung to her skirts. The hackney travelled slowly down the narrow, cobblestone streets. No one paid any attention to the hired coach or recognized the heavily veiled occupant within. Even so Morgana sat with her back pressed stiffly against the seat, well away from the windows and the dim light which sometimes streamed in from the flickering lanterns that lined the way. She had no wish for someone to remark upon her late-night journey.

She hoped she was not too late. The letter had specified no particular time of arrival. The hackney set her down in front of Madame Frampstead's establishment, and she paid the driver, telling him he need not wait for her. He drove off without a backward glance, well acquainted with the bawdy women who patronized that place of business. This one had been a little better dressed perhaps and veiled, but that was all.

Morgana drew in a deep breath and lifted the heavy brass knocker upon the door. She thought for a moment that the lion's head grinned at her wickedly, but it might have been only the flickering of the lamps, then the door swung open wide. A thin man with a nervous twitch in one eye and a high, pinched nose stood within.

"Your card, please," his voice was stiff.

Card? Of course, one had to have a membership card to frequent such an establishment. That way visitors could be screened so that the Bow Street Runners did not filter in by mistake.

"I'm afraid I have none," she stammered nervously.

"Then please be good enough to tell me your name and with whom you are here to spend the evening," the doorman had obviously heard this line before.

"That's quite all right, Sammy," the blonde woman Morgana had seen at the theater suddenly appeared from nowhere. "I will take care of this lady."

"Very well, madam," old pinched nose spoke again, his eye twitching.

"If you will follow me, please," the woman turned to Morgana.

Morgana had never been in a gaming hell before and could not help but be curious about it. She peered with interest at the rooms through which they passed, noting the rich red and gold of the furnishings and their ornateness. The drapes at the windows were very heavy and the carpet was so thick she felt she must sink in it. There were gold-veined mirrors everywhere and many naked marble statues followed her veiled figure with their sightless eyes. She recognized many of the noblemen present and a few of the women whom she'd seen onstage at Drury Lane. However, no one glanced her way as she hurried to keep pace with the woman she presumed was Madame Frampstead; they were too intent on the gaming and drinking. Many of the men had their bits o' muslin, as ladies of the evening were commonly called, perched on their laps as they wagered their monies in the games of chance: silver loo, whist, hazard, écarté, piquet, and faro. She could hear the rumble of dice at the hazard table and remembered that once Denby had told her that was how Rian obtained the house in Grosvenor Square. The tinkling of coppers sounded from the faro bank as she

302

passed, and she saw a rouge et noir table in one of the quieter rooms.

Finally Madame Frampstead led her up a curving flight of stairs to the rooms on the second floor. Morgana guessed correctly that these were reserved for extremely well-paying customers who wished to conduct their games of chance in private or to carry on a quiet tête-à-tête with their lights o' love.

"I hope you may not be sorry, my lady," the woman spoke for the second time all evening, then disappeared down the hall after opening the door to one of the boudoirs. Hesitantly, Morgana stepped inside.

"Come in and close the door," a voice spoke from the shadows.

Morgana did as bid, her eyes trying to adjust to the dim light of the flickering candles. It had been much brighter downstairs.

"Who are you and what news have you for me?" she

Lord Chalmers stepped out from the shadows then. Morgana gasped at the sight of the short, squat man who stood before her, his squinty eyes studying her excitedly. called out.

She recognized the man at once as Lord Chalmers.

"You may call me Harry, Morgana," he spoke softly, pursing his blubbery lips together in anticipatory delight. "I like your hair much better in its natural state," he said.

"My lord, I'm sure you did not bring me here to discuss my appearance. Your note said you might be able to save my husband's life. Pray tell, how do you intend to accomplish such a feat?"

"I have ways, my dear. In due time, in due time," he repeated. "I shall speak of them. Won't you be seated?" he indicated a chair. "Would you care for some sherry, a brandy perhaps?"

"No, nothing," she answered. "Please get to the point at once. I've no desire to linger in this establishment."

"The point is this," he circled her slowly, appraising her with deep admiration as though she had been a slave on a trading block or a horse at an auction. "I am quite aware that your husband was nowhere near Ireland in November. Ah, you wonder how I know this. I know because he held me up in Sussex just about that time, if I remember correctly. No, do not offer excuses or deny it, Morgana. You would not be here had you not known the identity of Gentleman Jack," Chalmers chortled. "Aye, 'twas the scar that put me onto it."

"Then surely you are aware that such a defense is impossible. They would hang my husband for highway robbery instead," Morgana was beginning to grow impatient.

"Not necessarily, my dear. I have friends who might be persuaded to impose a lighter sentence, especially in view of the fact that the Earl could obviously not have committed the crime of which he now stands accused. Treason is such an ugly word," his pig-eyes blinked at her rapidly.

He was fairly drooling at the mouth from her nearness. That fragrance, lilacs he believed it was, was most enchanting. He wished, however, that she would remove the veil and cape.

"What kind of sentence could you obtain?" Morgana questioned, and Chalmers could tell she was more interested than she pretended to be.

"Oh, most likely they would impress his lordship into the Royal Navy. 'Tis not an uncommon occurrence. The Earl is accustomed to life on the sea. He would no doubt find it much more pleasant than the gallows."

"I see." Morgana did not like the distinct manner in which he leered at her. "And what do you want in return for performing this good deed, my lord, money?"

Lord Chalmers threw back his head and laughed gloatingly, the fat on his belly bouncing up and down like waves of jelly. "Oh, no, my dear. I am a very wealthy man. I have no need of your gold."

"What then do you desire?"

His eyes raked her lustfully now. "Why you, my dear, of course. I have long admired your beauty."

Morgana gasped. She would not even entertain such a thought. The very idea was ludicrous in the extreme.

"I find myself unable to strike such a bargain, my lord," she said stiffly and made ready to leave.

"Not even to save your husband's life, Morgana? What a pity. I'm certain your husband will be most sorry that you didn't. Most sorry indeed when they stretch his neck from the end of a rope." He pulled the veil from her face. "May I?" his hands removed the cape from her person, his fingers trembling as he fumbled with the tiny buttons.

Morgana cringed as his fat fingers touched her shoulders and brushed her breasts. She thought of Rian. Would he really want her to save his life in this manner? Something told her that he would see her at the gates of hell before agreeing to such a plan. She became uncomfortably aware of Lord Chalmers's greedy gaze, hungrily intent on the display of rounded flesh which peeked from the bodice of her gown, and suddered with revulsion. No! She could not do it. Not even to save Rian's life could she allow this fat, balding pig to place his hands on her flesh and ease the lustful ache in his loins with her body. She saw with horror that his manhood was already bulging against the material of his pants and drew back in fear.

"Well, my dear?"

"If you touch me, I'll scream," she snarled at him. "You brutish lout! Think you that I would let you soil one tiny bit of skin my lord has kissed and loved? Aye, loved and lingered over longingly. Why, you're not fit to wipe the mud from his boots," she sneered.

Lord Chalmers's face went livid with rage and he struck her face with his fist. "By God, you bitch! You shall not speak to me in that manner. I, who have loved and adored you from afar. Your husband doesn't know the meaning of the word. He does not worship you as I do. By God, you'll not reject me again, Sally!"

Morgana cowered on the floor in a heap, her head spinning from the sharp blow. Why, the man was insane. He did not even know her name. What had he called her?

Sally, yes, that was it. He kicked her roughly with his foot and she doubled over from the pain.

"Get up, you whore! Get up, Sally Denby, that I may see you grovel on your knees before me."

Good God! This was the man who'd murdered Sally Denby, Brad's wife. It must be. Morgana saw with fright that he meant to kill her as well. He yanked her from the floor, his hands tearing graspingly at the material of her dress, baring her breasts to his leering stare. With a groan of pleasure, he fastened his mouth greedily upon the ripe mounds of flesh, his teeth biting deeply, hurtfully, into one breast. Morgana tore free of him with a scream. He caught her hair with one hand, yanking her back. She tripped and fell, pulling him to the floor with her. They rolled over in frantic combat, Lord Chalmers attempting to push the gown and many petticoats up over her thighs. With a low moan, Morgana managed to free one leg. She drew it up and kicked him squarely in the groin, and he fell backwards with a cry of pain. She tried to rise, but he recovered and grabbed her legs again, tripping her in the process. She sprawled upon the floor and he leaped on her, his weight nearly crushing her in the attempt. He was breathing heavily now. She could hear him rasping, wheezing, his breath hot and panting against her throat. She groaned. She could not fight him off. Her arms were not strong enough to push those mounds of fat. She struggled, flayed against him helplessly. She saw him fumbling with his pants and thought she must die. In his hurry to get them off, he loosed his tight grip and she managed to squirm away. Her hands grabbed a chair for support and her reticule fell off in her lap. With a sobbing cry of relief, she opened it and withdrew her little pistol. Lord Chalmers did not see it in her hand. He stumbled toward her, his pants sagging down around his knees. Morgana closed her eyes tightly and pulled the trigger. The gun went off with a deafening roar. Chalmers stared at her in disbelief, then crumpled slowly to the floor, one hand over the bloody hole she'd pumped in his fat belly.

"You've murdered me, you whore," he whispered hoarsely before he groaned and lay still.

Morgana was shaking all over. The sobs racked her body like the dry heaves. She expected the door to burst open any moment and the Bow Street Runners to come pouring in, ready to arrest her. Then she realized with a start that it was so raucously noisy downstairs no one had probably even heard the shot. With trembling fingers, she dropped the pistol back into her purse, sending a silent thanks to her husband for its provision. Then she buttoned on her cape with her quivering hands as she glanced nervously toward the door. She gathered her veil and bag, gave one quick, searching gaze around the room to be sure that nothing else of hers remained, and cautiously opened the door, ignoring Lord Chalmers's sprawling, thickset corpse with its slackened, drooling mouth.

The hall was clear. Apparently she had been right about no one hearing the scuffle or the explosion of the pistol. What to do? She could not go back the way she came, not with her hair in tumbled disarray and her gown in such a state. Rapidly she ran to the other end of the long corridor. A place like this had to have a back entrance somewhere. With a small cry of joy, she found she was right. She hurried down the dimly lit, winding set of stairs and let herself out into the night.

Chapter Twenty-two

Morgana fairly ran down the street, paying no heed as to the direction in which she travelled, glancing over her shoulder as though the devil himself pursued her. When at last she could run no more, she fell up against the wall of a building, panting and gasping for breath. She had no idea where she was. She had never been in this part of the city before and had not thought to study the way the hackney had come. For a moment, tears of despair filled her eyes, then she drew the edges of her courage together raggedly. A hackney had brought her here. A hackney could take her away again. She continued down the street warily, jumping at even the shadows the flickering lamps cast in the darkness.

She had not gone very far when two men leaped out at her from an alley.

"Lord, Charlie, 'tis a gentry-mort. A real looker, too," one of them said, eyeing her appreciatively.

"Nay, Pete, that ain't no gentry-mort. 'Tis more like

a liedy o' the evening, I'd say. 'Ow 'bout it, luv? Want to give us a little piece o' fun afore ye goes 'ome?"

Morgana was so relieved that they were not the law, she found she couldn't speak.

"What's the matter? Cat got yer tongue?" the one called Pete asked. "Lord, Charlie, she ain't even got any gewgaws on," he snorted with disgust.

"Mayhap she's got some money in that bag," Charlie answered. " 'Ow 'bout that, luv? 'And that pretty thing over 'ere."

Morgana woke up with a start. These men were trying to rob her, and not doing a very good job of it at that. With icy dignity, she pulled herself up to her full height, and stared at them haughtily.

"I'll give you my money if you'll just go away and leave me alone."

The two men punched each other craftily and watched eagerly as she opened her reticule. They were not laughing moments later when she pulled the little pistol out and told them to move along before she made it impossible for them to do so. She watched them skulk away, muttering to themselves about uppity females with loaded guns, and almost smiled. At any other time, the incident would almost have been funny.

Fortunately she spied a hackney a few minutes later and flagged it down. She gave the address in Grosvenor Square, then settled back in the seat, pondering what she must do. Obviously she could not remain at the house. Madame Frampstead knew who she was and would no doubt report her to the Bow Street Runners soon, if, indeed, she had not already done so. The thought that they might even now be waiting for her made Morgana's knees knock with fright. She did consider this highly unlikely, however. It seemed fairly absurd to assume that Madame Frampstead had even entered the chamber. If she went barging in on customers, they were not apt to return. Morgana decided that she probably had several hours before the crime was discovered and reported. Where was she to go and how was she to get there? She could go to Mandrake Downs, of course, but they would probably look for her there also. Besides, the place held unpleasant memories. Actually, she thought, the best thing to do would be to flee the country. A slow, contented smile curved her lips. Of course. That's just what she would do. She owned a ship, the *Sorceress,* and it was moored in London's harbor. She could go anywhere in the world.

Then she remembered with a frown that, although she was his wife, the *Sorceress* really belonged to Rian. What if the first mate, Harrison, refused to take the vessel out of port without the Earl? Perhaps she could bully him into it. But could she handle those men? She recalled how they'd acted on the voyage over and the way in which the close quarters and her beauty had affected them. What if she couldn't control them? She certainly had no desire to be raped by a gang of sailors.

Oh, if only Rian were here! He would help her get away, would probably go with her. How silly. If Rian were here, she wouldn't be in this fix. Suddenly she longed wildly for her husband's mocking smile and arrogant, careless grace. He was extremely adept at dragon-slaying. Slowly, carefully, an outrageous plan began to take shape in her mind.

"Wait for me here," she told the driver when they reached the townhouse. "I'll only be a moment."

She let herself in and hurried upstairs before the servants could see her. Morgana rearranged her hair, pushing the twisting mass of curls back into place. There was no time to change her dress, but she saw with relief that the cape covered most of the damage anyway. Just to be sure, she took her long cloak from the closet and tossed it over her shoulders. Then she gathered a couple of bandboxes and a portmanteau and rapidly stuffed them full with as many of her dresses and Rian's clothes as she could manage to squeeze in. She snapped the lids shut with a sigh of satisfaction, paused briefly to pick up the Chinese puzzle box and dash off a short note, then scurried downstairs.

"Bagley," she encountered the butler. "Have someone fetch Louis immediately. Lady Brisbane is ill and I must attend her for a few days." That excuse would explain the baggage.

"Right away, Lady Keldara. My condolences on Lady Brisbane's illness. Nothing serious, I hope."

"No, I don't think so. I believe she may be pregnant," Morgana confided errantly, hoping Anne would not be angry over the rumor that was sure to spread. Nevertheless, her lie had its desired effect, for Bagley's mouth dropped open and he blushed.

"You don't say."

There, that explained the odd behavior of her ladyship at this hour of night. No doubt she would remain at the Denbys for several days. She certainly seemed excited about something anyway. But then he'd never known a woman who didn't get excited about babies.

Morgana saw that Louis was out front and went outside to join him after bidding the butler a pleasant good-night.

"Louis," she said as he tossed the baggage into the coach. "You think a great deal of my husband, don't you?"

"Aye, m'lady, I do," he spoke bluntly, curious as to where this line of questioning was leading.

"Would you do something for me then, and tell no one what I've asked you to do?"

"Aye, if it's to 'elp the Earl, I will," his sharp face eyed her speculatively.

"Good. I want you to drive this baggage down to the *Sorceress* and inform Mister Harrison that he's to round up the crew and make ready to sail tonight. Then you're to deliver this message to Lord and Lady Brisbane," she handed him the note she'd written. It explained what had happened at Madame Frampstead's and what she hoped to accomplish this night. "Give it into no one's hands save theirs, Louis. 'Tis most important that no others read what it contains. After that, you're to report back here and inform that stiff-necked butler of mine that you delivered me safely to Lady Brisbane's residence. Is that clear?"

"Aye, m'lady," Louis cracked a smile at her remark

about Bagley. He felt ready to burst with pride at the trust she showed in him.

"And, Louis," Morgana turned. "I want you to know that, whatever happens, I've always been fond of you. No one could have a better tiger."

"Thank ye, m'lady," Louis thought she looked on the verge of tears and wondered what was amiss that she gave him such strange orders and bid him an almost fateful farewell.

He watched her ride away in the hired coach, clucking his tongue over her behavior, then moved to carry out her demands.

Morgana was worried, but she was also desperate. She knew this was a crazy scheme she had planned this chilly night, but she prayed it would work.

"Where to now, m'lady?" the hackney driver brought her back to earth with a start.

"Newgate Prison."

If the man thought her destination strange, he did not say so, but turned the coach around and headed toward the jail. He glanced at her briefly. Aye, she was a queer one, but as long as she paid the fare he didn't care if he drove her to the gates of hell and back. He didn't know how close he came to doing just that. At last, they reached the jail.

"Ye're sure ye don't want me to wait for ye, m'lady?" he eyed her pretty face wonderingly, rather concerned about leaving her there alone.

"Nay," she tossed him some coins. "Keep the change, driver."

"Thank ye, m'lady."

Morgana listened to the sound of muffled hoofbeats fade away into the darkness, then, drawing a deep breath, she pounded upon the doors to the main portal of the prison.

"Who goes there? Whaddya want?" a sleepy voice finally responded after what seemed like hours.

"Lady Keldara. I want to see my husband."

"Go 'way. 'Tis late."

"Open up. I have urgent business with his lordship.

313

If you don't open these doors immediately, I shall call the law," Morgana threatened determinedly in her nastiest voice.

The guard gave her a sour look as he opened the doors, but Morgana paid him no heed.

"You do not need to accompany me. I know the way," she told him icily.

"'Uh!" he grunted. "From what I understand this will be one o' the last times you 'ave to visit this place."

She cast him a withering glance, then started down the dark, narrow corridors, passing through the main jail before she reached the chamber where her husband was confined. Mister Crotchetts eyed her acidly.

"I wish to see my husband. Open this door."

The jailer grumbled under his breath, but took the ring of keys from his belt, selected one, and unlocked the cell. Rian started fitfully at the sound of the rusted hinges and threw his arm up to shield his eyes from the sudden, bright light of the lantern.

"Morgana!"

She drew the tiny pistol from her bag. "Do not make a sound, Crotchetts, or I shall blow your head off," she told the jailer softly.

He and Rian both stared with amazement at the weapon she held so purposefully in her hand, and Crotchetts's eyes fairly bulged out of his head with fright. He made a choking noise in his throat, but no words would come out.

"That's right, Crotchetts," she continued in the same soft voice. "Now take those keys and unlock the manacles on my husband."

Without a peep, he did as she said. Rian rubbed his chafed wrist and ankles vigorously, trying to start the flow of blood circulating again.

"Rian, take those keys away from that resident of a pigsty," she almost smiled. "I'm sure I do not need to warn you to keep out of my line of fire."

"Morgana, what do you think you're doing?" he

314

asked as he relieved Crotchetts of the ring of keys. "Have you gone daft?"

"Nay, my Lord. I'm breaking you out of jail, of course. Any fool can see that. I'm afraid you," she turned to Crotchetts, "will be forced to spend a most unpleasant evening in this filthy little cubbyhole. Be careful that the rats do not eat off your toes while you sleep," she mocked the horrified jailer, who immediately began blubbering for her not to leave him there.

"Heartless female," Rian appraised her coolly after they'd locked Crotchetts in despite his whining pleas. "Now what do you propose to do?"

It was a simple and brazen plan, so plain and bold, Rian agreed, that it would probably work. There were few guards in the prison at night and the passageways were so dark that Morgana hoped to smuggle her husband right out of jail and through the main portal.

"Funny how people miss what's under their very noses," Rian whispered in the wavering light. "Come on then."

They started down the winding corridor to the main jail encountering no difficulties until Morgana spied another turnkey.

"Hide yourself in the shadows," she hissed and saw her husband disappear. Then, "Good evening," to the approaching jailer.

" 'Ere. What are ye doing 'ere?" he demanded to know.

" 'Ere, luv?" Morgana altered her pattern of speech. "Why, one o' the prisoners, luv. 'E wanted a bit o' fun and the guard saw no 'arm in it. Most likely 'ad 'is palm well greased, I 'spect. Wouldn't ye, luvvy?" she nudged his ribs and gave him a broad wink. "Course, the prisoner got a little rough," Morgana allowed her cloak and cape to fall back from her shoulders slightly so the man could feast his eyes on the small amount of rounded flesh the torn material, which she held together with one hand, now displayed. "Me new dress is purt nigh ruint. Well, guv'nor, I'll jest be moseying on 'ome now," she saw the lustful glint in his eyes. Lord, what if he asked to purchase the wares she was supposedly selling? Before he even opened his mouth again, she said, "Blimey, I wouldn't be at all surprised but what that bloke gimme the French disease, too. 'E were filthy!"

She saw the jailer recoil in disgust and barely suppressed her choked laughter. To her utter mortification, she heard Rian gasp smotheringly in the darkness and surmised correctly that he was trying to do the same. She began to cough loudly, causing the turnkey no end of dismay when she managed to explain between rasps that she feared she had the consumption besides. He hurriedly bade her move along, then disappeared into one of the twisting passageways as fast as his legs would carry him.

"Rian?" she called softly.

" 'Ere, luv," he mocked laughingly from the shadows.

"Be still," she snapped. "That wasn't funny. We almost got caught because of you."

"I'm sorry, sweet," he apologized in the face of her worried frown. "It won't happen again."

They reached the outer gates of the main portal without further mishap and Morgana managed to distract the guard's attention long enough for Rian to slip through without being seen. She breathed a sigh of relief when the heavy doors banged shut behind them.

"Morgana, you are a constant source of amazement to me," Rian kissed the palm of her hand gallantly.

"My lord, if you stand here mooning over my charms and talents, we will never get away. Now come on!"

They ran from the shadows of the prison, twisting and turning down the narrow streets until they could see it no longer. Rian barely suppressing a nasty shudder at the sight of the gallows, for executions were conducted publicly in London. He wondered briefly how many would have gathered to jeer him at his hanging. Finally they paused to rest, Morgana gasping for breath and Rian leaning against the wall of a building for support, panting from the exertion. He ached all over and realized the months of confinement had taken their toll.

He glanced at Morgana's face in the blackness, partially illuminated by the light shimmering from the lamps, then with a sigh of great longing and desire, he bent his head and kissed her hungrily, all the months of pent-up waiting and wanting finding their release as his tongue ravaged the inner sweetness of her honeyed lips.

"Oh, love, love," he whispered hoarsely. "You don't know how much I've missed you."

To his surprise, she flung her arms around his neck and kissed him back feverishly, her small tongue entwining with his own softly, hesitantly.

"Mag," he groaned. "I cannot take you here upon the street like a common trollop, but I fear I cannot suffer much more of this sweet torture either."

They hailed a hackney and rode the rest of the way to the docks, her head upon his shoulder as they nestled tiredly in the seat of the hired coach. It had all been so easy. Morgana could scarcely believe they'd gotten away with it.

If Mister Harrison was dumbfounded to see them, he masked his surprise well, although he did exclaim fervently that he was glad the Earl was not to hang after all.

"I always knew ye were innocent, Cap'n," he spoke proudly. "And me and the lads will sail with ye to the ends of the earth if ye so desire."

Rian thanked him for his considerate opinion, then ordered him to shove off. With a wide grin, the first mate barked the command to the crew and set about to raise the sails.

"Look lively, lads," he called out to their scurrying figures. "We're heading for chopsticks and China dolls!"

"Do we not sail for Ireland then?" Morgana asked Rian, her arm about his waist. How good it felt to lay her head on his shoulder and let him carry the burden of the decisions once again.

"Nay, love. I must let this matter cool awhile before

317

we return home. 'Twill be time enough then to decide how to clear my name."

"And mine," she murmured worriedly, the murder of Lord Chalmers haunting her bonnie face.

"Eh? What's that?" Rian gazed down at her momentarily, his face filled with concern.

"I will tell you in the cabin, my lord. 'Tis not wise for other ears to hear."

"As you say, sweet," he wondered what could be troubling her. If he could get the charges against him dismissed, there would be no reason for any to be pressed against his wife for helping him escape.

Shivering quietly, Morgana stood upon the deck of the *Sorceress* with her husband's arm about her shoulders and watched as the ship slid slowly, silently out of port; and England faded mistily from sight.

Chapter Twenty-three

The night air soon turned cool. Tiny droplets of moisture formed, swirling into a grey mist that hung over the waters like a pale, hushed shroud. The waves struck the hull of the ship with a gentle slap as the vessel sliced forward into the darkness. Morgana shivered as the wind touched her with icy fingers, for she felt chilled in spite of the cloak which caressed her lithe body as though it had been her lover, and she was glad when Rian suggested they seek the warmth of the cabin.

He lit the lamps and sank gratefully into the warm tub of water Harrison had thoughtfully provided, scrubbing himself diligently in an effort to rid himself of the vermin which crawled upon him. When he had finished, he shaved as well.

Morgana studied his face carefully in the shadows, noting the fresh, hard lines left from prison life and the whiteness of the scar slashing across his cheek. His hair, as black as the chasms of a world without a sun must have been, hung shaggily unkempt, curling about the nape of his neck in soft tendrils. Prison had changed him. Once he had been languid, moving with careless, lazy grace; now he prowled like a panther with restless, suppressed violence.

His green eyes smoldered with hot embers as they raked her now, the desire naked upon his face sending little shivers of excitement tingling up her spine. How would it be, she wondered, if I now gave myself willingly into his arms? Would he later mock my weakness and use it to make me grovel at his feet? Aye, he would enslave my heart and keep me prisoner to his will, for then he would be certain that he had won this mad game we play between us. 'Tis the challenge that makes him hunger for me so and the knowledge that though he possesses me he has not chained that part of me which flies unfettered from his touch. He does not own my soul, and that is what he desires.

As always, she felt mesmerized by his gaze and when his fingers closed about her wrist to draw her near, she did not protest. Her lips trembled under his flaming kiss and she felt close to swooning. She did not realize how much she had missed the feel of his hard, demanding mouth upon her own.

Rian took his time, savoring the lush sweetness of her taste, quenching the thirst for her which had slowly grown upon him in prison. He could scarcely believe he held her in his arms. Morgana! He spoke her name aloud, and felt her quiver at his touch. His lips nibbled her ear gently, and he found that his hands shook with excitement and longing as he unfastened her cape, fumbling with the tiny buttons. He looked at the torn material of her gown and the teeth marks plain upon her breast with anger. What lustful roué had dared to trespass upon his beloved terrain? He raised his eyes to Morgana's, searching her emerald depths for some sign of her betrayal, and touched the wounded breast lightly.

"How came you by this, love?"

She shuddered in his arms and could not face him. "Oh, Rian, it was horrible! 'Tis what I wished to speak with you about in privacy. My God," she pulled away from his grasp. "Rian, I—I've killed a man."

Bit by bit between her racking sobs, the entire sordid story was told. He had no doubt from her tears and frightened face that it was true. So, Chalmers was dead. Rian was sorry only that Morgana had killed the man herself. He would have liked to strangle the bastard with his bare hands; still, he did not feel cheated. It was only as she continued with her tale that his heart hardened against her. Lord, what a fool he'd been. She had not saved him from the hangman's rope out of love as he'd hoped. No, he should have known. She desired only to save herself from the same fate and had needed his assistance. He cursed himself a simpleton a thousand times for believing that she'd wanted him.

Morgana finished speaking and cast herself, crying, upon his chest, but she found no tenderness in his embrace, for Rian's arms were like granite around her and his eyes were as cold as flinty steel when they looked upon her face.

"There's no need to be angry, my lord. Truly, Lord Chalmers didn't—" she faltered in light of his jeering gaze.

"Oh, I have no doubt that you saved yourself quite admirably, my dear," his voice was harsh. "I fail to understand why you thought to have need of me at all. Why, you could have strutted about this ship with a whip and lashed my crew to order. They would doubtless have been as defenseless against your fury," he sneered at her.

She drew away from him, the fear and puzzlement at his tone plain upon her face. "My lord, I didn't mean—"

"Do not seek to play me for the fool, Morgana. I know full well there is naught between us, naught between us," he repeated. "Save this."

His mouth closed down upon hers cruelly, forcing the parted lips open as his tongue pillaged the yielding gentleness within. His hands ripped at the torn cloth of her gown, finishing the shredding as it fell away from her body. He threw it on the floor, tearing savagely at her remaining garments, driven on by the ache in his loins, sharpened to a keen hone by his enforced celibacy, then forced her down upon the bed. He was wild in his hunger and fury, and hurt her with his roughness, undaunted when she cried out in pain and fear.

"No, Rian! Not like this, please," she begged him, but to no avail.

He clamped one hand cruelly over her mouth. "Do you plead for mercy, love, or do my ears deceive me? Can it be that you have missed me, have hungered for my kisses?" his low laugh grated. "You have them now and say me nay. What manner of deviltry is this?"

"I hate you!" she spat when his hand strayed to her breast, taunting the hard nipple which blazed under his touch. "How dare you treat me thus? I should have let them hang you!"

"No doubt you would have been a merry widow as you were before when you thought me dead," he muttered in her ear. "What poor buck did you have waiting in the wings this time, sweet?"

"A better man than you," she lied mockingly.

"Tell me, love," his hand tightened about her throat. "You have the most slender neck," he whispered. "Do you know that I could break it with my bare hands?" his fingers closed threateningly as if to throttle her. "How many lovers laid upon you thus while I languished in that hell?"

Morgana was really frightened now. God, did he mean to kill her? His black eyebrows were drawn together fiercely and his rugged face took on demonic proportions in the flickering lamplight. For a moment, she believed wildly that he really was the devil everyone claimed.

"No one," she gasped. "There's been no one, my lord. I swear it. I only spoke so to hurt you."

"To hurt me, Mag? I grow weary of the small wounds you seek to inflict upon my soul," his mouth traced wet circles upon her breasts.

She moaned and struggled beneath him as he leaned his weight upon her. He was too strong. She could not push him away. She reached up and raked his face, her nails leaving five bloody scratches upon the white of his scar.

"You bitch!" he breathed, grabbing her hands and pinioning them over her head. "Have you learned nothing? I told you once that I master those things I possess and I meant it."

"I am not a thing, my lord," she hissed. "And you will never master me."

"Ha!" he jeered. "I take you even now and you are powerless to prevent it," his hand dropped between her thighs, caressing gently though she sought to close her legs against this intrusion.

"You have no right," she whimpered softly.

"No right, Mag? By English law, you are my wife and by that same law, I own you. I can do anything I like with you, to you," he emphasized his words mockingly with his hand. "Aye, anything I like."

"No, Rian, please," the tears streaked her face as she felt the mounting of pleasure between her thighs.

" 'No, Rian,' what?" he spoke softly, rolling his body over on hers, his knees forcing her thighs open wider for his entrance. His shaft pierced her, sending waves of hot fire flooding through her veins. "Answer me, sweet," he panted hoarsely. "Say you want me."

"No, I—"

"Say it, by God, or I'll—"

What he would have done, she never knew, for just then she began to quiver, and the earth quaked and broke within her, sending tremors of exquisite pleasure coursing through her body over and over again.

"Aye, I do, I want you," she moaned before she gave herself up to the sweet invasion of his deep, slow thrusts.

Madame Frampstead crept upstairs softly and laid her ear to her brother's door. It was quiet, almost too quiet. Had Harry succeeded with his foul plan after all? Timidly, she knocked upon the portal, expecting to hear his loud, bellowing voice demand who stood without. But there was no answer save silence. Quietly, she turned the knob and went inside. The sight of her brother's gross, stiff, blob of a body stretched out on the floor, wallowing in its own pool of congealed blood, sickened her. She closed the door quickly and hurried to his side. Aye, he was dead, cold to the touch and as rigid as a rock. His blank, sightless eyes glared up at her recriminatingly from their little folds of fat. His mouth hung open as if in a state of dumbfounded shock, the spittle still upon his face. Maria Frampstead stared down at him, and then she threw back her head and laughed.

Lord and Lady Brisbane were none too happy about being rudely awakened in the midst of the night, especially when they'd spent a very late evening at Almack's and had only just retired. Nevertheless, when the maid informed them that Louis waited in the drawing room with an urgent message from Lady Keldara, they bestirred themselves to see what was the matter.

"I'm sorry if I've awakened ye," the tiger apologized upon seeing their state of dress, "but Lady Keldara insisted I give this letter into no one's hands but yours." He held out the sealed billet.

Brad tore it open while Anne read over his shoulder.

London, England, September 5, 1814

My dearest Brad and Anne—I write this note in utmost haste in hope that you will help me. This very eve Lord Chalmers revealed to me at a horrid gaming hell that he knew Rian was Gentleman Jack. He said he could save my lord's life and tried to strike a most abominable bargain with me. When I refused, he attempted to force himself upon me and I killed him. During the struggle, he made it known to me that he murdered Sally. You must get Madame Frampstead, for I'm sure she has the entire story and was in on it up to her neck. I have no choice but to flee the country or stand trial for this deed. If all goes well, my lord and I will be upon the high seas by the time you receive this message. Please try to help me. I am desperate!

Affectionately yours,

Morgana

The young couple read this rather disjointed missive with some confusion.

"Why, she says she's killed Lord Chalmers, Brad," Anne was aghast. "And that 'twas he who murdered Sally. How can this be?"

"Louis, where is her ladyship now?" Brad eyed the curious tiger askance.

"I don't know, m'lord. She told me to deliver some baggage to the *Sorceress,* then to bring ye that message. Then she took off in some 'ired 'ackney. Is it true that she kilt some lord?" his face looked incredulous. "Why, she didn't appear like she'd jest committed a murder. Cool as a cucumber, she were."

"Louis," Brad spoke sharply. "You must fetch the Bow Street Runners at once. Tell them to proceed directly to Madame Frampstead's establishment, that you have reason to believe a crime was perpetrated there this evening. I shall meet you there. And for God's sake," he gave Louis a stern glance, "babble of this to no one. If Morgana has succeeded in somehow getting Rian out of jail, they must have time to escape."

"Aye, m'lord. Right away, m'lord."

Brad hurried into his clothes and Anne helped him into his greatcoat.

"Oh, Brad. You will be careful, won't you? I know how much Sally meant to you," she bit her lip, "but we don't even know if this preposterous tale is true."

He glanced at her concerned pixie face and smiled reassuringly. "I'll try not to be gone too long, Anne."

And with that she had to be content.

Brad was almost as fine a whip as Rian, and the wheels of his curricle clattered furiously over the cobblestones as the vehicle careered wildly through the narrow, twisting streets, splattering mud and water as it went, for by this time, a light rain was beginning to fall. He hauled on the reins roughly, paying no heed when the high wheels of the curricle wobbled precariously and the coach reeled threateningly in the darkness. Louis had kept his word, for the Bow Street Runners were already at Madame Frampstead's when he arrived.

The pinch-nosed butler tried to block his entrance, but Lord Brisbane shoved him away angrily. "Where is Madame Frampstead?" he demanded.

"Upstairs, my lord, but—"

Brad did not wait to hear more. He took the winding steps two at a time, fairly stumbling into the crowded room. He could not believe the sight which met his eyes. Maria Frampstead was kneeling beside the dead body of Lord Chalmers, laughing hysterically, seemingly oblivious to the Bow Street Runners who were attempting to question her.

See here, you can't come in here. Who are you anyway?" one of them noticed Brad.

"Lord Braddington Denby, the Earl of Brisbane," Denby gave the man a cool stare. "I believe I may be of some assistance. 'Twas I who sent for you."

"Indeed? Then perhaps you'll tell us how you knew of this nasty incident," the Runner eyed the unpleasant sight grimly.

"I received this evening a rather puzzling missive from Lady Keldara—"

"The Irish rebel's wife?"

"Lord Keldara is not an Irish rebel," Brad spoke coldly.

"Do you have this message with you?" the Runner, Mister Smythe, decided it would be best not to argue the point.

"Unfortunately, no. However, that is not important. Lady Keldara informed me that Lord Chalmers," he indicated the fat corpse. "Had—er—attempted to force himself upon her and that she'd killed him, in self-defense, of course. She also insisted that this same man

326

was responsible for the brutal murder of my wife some years ago."

"Oh, she did, did she?" Mister Smythe looked at him skeptically.

" 'Tis the God's truth," Maria Frampstead wailed suddenly, grabbing everyone's immediate attention. They stared at her tear-streaked face as she began to sob and waited for her to continue. "Harry was mad. He belonged in Bedlam," she choked. "He loved your wife," she told Denby pleadingly. "He didn't mean to kill her, but he was out of his mind. He went to your house one night to beg her to run away with him and she laughed in his face. She'd never given him reason to believe that she returned his devotion. She started screaming and he struck her, trying to shut her up. She fell and hit the bedpost. The blow killed her instantly. He came to me for help and I gave it to him," she covered her face with her hands.

Mister Smythe gave her time to compose herself, then said, "Pray, continue, Madame Frampstead. Why did Lord Chalmers come to you for aid?" he helped her to a chair.

She spoke again on a calmer note, an almost serene, resigned expression coming over her face. "He was my brother. He—he bought me this place and he held it over my head, threatening to close it if I didn't do what he said." She shut her eyes tightly for a moment and prayed they would believe her, for she could not bring herself to tell these stern-faced men of their incestuous relationship. "Then a couple of weeks ago he ordered me to take a note to Lady Keldara, asking her to meet him here this evening. He was crazy, I tell you. Harry thought her ladyship had conceived some sort of devotion for him. It was the same thing all over again," Madame Frampstead started to cry again quietly.

"But why would Lady Keldara even consider keeping such an appointment, especially in your establishment? No offense, Madame Frampstead," Mister Smythe coughed discreetly.

"Harry said he could prove Lord Keldara wasn't the Irish rebels' leader like everyone thought. He told me he'd seen the Earl in Sussex in November and he intended to bargain with her ladyship."

"And what was this bargain?" Mister Smythe was becoming more curious and interested by the minute. He'd never been assigned to such a scandalous case in his life.

"Well," Maria Frampstead swallowed hard. "He said he'd tell the magistrate about seeing the Earl if—if Lady Keldara would consent to becoming his—his mistress. She must have refused and he attacked her. You can tell there was a struggle," she indicated the disorderly room. "Harry enjoyed beating things. He was extremely cruel."

"I'm afraid I'm going to have to take you into custody, Madame Frampstead," Mister Smythe spoke severely, but his expression was gentle. He felt rather sorry for the woman. He turned to Lord Brisbane. "I don't imagine there'll be any charges pressed against Lady Keldara, although she will have to make a statement. Leaving the scene of a crime is a serious offense, but it's a plain case of self-defense, and I'm sure the magistrate will take into account how distraught she must have been. With Madame Frampstead's testimony, she shouldn't have any trouble," he said. "Do you know where she is by the way?"

"No, I don't," Brad lied. "I'm afraid her message was so urgent and confusing that I hurried right here. I've no idea where she might have gone. I'm sure she only turned to me and my wife because her husband was in jail, and wrongfully, so it seems," he added.

"I'll see that it's brought to the proper attention," Mister Smythe promised.

It was a promise the Bow Street Runners did not have to keep, for by morning, all of London was abuzz with the news that the notorious Earl of Keldara had escaped from Newgate Prison, and that he and his wife had disappeared.

Morgana awakened slowly. She ached all over and there were purplish bruises on her throat and breasts. Why, she wondered, had her husband suddenly turned so cruel, become so rough? What had she done to provoke him so? She could not recall anything she might have said to cause his anger. Surely he did not hold the incident with Lord Chalmers against her. It had been no fault of her own and, besides, he'd killed many men. She herself had seen him slay two of them. No, that could not be the reason. What then? She did not know.

His hand was snarled in her copper tresses and she attempted gingerly to pull them from his grasp, but he opened his eyes lazily and grabbed her wrist.

"Nay, do not fly away just yet, my dove," he whispered softly.

"Please, my lord. You hurt me."

He propped himself up on one elbow and eyed the marks on her creamy flesh with distaste. It bothered him to see her pale skin so marred, but he did not blame himself for its occurrence. The wench deserved that and more.

"I will be gentle, love, when you learn to obey me," his voice was low as one hand traced tiny swirls across her belly.

Morgana lay very still, the fright and hatred plain upon her face. "I will not beg for mercy again, nor surrender to your embrace, Rian," she said stonily.

"Ah, but you will, sweet, you will."

He took his fill, but had no pleasure from it, for she kept her word and lay as still and silent as a statue, and he withdrew from her with some measure of disgust. With a muttered oath, he dressed and flung himself out of the cabin.

Morgana smiled mockingly to herself when he had gone, pleased that she had won some small amount of the battle against him.

Later, she dressed and ate the light breakfast Harrison served, then she went on deck for her morning walk. Rian eyed her with displeasure and had to repeat an order to Timmons, the bosun. Morgana tossed her curls haughtily and turned her back on him, and he clenched his fists at her insolence before he strode away without speaking.

"Good morning," she stopped to chat with Jeb briefly, for ever since she'd heard him play the guitar he had been one of her favorite crewmen.

"Morning, m'lady," his smile crinkled up the weathered corners of his eyes.

"I hope I'll be hearing the melodious sound of your guitar this evening," she said brightly.

"If it is m'lady's pleasure," he replied.

Soon the other crewmen gathered around, for unlike most sailors they had become inordinately fond of her ladyship and had decided that a woman on board the ship was not such bad luck after all, contrary to popular superstition. They begged her to tell them how she'd managed to break the Earl out of jail, and she gaily regaled them with the story. Rian, overhearing her remarks, got a most sour expression on his face. Damn the wench! Must she make a fool of him in front of his men as well? He walked over to the little knot of seamen, most annoyed by her behavior.

"Don't you men have work to do?" he growled.

They eyed his irate face with some surprise, then remembered his jealous temper and hurriedly recalled their most pressing duties, muttering their sorrowful excuses to Morgana as they went.

"Stay away from my crew," he spoke coldly, then marched away without another glance, thereby missing the pink tongue Morgana childishly stuck out at his retreating figure. With a frown, she returned to the cabin, cursing him for spoiling her fun.

He's the most beastly man I ever knew, she told herself silently, flopping into a chair. How dare he order me about like a slave? I won't stand for it! He struts about up there like some banty cock in a barnyard, expecting me to bow and scrape to his slightest whim. The devil with him, she grabbed the Chinese box, picking angrily at the elusive locks. I swear I'll make him rue the day he ever took me to wife. I shall blow hot and cold until he is daft with puzzlement, smile or frown as strikes my fancy till he is wild with confusion. I shall have my small revenge against him for this cat and mouse game he plays with me. She laughed aloud at the thought. He'll beg someone to hang him when I get through, she vowed.

That evening Morgana put her plan into operation, completely ignoring Rian's dark looks and fierce eyebrows. It would not do to smile upon him too quickly or else he would suspect what she was up to. So after dinner, she gave him a withering glance, gathering her cloak and hurrying out of the cabin before he thought to stop her. The faint, whispering notes of his guitar led her to Jeb's presence.

"Jeb," she spoke quietly. "Would you teach me how to play?"

If he seemed surprised by her request, the old seaman masked it well and said that he would be happy to instruct her. Thus it was that when Rian strode out of the cabin thirty minutes later in search of his wife, he found her holding Jeb's guitar, her fingers learning the patterns for a few simple chords. He stopped short in some consternation, having expected to find her flirting amidst a group of encouraging sailors. He could find no fault with her behavior, for her face was a picture of concentration as she strove to place her fingers on the right frets and strings while Jeb corrected her with patience, his conduct almost fatherly, for he was at least twenty years older than his young pupil. Neither of them noticed Rian in the shadows, and, after watching for a few minutes, he turned and walked away without speaking. If the wench wished to play the instrument, it did not trouble him. Perhaps it would give her something to do on the long voyage.

Now Morgana, with her husband's tacit approval, was able to continue her lessons. She was a willing and apt student, and progressed rapidly. Jeb soon found himself looking forward to the evening lessons. He had lost both a wife and a daughter in the Caribbean Islands, and his captain's pretty bride filled a void in his life. His face beamed with pleasure and pride when she was able to play her first song, albeit somewhat hesitantly and with a couple of minor mistakes. The look of delight on her face at his praise more than compensated for the hours of patient instruction he had provided. Although the crew teased him unmercifully and he became the butt of many risqué jokes, Jeb continued to look on Morgana as nothing more than the daughter he might have had.

It rained, grey and dismal, drizzling down from the overcast clouds like salty tears. Morgana gazed out of the window in the cabin pensively, the strain of the voyage beginning to tell. Rian had grown more sullen and withdrawn of late, scarcely speaking to her at all. Even his mocking remarks were better than this cold silence she was forced to endure. If she attempted to communicate with him, he turned on her like a snarling wolf, hungry to lay the blame on her hatred of him before he grabbed her roughly and sought to quell his desires with her trembling lips and creamy flesh. He went about his daily chores, brooding darkly, to the point of being curt with even his crew, causing them to wonder what had brought about his black mood.

Morgana bit her lip. It did no good to dwell on the matter. Perhaps it was not a good idea to antagonize him after all. She was starting to feel as though she toyed with a dangerous animal, a beast who might at any moment break the chains which held him and spring upon her ferociously, tearing at her slender throat. Unconsciously, her hands went to that white column, remembering the deadly sound of Rian's whispered words as his fingers had tightened there threateningly, and she wondered momentarily if it had been he who'd tried to kill her at Shanetara. It seemed so long ago, so far away, that she'd almost forgotten it. Had Rian?

Chapter Twenty-four

Morgana splashed about gaily in the bathtub. How nice it had been of Harrison to catch the rainwater in buckets for her and save it for her bath. She had indeed grown weary of the feel of salt water against her skin. The liquid was soft, silky, with a fresh, clean scent which mingled headily with the lilac fragrance she always used. She scrubbed herself fiercely, making her flesh tingle and glow warmly in the lamplight. Rian, hunched over his desk, muttered an oath under his breath as the quill he was using made a huge, dark ink-stain on the ledger. Damn the wench! He could not concentrate with her lolling in the tub, trickling water upon the floor. The aroma of her perfume drifted to his nostrils, wafting gently, enticingly. Morgana smiled to herself as he slammed the ledger shut and jabbed the quill back into the inkwell.

He pushed his chair back and turned to survey her mockingly. The water played about her rosy breasts enchantingly and one curl dripped and twisted about the nape of her neck where it escaped from the mass of tresses she had piled atop her head. She lathered herself luxuriously with the scented soap, holding the sponge high as she squeezed it, allowing the bubbling droplets to trickle down her throat and breasts, paying no heed to Rian, seemingly intent on this pleasure. She lifted one leg daintily, her breasts cutting wide arcs in the water as she stretched her arms down its length, rinsing her toes. She turned her head away from his gaze, noting the desire that flickered in his eyes, not wanting him to view the triumphant smile which lurked about the corners of her mouth. Aye, she thought, look well, you fool, and see that I am a woman and not the thing you call me.

Slowly, sensuously, she eased herself from the tub, draping the folds of a linen towel about her silken, shimmering, dripping flesh. It clung to her curves invitingly as she pulled her hair free, allowing the cascading mass to tumble down her back. With her brush she began to stroke the fiery tresses, her green eyes slanting under half-closed lids as they met Rian's reflection in the looking glass.

She parades before me as though we were lovers, Rian mused silently. Does she seek to seduce me? Why this sudden change of heart?

He took the brush from her hand and began to comb the tangled locks himself. A stiff, frozen mask fell upon Morgana's face. Brilliant, she thought remotely as she saw herself in the mirror. I should have been an actress. She pulled away from his touch.

"I am capable of completing the task of grooming myself, my lord," she spoke coldly.

He glanced at her face, devoid of all expression, with some measure of surprise, for only a few moments past her lips had been inviting, he could have sworn.

What manner of game is this, he wondered? Does she not realize how the sight of her thus must stir me? She flaunts her creamy breasts before me, then becomes a marble statue when I but lay my hand upon her. Does the wench seek to drive me daft? Aye, his eyes, narrowed in sudden, dawning light, and a mocking smile played about his lips. She seeks to tempt me with with her charms, then lie beneath me like a cold sculpture so that she may laugh at me when I find no pleasure in her arms.

He tossed the brush on the table and seized her wrists, pulling her to him. Morgana closed her eyes tightly, prepared for his rough rape. To her surprise, his mouth came down on hers gently, teasingly, his tongue parting her lips softly. He wrapped his hands in the mass of copper curls, twisting her face up to his so that he could hold her still as his lips travelled to her temples and ears, then down her throat to her breasts as he loosed the towel and it dropped to a crumpled heap about her feet. He kissed her endlessly, lingeringly, hungrily until she thought he would never stop, till her mouth trembled beneath his and she felt the ache of desire sweep through her traitorous body and gave a low moan. His hands cupped her swelling breasts as he buried his face in them, his mouth upon the engorged nipples before he dropped to his knees and his tongue sought her even there, between her thighs, his fingers caressing the rounded curve of her buttocks.

Morgana could not help herself. Her fingers fastened themselves in his hair, pulling him to her. His kisses traced their way back up her belly, leaving her quivering, demanding, and unfulfilled, her body screaming its need of him. God! What was he doing to her?

And then she was in his arms and he was carrying her to the bed, pausing only to take off his clothes before he slid in beside her and parted her thighs. Sobbing, she put her arms around his neck and forgot everything as he smiled down into her eyes, strangely, triumphantly, and drove home within her.

Morgana was awakened by a crashing roar which sounded like thunder booming in the sky. It's going to rain again, she thought, trying to free herself from Rian's strong embrace, one hand tangled in her hair as his knee rode randomly between her thighs. She was not prepared when her husband roused himself and flung himself from the bed like a madman, pulling his pants on with great haste before he slammed out of the cabin, yelling at her to stay put. She pulled the sheet up over her nakedness, cringing in fear. What had she done to cause this sudden outburst?

There was another crash of thunder, and she sprang from the bed and dressed. Rian knew she was terrified of storms. How dare he leave her here alone to brave its fury? She heard him shouting orders at the crew and the pounding of feet across the deck as they scrambled to obey. With a brief pause, remembering his anger the last time she'd disobeyed him, Morgana left the cabin in search of her husband. Why, there isn't a cloud in the sky, she stared confusedly at the blue horizon. Just then there was a puff of white smoke and the thunder rang again, rocking the *Sorceress* and drenching Morgana with the sudden spray of water which followed. She saw a ship in the distance through the clearing mist of fumes and realized with a sudden terrifying clarity that they were being fired upon.

Good God! Had the British army come this far to arrest them? The men were loading the cannons on the *Sorceress*, and she knew they meant to fight. Even now one cannon spoke with a loud roar as the sailor lit its fuse, belching flames and smoke as it sent its contents hurling toward the other vessel. There was an answering blast from the attacking ship and the *Sorceress*'s spanker mast toppled, the crossjack in shreds. Morgana grabbed the rail for support, cowering at the flying debris, when Rian spied her and bellowed angrily at her to get below.

Once in the cabin, she paced the floor nervously, wondering what was happening on deck, cringing every time a shot was fired and the *Sorceress* quivered sickeningly on the rolling waves. After what seemed like an eternity, she heard the crew give a roaring cheer and surmised that they had won, at least she did not hear the sound of grappling hooks against the side of the vessel and although they had slackened speed, she knew the damaged mast could have caused that.

Rian came in a moment later, hot and tired, and

covered with gunpowder, the sweat dripping slowly down his chest. He eyed her with distaste.

"You little fool. You might have gotten killed up there."

"I didn't know we were under attack," she returned his cold stare. "I thought it was a storm and I was frightened. Was it—was it the British army, Rian, come to arrest us?"

He saw the fear in her eyes and her scared, white face, and his voice softened. "Nay, love, though doubtless you would have wished it had they boarded us. 'Twas a Barbary gunboat. I hate to think what those marauding pirates would have done with the likes of you."

Morgana shivered under his gaze. She'd heard tales of the Moorish pirates, how they sold the women on blocks into slavery and turned men into eunuchs.

"There's no need to worry, sweet," Rian put his arm around her. "The *Sorceress* is well armed, and I have withstood worse attacks. I was planning to put into Cádiz anyway for supplies. It will delay us more than I like to repair that damaged mast, but it can't be helped."

Morgana was so relieved that he did not beat her for being disobedient that she made no protest at all when he led her to the bed, leaving wet, sweaty streaks of black gunpowder across her breasts and belly.

Cádiz was teeming with people, for it was one of the few cities that had managed to resist successfully the French siege during the Penisular War and was the seat of the Spanish Cortes, the representative assembly composed of the clergy, nobles, and burghers. Morgana had never been to Spain and now she gazed with frank delight upon its dark-haired citizens, white-washed houses with red-tiled roofs, and the funny little donkeys Rian told her were called burros. They plodded through the narrow streets heavily burdened with baskets full of wares, their tails whisking briskly at flies and their sleepy lids almost half closed in the heat, seemingly oblivious to the noise around them. Here and there ragged children played, their smiles white in their brown-skinned faces, while the peddlers hawked their goods in shrill Spanish voices, and a blind old man on one corner near the cathedral begged for alms. Rian tossed him a couple of coins as they passed.

Harrison had been dispatched to see about repairs for the ship, and Rian permitted the rest of the crew shore leave, for they had grown as tired as he of the bland diet of scanty provisions they'd left England with.

Morgana hung on Rian's arm gaily, ignoring the curious stares of passersby, and drank in the sights with joy. They walked past a group of peasant women washing clothes in the fountain in one of the squares, chatting amiably as they worked. Occasionally a small child ran up to them, begging to show them the city or perform some other service. Rian would give each of them a copper and tell them that he did not need their help at the moment. Morgana watched face after face light up as their grimy fists closed over the coins before they scattered into the crowd.

Her husband had promised to take her to the marketplace. She strolled among the crowded booths, pinching the fruit and vegetables to be sure they were ripe, but not too ripe, then Rian dickered with the vendors, for he spoke fluent Spanish and Morgana knew none at all. He never ceased to amaze her. She marvelled at the ease of his manner with the peasants. Soon she had a basket filled to overflowing and Rian told the last child who approached them that he might carry la señora's purchases if he were careful. The lad beamed delightedly, saying, "Gracias, señor," and lugged the heavy burden along behind them with utmost care.

They paused before a booth hung with brightly colored skirts and serapes, and Morgana insisted on buying several, along with some frilly, scoop-necked blouses.

"For, you know," she told Rian, "that I did not bring many clothes in my haste and what few I had you have torn from my back."

He was not daunted at all by her tone of voice as he laughed mockingly and said that she would just have to learn to undress faster. Nevertheless, he paid for them and the clothes were added to the little Spanish boy's growing bundle.

"Rian," she glanced at the lad with some concern. "Do you not think you should help him, or at least hire another child to carry some of the load?"

"Nay, love. He would be most insulted. Besides, at this rate, I shall run out of money long before the lad tires of his burden."

Morgana gave him a frowning glance and tossed her curls defiantly. "No doubt they have a gaming hell somewhere in this city where you can replenish your purse easily enough."

"Are you so eager to be rid of my company, sweet?" his hand went about her waist as he kissed her ear.

"Stop it, Rian, people are watching." She tried to pull away from him, and he laughed and let her go.

He bought her some bangles though he said they were cheap and would tarnish, but she liked the tinkling sound they made upon her wrist and told him she didn't care. But he put his foot down when she asked to purchase a cage with two canaries, saying he damned well wasn't going to listen to that racket during the entire journey and that the birds probably couldn't withstand the long voyage anyway.

Finally he suggested they go check into a hotel and freshen up, for it would soon be time for dinner. She readily agreed to this, wanting to try on her new clothes and take a bath, and soon they were installed in a very quaint white-washed building with wrought-iron balconies.

"Well, how do you like Spain?" he asked after paying the small lad for his services and depositing Morgana's many bundles on the bed in a heap.

"Oh, I think it's wonderful, Rian," she said, busily poking through the packages. At last she found the one she wanted and carried it off to the bathroom with her, two giggling chambermaids having prepared the water for her toilet.

They studied her curiously with their dark eyes. Morgana tried to explain to them that they need not stay to help her, but she could not make them understand. Their fingers worked busily at the hooks of her gown and shoes, then they pinned her hair up with a great deal of chattering and laughter, none of which she could understand. They seemed to be enchanted with her copper curls, saying, "Su pelo rojo es muy bonito, señora."

When she'd finished with her toilet, they helped her into the multicolored skirt and white blouse, and showed her how to lace up the sandals she'd seen and made Rian buy at the last minute. They nodded their heads, smiling brightly at her appearance, exclaiming their approval in gay voices as Morgana spoke the only Spanish word she'd learned all day, "Gracias."

At last they left and she went into the adjoining room to find Rian. He was slouched in a chair and, of all things, smoking a cigar. She stared at him in amazement, for she'd never seen him smoke, and only observed that he took a pinch of snuff upon occasion.

"You look like a gypsy wench, love," he said upon noting her attire, for when she walked the ruffled skirt showed a well-turned ankle and the low-cut camisa clung to her breasts revealingly. "I shall have to take my pistols with me this evening, lest some hot-blooded Spaniard attempt to take advantage of your obvious charms."

He pulled her onto his lap, his kiss tasting of tobacco and wine upon her lips, before she laughed shakily and pulled away from him, insisting that she did not want to have to take another bath and besides, "I'm famished," she claimed, blushing under his approving gaze.

They ate outside in the garden of one of Cádiz's more popular restaurants, dining on hot corn tortillas filled with spicy meat and smothered with melted cheese, and rice with jalapeño pepper which made Morgana reach hurriedly for her wine glass to ease her flaming mouth. The night air was still, filled with the heady fragrance of exotic flowers and the throaty melodies of the many birds which mingled pleasantly with the strains of a flamenco guitar someone played in the darkness.

Rian sipped his wine and lit another cigar, inhaling

deeply, watching as Morgana reached out and broke a white blossom from its stem, placing it behind one ear. She glanced across the table at him, and for one fleeting moment their eyes met and locked, and something flickered, stirred so that neither one of them even breathed for the barest instant of time, then a clattering of castanets broke the spell as two dancers began the traditional flamenco steps; and Morgana turned away as Rian swore softly in the night.

They walked along the beach for a time, but neither one of them could help remembering that night upon the sands in Ireland, and so finally they returned to the hotel.

In the morning, they exercised the horses, for Louis had thoughtfully remembered to board Lucifer and Copper Lady as well as the baggage Morgana had entrusted to him.

Four days later, they were again at sea; and Morgana had only the lovely ebony guitar inlaid with mother-of-pearl that Rian had given her as a surprise their last night in Cádiz to remind her of the enchanting spell of Spain.

The wind filled the sails gently as they left Cádiz. Morgana stood at the rail, the spray of salt water cool and refreshing against her face. She breathed deeply, running her tongue over her lips, savoring the taste of the sea. They journeyed to Africa, carefully skirting the coastal areas of the Barbary pirates, the dark Moors who'd attacked them once before. The days and nights ran in a steady stream, and Morgana drifted like the ship upon the sea, waiting, wondering. Rian seemed strangely subdued, but she did not know the reason for his aloofness.

She dared not ask him about it for fear that he would turn bitter and mocking. She thought about his many moods at night when she sat against the rail of the *Sorceress* with Jeb and the melodies of their guitars echoed in the stillness of the evening. For the first time in her life, Morgana began to have an inkling of what the man she had married was really like. But she did not recognize the demon which drove him on any more than she realized why she deliberately obscured her own understanding of him with hatred.

Only when they lay in the darkness together did she accept the intensity of her need for him.

She tossed the book she was reading onto a table. She could not keep her mind on its contents anyway. What was the matter with her? She could hear Rian above on the deck, pacing back and forth like a caged animal, restless, haunted. Morgana played with the puzzle box for a time; but, as always, its secret eluded her and she soon gave up the attempt. At last, she picked up her cloak and went out on deck, standing in the shadows of the tall masts.

Aye, there he was, studying the stars, his tall figure outlined against the black of the sky by the silver moon. She did not walk up to him, but instead watched him covertly. He was like the Chinese box he'd given her, elusive. She shivered as the night breeze swept through her cloak with its chilly fingers, and Rian noticed her for the first time.

"What are you doing out here, Mag?"

"Watching the stars, like you," her voice was soft, searching.

"They are beautiful, are they not?"

"Aye," she replied.

He pointed out several constellations to her, many of the names reminding her of the romantic Grecian myths.

"They say we are each born under particular stars and that is what shapes our destinies," Morgana mused aloud.

"Aye," he answered. "We were both born under the sign of Pisces."

"But you are eleven years older than I am. I'm twenty-three now, and you are thirty-four. I don't understand how one small group of stars could affect two lives so far apart."

"I do not know either, sweet, but it has, has it not?

342

'Twas fate which brought you to Ireland and made you my wife," he gazed down at her.

"Nay, 'twas the iron will of an old man and your own desires which brought that to pass, Rian. I shall never believe otherwise," she pulled her cloak more closely about her.

"Who is to say, love, whether we make ourselves what we are or we become so because fate has intended it?"

"You are a man, my lord. You make your own rules, ignoring those society has set down for us. Is that destiny or your own arrogance?"

"Mayhap a little of both. I take those things I desire and no man shall say me nay," he put his hands upon her shoulders. "But perhaps that is because I have lived long enough and travelled far enough to understand that one must sometimes take chances regardless of the cost. Others sit and wait in the shadows, watching life slip by because they are too cowardly to seize opportunities. Aye," he spoke softly, his green eyes searching her face. "My pride and my arrogance may be to you unbearable, but those are the very qualities by which I survive, my lady. My wits and daring are sometimes all I've had to rely upon. I do not know where one's soul goes, Morgana, after its body has long since turned to dust, but I never want to stand before a god on some judgment day and say that I've wasted my life."

"And do you not believe that there is such a god, my lord?"

"I don't know, love," he answered truthfully. "I told you once before that I live only for today and for the heritage I hope someday to leave to my children."

"Perhaps we shall never have any, Rian," his nearness was causing Morgana's heart to flutter again.

"Then, my lady, there shall be none to reap the harvest I sow and strangers shall rule at Keldara, and gaze out over the green lands I now hold."

"That would hurt you then, Rian?"

"Shall I answer that question, madam?" he suddenly yanked her to him roughly. "Do you seek to pry into my mind to find some new way in which to injure me? Think you that it does not grieve me to have a wife who despises me and wants no child of mine?"

" 'Twas you who chose to wed me, my lord. 'Tis you who can free me from this bond of bitterness," she turned her head away.

"Nay, Morgana, you yourself hold the key to the golden cage you claim I have placed around you. You have aught to do but unlock the door."

"You speak in riddles, Rian. I don't understand you."

"Then that is your misfortune," he released her.

She glanced at his dark face momentarily, wondering what it was that he sought to tell her, then with a small cry, she ran to the cabin.

Several days later they sighted the coast of Africa where they would put ashore. The Slave Coast was marked vividly by the wild, unbroken line of surf and beach which swept savagely into the dense green of the jungle, the cottonsilk trees, the tamarinds, the fedi palms, and the mangroves.

The *Sorceress* halted several yards away from shore and Rian indicated that this was as far in as the ship would sail, explaining that the horses could not be brought ashore, for the deadly tsetse flies would kill them.

"Morgana, go into the cabin and put on your most comfortable clothes. No layers of petticoats or corsets. You will have a hard enough time breathing in this humidity. And put on your stoutest high-topped boots," Rian ordered.

She did as he asked, glad that she was not to be left behind. But she felt a momentary chill of foreboding when he handed her a slender dagger, saying only, "Africa is a savage country, Mag. You may have need of this." It rode casually against her thigh where she strapped it, giving her some slight sense of security and reassurance.

They lowered one of the longboats and she climbed

down into it, aided by the willing hands of the many men who accompanied them. Harrison was left in charge of the ship. They rowed toward the shoreline, headed for the mouth of the huge river that poured into the ocean. They travelled steadily up its winding course, deep into the steaming mesh of growth. The dark stillness of the land was broken by the chattering cries of the monkeys as they swung from the twisting branches of the palms, sending multitudes of brightly colored birds screaming toward the sky. Bullikookoos crowed raucously from the treetops and once in awhile a cry like that of a woman screaming would pierce the air. Rian said it was a leopard.

Morgana had never seen a black man before and the sight of her first one was not pleasant. He was floating face down in the river, a huge hulk of rotting decay, the nappy head matted with twigs and leaves. She glanced at her husband, a sick feeling churning in her stomach.

"Slavers did that. Either the man was sick or a cruiser spotted them," he replied to the question on her face. "Slave trading's illegal, Mag. But the law can't do anything about it unless it catches the slavers with the goods, so more often than not they simply throw the evidence overboard."

"But—but these are people," Morgana stammered.

"Not to the slave traders, sweet."

It soon appeared that Rian's reasoning was correct because they encountered several more bodies along the way, as well as pieces of floating flesh which had rotted away from the corpses. Many scaly tree trunks lay in the river along with the dead men, but Morgana discovered to her horror that these occasionally sprang to life furiously with huge, gaping jaws and cold, beady eyes.

"Crocodiles. Keep your hands well inside the boat, Mag," Rian warned casually but did not appear to be too concerned.

The thick moss which covered various parts of the river clung to the oars as green slime. The men rowed forward, the steady splash of the oars punctuated by the strange calls of the wildlife, the only sounds in the ominous, heavy silence.

"There she be, Cap'n, Bobosanga," one of the men raised an uplifted hand.

Morgana followed his gesture and was surprised to see a scattering of low huts clustered along the river's edge. The buildings were made entirely of bamboo, and some of them were plastered with a thick, caked mud as well. Several longboats made their way between a vessel, the *Dragon Queen,* which was anchored in port, and the docks. Morgana saw that they carried cargos of blacks, all chained together like animals.

"Rian, you do not trade in slaves. Why have we come here?"

"There is much to buy besides slaves, sweet. You will see later on."

They pulled ashore and were met instantly by a multitude of Africans clamoring for gifts and cracking their fingers together in a form of greeting. Many of them stared at Morgana with unconcealed curiosity, for the sight of a white woman was indeed rare. She saw Rian toss them many of the beaded necklaces and some of the bolts of gay material he'd purchased in Cádiz for this purpose. They grinned broadly upon receipt of the presents, then stepped back a little distance to make way for a hulking man with yellowish skin. Morgana realized at once that he was a mulatto, for both Spanish and negroid characteristics mingled almost grossly in his face.

"Captain McShane," he spoke perfect English. "Welcome once again to Bobosanga." The man's eyes strayed toward Morgana questioningly.

"Don Mojados, greetings." Rian disembarked from the longboat and shook the mulatto's hand, then turned to help Morgana alight.

She stared at the huge man with as much curiosity as he displayed toward her, noting the sharp contrast between the kinky hair and thick lips and his rather hawlike nose and high cheekbones.

"Don Mojados," Rian broke this silent perusal. "Allow me to introduce my wife, Lady Keldara."

"Ah, 'tis indeed a pleasure, my lady," he at once bowed low over Morgana's hand. "You must forgive me for staring, but it is not often that my eyes are treated to the sight of a white woman in this land, especially one with such beauty as yours. Come this way, please."

He led the way to one of the larger huts, pulling aside an animal skin flap so that they might enter. There were many other such skins on the floors, as well as huge cushions of fine silk and small bamboo tables. In one corner was a grass sleeping mat.

"Sit down, sit down," Don Mojados waved an impatient hand. "So, you come to trade with me?" he inquired of Rian after they had been seated on the cushions and served a refreshing fruit drink by a comely black girl.

"Aye, as always."

"I take it then that you still have no desire to bargain for slaves?" the mulatto wiped his brow with a large handkerchief.

In the steaming humidity. Morgana could feel her loose camisa sticking to her shoulder blades and the sweat trickling down the hollow between her breasts. The high boots chafed her legs and she cursed Rian silently for making her wear them.

"Nay, Don Mojados. The usual goods suit me just fine. Blackbirding is a nasty business."

"But a very profitable one, no?" the man laughed, his belly heaving greatly in the attempt. "Still, if you have no stomach for it, I shall not argue the point. You are fortunate. Another caravan is due to arrive in a matter of days. You may retain this hut for your own use as long as you like. Naturally, I shall expect you as my guests for dinner. This is Bawku," he presented the black girl who'd brought the drinks earlier. "My third wife. She speaks English and shall attend your needs."

After the strange man had left them, Morgana stretched wearily out on the mat, the heat making her extremely drowsy. Rian said he must go and check on the accommodations for the crew members who had come with them, and left the hut shortly afterwards. She did not know how long she slept before she was awakened by what she thought dazedly sounded amazingly like giggles. She turned and saw several black women peering at her through a crack in the hut. One of them giggled again. She sat up and they stepped away from the small building in some fear. Morgana called to them, motioning them to come inside and, after some initial hesitation, they filed in and sat regarding her in solemn silence. Evidently they spoke no English.

Bawku came in just then and a smattering of guttural language followed, after which she turned to Morgana.

"They wish to know if your hair is real," she explained rather timidly. "Please excuse their bad manners. I will send them away if you wish. I did not know they were disturbing you."

"No, let them stay," Morgana was curious about these women who appeared before her, naked to the waist, their lower halves covered with grass skirts. Some of them held lighter-skinned babies to their breasts, and she realized that most of them were mulatto children, offspring of the slave traders probably.

She carried on a conversation with them for some time, with Bawku acting as interpreter, but the women scurried away quickly at her husband's return, giggling again as they averted their eyes from his face and hurried past him.

Dinner that evening was a feast. There were chickens stewed with almonds and rice, whole suckling pigs stuffed with grapes and tamarinds, yams drenched in goat's milk and honey, and fresh coconuts that Rian showed Morgana how to crack and scoop out for the white meat within. There were all kinds of syrupy liquors—palm wine, creme de cacao, and absinthe.

Afterwards, they were entertained by African musicians bearing strange instruments—drums made of skins drawn tight over the drums and guitar-like instruments strung with animal gut. It was not music as Morgana knew it, although the chants accompanying the din were haunting. A coal-black girl with sinuous limbs and gleaming skin danced by the firelight, slithering like a snake to the stirring rhythm. She had long ebony hair which hung freely down her back. It was curiously straight, in sharp contrast to the nappy heads of most of the other women. Her eyes were dark and slanted, and her moist lips had been smeared with some kind of berry juice to make them richly red. She was virtually naked, wearing about her waist a white sash just long enough to hide her womanhood. There were glittering bangles on her wrists and ankles, and huge, gold hoops dangled from her pierced ears. One side of her face had been scarred so that the flesh formed tiny beads of skin which stood out in an intricate pattern across her cheek.

Her belly undulated, seeming to have a life of its own as her hips swayed sensuously in the flaming light, buttocks rounded and firm as she whirled, breasts small and pointed. She was tall, with long, slender legs, and bare feet which almost appeared to float over the hard ground as she danced.

"My second wife, Talorza," Don Mojados murmured in the darkness. "Her father was a Moor and her mother a Dahomean. She is not as bright as Bawku, perhaps; she speaks no English and refuses to learn, but, as you can see, she has her charms."

Morgana could not get used to the idea that Don Mojados had five wives. She found the practice rather distasteful and wondered if his brides were not all jealous of one another, though how any of them could have wanted to wed the burly man was beyond her understanding.

The music jangled abruptly to a halt and Talorza collapsed gracefully upon the floor of the hut amid much applause, then she rose and inclined her head proudly in acknowledgment, leaving the hut without a word. Everyone seemed a little relieved at her departure and Morgana noticed that beads of sweat had formed upon the brows of many of the men present, including her husband's.

When they retired to their hut for the evening, she stripped the garments from her body, ignoring the desire which flickered in Rian's eyes, and sponged herself off with the tepid water Bawku had thoughtfully left in an earthen bowl. Then she stretched out upon the sleeping mat, letting the heavy net which was draped around it to keep out the insects fall back into place. Rian smoked a cigar and after a time, he, too, stripped and washed, then slid in beside her, making them both sweat in the darkness as he pressed his lips upon hers and took possession of her.

In the days that followed, Morgana learned much about the Africans and their way of life. She discovered that the slavers did not go into the jungle to hunt down the black men as she had thought, but simply sat and waited for the caravans to arrive; for it was the blacks themselves who sold their own people into slavery, bartering away captives from rival tribes or sometimes a shrewish wife whose tongue they could no longer endure, or an overly ambitious son who sought to become chief before his father's death.

She met the rest of Don Mojados's wives: Nako, who was scarcely more than a child and whom the mulatto had married primarily out of pity in order to keep her from being ravaged by a group of drunken slavers; Lakhamané, the fourth wife, who was like Bawku, sweet tempered and bright, of the Fulani tribe, who had skin almost the color of honey; and Kolokani, the first wife, whom everyone in the village feared because she was a voodoo priestess and spent hours with the juju man, concocting potions and calling on Damballa and Legba to aid her with their spirits.

Kolokani warned Morgana of the evil spirits that could eat one's brains or breath, and blow out the light behind one's eyes. The Mamaloi made Morgana a little Ouanga packet and told her to wear it always to protect her from the evil ones. Morgana put it around her neck, the leather pouch falling down between her breasts. Rian laughed at her and said it was foolish, and besides the roots in it stank, but she did not wish to make light of Kolokani's religion and refused to take it off. After a time, he ceased to tease her about it. But Morgana could not like Gberia, the juju man. She did not know why Don Mojados tolerated him, for he frequently charged the blacks with some crime, after which he insisted that the accused drink a bowl of sassywood to prove his guilt or innocence. Since the bark juice was poisonous, the man he indicated generally died. She told Rian that she thought it was positively disgraceful for Don Mojados to allow it to continue.

"He can do nothing about it, sweet. 'Tis their way of life," Rian explained.

Nevertheless Morgana ignored the juju man when she saw him and felt vaguely uncomfortable when he peered out at her through the slits of his plumed mask.

Some days after the McShanes's arrival, a tatooing of drumbeats echoed through the jungle to signal the arrival of the caravan. Don Mojados immediately sent out fanda and bungee, or dash as it was sometimes called, food and wine, and presents to impress the chief of the caravan favorably before bargaining.

Bawku told Morgana that there would be a grand colungee and much palaver as the men dickered over the goods once the coffle arrived. To Morgana's surprise, she saw that what she had been told about the blacks selling themselves was entirely correct. The only difference between the leader of the caravan and the slaves in his coffle were the tethers upon the slaves' throats. Those doing the selling strutted around with short lashes which they were quick to use if one of the slaves got out of line.

There were also some women with the coffle who bore huge baskets of goods upon their heads. It amazed Morgana that they were able to balance these heavy baskets perfectly as they walked. No doubt these contained what Rian hoped to buy.

Don Mojados's men immediately ran forth upon sighting the caravan and began the custom of dashing, and they greeted one another by cracking their fingers enthusiastically.

Morgana was glad that the caravan had arrived. At last, Rian could get what he came for and they could return to the *Sorceress*. There was something oppressive about this dark land that threatened to engulf her if she stayed here much longer. She didn't know if it was the heat or the weird chanting at night that disturbed and frightened her most but she was eager to leave.

She had not bargained, however, on the African people's love of show. First the chieftain spent a great deal of time explaining the exact nature of his visit to Bobosanga. Drinks and cigars were served while Don Mojados lounged patiently in his chair, listening carefully even though both he and the chieftain knew precisely what business was to be transacted. Then there was the usual feasting, and once again Talorza danced. The celebration dragged on into the night and Morgana grew weary, leaning her head tiredly on Rian's shoulder. She knew without asking by this time that there would be no bargaining for goods this evening.

"How long does this go on?" she yawned, covering her mouth with her hand and casting a quick glance about to be sure no one had seen. The Africans were tireless it appeared.

"It depends usually on what the chieftain thinks he can get for his coffle," Rian informed her. "Outtaye is shrewd and drives a hard bargain. This might last for days."

Morgana did not realize she had fallen asleep until Rian shook her awake. "Come on," he hissed in the darkness.

She stmbled after him blindly, tripping once or twice before he put out a hand to steady her. Once inside the hut she fell onto the sleeping mat without even bothering to remove her clothes.

"Get up from there," he ordered.

"No! Leave me alone," she finally decided that the palm wine she'd drunk was as bad as a drug, she felt so weary.

He laughed softly. "Do you wish me to strip those garments from you, my lady?"

She rose tiredly then and dragged the clothes from her flesh, for she had brought very few with her and could not afford to have him rip any, which he would doubtless do if she did not obey and quickly.

"Perhaps I should have brought you here sooner, Mag. You aren't usually so quick to obey." He seemed amused.

" 'Tis this horrible place. There's something foreboding, evil about it. This place is dark and twisted. I feel that the jungle is eating me alive."

"Hush Mag," he pulled her into his arms, kissing her gently. "It has the same effect on me, also. 'Tis like a slow erosion of the mind. No white man can live here for long. That is the secret of Africa's survival. We'll be leaving soon."

He stroked her hair and wondered if Kolokani had been preaching more of her voodoo magic to his wife. Still, Mag was right. There was something somber in the air.

Rian pressed his mouth against Morgana's and was surprised to find that her lips clung to his gently, almost trustingly. No doubt it had something to do with the amount of potent palm wine she'd drunk, but nevertheless he felt oddly pleased; and when she did not protest, he led her to the sleeping mat and lay down beside her.

His hands roved over her flesh, caressing the soft curves and the rounded breasts; and, as always, the touch and smell of her aroused his passions quickly. He spread her thighs, stroking gently until he knew she was starting to respond. She gave a soft, trilling cry as he entered her, arching her hips to receive him as he drove deep within her, murmuring huskily in her ear. For that precious, fleeting moment, Rian knew the sweetest joy on earth and joined her cry with his deeper one, then he lay still, kissing her face and throat as he buried his lips in the soft, billowing cloud of her fiery tresses.

Rian opened his eyes slowly. The bright gold of the African sun steamed through the cracks in the hut like hot, melted ore, but that was not what had awakened him. He cocked his head. There it came again, a loud, urgent shouting and the hard, running throb of bare feet against the ground. He pulled on his pants, pausing briefly to study Morgana's sleeping face, now so childishly innocent without its hard mask. He wondered if he would ever understand the enigma of his wife. Last night she had been almost loving in his arms.

Don Mojados was already in the square when Rian stepped outside. A crowd of blacks had gathered, as well as his own crew. They were listening intently to the somewhat incoherent, breathless pleas of a young white man who knelt on the earth in the middle of the circle. He was a priest, Rian saw with surprise.

"You must come, Don Mojados," the minister was saying. "We are desperate and truly fear for our lives."

"What goes here?" Rian asked, passing through the clearing made as the others stepped aside for him.

"Forgive me. I am Father John, sir. I'm here to beg the aid of Don Mojados."

"I'm the Earl of Keldara," Rian introduced himself. "What seems to be the trouble, Father?"

"Forgive me, my lord," the priest spoke again. "But I'm from the mission farther north. Father Samuel asked me to come, for he is too old to have undertaken such a journey. The natives have grown increasingly restless of late and Father Samuel fears they might do some harm to the mission. We could not defend ourselves and need assistance to quell the disturbance. My lord, we have two nuns with us," the young minister's eyes were beseeching.

"You say there has been no attack as yet, Father?" Rian asked.

"No, my lord. But the natives have been so different lately. We had been making excellent progress, but most of them suddenly stopped coming to mass, and the little ones no longer frequent the school Sisters have established."

"Old ways die hard, Father. Maybe Damballa and Legba are too strong for your god to oust. Don Mojados," Rian turned to the burly mulatto. "Do you mean to send aid to the mission?"

"Captain McShane, I am a good man, but I cannot be

sending men off on what might well be a wild-goose chase. I have a business to run. Outtaye will sell his slaves elsewhere if I leave Bobosanga now."

"As you wish. I shall take my crew to the mission. I trust you will choose the goods of the type you know I desire and have them delivered to my ship?"

"But of course, Captain McShane."

"Oh, thank you, my lord," the priest took Rian's hands gratefully. "May God's blessing be upon you."

"Save your prayers for someone who needs them, Father. I'm the devil himself, or haven't you heard?"

With that, Rian walked away curtly, calling to his men, leaving the stupefied priest to wonder what manner of man the Earl was to risk his life for people in service of the God he did not worship.

Morgana raised herself on one elbow, blinking rapidly at the sudden shaft of sunlight which split the hut as Rian entered. She saw at once that something was wrong, for his face was set in a hard, grim line. She drew the light sheet up to cover her nakedness.

"What is it, my lord?"

Briefly, as he threw his clothing into a bundle, Rian explained the situation. "I must go, Mag. It may be nothing, but I've seen what these blacks do to captives. 'Tis not pleasant."

"But you can't just leave me here!" she cried. "You can't! I can't stand it here, Rian. You promised we'd go."

"I know, sweet, and I'm sorry, but there are two nuns at that mission. White women, Mag. I just can't let the natives take them. You'll be safe, Morgana," he shook her arm off gently. "Samson will guard you with his life. I'm leaving him here with you."

The hulking giant of a crewman was called Samson by the rest of the sailors because of his size. It was rumored by the men that he'd killed many opponents with his bare hands. Morgana shivered silently.

"Please, my lord, something will happen to me, I know it. Don't leave me here," she bit her lip.

Rian laughed. "Mag, I've told you a million times that your imagination runs away with you. I'll be back before you know it."

He walked away with the young priest, his crew trailing single file behind him. She watched until he disappeared into the dense, steaming growth of jungle. Then she sank down upon the sleeping mat and cried hot, angry tears at his departure. The beast! He would leave me here with these savages, that burly mulatto and his voodoo queen wife, she thought sulkily, then immediately felt contrite, for they had been kind. Ha! Mayhap he does not even intend to return; she was suddenly anxious, all her old fears returning. Perhaps this is how he means to be rid of me.

She tried to calm herself down and presently sent for Bawku to pour her a sponge bath in the earthen bowl, somewhat reassured when she spied Samson's great figure just outside the door, a heavy sword in his hand.

"Just look at me, Bawku," she fumed angrily upon seeing her reflection in the looking glass. "I look like an ugly old hag. No wonder my lord goes off seeking new interests."

Her red hair was tangled and hung straggling down her back, and her face had burned and peeled.

"There, there, my lady. I'm sure it is no such thing," Bawku soothed gently with her silken voice. "Such delicate skin. You were not made for our African sun, I'm afraid. I know a plant whose juices will restore the moisture to your face, and you can wash your hair. Then you'll feel better, no?"

"Aye, perhaps," Morgana was still feeling sorry for herself.

"Of course you will. Come, let me help you. I swear the Cap'n won't know you when he returns."

Morgana continued to grumble under her breath, but she allowed Bawku to do as she pleased and was mildly startled to find that the woman did indeed know exactly which plants might soothe the burning flesh or cleanse the soiled hair.

"Such fine hair," Bawku talked as she washed, her

nails scrubbing Morgana's scalp expertly. "And such a beautiful color. The other women thought it was a wig at first."

"Aye, I remember," Morgana smiled briefly, recalling the curious giggling of the African girls the day they'd come to the hut.

When she had finished, Bawku wrapped Morgana's head in a clean tropical white towel, then massaged her flesh with the pulpy juice she'd extracted from some plants earlier.

"Um, that feels good, Bawku," Morgana purred, closing her eyes.

"You wait and see, my lady. This what Talorza uses to make her skin shiny, make it glisten all over."

"She's so strange, Bawku. I've never heard her speak."

"Bah, that one. She thinks she is too good for the rest of us. She dance and smoke the dreamy grass. She not here most the time. Her body here, but her spirit not in shell. Very bad. Legba come one day and eat her breath if she not careful," Bawku prophesied darkly.

"Dreamy grass? What's that?"

"Bangi. It makes the spirit wander, like too much palm wine, leaves shell empty. Legba come and blow out light behind one's eyes someday. Kolokani say it is true."

"No, Bawku, it must be some kind of drug, that's all," Morgana was beginning to feel sleepy again.

Tiredly, she closed her eyes.

The air was hot and still, with the heaviness of an impending storm. Rian hacked with his dagger at the overhanging branches with their wide leaves. Sweat poured into his eyes and the mosquitos plagued him and the men unmercifully. Only the few blacks who travelled with them seemed unaffected by the droning insects. The path they followed to the mission could not even be called that, it was so overgrown with the jungle. He wondered how the priest had ever found his way to Bobosanga. Well, no doubt the man knew the territory well. He'd said he'd lived here for five years, trying to convert Africans to

Christianity. Rian thought it must be a thankless and difficult chore, highly unrewarding to say the least. He'd never seen any Christian black men, but then, he almost smiled to himself, he didn't really know any Christian white men either.

They camped beside the riverbank, lighting a fire to keep away the wild animals that prowled restlessly at night, each man keeping his weapons close to his side. Rian checked his duelling pistols, to be sure they were loaded and ready for use, and that his rapier and dagger were within his reach.

He closed his eyes, unaware that the young priest studied him curiously in the darkness, wondering what this unusual man was thinking. Rian had long ago learned how to sleep guardedly with one ear cocked for any unexpected danger. Only when he felt completely safe could he relax and fall into a deep, almost drugged slumber. Morgana's angry face floated into his mind. Lord! She hadn't been happy about him leaving her there at Bobosanga almost as though she really cared about his leaving. No doubt he would feel the sharp bite of her tongue upon his return.

They travelled two more days before they reached the mission, or what was left of it, for they were two days too late. It had been burned to the ground. The two nuns were staked out spread-eagled on the ground, spears driven through their palms and feet. Rian didn't need anyone to tell him what they'd suffered before dying. The thick, congealed blood had attracted hordes of ants which covered the corpses like a tiny army, crawling in and out of the nostrils, mouths, and eye sockets of the women, as well as various other places.

"Oh, my God!" Father John moaned and immediately turned away to retch chokingly.

"Where was your God when this happened, Father?" Rian spat bitterly, kicking at the pearly rosary which lay in the dust.

They found Father Samuel a little farther on, tied to a tree. He'd been disemboweled and his throat had been slit. He was still clutching his Bible in his stiffened, rotting hands.

The few blacks who'd been loyal to the mission were dead, too, decapitated and thrown in a little pile on which sat several vultures, gorged with the feast the natives had so thoughtfully provided.

Rian swore at them angrily and they scattered, crowing raucously, flapping their large wings as they hovered nearby, waiting for him to leave.

"Come, lads, start digging and let's get these people buried," Rian turned to the crew.

"But, Cap'n," one of the men began, staring with horror at the putrefying carrions.

"I said, let's get these corpses in the ground," Rian's eyes narrowed dangerously.

"Aye," the man shuffled off.

They sharpened several bamboo trunks and managed to scoop out some shallow graves in which they placed the dead bodies, after which Father John read some words from his Bible. Rian worked right along with the rest, cursing silently to himself. Damn fools! Should have known better, he thought angrily.

The jungle was strangely silent through it all, only the rustle of the cottonsilk trees and brief spurts of monkey chatter breaking the uneasy quiet. A lizard darted through the brush. Then the storm broke, the clouds swirling, darkening, as they spewed forth the driving rains. The men finished stacking the stones on the graves so that no wild animals would dig up the corpses, then they scurried for the cover of the wide palm leaves. Rian, crouched beneath the semi-shelter pondering the remains of the pitiful mission was suddenly struck by a dark, chill sense of foreboding.

Chapter Twenty-five

Morgana was in the hut when the howling Ashanti warriors came, painted and half-naked, descending upon Bobosanga with sharpened spears and arrows. She heard the shouts and ran to the flap to peek out, and dropped it shut immediately at the sight, her heart pounding wildly.

No one could have been more surprised than Don Mojados. He was lounging in a hammock, sipping syrupy fruit juice from a coconut shell, smoking a cigar as little Nako fanned him indolently. In all his life, he had never been so astonished, for Bobosanga had thrived on the banks of the African river for three years and such a thing had never happened. He fell from his hammock and little Nako dropped her palm fan in the dirt, screaming as she ran.

Don Mojados shouted orders to his black servants who were shrieking and attempting to escape into the jungle. The warriors were cutting them down like animals, crowing each time one fell victim to a spear. The Ashantis set fire to the village and the dry bamboo buildings went up in smoke like blades of grass. Outtaye was defending himself bravely, as were the members of his caravan, but they, like everyone else, had been caught off guard.

Morgana ran from the blazing hut, standing in the square miraculously unharmed in the confusion, tears streaming down her cheeks. Samson turned from his desperate battle to call to her, and a spear pierced his chest. He staggered to the ground, blood spewing from the mortal wound.

The battle was soon over, and the dead lay thick and bloody upon the ground, many with heads and limbs severed from their trunks. Some of the women had already fallen victim to the warriors. Morgana saw Bawku struggling with two of them. Without thinking, she ran to her friend's aid.

"Stop it! You monsters," she cried, tearing at them, clawing at them furiously.

It was then that a black man, taller than the rest and magnificently attired in a bone breastplate and loincloth, his face painted with multicolored slashes of dye, a high, plumed headband around his forehead, approached and barked an order. Immediately, the entire village fell silent.

Morgana stared into his savage dark eyes and felt a tingle of apprehension run up her spine. The warrior studied her intently, feet planted wide apart, then reached out and touched her long red hair. She stood immobilized by fear and horror. He muttered something she could not understand, then two others came running up with long strands of liana vines. The chieftain, for surely he could be none other, fashioned these into a braid and wrapped them roughly about Morgana's throat as she cringed in fear, then Don Mojados' five wives were bound to her so that they formed a chain. None of them could move or run away without dragging the others with her. Outtaye was bound separately. Morgana reasoned correctly that the warriors recognized him as a rival chieftain and meant to hold him for ransom. Don Mojados himself the

Ashanti tortured slowly, and it took him a very long time to die.

The sharp point of a spear jabbed Morgana's side none too gently and she trudged forward, the vines cutting into her throat as she sobbed. Nako and Lakhamane screamed and babbled incoherently. Kolokani called to her voodoo gods under her breath, cursing the lives of the warriors with zeal. Bawku trembled and tears streamed from her eyes. Only Talorza was as still and proud as a statue, her stony face showing no signs of emotion.

As they walked out through the remains of the village past the decapitated corpses and the gross, burly body of Don Mojados, whose intestines spilled forth into a little heap on the ground, the rains descended with a roar.

BOOK FOUR

The Bitter Memories

Chapter Twenty-six

The Jungle, Africa, 1815

The blinding rain stung Morgana's face, mixing with her bitter, frightened tears. The natives paid no heed to the torrent, prodding their captives forward, using the tips of their spears in none too gentle encouragement. On and on through the wet, slapping leaves of the palms they trudged. Morgana often stumbled and fell in the slimy forest, only to be yanked to her feet again roughly. Her long, red tresses dripped with the heavy rain and became plastered down against her head. Her clothes were soaked to the skin, and the liana vines rubbed her throat.

She studied Bawku's nappy head, bright with the droplets, before her. That was almost as far as she could clearly see. Once she tried clawing at the thick vines which held her prisoner, but they were as strong as rope and she could not loose the heavy strands. After a time, it no longer even mattered. Nothing mattered at all except for being able to put one foot in front of the other without slipping and falling, without losing sight of Bawku lest they all pull in different directions and strangle themselves. She ceased to feel the driving rain, the choking vines about her throat, the aching muscles in her legs. She decided that this numbness must be some form of protection, for this empty, wooden daze had aided her in earlier crises.

When night fell, the procession halted, taking what shelter was available under the spreading leaves. Morgana dropped tiredly to the ground, resting her head against the trunk of a tree, the others sprawling beside her. The rain drummed on incessantly. The Ashanti didn't even attempt to light a fire, and as Morgana watched them take pieces of fruit from some of the baskets a few carried, she was suddenly conscious of her own gnawing hunger. The tall one, as she had come to think of him, the chieftain, offered her what remained of his own meal when he had finished, but she found she was unable to touch the pieces of half-eaten fruit, and he turned away with a grunt, tossing them into the underbrush.

She slept, only to be awakened crudely a few hours later, the rain still pouring. She and Don Mojados's wives took care of their personal needs together. There was no other way. Morgana thought she had never felt so humiliated in all her life, squatting in the African bush with five other women and trying hard to ignore the warriors who stared at them disinterestedly. She was thankful for the long skirt she wore.

She wondered dimly about her husband and his dark, mocking smile lingered in her thoughts. He would not have been afraid. He would have kissed away her fears with his searing lips, and laughed in the face of the danger. The thought helped her somewhat, although she didn't know why, and she stiffened her small shoulders squarely and trudged on.

The hours turned into days, and the days into weeks, and still the rains descended from the heavens, steadily, droningly. Morgana could not remember when she last had been warm and dry, when she had not walked unceasingly, when she had not slept with her back against a tree, and had not eaten leftover bits of dried fruit and been grateful for them.

No one talked. She could not understand the Ashanti language, which seemed to consist mainly of threatening gestures and grunts. She did not know that they were an intelligent, proud race, well known for their finely crafted goldwork. The captives were too tired, too uncaring, too frightened to speak among themselves. Morgana almost forgot that she possessed a voice, a voice capable of laughing, of crying, of singing.

Once, she had been a foolish, selfish woman, basking in the bright lights and gaiety of London, taking for granted those things that Rian had lavished upon her. Now Morgana saw with a sudden bright, startling clarity that those things she had thought treasures were only bits of tarnished gold, worthless; things that lost their meaning once she possessed them. She understood all too clearly why Rian had considered them as unimportant as those who valued them. What was it Rian had said one night, about the only things worth having were things no one could take away from you? Something about the heart and the soul? Why couldn't she remember now? For some reason she wanted desperately to recall the words he'd spoken. It was no use. She had scarcely listened then, her hatred of him deafening her to what he said.

Weak and exhausted, she travelled ever onward, to what destination she did not know. Did they intend to kill her, these African savages? Then why had they not done so already? The way that tall one looked at her sent shivers up her spine. It was a look women have recognized in men since the beginning of time, the jarring, shocking, exciting, frightening, caressing glance of desire. Men and women killed for it, died for it, built empires and destroyed them for it. And Morgana was alive because it existed in the eyes of a tall black African.

His name was Kassou, but Morgana would never know that, and he was indeed a proud chieftain, as was his father before him, and his grandfather before that. A prince of a race the British must battle for almost a century to conquer and which even then would not ever

369

be totally subdued. Kassou was handsome, regally so, with fine dark skin, and proud, flaring nostrils. He was the husband of seven wives and the father of many children. Privately, he had often thought they were all more trouble than they were worth, and sometimes with a frustrated sigh, he would think that perhaps the white man's way of only one spouse was best. Seven women were not more fun, they were a thousand times more disruptive than just one. They quarrelled among themselves like chattering magpies, fought like tigers for their children, and sulked if he did not take them every night upon his sleeping mat during their respective weeks. He never knew a moment's peace.

Legba, but the pale woman with the hair like fire intrigued him. He had never seen a white woman before, although he had upon several occasions seen white slavers. Only those two females in the strange black robes had been white, he reminded himself sharply, remembering. Funny little creatures with beads in their hands with which they prayed to their god. What kind of god settled for a string of beads, he thought wonderingly? In his village, the gods were worshipped with many rituals, food, and gifts, sacrifices. A very poor god, he sneered to himself, who is not fed and receives no presents.

The white woman's hair lay dank and dark down her back in the rain, but he noted the curve of her breasts with interest beneath the thin blouse she wore. A foolish custom. How did her skin breathe? How did the sun's rays reach it? Well, obviously they didn't or she would not be so pale. But she had stamina, he admitted grudgingly. She had ceased to scream or cry like the others; she was silent like the tall one who looked Arabic. That one had not made a sound. Perhaps he would give that one to Djibasso, his first friend, who seemed to like the woman well enough. But the white one Kassou would keep for himself. He would be the envy of all the Ashanti. Not one could boast of such a woman. Or maybe he would present her to the King at Kumasi. Such a gift would surely raise him in his monarch's esteem. He almost smiled. The others, of course, he would sell to the blackbirders, the slavers.

Kassou sighed as they continued, the rain falling steadily. Soon, the season would pass as it always did, leaving him to wonder if what came next was not even worse. The summer would be hot and humid, and the heat did strange things to men and to the animals as well. Kassou's mind wandered back as he walked to the summer just before the Ashanti ceremonial rituals that would proclaim him a man.

He and Djibasso had been hunting when they heard the piercing scream of the leopard. His village had been without meat for weeks, surviving on what vegetables and fruit they could glean from the forest. The leopard suffered from hunger also, only slow starvation could force it so close to the camp of humans. Kassou could almost feel the sweat on his brow now, in spite of the rain, as he and Djibasso had faced the beast. Its soft pads made gentle thuds upon the earth as it prowled back and forth like a caged animal. Kassou stood stock-still at the sight and cautioned Djibasso not to move, but they were upwind of the animal and its sensitive nostrils caught the smell of fear in the air. It turned and leapt, springing high into the air as it fell upon its prey. At that instant Kassou had begun to function again, his hunter's instinct overtaking his fright. He raised his spear and drove it through the beast's heart. The animal shuddered and lay still.

How proud his father had been that Kassou, not yet even a man, had committed such a feat of bravery. They skinned the leopard. Even now its furry pelt adorned Kassou's hut, a symbolic reminder to his people of his courage.

Kassou turned his eyes upon the red-haired woman again. Would she be impressed? Morgana saw his glance and shivered. She must escape and soon!

Rian insisted that his men move as fast as possible in the blinding rain, driving them with a fury they could not understand. Even he did not know why he pushed them so hard, except for the intangible feeling of dread which had crept over him and enveloped him. He cursed them all without provocation, causing the priest to mutter prayers for the Earl's lost soul as they hacked their way back to Bobosanga.

It took them almost a week because of the rain, and when they got there, what was left of the village was almost totally unrecognizable. The charred remains of the huts were small piles of muddy ashes and the bloated bodies of the dead were swollen and rotted.

Rian stared at the disastrous scene and went momentarily berserk. He flung himself to his knees in the center of the village, howling ominously as he beat on his chest with tortured fists. His men gazed at him in disbelief, for never in their lives had they seen their captain behave in such a manner, and they feared for his sanity. With a knowing glance among themselves and heedless of the rain, they began to examine the corpses, searching for some sign of the flaming tresses and pale white skin that had been the captain's wife. They found none and they trembled with fear when they spied Samson's body, each unwilling to be the one to tell their captain that they believed his wife had been taken prisoner by the Ashanti warriors or was even now lying dead in the jungle.

"Better off dead than a captive of those animals," one of the crewmen spoke darkly. "Poor lass."

"Aye, she were a bonnie thing, our lady," another agreed. "Brave-hearted, too. I seen her give the Cap'n as good as he sent."

The others nodded knowingly, as if this were no mean feat, for they all stood somewhat in awe of their captain.

Rian did not hear these comments, although the men were fairly shouting because of the pouring rain. The only thing that reached his ears was the memory of Morgana's pleading voice. *Don't leave me here,* she had said. *And I* laughed, he thought bitterly. *I never dreamed the Ashanti would come this far, would attack Bobosanga. She was dead.* His winsome, laughing, sulking, sensuous wife was dead, and he had no one to blame but himself. Himself and his damned arrogance. He had killed her as surely as if he'd wielded the spears carried by those ravaging savages.

He wept hot, bitter tears, but his men could not see that. Rian felt a hand upon his shoulder and raised his face to Father John's.

"My son," the priest cleared his throat and wished he didn't have to yell. "Pull yourself together. Your wife may still be alive."

"Nay. I've killed her," Rian choked on the words and the priest barely understood him.

But he understood well enough the raging torment he saw in Rian's eyes that soon hardened into a blinding desire for revenge.

"I'll kill them, every last one of them," Rian's eyes narrowed with determination. "I'll hunt them down like dogs and slay them if it takes me a lifetime. I promise you, Father, her death shall not go unavenged."

His men could not convince Rian that there was a chance Morgana might still be alive, nor could they reason with him to remain in the village and get some rest. He was like a man possessed, and nothing they could say would change his mind about setting out after the Ashanti warriors immediately.

"But, Cap'n, we don't even know which direction they may have taken, and besides, we're exhausted," one of them tried.

"I have no doubt that the Ashanti are returning to Kumasi, their capital city. Those of you who do not wish to follow me may return to the ship," Rian's voice was hard, cold.

None of them did, however. The thought of what Harrison would do if they returned to the *Sorceress* without the captain under such circumstances made such a thing unthinkable. They groaned silently and hauled their weary bodies after Rian, privately believing that the loss of his wife had unhinged the captain's mind.

They could not follow the exact path of Kassou's warriors because the rain had wiped away all the tracks, but Rian had a general idea of the direction they must have taken and he allowed his instincts to be his guide. His face was stony, and he walked and acted like a dead man. He had no mercy on his crew, and he himself appeared to be inexhaustible. His mind wandered and he asked himself a million times why he travelled on instead of returning to the *Sorceress*, for revenge was useless. It would not bring Morgana back to him. He saw her frightened face behind every rock and tree, and the sound of her pleading voice echoed in his mind relentlessly. He despised himself.

For now, when he believed her dead, he was able to admit to himself that he really did love her, loved her beyond all reason, and it was like a blinding fury that started in the pit of his stomach and travelled to his heart with a pain that was almost unbearable. And, yes, he had been afraid to say it, afraid that she would hurt him, mock him as he so often did her. Aye, he had wanted her and loved her with a passion that had almost driven him mad because she didn't return his love, and he had sought to strike out against her because of it. You're a fool, Rian McShane, he cursed himself bitterly, and he vowed that if by some slim chance she was still alive and he found her, he would tell her what was in his heart.

Kassou's village was some distance away from Kumasi and it was there that he took his captives. Morgana cringed as his strong hands cut the liana vines from her throat and shoved her roughly into a hut, separating her from the others. There was a fire going inside and she stumbled toward it, trying to drive the chill of the rain from her body. She sank onto the ground wearily, falling asleep almost at once. She was awakened sometime later by the sound of drumbeats and the chanting of the tribe. With a start, she realized that night had fallen. She was still alone in the hut. She timidly lifted the skin which covered the door to peek out and dropped it shut again at once, for two warriors with spears stood guard. There was no one else in sight, and she was able to determine that the noise was coming from a large hut in the middle of the village.

Morgana shivered and crept back to the fire. She was despearately afraid and wondered what the savages intended to do with her. She remembered the look on the tall one's face and shuddered. Her dazed mind was beginning to clear, the numbness being replaced by the instinct to survive. She had to get away at once while the natives were still celebrating. She might not get another chance. But how? Morgana searched the hut, but saw nothing to use as a weapon. Then with a slight shock, she felt the blade which rode against her thigh under her skirt. Her fingers frantically loosed it from its sheath. There had been no opportunity to draw it before because she had been watched so closely. She considered using it on the two guards outside the hut, but soon decided that she could not kill them both. Her strength was no match for theirs and they might easily arouse the village with their cries. She glanced at the walls of the hut. They were made of bamboo lashed together with vines. Morgana tested one section. It was sodden with rain and bent easily under the small weight she leaned against it. With a sigh of relief, she took the small dagger and set to work, cutting the vines as quickly as possible. In a short time, she had sliced enough of them so that she could push out part of one wall wide enough for her to slip through. Her heart pounding wildly, Morgana stepped out into the darkness and the rain.

Hesitating only briefly, she set off toward the dense undergrowth of the jungle, not daring to ask herself if she could even survive its savageness alone. She ran blindly, having no sense of direction, intent only on putting as much distance as possible between herself and the village. The days of walking had strengthened her leg muscles and now she moved swiftly through the brush, for she had no idea when they might discover her disappearance and whether or not they would pursue her.

That first night she barely slept, climbing up into a tree which she shared with a couple of angry monkeys. They chattered at her fiercely but left her alone after a few menacing gestures, swinging up to the higher branches to watch her with curious dark eyes. She dozed fitfully and at the first sign of daybreak was on the move again, driving herself hard. She snatched a few pieces of fruit, eating while she travelled. Her one thought was to find the river which wound through the jungle and follow its course back to the ocean. She dared to hope that she would be able to hail the *Sorceress* from the shore.

Morgana was grateful for the first time for the rain which fell steadily, for very few things stirred in the jungle because of it. She had roughly determined her position now, although the first light of day was very pale, and she turned southward, positive that sooner or later she would reach the shoreline of Africa.

Kassou was very angry when he discovered her disappearance, but he did not attempt to follow her, knowing that it would be impossible in the rain. He shook his head sadly. The red-haired woman would surely die. Three days later he slaughtered all of the captives except Talorza. He could not bear to look at them because they reminded him of the one with the white skin and green eyes.

After some days of travel, Morgana breathed easier, sure that the warriors did not intend to come after her now, but she did not lessen her caution, for there were other tribes in the jungle and she had no desire to fall prey to any of them. She was glad she wore the stout boots Rian had insisted upon, for the jungle was infested with snakes, and the boots were good protection against the sudden quick darting of fangs. The first time a snake struck, she had almost swooned, staring petrified at the slick, beady eyes of the creature before grabbing a stout stick and beating it to a bloody pulp upon the ground. She'd yanked her boot off and found to her immense relief that the snake's fangs had not been able to penetrate the wet leather. Now she scarcely even worried about it, although she took infinite care not to linger under branches, for she had learned quickly that pythons dropped out of them, coiling around their prey until they choked the life from it.

One morning she woke feeling that something was

different. The dense undergrowth was quiet, and she realized with a start that the rain had ceased. The golden African sun spilled across the land like melted butter, radiant in its new-found glory. She was glad, because she assumed the going would be easier now, but she soon discovered that this was not the case at all. The wild creatures crept from their hiding places to venture abroad in search of prey. Leopards screamed in the night as they prowled in the darkness and more than once Morgana saw their strange, slanted eyes gleaming in the moonlight. Instinct guided her and kept her absolutely motionless at these times, allowing her to breathe a sigh of relief only when the beasts had disappeared.

Her pale, burned skin darkened to honey under the sun, and her clothing became so ragged that she cut most of it away, binding up the long skirt so that her legs were not hampered by the material now. She often wondered how it was that she remained alive, and indeed it was only her own tenacity and miraculous luck that kept her that way. She understood clearly what Rian had been trying to say when he'd told her that sometimes all he had to survive on was his wits, his instincts.

She ate nothing that she had not seen the chattering monkeys consume, for she was afraid she would accidentally poison herself in her ignorance, and she reasoned that if it did not kill the furry beasts, it would most likely not harm her either. But she lost a great deal of weight on such a diet, her rounded curves sharpening to angles.

Once, she caught a glimpse of herself in a stream as she bent to drink and she did not recognize the sharp, pinched reflection that stared back at her, its hunted green eyes too large in the thin face. She gasped, horrified, as another image appeared in the water and she whirled to face an African native. One dark hand reached for her and without even thinking, she pulled the little dagger from its sheath against her thigh and drove it into his chest. He didn't make a sound as he staggered backwards in surprise, blood dripping from the motral wound as he fell. Morgana did not wait to discover if there were others with him. She yanked the knife from his slackened grasp where his hands had sought to remove it, pausing only to wipe the blood away with some leaves before she returned it to her thigh and fled into the underbrush. She felt shaken by the incident, but the long African nights and her furtive struggle for survival had taken their toll. She felt no remorse at all about what she'd just done. Not even the cries of the vultures that soon circled overhead moved her.

Morgana slapped angrily at the mosquitos that bit her tender skin leaving ugly, red, swollen marks upon her flesh, but there was little she could do about the other insects, the ones that crawled inside her clothes in spite of the many times she stopped to shake them out or squash them.

Her eyes puffed up and ran in allergic response to bites, and just when she thought nothing worse could possibly happen, the locusts descended. They came in swarms, in droves, darkening the sky with their millions of buzzing bodies. They got into everything, into the water, into the fruit, into her eyes and mouth, and there was nothing she could do to stop it. She vomited pieces of bugs she had swallowed and still more came. The birds died from overeating and rotted on the ground.

She cried when she stumbled into the open savannah lands, realizing that she had been travelling in circles, and fell upon the earth as a merciful blackness invaded her consciousness.

Rian glanced at the clearing sky with relief, for now he would be able to follow the Ashanti much more rapidly. The rains had depressed him, made him bitter and remorseful. Lines of strain showed about the corners of his eyes and mouth, but he gave himself no quarter nor any of his men. At another time, he might almost have laughed at the odd little procession of exhausted, straggling men, dragging a tattered priest along with them through the bowels of the African jungle. In fact, the more he thought about it, the funnier it became, and at last he did laugh, his raucous howls echoing strangely in the underbrush. His crew shook their heads and cast knowing glances at each other behind his back. Aye, the captain was daft. Just listen to the sound he was making, their silent eyes turned to each other fearfully. 'Twas the devil's laughter, for surely no sane man could find mirth in a situation so grim.

But Rian refused to listen to their suggestions that he needed some rest and did not explain his odd outburst. He shook himself mentally, however, trying to get a grip on his emotions. It would not do to lose control of himself. His men might mutiny and refuse to follow him, and he would need their help later on. Indeed, their sullen faces informed him that they might already have discussed such a plan of action; and with a sigh, he suggested an early night. This seemed to restore their spirits somewhat, but Rian slept with his duelling pistols loaded and his rapier and dagger within easy reach.

This proved to be an excellent precaution, for in the night one of his men attempted to slit his throat. At once he roused himself, flinging the assailant off with a curse. The two men grappled on the ground briefly before Rian's own weapon drove home.

"Now," he faced his men angrily. "Is there anyone else who wishes to challenge my position as captain of this crew?"

Silently, one by one, the men returned to their beds, not daring to meet their captain's eyes. None of them desired to meet with the same fate that Thompson had just suffered.

Some days later they sighted the Ashanti village. Rian snaked forward on his belly to get a better view of the layout. He saw no sign of his wife, but he did spy Talorza, the dancing girl, and knew that he had come to the right place.

The Ashanti were unprepared for attack, which was in Rian's favor, for their warriors outnumbered his crew almost three to one. With the element of surprise on his side, he fired all their buildings almost simultaneously;

and in the confusion of the burning huts he and his men swept into the village, killing as many of the warriors as was possible. The battle was long, bloody and savage; but in the end Rian and his crew prevailed because they had the advantage of firearms and many of the Ashanti were frightened by the weapons and ran off into the jungle.

His mouth tightened into a grim line of determination, Rian lined up what prisoners remained and attempted to question them, using Father John as an interpreter. When they refused to answer, he slit their throats. Three warriors died in this fashion before he approached the fourth. This one was taller than the rest and looked him squarely in the eyes, showing no signs of fear. Aye, Rian thought, this one would be their leader. He turned to the priest.

"Tell him that I know he is their chief. Say also that I am chief among my men and have great respect for such courage. Tell him that I challenge him to a test of strength. If I win, he will tell me what has happened to the red-haired woman. If I lose, he and his people will go free."

"But, my lord—" the priest protested.

"Tell him!"

The African sun was hot, the heat of the blazing huts made the village an inferno. Rian wiped the sweat from his eyes as he stripped to the waist, then picked up an Ashanti spear and shield. He faced his opponent, knowing that this was the one battle in his life that he must win. The image of Morgana's slanted green eyes haunted him and he forced it from his mind with difficulty. He must know if she were dead or alive; and if these savages had killed her, he would slay every last one of them. The Ashanti chief circled wearily and with the first clash of spears, Rian felt his heart sink. It would not be an easy fight. This was no drawing room dandy grown soft from too much liquor and too many women. This was a strong, virile warrior, a man used to battle and primitive conditions, a man whose body had grown tough and lean in the fight for survival in the African jungle.

Time and again spear met shield and retreated to lunge again. Rian could feel himself faltering, but his pride and his heart kept him on his feet as he stared into the chieftain's dark eyes.

His men shuffled nervously, readying their own weapons, for in spite of what the captain had said, they meant to murder these savages if he was killed.

It was only by the queerest turn of fate that Rian won, and indeed years later when he told the story, he would not claim credit as the victor at all. Among the huts set afire was the one belonging to the medicine man. A pit viper kept there in a woven basket managed to escape the flames and slithered out into the center of the village. Both men halted abruptly at the sight of it, then strove to drive each other closer to its venomous fangs. The viper coiled and struck, sending its deadly poison into Kassou's ankle. The chieftain stumbled and fell as the snake lashed out again. Rian drove his spear into the creature, then hurled it into the underbrush. He knelt beside the dying Ashanti warrior.

"What does he say, Father?" his ears strained to understand the soft-spoken words.

The priest hurried to Rian's side. "You are the chosen. Damballa has said it is so. The red-haired one escaped, fled into the jungle. By now, Legba will have blown out the light behind her eyes."

Kassou moaned and lay silent, and quietly Rian closed the dark eyes forever. There was no doubt in his mind now that Morgana was dead. If she had escaped, she would not have been able to survive in the African wilderness. Legba would indeed have blown out the light behind her lovely emerald eyes, as the chieftain had said.

He made no move to stop his men when they slaughtered the rest of the warriors and forced the screaming women to the ground, taking their pleasure of them before they silenced them for good, then looted what remained of the village.

Rian felt emotionally drained and empty. His mouth

was so dry he couldn't swallow. He continued to kneel beside the dead chieftain until the sound of the priest's voice returned him to the present.

"My son, these are human beings your crew is violating and murdering. You must stop it."

Rian shook off the man's arm and strode away angrily. Some of his men saw him going and hurried to catch up with him. Not a one of them looked back at the burning Ashanti village strewn with bloody carrions. One small child who had somehow managed to escape notice wandered out into the center of the village and cried loudly, not understanding that there was nobody to answer his call.

Chapter Twenty-seven

Somewhere in the dim recesses of her mind Morgana decided she must have died and gone to heaven, for she thought she saw a tall blond angel bending over her, his crystal-blue eyes filled with concern, but then the image faded as she again slipped into unconsciousness. Her vision had not been an angel, however.

His name was Taylor Jones and he was very much alive. He was a trapper and trader by nature, a generally quiet, soft-spoken man. He had been out hunting with some of the natives, and the last thing he'd expected to find was a half-dead wench with matted red hair and a face so bitten by insects it was almost unrecognizable. He lifted her up gently, calling to the natives to bring the litter which had been intended for game. He placed her in it without much hope, for he believed she would surely die before the night passed, but nevertheless he carried her back to the natives' village.

There he stripped her and bathed her body tenderly, shaking his head over the condition of her flesh. He made a poultice, spreading it over her skin, then wrapped her in tobacco leaves to draw out the stings of the insects. He sat by her side all night, cradling her head and wondering who she was and how she came to be out on the open savannahs in such a condition. He wiped her feverish brow with a wet cloth and pressed her cracked lips from time to time. It seemed to ease her pain, for she grew less restless, although she continued to cry out occasionally.

Taylor watched her silent battle for survival with admiration, for she clung to her fragile life with determination. By morning, he was sure that she was going to live.

Morgana lay in her unconscious state for several more days, and through it all Taylor sat and watched, and nursed her as though she had been a small child. He held her hands when she called aloud, and spoke to her quietly with his soft, slurring voice, wondering all the while why it even mattered to him whether or not this forlorn little wench survived.

But Taylor was the kind of man who mended broken birds' wings and set them free once they could fly again. He could not abide to see anything suffer, and he felt a strange pity for the red-haired woman. With immense relief he saw her eyes flutter open slowly some days later. For a moment, he felt as though he were drowning in their dark emerald depths. They were too haunting, too mesmerizing, and Taylor felt feelings stirring that he had thought long dead. Then she smiled, and her smile was as beautiful as her eyes, soft, winsome, showing white, even teeth.

"Am I in heaven? Are you an angel?" she asked weakly.

He almost laughed aloud at her questions. "Nay, though for a time I feared that would be your fate."

Morgana studied him quietly for a moment. He was a big man, like a cuddly stuffed bear with his unkempt hair and his beard and moustache. His crystal-blue eyes were serene and serious, as though he had suffered much in his lifetime. He did not turn away from her gaze, but returned it steadily. He looked to be about twenty years older than she.

"Do you have a name, lass?" he asked finally.

"Morgana."

"'Tis a mighty purty name, Morgana. Mine is Taylor Jones. But there, you're tired and it won't do for me to talk with you now. You get some rest."

Morgana blushed under his gaze, suddenly aware that she was wearing nothing beneath the light sheet which covered her body, and that her skin had been smeared with some kind of salve, and bound with leaves. It felt good. The stinging sensation was gone. She closed her eyes and drifted back to sleep, pondering this strange turn of events. Who was this big man who treated her so kindly, and where was she?

In a few days, she was able to sit up and consume the light broth Taylor offered her.

"And how are you today?" he queried upon entering the hut.

"Much better, thank you," she responded, sipping the hot brew.

She discovered that he was from America. He owned a plantation in Virginia, which explained his drawling speech, that was run by his brother. He himself preferred a life of travel since the death of his wife some years before.

"Aye, the place got kinda lonely without her and my brother said he'd look after things if I wanted to get away for a while. That was seven years ago. I've been on the move ever since, trapping and trading. Got me a fine vessel, the *Lucky Lady,* she's called. I sail all over the world and put into Virginia about once a year to see how things are going and to sell my goods. But there, that's enough about me." His eyes suddenly looked startled, as though he were amazed to find himself talking so freely.

Indeed, it had been a long time since Taylor had spoken so many words at one time. He was normally very quiet, preferring to listen and learn while others rambled on about themselves.

"What about you, Morgana? How came you to be

half-dead in this savage land? This is no place for a woman."

Wanly, she told him the story of her capture and escape. It was a wild, incredible tale, but he did not press her for details, giving her time to compose herself when the memories brought tears. When she had finished, he spoke again.

"And your husband, you do not know where he is?"

"Nay. I fear he must think me dead, sir. Doubtless he has returned to his ship. He did not—things were not going well between us," she ended lamely.

"Morgana, have you thought—has it occurred to you that he may be dead himself?" Taylor tried to make his words as kind as possible.

"Aye, I've thought about that, but I can't believe 'tis true. I don't know. I'm tired."

He stroked his beard thoughtfully. He'd experienced a momentary sinking of heart upon learning that Morgana was married, but now it seemed that the union had been an unsatisfactory one. Still, she had called her husband's name when she'd been unconscious. It gave him pause, and he did not quite know what to do with her. Privately, he believed her husband was probably dead. He'd seen what those murdering Ashanti warriors did. Taylor took the empty bowl of broth from her outstretched hands.

"There's a good girl. Tomorrow we'll see about getting you some proper clothes and decide what needs to be done about this rather remarkable situation."

He turned away, noting her embarrassed blush at the mention of her garments, and quietly left the hut. Morgana lay still for a long time after he'd gone, her mind in a turmoil over this strange, gentle Yankee who'd saved her life. He was like no other man she'd ever met, and she did not quite understand him or know how to react to him. Was it possible that Rian *had* been killed? Her heart gave a queer jerk of pain. Nay, he was like a cat; he always landed on his feet.

In the morning, as he had promised, Taylor brought some clothes.

" 'Tis the best I could do, Morgana," he apologized as he held out the garments. "They're not exactly fitting for a woman, but 'twill be better than nothing at all. They belong to one of the young lads in my crew."

Morgana took the breeches and shirt, murmuring a polite thanks as she did so, but he had already gone. She saw that Taylor had also thoughtfully brought some water so that she might bathe, and this she managed to accomplish somewhat shakily, peeling away the leaves and washing the salve from her body. It took her a few moments to become steady on her feet again, but at last she was clean and dressed. She noted with a slight wonderment that he had even patched the soles of her boots where the sodden leather had rotted away.

She discovered that the breeches fit rather snugly as she bent over to stuff the cuffs inside her boots, and the light linen shirt clung to her breasts somewhat revealingly. But it did not really trouble her. By now, she had grown used to the idea that Taylor had seen all that she possessed when he'd undressed her and tended her hurts. Finding no comb or brush, Morgana ran her fingers through the mass of tangled copper curls, tugging them into some semblance of order. Then she stepped outside.

She closed her eyes immediately against the sudden glare of the hot African sun and it was some time before she was able to open them again, squinting in the bright light.

"Well, you're up and about, I see," Taylor approached her.

"Aye, thanks to you. I'm very grateful."

"Ah, shucks," he seemed embarrassed by her gratitude. "All I did was help you out a little. You're the one who hung in there so bravely."

"Nevertheless I owe you my life, Taylor," she smiled at him. It was the first time she'd called him by his Christian name.

"Oh, by the way, I have that little dagger of yours. A rather nasty weapon," he appeared surprised that she should have possessed such a thing.

"And most useful at times," Morgana spoke wryly, remembering with a shudder the times she'd had to use it.

"Aye, perhaps," he conceded, handing it back to her. "Still, 'tis hardly the sort of thing one would expect a woman to be carrying."

"But if I hadn't had it, I'd not be here. Events have a way of changing people. I doubt I'll ever again be like other women nor do what people expect of a woman. You may soon be wishing you'd left me on the savannahs," she cautioned him.

He did not answer, merely staring at her briefly before he strode away, leaving her to ponder his odd manner. The truth was that Taylor considered her to be a remarkable woman and seeing her attired almost presentably had brought home to him most rudely the fact that she was also a very beautiful woman. Even the slight marks which remained from the insect bites could not disguise that, and those would fade with time.

When Morgana hurried after him, he slowed his pace a little, for she was not yet well enough to keep up with his long strides and he did not want to tire her.

"Why do you follow me, girl? You should be in the hut resting," he grunted.

"Why not? I'm tired of being indoors, and I want to see what you do all day."

He sighed, but allowed her to go with him. Thereafter, it became her habit to accompany him every morning, causing the natives to ponder the strange couple wonderingly. Taylor showed her how to skin, clean, and dry furs, something at which Morgana soon became very adept. She did not really enjoy scraping the hides of the animals and stretching them taut to tan in the sun, but she was always ready to absorb all kinds of new knowledge and she decided that this might be helpful if she were ever to become lost in the wilderness again. She learned how to inspect goldwork and ivory, looking carefully for quality craftsmanship, and how to determine if the pieces were genuine. Taylor bartered expertly with the natives, but if

Morgana admired something, he bought it, not even haggling over the price.

Morgana regained her strength slowly; and when she was able, she learned how to cook from the native women who prepared Taylor's meals. They showed her which plants were good for seasoning and which ones were poisonous. Soon she could make monkey stew as well as any of them, although she steadfastly refused to boil the heads down. Nor would she use the hands and feet in her dishes, claiming they looked too human. She shuddered when Taylor informed her that some of the bush tribes actually ate people.

Taylor sent to his ship for bolts of material that Morgana cut and sewed into dresses for herself in the evenings. She would glance up often from her work, thinking how domestic everything seemed with herself sewing and Taylor solemnly puffing on his pipe contentedly. Why, we might be an old married couple, she thought with some amusement.

One night he amazed her by suddenly throwing his dish across the hut at supper. "For God's sake, woman, why do you busy yourself like an Indian squaw? It's unsuited to a woman of your position."

Morgana stared at him, wondering the reason for this outburst. "I merely sought to please you because you've been so kind to me. However, if you don't wish me to cook for you, I shall not do so again."

She squared her small shoulders and strode across the room to sit upon the sleeping mat, turning her back on him in a huff. It was so quiet she thought for a moment that he had returned to the hut he'd shared with his men since giving her his own. Then she felt his strong hands on her shoulders.

"I'm sorry, lass. It's just that—for God's sake, Morgana. What am I going to do with you? My business here is almost finished and I must be setting sail soon. I can't just leave you here, and 'twill be impossible for me to return you to Ireland. I go to China from here."

"Take me with you, then. I'll find a way home," her

voice was low, the words Rian had spoken to her one night about carving out one's own destiny or accepting the whims of fate echoing in her mind. "Take me with you. I will find a way," she repeated softly.

The hot air was cooled by the ocean breeze as they moved slowly away from the African coastline. Morgana stood on deck, her eyes searching the horizon for some sign of the *Sorceress,* but there was none, and she realized with a sinking heart that Rian had left her. Perhaps she would never see him again. Crystal tears slipped down her cheeks. He probably hadn't even bothered to look for her. She brushed the salty droplets away angrily, hurriedly, at Taylor's approach. At least he was kind to her, and he had not once attempted to touch her.

"Your cabin's ready, Morgana," he said gruffly. "I've made arrangements to take my first mate's lodgings, so that I'll be close by. Some of my crew are superstitious about having a woman on board. I wouldn't want any harm to befall you while you're in my care."

"Thank you, Taylor," she answered and followed him to the cabin.

It was not as spacious as the one on the *Sorceress,* and had only a narrow bunk, but it would serve well enough. There was a mirror and on the dresser lay a brush and comb.

Morgana cried with delight upon spying these two items, and when Taylor closed the door, she was seated before the looking glass, busily working on her unruly locks. He almost smiled to himself. He was unsure that he had done the right thing in bringing her with him, but he told himself for the hundredth time that he'd really had no other choice.

The days that followed soon settled into a smooth routine, causing many of Taylor's doubts to fade. Morgana fit in easily, much to his surprise and that of the crew, for she had learned the ways of a ship from her trips on the *Sorceress,* and she knew exactly when she might stroll upon the deck in the morning without disturbing the men at their toilets, and that certain parts of the vessel were not to be explored under any circumstances. She was always courteous and did not ask incessant questions; and although she always had a ready smile, she did not flirt with any of the sailors or encourage their attentions. She bandaged cuts and scrapes and advised the cook on new methods of preparation so that the monotonous diet was varied. The crew soon both accepted and respected her.

In the evenings, she shared her meals with Taylor and sometimes his first mate, Matthews, and the boatswain, Richardson. She kept them entertained with her tales of London life and they regaled her with stories about America, of which she knew very little.

"But I thought 'twas all a vast wilderness filled with savage Indians," she turned her wide, innocent eyes upon them. "I was very surprised to learn Taylor had a plantation there."

They dissolved into laughter at this, while Taylor patiently explained that much of the land was as civilized as London, and that Virginia society could be, in fact, even more snobbish. She digested this thoughtfully, smiling when they teased her about her ignorance. Through it all, Taylor studied her, and there grew in his heart a desire he had not known for many years. He felt extremely frustrated by a situation over which he had no control.

He would have liked to court Morgana, but always in the back of his mind lurked the fact that she was married. He argued with himself, telling himself that no one in Virginia would know this, that he could return to his plantation, settle down, and raise a family. What difference did it make if they did not have the everlasting blessing of the church? Besides, he felt sure in his heart that Morgana was a widow, in spite of the fact that she refused to accept the fact. It did not seem possible that anyone could have survived a battle with the Ashantis, especially with nothing more than a handful of men to aid him. But then he would sigh and tell himself truthfully that he did not even know how the woman felt about him. She was as elusive as a shooting star, veiling her eyes with those bristly black lashes whenever he sought to find out in a roundabout way what she was thinking.

For her part, Morgana lay awake in the night, tossing restlessly upon the narrow cot, kicking the sheets off and finding herself drenched with her own sweat, craving the sweet release she had known with Rian. Where was her husband? Had he already found another woman to warm his bed? She considered this to be most likely. If he thought her dead, he might have remarried. She could not even be sure that she was still the Countess of Keldara anymore. How bizarre it would be if she were to return to Ireland and find another in her place!

Morgana drew in her breath sharply as Rian's image floated into her mind, his mocking smile, his damned arrogance. She could almost taste his searing lips on hers, hear his taunting voice as he teased her into admitting that she wanted him, feel the little muscles ripple along his back as—"Damn you, Rian McShane!" she swore softly. She could almost see him standing before her, his feet planted wide apart in that swaggering stance, gazing at her in that peculiar manner he had. "Damn you to hell and back!" she swore again, then flounced back to bed, turning her back as she drew the sheet up over her nakedness. But his laughter echoed in her ears as his teeth nibbled gently, his hands moved upon her flesh, and he wrapped her long red hair about his throat, whispering huskily in the darkness.

There is always this between us, he had said, and you will remember all that I am as long as you live. I know you in a way no other man can, love.

Love, love, love . . .

The word drummed in her head until she could stand it no longer. With a cry, she pulled the pillow over her ears, trying to shut out the sound. It was a long time before she was finally able to get to sleep.

A smile played about the corners of Taylor's mouth as he watched his crew trying to string a clothesline between two of the masts and arguing over the best way to accomplish this. Morgana waited most patiently, a basket full of wet clothes against her hip. The men usually just tossed their garments over the rails of the ship to dry, but she was afraid hers might be swept away by the wind and she had very few dresses. Finally a decision was reached and soon her gowns fluttered gently in the breeze. The men turned away, faces red, at the sight of her flapping undergarments and Taylor smothered his laughter with difficulty. Then he sobered again, trying to determine whether or not Morgana would accept the proposal he planned to make to her this evening. He had been thinking it over for some time. Lord, she was a fetching sight this morning, her hair swept up on top of her head in a small knot. She smiled brightly at some of the more bashful sailors, asking if one of them would mind holding the heavy basket for her. At once, several of them stepped forward and almost came to blows over who was to help her. The chosen one gave his fellow crewmen a cocky grin of victory.

Taylor shook his head ruefully over her antics and clucked his tongue, but privately he was very proud of the way she'd taken to his ship and how much his men adored her. She was smart, too, and he was sure that she would have no trouble at all in running the huge household on his plantation should she accept his offer.

The wind billowed in the sails, sending them swiftly southward toward the African cape. Sometimes they ran into blackbirders, but Taylor always steered clear of them whenever possible. He disliked slaving and his own plantation was worked by hired men, a situation of which, he informed Morgana, his brother heartily disapproved.

"You have no slaves then?" she glanced at him questioningly as she retrieved her empty basket, swinging it lightly by her side.

"Nay. 'Tis bad business, Morgana, this dealing in men. Evil, in fact. But there, we all have our differences and my brother's a good man, for all that he would have me traffic in slaves. He's young and does not realize how abominably the poor devils are treated by these blackbirders, forced onto ships by the thousands, stuffed in the holds with little food or water. The air down there is foul enough and with hundreds of sweaty bodies chained in the hull, there's scarcely room to breathe. It breeds sickness and disease, and if that doesn't kill them, the crew does, beating the men half to death and using the poor wenches nightly—but there," he caught himself sharply. "I should not be telling a gentlewoman such things," he concluded, seeing her concerned face.

That evening Morgana pushed her chair away from the table with a sigh, sipping her wine slowly. Everything was so peaceful. She watched as Taylor tamped the tobacco down in his pipe and lit it, sucking contentedly on its stem. She was somewhat surprised when he leaned across the table and took her hand.

"Morgana, I've been doing some hard thinking about your situation," he began slowly. "I know you don't believe me, but I fear your husband is dead. We surely would have spied his ship by now otherwise. No—" he raised one hand. "Let me continue. I've gleaned from what you've told me that your marriage wasn't exactly a happy one anyway. As you know, I've been a bachelor these many years since the death of my wife, but there comes a time when a man starts thinking about settling down. I'd like you to come to Fairoaks with me, Morgana, as my—as my wife."

Morgana was stunned. "But, Taylor, we don't know that Rian's really dead," she was slightly appalled by his suggestion. "It wouldn't be legal."

"I've thought about that, too, and it doesn't matter. We can be married in the church at Norfolk and no one need be the wiser. You needn't answer me right away. Give yourself some time to think it over. I—I've come to love you, Morgana. I promise you won't regret it if you decide in my favor. That's all," he released her hand gently.

She sat for a long time, thinking about what he'd said after he'd closed the door softly behind him. Was there really any reason for her to return to Ireland? Suppose Rian were dead? Suppose he were alive and she went home to find that he no longer wanted her? Had she ever really been happy with him anyway? Here was an ideal opportunity to slip away without having to answer to anyone. Morgana McShane could die here and now, and Morgana Jones could travel to Virginia as mistress of Fairoaks, one of the largest plantations in the county. She would never have to worry about another thing as long as she lived. Taylor would treat her well, she felt sure of that. If events had decided her fate for her at last, perhaps it was all for the best.

One week later Morgana told Taylor that she would marry him. He took the news with outward calm, planting a light kiss upon her cheek. Immediately afterwards, she began to wonder if she'd made the right decision, but the more she thought about it, the better she felt about it. It was as if a heavy burden had been lifted from her shoulders.

She and Taylor spent many evenings discussing the wedding plans and although Morgana would often feel a twinge of guilt at these times, she refused to let it disturb her. She begged Taylor to tell her about Fairoaks, which he did with relish, for he was extremely proud of it and the heritage behind it. Morgana would curl up in his lap like a child, sometimes tweaking his beard when he became too serious, laughing gaily at the look of dismay which appeared on his face. She told him that he reminded her of a big, furry bear, and he remarked that she'd best behave then if she didn't want to get bitten.

He was correct and mannerly at all times, never seeking to seduce her; and though she lay restlessly in bed at night, she found that she could not bring herself to travel the few short steps to his room.

Only one quarrel marred their newfound happiness. It occurred when Morgana sought to investigate the state of Taylor's finances, for she wished once more to have the freedom of managing her own money Rian had given her. Taylor clucked his tongue and told her not to worry about it.

"But, Taylor, I have a right to know these things. I am quite capable of managing my own affairs," she said, momentarily irritated by his stony face.

"Nay. A woman's place is to manage her home and

her children, Morgana. There's no need to trouble yourself about business matters. I'll see to all your needs."

"But, Taylor," she tried again more gently. "I'm used to doing these things for myself."

"Aye, and look where it's gotten you. I declare, Morgana, I don't know what the folks back home would say if they knew about your rather colorful past," he clucked his tongue again.

This really made her angry. "Well, I'm certain you do not mean to tell them," she stormed. "Indeed, what would they say if they discovered we were not legally wed and that all your children were bastards?"

"Morgana! You must not say such things," he warned her solemnly.

"Oh, and why mustn't I?" she flung herself out of his grasp. "I don't intend to guard my tongue and pretend that I have no mind of my own when I'm able to think just as well, if not better, than most men."

"We'll talk about this later," he moved to leave the room.

"No! We'll discuss it now. What shall you do, I wonder, if by chance my real husband shows up at your plantation, disrupting your peaceful existence?"

" 'Tis unlikely to occur. You yourself said he probably believes you dead, as doubtless you would be if I had not happened along. Besides, there's no use in worrying about things which might never come to pass."

Morgana cursed him silently under her breath after he'd gone. How dare he behave as though she were incapable of managing her finances. She longed to pull his beard and tell him what a stubborn, narrow-minded fool he was. At least Rian had never treated her in such a manner. He had always respected her opinions and encouraged her to voice them. In fact, now that she thought about it, Rian had a lot of good qualities she hadn't appreciated. She made a face at herself in the mirror, then bit her lower lip sulkily. Well, once they got to Virginia and Taylor's hands were tied, they should see whether or not she sat at home like a meek little mouse.

She almost laughed aloud at the thought of Taylor's

face should she disclose to guests in their home the true nature of their relationship. No doubt half the women in the room would swoon at the very idea! Then she rebuked herself for such thoughts. Taylor certainly did not deserve such treatment, especially after he'd been so kind to her. Still, she couldn't help wanting to shock him out of his obstinacy.

Ah well. Once she had him where she wanted him, she would set Virginia society on its ear and do exactly as she pleased. To hell with all of them. She pulled out a bottle from Taylor's private stock and poured herself a stiff glass of brandy. Then, knowing how his eyebrows would rise if he discovered her drinking, she hurriedly rinsed her mouth out with some lavender water.

When he came in for dinner, Taylor wondered why Morgana smiled at him like a cat who's just finished a nice bowl of cream, but at least she wasn't still angry as he'd feared she would be. She seemed content to sit on his lap and gaze at him innocently with those wide emerald eyes. It made him distinctly uneasy, however, that a woman should have been blessed with such a quick, scheming mind. Her teasing bothered him when she tweaked his beard and told him she just couldn't wait to see Fairoaks.

"Shall I have to affect a drawl?" she asked sweetly. "How's this? Why, Taylor, honey, I just don't understand how you-all manage to run this huge farm."

"That's enough, Morgana. This behavior doesn't become you."

And upon seeing his rather sad face, Morgana sighed contritely. "I'm sorry, Taylor. It's just that I do so want to fit in with all your friends and everything," she lied. "How do you suppose they'll feel when you come home with a bride on your arm, and an Irish Tory at that? They shall all compare me to your wife. Perhaps I shan't be able to take her place. People tend to ascribe virtues to those who have died that those who follow cannot match."

Taylor stared at her with sudden understanding in his eyes. So that was it. She was just worried about how his friends would accept her and if he was still in love with his dead wife's image. This was something he could easily cope with and he seized upon it eagerly.

"Now don't you worry about a thing. Janet didn't know those people long enough for them to form any opinion of her. She died right after the plantation was finished, scarcely lived in it a year. And I have sense enough to realize that you're nothing at all like her, Morgana. I don't attempt to compare you with her, so you can set your mind to rest about that."

Morgana lowered her eyelashes so that he couldn't tell what she was thinking, remembering that Rian always said that her eyes gave her thoughts away so easily. How simple it was to fool Taylor. She would soon have him wrapped around her little finger. Then she smiled at him waveringly, murmuring her thanks, before she kissed him lightly and sprang away from his grasp.

"Come, let's play a game of cards," she challenged him invitingly.

And just so that he would not get to wondering how clever she really was, Morgana let him win all three rounds before he insisted they call it a night.

The waves slapped gently against the hull of the ship as the *Lucky Lady* plowed forward in the waters, passing the cape of South Africa in the darkness. Morgana closed her eyes dreamily as she pulled the sheet up over herself, unaware that Rian's ship lay moored in the harbor of Cape Town, so near and yet so far.

Chapter Twenty-eight

Rian stared morosely at his glass of whiskey, giving the slatternly barmaid who winked at him such a fierce glance of disgust that she backed away quickly, apologizing under her breath for having disturbed him. He scowled at her again before returning to his contemplation of the amber liquid. He had been sick with grief, but he was starting to recover now. God, when he remembered how crazy he'd been . . .

He hacked his way through the tough, clinging vines of the African jungle, not looking back to see if his men were following. He was certain now that Morgana was dead. He had held so tightly to a slender thread of hope only to have it snapped in half irretrievably by a dying man's words. He would never have her again. Never again would he hear her bright, lilting laughter, taste her sweet, honeyed lips, gaze into the depths of her dark emerald eyes. The one woman he'd ever really wanted, aye, and loved, was gone.

His search party wound its way back to the river and

from there to the shore. The Ashanti had burned the longboats moored at Bobosanga, so it had been necessary for them to light a fire on the beach to attract the attention of those on the *Sorceress*. Harrison had promptly dispatched another dinghy to fetch them. They were half-dead on their feet, covered with insect bites. One man still bled from a wound received in an encounter with a hungry leopard. He died shortly after they got back on the ship and Harrison instructed the men to throw the body overboard. The rest he sent to sick bay. But there was nothing he could do for the look of death he saw in his captain's eyes.

The men who'd followed Rian told Harrison as quietly as possible what had happened, and informed him that the captain had not spoken one word since they left the Ashanti village. Mister Harrison shook his head solemnly.

"Aye, I knowed no good would come of his taking the lass to that savage place. The poor girl, God rest her soul. She's gone and there's nothing we can do about it," he told them. "But I've never seen the Cap'n in such a state. I fear he's lost his reason."

The others nodded in silent agreement.

"We must all pray for him, Mister Harrison," Father John spoke up.

He had accompanied the crew on board, seeing no other course of action open to him. He intended to disembark at Cape Town, where he knew there was another mission.

"And hope that he regains his sense quickly," the priest continued speaking about Rian. "I believe he blames himself for Lady Keldara's death. He must have loved her very much."

"Aye, well, we must do the best we can," the first mate nodded solemnly.

Rian sat in the cabin and saw nothing but Morgana's winsome face. He drank and drank, but even the large amount of whiskey he consumed could not drive her image from his tormented mind. He played with the puzzle box for hours on end. He sent his meals back to the galley untouched. He neither bathed nor shaved, and the lines in his face grew hard with strain, the scar on his cheek showing white against his tan. When Harrison ventured to peek inside, Rian cursed him angrily and informed him that he would shoot the first man on sight who dared to show his face to him again.

The first mate crept away, more concerned than ever. Below, the crew grew restless and uneasy, and bolder because Rian took no interest in the ship. Some of them dared outright to disobey Harrison's orders, muttering mutinously when he had them whipped and thrown in chains. The first mate became suddenly aware of how dark the passages in the ship were and how easy it would be for one of them to put a knife in his back. He feared that they intended to revolt at the first opportunity. The men no longer included him in their discussions and fell silent when he approached them, only to begin whispering once again when his back was turned.

He and Timmons, the bosun, discussed the possibility of a mutiny in the evenings over supper.

"I tell you, Timmons, I don't like the looks of things around here. I sure don't. Cook says someone raided the galley and stole most of the supplies as well as the water rations."

"Aye, I think we'd best prepare ourselves for an attack," Timmons's face was grave. "The first thing we'd better do is lock up those rifles the Cap'n keeps on board."

Immediately they hurried to the stronghold. Too late! The lock on the strongbox had already been forced and its precious contents stolen. They looked at each other solemnly.

"They'll hit us at night," Harrison reckoned. "When they think we're sleeping. I'll take the first watch."

"Don't you think we should inform the Cap'n of this, Harrison?" Timmons ventured fearfully.

"I'm telling you he said he'd shoot the first man who showed his face in that cabin. I believed him, lad. You didn't see the look on his face, like he's dead inside and don't care what happens to him. He loaded those duelling pistols and keeps them by his side constantly. Even drunk, the Cap'n's a better shot than most men are sober. I don't care to feel the bite of steel in my gut if I can help it. I've followed the Cap'n a long time, but I've never seen him like this before. I just don't know what to do," Harrison's face was perplexed.

"Aye, well they're a greedy lot, this crew. No doubt they hope to take control of the ship and get rich off the cargo the Cap'n has stored in the hull. His horse alone must be worth a fortune. I think we can count on Jeb to help us," Timmons offered. "He was pretty cut up about the lady's death. You know she was like a daughter to him in spite of the way we teased him. He ain't touched his guitar since he heard the news."

"And Cook, too. Cook don't like the way things is going around here either," Harrison said. "He sailed on a ship once before on which the crew mutinied. Told me it was something he'd never forget. After the slaughter, them that survived liked to starve to death because some idiot heaved all the supplies and drinking water overboard."

"God!" Timmons shuddered. "I hope none of these boys was fool enough to have done that. A lot of them's too sick to fight, so perhaps we'll be able to stand the others off. Call me when you're ready to change guard shifts."

"I will," Harrison promised.

The mutiny came at last, the sudden quick-hushed voices, the pounding of feet, and Harrison was ready for them. He had his own pistols loaded and primed, and roused the other loyal men immediately. He, Timmons, Jeb, Cook, and Father John, a last-minute recruit, barricaded themselves in the first mate's cabin. Anyone who sought to get at them had to come through that door. And they did. As soon as one man fell, another took his place. They poured in without regard for their own dying crewmen, stepping on their bodies as they came. The men inside could not reload their pistols fast enough and soon the mutinous crew invaded the room. At such close quarters, they drew their rapiers and the battle became even bloodier.

Rian roused himself from a drunken stupor. "What the devil?" he roared, rolling his bloodshot eyes. He grabbed his pistols and stormed out of the room, intent on murdering whoever was making that dreadful racket. It took him a moment to realize what had happened. The crew had not thought to secure him in his quarters because they all assumed he'd gone mad with grief. Now he came at them like a crazy man and they were convinced of it. He felled two of them with his pistols, then drew his rapier to join in the melee.

Time and again his sword flashed, scraping steel against steel, driving the point home. At last, the remainder of the men threw down their weapons and surrendered, facing their bearded captain sullenly.

"What in the hell is the meaning of this, Harrison? Why did you not notify me that the men were about to mutiny?" Rian wiped his blade off carefully and gave his first mate an angry stare.

"Begging your pardon, Cap'n, but you said you'd shoot anyone on sight who entered your cabin. You haven't been yourself, Cap'n. No offense, Cap'n," Harrison added hastily under Rian's piercing gaze.

"Clap these men in irons," Rian growled.

"Begging your pardon, Cap'n," Harrison said again and swallowed hard. "But if I put all these men in the brig, there won't be anyone to man the ship."

"Then hang the ringleaders from the yardarm. Leave them there until they rot, and put the rest of these men back to work! Anyone who complains is to be keelhauled. Is that clear?"

"Aye, Cap'n, right away, Cap'n," Harrison almost smiled. Now the captain was sounding like his old self again.

They moved hurriedly to carry out his orders, throwing the dead overboard, executing the ringleaders (whom they discovered with no trouble at all since their own crewmates gave them away), and sent the remainder of the men back to their duties. Having accomplished this, Harrison reported at once to Rian's cabin.

"I've taken care of everything, Cap'n. Here, let me see about that wound." He examined a cut in Rian's arm carefully, pushing the younger man's hand away when Rian sought to stop him. "Best pour some whiskey on it. No use in taking chances."

"Stop fussing over me like a mother hen!" Rian snatched his arm away impatiently. "I'll get some alcohol on it, that is, if I have any left."

" 'Twill be a miracle if you do," the first mate said under his breath.

"What was that?" Rian raised one eyebrow demonically.

"I said it would be a miracle if you did," Harrison almost shouted. "Sitting up here swilling it down as though it were water. 'Tis a wonder you're still alive yourself. I seen you madder than a hornet, and I seen you slit men's throats, but I ain't never seen you sitting around wallering in your own self-pity before," Harrison finished defiantly.

"That will be quite enough," Rian's words were clipped. "Now get out of here!"

"Aye, Cap'n," the first mate slammed the door with a decided bang.

The Earl stared into space a long time after Harrison had gone. The first mate was one of his oldest friends and Rian had a great deal of respect for him. It angered him to have Harrison turn on him so sourly, especially when he knew the first mate was absolutely right. Rian was thoroughly disgusted with himself. He'd drunk himself into a head-splitting stupor, ignored his ship, and allowed his men to mutiny. He hadn't bathed or shaved in weeks. He looked at himself in the mirror and could not believe what he saw. Morgana would have cringed from his very touch.

Morgana! The thought of her was driving him crazy.

He'd have to get over her, lay her ghost to rest. With a bitter oath, he yelled for Harrison to bring him some water. The first mate was glad to oblige, having discovered where the missing rations had been hidden.

At the first light of morning, Rian appeared on deck, neat and cleanshaven. The sight of him, obviously in full possession of his faculties, stilled whatever mutinous thoughts remained in the minds of his crew. He took command of the helm, informing Harrison that they would be putting into port at Cape Town to replenish supplies and leave Father John at the mission.

Harrison muttered a noncommittal, "Aye, Cap'n," but Rian saw that the first mate had been smiling as he turned away.

The Earl drew himself back to the present sharply, tossing a few coins on the table to pay for his whiskey before leaving the Cape Town bar. He frowned. He might as well return to the ship. It would do him no good to try and find some whore with whom to spend the rest of the night. No woman he saw had that copper hair, those emerald eyes. "Damn you, Morgana!" he swore softly as he walked along the wharf in the darkness. He stood on the docks for a moment, watching quietly as the tall, white sails of a ship which was passing through the waters glistened in the distance. He could barely discern the name of the vessel in the shimmering moonlight. The *Lucky Lady*. He hoped she was as aptly called as the *Sorceress*.

"I bid you safe passage, madam," he drawled mockingly, drunkenly, to the vessel before strolling up the gangplank to his own ship.

India! The very name shimmered like the garments worn by the dark-skinned natives. The women wore veils over their faces and some of them had bright jewels upon their foreheads. Morgana drank in the sights eagerly after Taylor consented to allow her to disembark from the vessel. Many of the men were garbed in white robes and some of them had their heads bound in turbans.

"Come on, Taylor, let's go shopping or sightseeing," Morgana yanked on his arm, trying to pull him with her.

"Morgana, stop it, please! I have business to attend to and I won't have you running through the streets like some common wench. I've sent a message to the Maharajah Bhavnagar and he's invited us to dine with him this evening. Wouldn't you rather do that?" he glanced at her pouting face anxiously.

"Oh, very well, but if you sit there and talk business all evening, I shall positively scream with boredom," she informed him, thrusting her jaw out defiantly.

Taylor sighed. "I thought you were interested in my business dealings. Have you changed your mind?"

She didn't reply and he smiled knowingly to himself. She had grown bored with finances, of course, just as most women did. He had nothing to worry about after all.

To Morgana's surprise, the Maharajah lived in an awesome palace with crested domes, tall spires, and minarets.

"It reminds me of the Brighton Pavilion in a way," she breathed as they were ushered through the long halls. "You know Prinny is having it redone Oriental fashion."

"Now just how would I know such a thing?" Taylor rolled his eyes at her disbelievingly. "Really, Morgana, sometimes you say the damnedest things. I pray you hold your tongue at dinner."

Well, I shan't if you continue to treat me so shabbily," she pouted and tweaked his beard, much to his chagrin. "I daresay the Maharajah will find me amusing, even if you don't."

"For God's sake, Morgana! I transact much of my Indian business through him. If you do anything at all outrageous, he will refuse to see me again."

Morgana flushed under his exasperated stare. Really! Taylor had no sense of humor at all. She promised to be on her best behavior, then tossed her curls arrogantly, cursing under her breath. Sometimes he reminded her of a fussy old maid. If only he would be more daring!

She found the Maharajah Bhavnagar extremely fascinating and not at all the rather savage person she had expected. He was very distinguished-looking and spoke flawless English. Dark, swarthy, and charming, he seemed to be as taken with her as she was with him and couldn't keep his eyes off her as they settled upon the satin pillows around an intricately carved bamboo table.

Morgana looked enchanting in the dress she'd made up from some of the material from Taylor's ship. It was a simple pattern; after all, she was not a seamstress, but the silky black set off her creamy skin to perfection and made her green eyes snap like sparks, accentuating the bristly lashes which so heavily veiled the emerald jewels. Her fiery tresses glowed like burnished copper.

Taylor frowned as he watched the two of them laughing together. Morgana's cheeks flushed when the Maharajah leaned forward to press a piece of fruit upon her. She bit into it lustily, noting the manner in which his eyes darkened with pleasure at the sight of her small white teeth and sensuous lips. When he suggested that she might like to stroll through the palace gardens, she readily accepted, ignoring Taylor's disgruntled glance. The silver strands of her laughter rippled gaily in the night, drifting through the open archways tantalizing Taylor. What were they doing out there, his fiancée and the Maharajah? They had not asked him to join them. He sighed. If only he could get her to Virginia, to Fairoaks. He was sure things would be different there.

The perfume of flowers wafted exotically in the night. Morgana felt Sirsi, as the Maharajah had begged her to call him, glance at her invitingly and her heart began to hammer slowly in her breast. He was standing in the shadows and for a moment she imagined that he was Rian. Rian in the gardens at Shanetara speaking of the witching hour. A clock chimed. *Aye, you could bewitch a man with those eyes of yours.* She flinched. *I shall have a bruise there in the morning. Aye, I have placed my brand upon you. See if any dares challenge me for the right.*

"Morgana. You haven't heard a word I've said," Sirsi's dark eyes brought her back to the present with a start.

"I—I'm sorry, Sirsi. I'm afraid I was somewhere else, another time, another place," Morgana apologized contritely.

"'Tis of no consequence. I merely asked if you would care to remain at the palace during your stay here?"

"Why, yes, that would be lovely, but you must check with Taylor. I'm afraid he doesn't like my making decisions on my own."

"But that is only proper. 'Tis a man's right to rule over his domain," Sirsi's smile flashed whitely in the darkness.

"And if he be not fit to reign?" Morgana challenged him teasingly, but there was a note of seriousness in her voice.

"Then another shall take his place," the Maharajah broke a blossom from its stem and tucked it behind her ear.

The motion jarred the bush lightly and petals showered over his tunic like tiny stars in the moonlight. Morgana's spine tingled warmly at his touch as she smiled into his face and suddenly wished his eyes had been green instead of brown.

"I'm haunted by a demon, Sirsi. Shall we not go in now?"

The Maharajah followed her slowly, wondering what had brought about her sudden change of mood. He had been told that all Englishwomen were cold, but there was a fire he sensed in Morgana and he longed to fan it into a flame of desire.

Taylor was displeased at the sight of the flower in Morgana's hair and the loose petals trailing over Sirsi's tunic, and he took rather perverse delight in drawing the Maharajah's attention to them somewhat sarcastically.

Sirsi smiled and brushed the petals with an indolent

hand. "Your fiancée is most charming, Captain Jones. I have told her that my stables will be at your disposal for the duration of your visit, and I beg you will remain in the palace as my guests."

The sea captain saw no other choice but to accept. To refuse the hospitality of the prince would be extremely rude, and it would not be wise to insult the Maharajah.

In the days that followed, Morgana was often Sirsi's riding companion across the lands of his small province. He introduced her to his wives, Jind, Dhoraji, and Amreli, and when she was not out riding, she spent many hours in the women's quarters. Sirsi's wives were enchanted with her and they clamored around her most inquisitively, much as Don Mojados's wives had done. Morgana found that she still could not get used to the idea of a man having more than one spouse. It seemed so primitive and pagan, but the women treated her so courteously she could not bring herself to be other than kind to them in return.

Jind was the youngest, slight and sultry, with a mouth like red wine and eyes that slanted mysteriously. She had long dark hair and her nose was pierced and bore a small diamond. They all had pierced ears and had begged Morgana to allow them to pierce hers, but she steadfastly refused.

Dhoraji was older and apt to be a trifle trying sometimes. She was the mother of the prince who would someday inherit Sirsi's kingdom and she never let the other two women, who had borne only daughters, forget it.

Amreli's face was hawklike, not really even pretty, but Morgana saw that she had a certain sensuality which might have attracted a man like Sirsi.

Sirsi. How easily his name rolled off her tongue. He was cool, but she suspected there was a great deal more to him than the exterior he so regally maintained. She caught a glimpse of his temper one day when an Untouchable woman attempted to feel the fabric of her dress in the marketplace. He would have had the girl whipped had Morgana not intervened. It was difficult for her to

409

understand the caste system in India, for, except for her dress, the woman could have been one of Sirsi's wives.

He entertained her royally, much to Taylor's disgust. The captain was growing impatient with the Maharajah and longed to get his business transacted so that he might sail again, but always the prince delayed, saying there would be time enough for business later on. Taylor suspected that it was Morgana who delayed the matter, but there was no help for it. If he attempted to broach the subject, she merely laughed and told him not to be so stuffy.

She had her fortune told by an old man who read the bumps on her head. His words disconcerted her so that she shivered in the bright Indian sun and turned away after tossing the man a few coins. From the piles of bright fabrics in the marketplace, she selected some to be made into saris for herself. And she eyed the hooded cobras which slithered upward from the flute players' baskets with a twinge of fear, remembering the pit vipers of Africa.

Several days later, Sirsi suggested that they journey to the city of Agra to view the Taj Mahal, and they set out with a large retinue from the Bhavnagar palace, escorted by several armed guards. Jind and Amreli accompanied them in litters, as they did not care to ride. Dhoraji preferred to remain at the palace, having seen this wondrous sight many times before. Morgana handled her small mount well, having become used to the horse's temperament over the past few weeks and was surprised to learn that Taylor was as at home on a horse as he was on the deck of his ship, for he had not once accompanied them before. She was glad of the flowing burnoose which guarded her skin from the sun and dust as they travelled, but on occasion she eyed with longing the ease with which Jind and Amreli journeyed. It would have been nice to loll in one of the curtained litters fanned by palm leaves. But then she would not have been willing to give up this chance to remain at Sirsi's side.

He looked very handsome upon his white stallion, and when his warm glance fell upon her more than once during the day, color rose in her cheeks most becomingly. Aye, he was a fine figure of a man and he invaded her thoughts more and more, especially at night when they stopped to erect the huge, silken tents and roll the carpets and pillows upon the ground. She tossed restlessly, imagining herself an Indian princess, and sometimes when she could not sleep, she strolled upon the desert sands and studied the stars. Once she saw the Maharajah standing in the shadows of his tent, watching her in the darkness, and she hurried back to bed, her heart pounding oddly.

When, some days later, Morgana at last set eyes on the Taj Mahal, she thought it must surely have been the most beautiful building she'd ever seen. It was a perfect, white marble jewel, so delicate, so majestic, that it almost took her breath away. She stood in the archway and marvelled at its loveliness. Even Taylor seemed awed.

"Tell me, Sirsi. Tell me the story behind this. Who built it and why?" she begged eagerly.

"It was inspired by love," the prince told her, and went on to relate one of the most beautiful tales she'd ever heard.

"The Taj Mahal took eighteen years to build and was finished in 1648. The king who ordered its creation, Shah Jahan, once ruled a vast Moslem empire in India, of which Agra was the capital. He invited artists and architects from every country to build his marble city. He owned huge chests of rubies and gold, and his royal stables contained thousands of horses and hundreds of elephants. But the one treasure which the King prized above all else was his beautiful wife, Mumtaz-i-Mahal, which means The Chosen of the Palace," Sirsi's voice was soft.

"As you know, Morgana, it is our custom to have many wives, but for Shah Jahan there could be only one. It is said that he and Mumtaz-i-Mahal were never parted for even one day during the entire eighteen years of their married life. But destiny intervened with a cruel hand, turning this great romance into a tragedy. The Empress was stricken with a fatal fever and died. For days, the palace feared the King would die, too, for he refused all food and not even his children dared speak to him. At last, he summoned his best architect, Usted Isa, a Persian, and commanded the man to construct a tomb for the body of his beloved Queen. The King spent much of his treasure on the Taj Mahal, which means the Crown of Mahal," Sirsi translated. "And he poured all of his grief, tears, and love into it as well."

Deeply moved, Morgana listened in silence as the Maharajah continued.

"It is said that the tomb contains a soul, Morgana. Legends say that if two lovers chance into the gardens on the night of a full moon, they may see the sepulcher fade into the mist, and for one breathless moment glimpse the radiant image of Queen Mumtaz-i-Mahal before she evanesces into moonbeams shimmering in the fountains."

"And Shah Jahan, what happened to him?" Morgana asked as she gazed at the woven canopy of ten thousand pearls folded over the casket of the Empress.

"Ah, that part is sad, also, for immediately after the tomb was finished, the King's son led a rebellion against the throne and put his father in prison. Shah Jahan remained there for seven long years while he waited for death. At last, when he lay dying, he requested the soldiers to carry him to a balcony in the prison at dawn so that he might see the Taj Mahal once again before he died. His request was granted and the old man closed his eyes forever, content that he would soon be rejoined with his one true love," Sirsi ended.

Suddenly Morgana felt very empty and to her surprise, she found she was weeping for the star-crossed lovers, and for herself.

"Why, Morgana, I've made you cry," the Maharajah was genuinely upset. They had somehow drifted away from Taylor, Jind, and Amreli, and were quite alone in this particular section of the tomb. "Here, you mustn't be sad. All of this happened many years ago. I did not mean to distress you."

"I'm sorry, Sirsi, I just can't seem to help myself," she sobbed, taking the silk handkerchief he offered.

She wiped her eyes and did not protest when his arms went around her, pulling her close to him for comfort. She wondered if Rian had ever seen the tomb. He would have understood exactly how she felt at this moment, and yet she found this strange that it should have been so. Still, he had understood the time she'd seen the ghosts at Shanetara and he had spoken of their love for one another. The sound of footsteps echoed dimly in the hall and they broke apart as the others approached.

"We've been looking all over for you," Jind told them sulkily.

"Why, Morgana, have you been crying?" Taylor glanced at her suspiciously.

"It was my fault," Sirsi explained. "I told her the story of the tomb and it upset her. There, are you feeling better now?" he turned to Morgana.

"Yes, thank you."

Jind's face relaxed at this bit of information and she was able to view Morgana more kindly. "Yes, 'tis very sad, is it not? I myself cried upon hearing the tale for the first time. Come, let us leave this place of death. I'm famished."

Morgana was so lost in her thoughts that she scarcely spoke to any of them on the journey home. Taylor tried to amuse her, but he could do nothing to shake her melancholy mood.

One night she awoke to find herself drenched in sweat, the light sheets clinging to her skin stickily. She knew what was wrong with herself, but refused to admit that she missed Rian's lovemaking, the feel of his lean body next to hers, the touch of his searing lips. He had awakened her passionate nature and now she hungered for fulfillment. Jind and Amreli slept on, undisturbed as she pulled back the flap of the tent and stepped outside. The eunuch who guarded the women stirred slightly, but merely nodded his head upon seeing that it was only the Englishwoman. The cool desert breeze felt good against Morgana's flesh and the sand was cold against her bare feet. She seemed to float in the moonlight as she walked through the silent camp. A movement in the shadows caught her attention, and Sirsi stepped from the darkness.

She parted her lips and spoke softly, "Sirsi, I—"

Morgana did not have to say more. The pressure of his lips upon hers stilled whatever else she might have whispered. She flung her arms about his neck and he carried her into his tent. He laid her softly among the pillows and his hands were gentle, unhurried, as he loosed the ribands of her negligee. She felt no shame as he pressed his mouth to her breasts, moaning her name huskily, and his hand explored the softness between her thighs. She quivered at his touch, drawing him to her, fumbling with the cord which bound his robe. At last, she pulled it free and her fingers found his eager maleness, urging him on. She gasped quietly when he entered her, then matched his pacing with her own desires, telling herself that it was only a trick of the moonlight that made his eyes glitter green in the darkness.

Morgana sighed, contented, as the first pale streaks of dawn lit the sky. She yawned and stretched, running her hands down the length of her sated body. Bathing in the white marble tub, she was glad that Jind, Amreli, and Dhoraji still slept. Sirsi was a good lover. Strange, though, that he should have been the first man to whom she'd given herself willingly. Wearing a cool, flowing sari, she wandered the gardens of the palace, pausing to pluck a blossom. She twirled it idly in her hands. She had nothing important to do. Later on she would send one of the servants to fetch her a tall glass of fruit juice and she would linger for a time on the patio. It was the nights that counted now, the nights when she could slip from the women's quarters, past the carefully averted eyes of the eunuchs, to the arms and lips of Sirsi. No longer must she lie awake, longing for love.

Sirsi grew more enamored of her with each stolen moment, begging her to remain with him and constantly devising some new way to postpone her leaving.

"You cannot mean to marry Captain Jones, Morgana," he whispered one evening. "When I think of you in that old man's arms—"

"He's not that old, Sirsi, and, he doesn't have three other wives," she teased him.

"Ah, Morgana, you know that I cannot set them aside for you; but I swear if you stay, I shall go no more to the women's quarters. I'll treat you like a queen. You shall have your own rooms and servants, anything that you desire."

"But I should be little more than a concubine, Sirsi," she protested, then gave herself over to his searching lips.

The scent of jasmine hung heavy in the air, mingling with the sweet fragrances of the other flowers. It was almost overpowering in the heat. Morgana closed her eyes briefly, allowing the perfume to invade her nostrils.

"The flowers are beautiful, but you, my dear, are the loveliest blossom in the garden."

Morgana whirled, startled at the sound of the voice so near. A tall man stood behind her, his dark eyes raking her appreciatively.

"Who are you? What are you doing in these gardens?" she glanced around anxiously, but there was no sign of anyone else. She was quite alone with the stranger.

"A nomad bandit. I understand you are the Maharajah's latest mistress and I intend to kidnap you and hold you for ransom," his white teeth flashed in a smile.

"My God!" she backed away from him warily. "Guards! Guards!"

In a matter of minutes, they were surrounded by soldiers from the palace. To her surprise, they did not arrest the intruder as she had expected, but fell on their knees in front of him.

"Are you daft? Arrest this man at once," Morgana told them angrily.

The stranger clapped his hands together, laughing. "Leave us, please."

"Yes, my lord," the soldiers bowed and disappeared, giving Morgana silent looks of puzzlement as they passed.

She stared at the man who had dismissed the guards so easily, the fear evident in her face. "Who are you?"

she asked again, preparing to take flight. If only she could get to the palace. Damn those soldiers! How dare they leave her here with this bandit?

The intruder laughed again. "I'm sorry. Perhaps it was a bad joke on my part. I am Hassan, the Maharajah's brother."

Morgana almost choked with relief, then her eyes narrowed angrily. "That wasn't funny. Why didn't you just say so in the first place instead of scaring me out of my wits?"

Hassan shrugged. "I merely wished to see if you really are the fiery wench the palace claims."

"And am I?" she was starting to relax now. Sirsi's brother had inherited the Bhavnagar charm, it seemed.

"Perhaps. Come, shall we go inside?" He offered her his arm.

"As you wish, my lord."

They were met at the archway by Sirsi and Taylor.

"Hello, Hassan. I did not know you had returned," Sirsi studied his brother briefly.

"No doubt you find it a most unwelcome surprise," Hassan remarked dryly.

"Morgana, what was all the commotion out in the gardens?" Sirsi ignored his brother's statement.

" 'Twas nothing, Sirsi. Just a little misunderstanding. I'm sorry I called for the guards. I thought Hassan was a bandit and was momentarily frightened."

"You are unharmed?" Sirsi questioned rather sharply.

"Aye," she nodded.

"Good. Captain Jones," he turned to Taylor. "I have business to discuss with my brother. I trust you will excuse us. I shall expect you and your lovely fiancée for dinner as usual."

Taylor accepted the dismissal graciously, reaching for Morgana's hand as he led her away. She saw Hassan's eyebrows rise questioningly for a moment, but it was not until she was halfway down the hall that she remembered that he had called her the Maharajah's latest mistress. He knew! Somehow he knew.

"Well, Hassan. What brings you to India? I believe you still had one more term at school," Sirsi's voice gave no hint of the anger he felt. "Have you been expelled again?"

"Yes, but what the hell? It was an accursed dull place anyway," Hassan flopped on a chair, impervious to Sirsi's frown.

"Hassan, this is the third time you have been thrown out of an academy. I do not like to see my money wasted. What was it this time? Women?"

"As always, brother. What else?" Hassan frowned now. Sirsi was going to be difficult, it seemed. "There are other universities."

"I do not intend to find another school for you, Hassan," Sirsi gazed at his brother coldly. "You grow more dissolute all the time, with your women and gambling. My accountant informs me that you are heavily in debt."

"Yes, but I'll come about. 'Tis of no importance."

"It is important to me. You give the Bhavnagar palace a bad name and the people lose their respect for us. I won't have it, do you understand?" he waited for his brother's curt nod. "Very well, then. I've made up my mind in this matter. The nomad tribes have become bolder in their attacks on my caravans. Twice this month they have cost me heavily. One piece of jewelry that I valued very highly was stolen," he paused, remembering the fire opals he had intended to give Morgana. "I have, therefore, decided that you will lead a detachment to the north of the province. I expect you to subdue these outbreaks of violence and see that peace is restored in my Kingdom. You will leave in a fortnight. Perhaps you will find army life more to your liking. That is all."

Hassan caught his breath sharply. "And perhaps I shall be killed. You'd like that, wouldn't you, brother? Always you manage to find some way to keep me from the palace. Do you fear me, brother? Are you afraid that I might wrest this throne from your grasp?"

"No, Hassan," Sirsi gave him a penetrating stare. "But I have no doubt that you would try, and I have no

417

desire to hang you for treason. Go and make ready to depart. I am not speaking to you as your brother, but commanding you as your King."

Hassan turned at the door. "Oh, by the way, brother. I find your latest mistress most enchanting. Captain Jones, of course, remains in ignorance of the affair?"

"One of these days you will try me too far, Hassan," Sirsi's words were clipped.

Hassan laughed unpleasantly, then slipped quietly through the archway. Sirsi stared after him coldly. Damn Hassan! How did he always manage to know everything that occurred within the palace walls?

Taylor cleared his throat nervously. "Would you care to go to the marketplace, Morgana? I've some free time, it seems, and would enjoy your company."

She started to decline, then it occurred to her that she had spent very little time with Taylor recently. "Why, yes, I'd like that," she smiled at him and was rewarded by the sudden warmth in his eyes.

Her nerves raced guiltily. What a tangle. She didn't know how it had all come about. Here she was sleeping with one man, engaged to another, and married to a third. Oh, how did she always manage to get herself into such scrapes? And now that horrible man, Sirsi's brother, knew. She wondered if he would keep his silence.

Taylor took her arm to help her mount, and it was all Morgana could do to keep from cringing at his touch. If he noticed her sudden stiffening, he gave no sign, however. God, how could she do it? How could she marry him and live in Virginia on a backwoods farm when she had lain in the arms of a prince? She found herself comparing his stocky body to Sirsi's lean figure, and shuddered. Taylor would no doubt consider it his duty to take her to bed, but nothing more. He would be shocked to discover the depths of her passionate nature. For the first time, she began to feel sorry that she had accepted his proposal so hastily. If only she hadn't been so desperately alone! She should have given the matter careful consideration.

Suddenly Taylor's anxious voice brought her back to reality. "Morgana, we must go back to the palace."

She noticed for the first time that the marketplace was filled with throngs of people, pushing one another. From her perch upon her stallion, she could at last glimpse what had caused the furor. A gallows had been erected and the soldiers were evidently getting ready to conduct a public execution. They had shoved the prisoner forward roughly and Morgana saw that he had been bound and blindfolded.

"Morgana," Taylor spoke again. "We must get out of here. This is no place for a woman."

A morbid curiosity seized her and she ignored his urgent pleading, digging her heels into the sides of the horse so that it pressed forward into the crowd. She had never seen a hanging before. The throng gave way at the sight of her and she was able to reach the foot of the steps at the gallows, unaware that Taylor was still behind her trying to get through the crowd. She watched, fascinated, as the soldiers lowered the coiled noose over the victim's head and tightened it, and for a moment, she saw not the plain Indian peasant, but Rian, Rian bound and blindfolded in front of Newgate Prison. There was a crash as the floor dropped out from underneath the victim's feet and the rope jerked sickeningly, followed by a softer snap of the man's neck. It was over in seconds. Morgana did not know that she had screamed, but Taylor heard her cry over the noise of the crowd and knew a sudden disheartening feeling. The word had been sharp, clear. *Rian. Rian,* she had cried.

"Not very pleasant, was it? I'm surprised that you stayed to watch."

Morgana turned to find Hassan beside her. He was mounted on a beautiful chestnut horse.

"I—I don't know why I did exactly, except that I once knew someone who was going to be hanged. I wanted to see what it was like," she explained lamely, reining her horse away from the sight.

"And did they hang him, your friend?" Hassan's eyes probed her face.

"No."

"He was most fortunate then. Do you return to the palace now?"

"Aye, I suppose so. Taylor was—oh, dear," her eyes searched the crowd anxiously. "I've lost him." He was nowhere in sight.

"Never mind. I'll ride back with you, if you wish."

Morgana thanked him, glad of his company, for the crowd was growing more and more unruly and she was slightly afraid of the curious Indian peasants who watched her so sullenly. She knew they would not dare to attack her in the presence of the prince's brother.

Hassan studied his brother's mistress curiously from under half-closed eyelids. She did not appear to be in the least upset at the sight of the hanging she'd just witnessed. Most women would have fainted, and he guessed that she must have seen far worse in her lifetime. He wondered what lay beneath the cool exterior she so steadfastly maintained. He saw easily why she had attracted his brother's attention. The deep emerald eyes starred with jet lashes, the sulky red mouth that just ached for kisses, the slender white throat. His eyes strayed lower to the curve of her breasts and the small waist he could have spanned with his hands. Yes, she was a woman well worth a prince, and perhaps a kingdom, his mouth curved into an unpleasant smile at the thought which had just occurred to him.

"Why do you study me so thoughtfully, Hassan?"

He saw that her eyes were cold, like ice, and that she had taken him in just as measuringly. The wench was no fool and he suspected that an extremely shrewd mind lay behind her seemingly innocent face. His eyes narrowed speculatively. Unlike most Indian men, Hassan respected a woman with brains.

"I was wondering what a woman like you sees in my brother?" he replied with a slow, inviting smile.

"Perhaps the same thing I see in you," she answered, pleased at the sudden startled look which crossed his face. If he wanted to play games, he would soon learn that she could match wits with the best of them.

She dug her heels into the sides of the horse and galloped down the narrow, twisting streets, causing the peasants to scatter at her approach. When she reached the stables of the palace, Hassan was already there, an amused smile on his face. She did not seek to reward him further by asking how he had beaten her there. His hands were warm around her waist as he lifted her from the saddle, and he stood looking at her momentarily before he at last released her. They walked into the palace only to be met by Sirsi, a frown on his brow. Morgana did not stay to hear what followed, but excused herself quickly, hurrying up the few steps to the women's quarters. Only the first hard remark caught her ears.

"Keep away from her, Hassan," Sirsi had said.

At dinner, Morgana apologized to Taylor for losing him in the crowd, and explained that when she'd turned, he had disappeared. He accepted this taciturnly, stroking his beard with a calloused hand. He was beginning to grow accustomed to her fits and fancies. Nevertheless his eyebrows rose when she mentioned that Hassan had been kind enough to escort her home. He had taken an instant dislike to the young prince.

"Perhaps in the future you will not be so headstrong, Morgana. I warned you that an execution was no place for a woman."

"Quite right, Captain Jones," Sirsi sipped his wine and gave his brother a quelling stare.

"Oh, well, no harm was done," Morgana said to no one in general and continued with her meal, ignoring the speculation in Hassan's dark eyes.

Morgana lolled in the spacious white marble tub, enjoying the scent of lilacs Taylor had managed to obtain from one of the ships in port. Jasmine floated in the water, mingling with the lilac perfume. She called for more hot water and Ajmer, her servant, obediently poured in another steaming bucketful. Finally she sighed and decided she really should get out now. It seemed such a shame to leave the lovely water, but it was growing dark and Sirsi would expect her as usual. She climbed the marble steps and allowed Ajmer to towel her dry with a soft square of linen. Then she lay on a nearby bench for a massage with perfumed oils, her muscles gradually relaxing under the servant's experienced hands. When that was finished, she rose, selected a gown of vibrant red and stood quietly while Ajmer draped its shining folds around her. Normally she could not have worn the color, but this particular shade danced under the flickering lights, catching the glint of her coppery curls in its threads. When she moved, it seemed as though she walked in a column of fire.

"Thank you, Ajmer, that will be all," she dismissed the girl for the evening.

She pulled one of the jasmine blossoms from the water, drying it carefully before she tucked it into her hair and slipped out onto the veranda. Behind her she heard the sounds of Sirsi's wives as they came in from dinner. She suspected that they knew about her and Sirsi, but they gave no sign if they did. They laughed and called to her, begging her to come play for them. Sirsi had given her a sitar, and as it was not unlike her own guitar, she had learned to play the instrument easily. It was not melodious like the guitar, having a peculiar, almost flat ring to it and the reverberation was much sharper, almost a buzz; but she enjoyed playing it and was glad to amuse them.

The song she chose was haunting, and although her pronunciation of the strange Hindustani words was accented, she still sang them fluently enough to be understood. Jind had been teaching her the language in the evenings. Her soft, lilting voice floated out into the gardens where Hassan stood against a tree trunk, his eyes upturned to the women's quarters; along the veranda where Sirsi lingered in a carved archway; and down the hall where Taylor sat in his room going over his accounts.

And as his ship sailed out to sea
She stood upon the sands and cried;

And sighing, lifted one fair hand
To wave her love goodbye.

Morgana's voice trilled, wafted, soared in the darkness, then fell in sadness; and each man, for his own reasons, was profoundly discontented.

Morgana didn't know how it had happened. One minute she had been lying in Sirsi's arms, knowing she must slip away before the dawn touched the sky. Then she had been walking along the veranda to the women's quarters when a hand had been clamped roughly over her mouth, almost suffocating her in the attempt. She struggled against her assailant, but it was no use. He stuffed her into a bag and threw her over a horse. Now she was being tossed bruisingly against its sides as it galloped over the desert sands. She knew it had to be the desert because the horse's hooves sank and thudded softly, unlike the hard clattering on the roads in Bhavnagar. But who had taken her or why, she had no idea. She tried screaming once or twice, but to no avail. Her captor either didn't hear her or chose to ignore her cries. After what seemed like hours, she became aware that the sun had risen and that it was growing extremely hot. She felt as though she were going to suffocate and the sweat dampened the back of her neck and poured into her eyes, blinding them with the stinging wetness. Her head ached and the blood rushed to it until merciful blackness descended.

When she became conscious again, something cool had been pressed to her forehead and for a moment Morgana thought she was in the large salon at Shanetara, and that Rian had just rescued her from the dungeons. Then her eyes fluttered open slowly and she stared into Hassan's amused face.

"You! My God! What have you done? You must be mad," she tried to rise.

"Patience, my little lotus blossom," he smiled at her wickedly, then pulled her hands out and bound them tightly.

Morgana tried to yank away, but he was very strong. She saw that what she had thought to be a bag was in reality a scrap of carpet. No wonder she had almost suffocated! Hassan had rolled her up inside the heavy material. God, the man was crazy. What was he going to do with her?

"I shan't harm you," he said as though he'd read her thoughts.

"Shan't harm me?" her voice sounded hysterical and she sought to control it. "You fool! You almost killed me." She felt bruised and battered all over. "Why have you done this insane thing?"

The wet cloth he had pressed to her forehead fell away as he yanked her to her feet, ignoring her question. "I'm afraid you'll have to ride astride," he told her. "I could hardly request a sidesaddle without raising eyebrows."

He tossed her into the saddle, taking the reins from her grasp when she reached for them, tying them to the pommel on his own horse. Then he mounted and whipped up his stallion. Morgana saw that she must either hang on to the saddle or be thrown and trampled upon, and with her mouth set in a grim line of determination, she grasped the horn tightly, gritting her teeth at Hassan's rapid pace.

He'll kill us, she thought, noting how lathered the horses' coats had become in the heat. He's mad!

The sand flew as the horses' hooves dug in, floundered, and pulled free again, lunging as they galloped. Hassan paused only briefly once or twice to give her a sip of water, shaking her roughly when she tried to do more than wet her mouth with it.

"You'll make yourself sick," he said angrily, clamping the lid back on the canteen.

She looked at him dully, her eyes filled with hate, and said nothing. He scanned the horizon, seemed satisfied with what he saw, and mounted again.

It was late when they finally came upon the nomad tribe. Night had long since fallen and Morgana was shivering as the cool breeze swept over the desert. She was only too glad when Hassan pulled her from the saddle and pushed her into a tent. She fell onto the cushions on the floor with a sigh. He spoke quickly and rapidly in Hindustani to some men who appeared, but she could not follow the conversation; then he sank down beside her.

"Tired?"

"You must know that I am," she told him hostilely.

"Poor lotus blossom. It can't have been much fun for you."

"Hassan, why have you done this thing?" she tried again. "Surely you know how angry Sirsi will be."

"I certainly hope so. I intend to hold you for a great deal of ransom."

"Oh, Hassan," she spoke wearily. "Not another one of your jokes."

"I assure you it is no joke, Morgana," his face twisted sardonically in the moonlight.

With a rising horror, she saw that he was actually serious and quite suddenly began to cry.

"Shut up!" he snarled sharply. "Do you want the whole tribe to hear?"

"I don't care," she sobbed. "You beast."

To her surprise, he merely laughed and cut the thongs which bound her wrists. In another minute, a young woman appeared bearing a tray with several slabs of meat and pieces of fruit. She studied Morgana sullenly, then spoke to Hassan in rapid Hindustani. At last, she smiled and left, setting the tray down before going.

"That was Krishna," he indicated the departing figure. "My woman."

"But she's a nomad," Morgana stammered. "I thought such things were forbidden among your people."

"That is true," Hassan replied solemnly. "But I wanted her. Besides, I cannot allow my religion to stand in the way of my ascension to the throne. One chooses one's friends where one must," he shrugged. "With the money I get for you, I will be able to lead a rebellion to oust my brother from the throne."

"But you must have money of your own," Morgana spoke, puzzled. "After all, you are a prince, too."

"No." The word sounded bitter. "I must depend on

Sirsi for everything I have. It was my father's wish. I have nothing that my brother does not give me. When I arrived in Bhavnagar last week, he was very displeased with me. He said he wanted me to lead a detachment to subdue the nomad people in the north of the province. He is a fool! The nomads attack his caravans under my orders. Does he think I'd put a stop to that?"

"That does not sound like the Sirsi I know," Morgana reached for another piece of meat, trying to appear calm although she was growing more frightened by the minute. She had to get away and warn Sirsi of his brother's plans.

"Ah. You do not know him as I do, lotus blossom. He's ruthless and cruel, and sees me as a threat to his power of the throne." And rightly so, Morgana thought. "He would stop at nothing to be rid of me."

"Sirsi is not like that, I tell you," she insisted.

Hassan merely laughed unpleasantly and tied her up again. "Sorry, little lotus, but I cannot have you escaping. Sleep well," he said and disappeared.

She tossed and turned for a while, attempting to loose the knots which bound her wrists and now her ankles, but it was to no avail. Hassan had tied them tightly. She cursed him silently under her breath for a while, then slept at last, sure that Sirsi would send for her immediately.

Days passed and when the Maharajah did not send the ransom money Hassan had demanded, Morgana began to grow very worried. Hassan bore a dark frown upon his face which boded ill for her and spoke sharply to her if she attempted to question him.

"Naturally my brother must hunt for you first, lotus," he persisted in calling her that foolish name. "But he will pay in the end. He knows he cannot find me here in the desert. He will pay," Hassan repeated.

But Morgana was not so sure anymore.

Chapter Twenty-nine

Amreli smiled secretly to herself. The entire palace was in an uproar over the Englishwoman's disappearance. She remembered the way it had been when the messenger arrived bearing Hassan's note demanding the ransom money. La! How angry the Maharajah had been. And poor Captain Jones. He'd looked absolutely sick with grief and worry, but it did not faze Amreli. Jind and Dhoraji are fools, she thought, that they cannot see what is going on beneath their very noses. Do they not know that the Maharajah is sleeping with the red-haired woman? Why, she might even be on her way toward becoming the fourth wife in this household. No, pretty, sultry Jind would not care, nor would Dhoraji, whose son would someday rule Bhavnagar. But she, Amreli, cared. She would not stand by and see the prince drawn into the fair Englishwoman's arms.

So when Sirsi questioned his wives about Morgana's disappearance, Amreli gazed at him with large, innocent eyes and said, "But, Your Highness, I was awake when Hassan came. He did not force the young Englishwoman to go with him. She went willingly."

Sirsi shook his wife until she thought the teeth would rattle out of her head. "What are you saying, woman?" he asked angrily, drawing his breath in with a sharp hiss.

"I tell you, I saw," she tossed her head back proudly. "Hassan came for her and—I'm sorry if this is painful for you, Captain Jones," she gave him a pitying glance. "But Lady Keldara went to Hassan of her own free will. I saw her press herself against him and she—she kissed him on the lips and then they rode away," Amreli finished defiantly, as though daring Sirsi to claim that it wasn't true.

Taylor struggled with his emotions valiantly. "I can't believe it. You're lying," he told the Indian woman.

"Why would I lie? Answer me that, then," she replied haughtily.

The sea captain knew of no reason and felt momentarily defeated. "Your Highness," he turned to Sirsi. "Surely you do not believe this tale. My fiancée has been kidnapped. I demand that you pay the ransom at once."

"You demand, Captain Jones? You forget yourself. I am master here," Sirsi answered coldly. "My brother hates me. Perhaps he has somehow managed to convince Morgana to aid him in this ridiculous plan. I find it difficult to imagine myself, but I cannot discount that possibility," Sirsi frowned, perplexed.

Had she done this to him? Had Morgana suddenly grown tired of him and thrown her lot in with Hassan? Perhaps. If Hassan had offered to marry her . . . promised her a kingdom in return for her help? What woman would not have jumped at the chance? His eyes narrowed seethingly. Amreli was right. His own wife, she would have no reason to lie.

He dispatched the soldiers to begin searching for the couple, then told Captain Jones he had no intention of paying the ransom until he had further evidence one way or another in the affair. Taylor grew livid with rage and fear, but there was nothing he could do.

The days dragged by, and still the soldiers found no sign of Hassan or Morgana. Another messenger arrived with a second, more threatening note which contained a lock of copper hair. Sirsi almost cried when he saw it. Could it be that he was wrong and Amreli had lied? He felt shaken and began to doubt himself and his decision. The note said that if he did not pay, a finger would be delivered next. He shuddered, remembering the way Morgana's slender fingers had curled in his hair, had pulled him to her. Taylor pleaded with him, cajoled him, and finally offered to pay the ransom himself.

"How much does your brother want? Name it and I'll pay it myself," Taylor said.

"I doubt if you could raise the amount, Captain Jones. It is a king's ransom my brother demands, a great deal even to me. In your American money, five hundred thousand dollars."

Taylor gasped. He knew of no place to get such a sum of money, not even if he sold his plantation and ship both.

"What can we do, then? Have your soldiers discovered nothing?"

"No, nothing at all. Hassan knows the deserts well, and he is friendly with many of the nomad tribes. I'm afraid this was my doing. I sent him to France and England to be educated, and he learned to despise our caste system. He would as soon bed an Untouchable as a princess, incredible as that seems."

Six days later the Maharajah received another packet. Inside was a small, bloody finger.

Morgana shrank away as Hassan approached her with the knife. "What are you doing?"

"I merely want to cut off a lock of your hair. My brother does not seem to believe you are in danger, little lotus."

"And am I?" she asked nervously.

"Did I not say I would not harm you? I always keep my promises, Morgana."

He sliced off one curl and folded it up in a packet, calling for Abu to come and deliver the message.

Several days later Hassan strode in and asked Morgana if she was ready to take her bath. Every day he escorted her to a nearby pond so that she might wash. He smiled. The first time she'd been very angry, then pleading as she begged him to turn his back. But he had lounged against a boulder and told her to get on with it or continue to look like a savage. Her creamy skin was black with dirt and her hair tangled like a gypsy's. Morgana took one look at her reflection in the water and indignantly peeled off the sari she wore, heedless of Hassan's appreciative stare. She waded into the water and scrubbed herself vigorously, surprised that he left her alone. She had fully expected him to rape her.

Now she no longer worried. No doubt Krishna kept him busy enough. Dropping her clothes with no hesitation at all, she walked into the water until it covered her firm, rosy breasts, gasping in the shock of the pond's coldness. When she had finished her bath, she waded out and donned her garments again. She was free to come and go as she pleased, but always someone lurked nearby to guard her. Only at night did Hassan tie her up as before, leaving her alone in the darkness of the tent. She knew he spent his nights with Krishna; and she wondered whose tent this was that she occupied. Had Hassan given it up for her? Ah well, she shrugged her shoulders indifferently. It probably belonged to Abu or one of the other men. Morgana didn't care as long as they left her alone.

Hassan studied Morgana quietly in the soft light which lit the tent, his gaze falling to her long, slender hands. How could he do it, cut off one of those slim fingers? He picked up the knife. He must do it, otherwise his brother would not send the money. Very slowly he moved toward her.

"What do you want, Hassan?" she spoke sharply. "Another lock of my hair?"

"No, little lotus, I'm afraid that was not sufficient."

Morgana shrank away at the wicked, pained look upon his face. "What is it, Hassan? You promised, you promised you would not harm me," she was suddenly very afraid.

"I know, Morgana, but I must send Sirsi something which will convince him that I mean business," his voice sounded deadly. "I mean only to cut one small finger. It will not hurt long, I promise you."

She screamed then, and screamed again, rising to run away. He grabbed her and they stumbled and fell among the pillows, the loose robe she had wrapped around her after her bath falling away to expose the creamy whiteness of her breasts. Hassan gasped greedily at the beauty bared before his face and felt a quickening in his loins. Yes, she was beautiful and she had lain with his brother. Before she realized what was happening, Hassan held the knife to Morgana's throat.

"Be still," he muttered, then pressed his mouth to the soft, ripe mounds, nibbling their pink tips gently until they swelled in response. His free hand moved to push the folds of the robe away, then travelled downwards to the white flanks, caressing, probing. Morgana moaned.

"No, Hassan, please."

"You gave yourself freely to my brother. Do you come less willingly to me?"

"You hate him, don't you?"

"Yes, I despise him. Taking you will be a pleasure, little lotus," he fumbled with the tie of his loose trousers.

She cried out once when he thrust boldly between her thighs, then his mouth moved to cover her own with his hard kiss. She tried to protest, but the sharp prick of the knife he still held quickly dissuaded her from calling out again.

When he had satisfied himself, Hassan rolled over to one side, keeping her pinioned to the ground with one leg wrapped strongly about her thighs. His face was flushed and angry.

"I cannot believe that you lie so still and unresponding beneath my brother, Morgana," he swore at her softly in the darkness.

"If you are displeased, then perhaps you should seek the arms of your woman, Hassan," Morgana spoke sarcastically. She ached where he had so brutally violated her.

"Krishna? She means little to me, but I must keep her happy or the nomad tribe will not follow me. Besides, her brother is very powerful and can raise an army whenever I desire. If giving her pleasure keeps her brother under my thumb, why not? One woman is much like another."

Morgana shuddered in the darkness, realizing he was absolutely ruthless. He would never return her to Sirsi so that she could give away his plans. He'd meant to kill her all along and she had as yet discovered no means of escape. They were interrupted just then by a loud wailing. Hassan swore angrily, reaching for his garments.

"What the devil? Do not try to run away, lotus blossom," he ran his hands over her breasts and between her thighs once more. "I shall return soon and then we shall discover what makes my brother desire you so."

She cringed as he laughed in her face, then, after binding her hands to one of the tent posts, disappeared into the night.

"Abu, what goes here?" Hassan called to one of his men.

"Pali's dead."

Hassan followed him to the tent. Pali was the wife of one of his best men, Shivpuri. She had been stricken with some kind of fever several days ago, but no one had thought she would die. Shivpuri was still wailing, a sad, mournful sound as he knelt beside the body of his wife. Krishna and some of the other women were there, washing and dressing the corpse for burial. Hassan stared at Pali's pale face unemotionally, ignoring Krishna's searching glance. Then to the utter horror of everyone present, he raised one of the girl's lifeless hands and cut off the little finger. Shivpuri stared at him, numb and speechless with shock and rage, then he bellowed and sought to attack his leader. Hassan brought his knife up sharply.

"Don't be a fool! She'd dead, and this small token will bring us the money we need to attack the palace and capture the throne," he hissed.

Shivpuri shook violently for a moment before he turned away and again subsided into sobs. Hassan handed the small piece of flesh to Abu, who almost retched at the sight.

"Go now to my brother. Tell him the next time he will receive the rest of the corpse. Tell him I grow weary of waiting for the money."

Hassan returned to his tent and smiled as he gazed down into Morgana's frightened face. There were red streaks about her wrists where she had attempted to loose the cords which bound her.

"So, little lotus blossom, it will not be necessary to cut off one of your fingers after all. How fortunate for you," he continued to stare at her naked body sprawled out upon the cushions. "You are lovely. I wonder that I ignored your obvious charms this long," he said before he once more loosed his garments and forced himself upon her.

Sirsi gasped as the withered, rotted, bloody finger rolled out of the packet into his lap. He could scarcely bring himself to touch it. God! How could Hassan have been so cruel? He stared at the young nomad who had brought it.

"I ought to kill you for this," he hissed.

"If you do, Your Highness, the red-haired woman will suffer the same fate. If I do not return, Hassan has promised her a very slow and unpleasant death," Abu met the Maharajah's eyes, so cold and dark.

Abu knew they would let him go as always, and as always he would outwit the foolish soldiers they sent to follow him. He thrust out his jaw defiantly. He was not afraid.

"Please, Your Highness," Taylor's face was anguished. "Give your brother the money. You heard what the boy said. They'll kill her."

"They will doubtless kill her anyway, Captain Jones," Sirsi's voice was low, defeated. "Jodhpur," he finally called to his servant. "Bring me my jewel chest."

Abu gasped when he saw the glittering display within. The chest itself must be solid gold. Hassan would be very pleased, and perhaps Shivpuri would forgive him for cutting off his wife's finger. He gathered up the chest quickly, holding it close as he rode away from the palace.

Morgana sobbed quietly. Almost a week had passed and still Abu had not returned. She had been horrified when Hassan had explained why he did not need to cut off her finger. God! He was mad. He would surely kill her. Every night now he came and forced himself upon her, laughing cruelly when she could not fight him off. Twice he'd beaten her. She was going to die here in this horrible Indian desert.

"Hush, foolish one."

She looked up to see Krishna holding one finger stealthily to her lips.

"What do you want?" Morgana asked dully.

"I've come to help you get away, but you must do exactly as I say," the nomad woman spoke softly.

Morgana nodded, too confused to think, and hope lit her eyes. Help had arrived, it seemed, in the unlikeliest of guises.

"Hassan is away on a raiding party. We must hurry. He will return before dark," Krishna explained as she cut the thongs that held Morgana captive. Hassan had begun keeping her tied up all the time now.

Morgana followed the Indian woman out of the tent, careful to make no sound that would arouse the attention of the men who remained in the village. When they had reached the edge of the encampment where the horses were tethered, Krishna pulled one of them free.

"I can get you no saddle. Go, ride quickly now. I

will loose the rest of the horses and scatter them to distract the men's attention."

"Why are you doing this, Krishna?" Morgana asked as she threw herself upon the stallion's back.

"Why? Do you think I don't know what goes on in your tent when the night falls? Why Hassan comes no more to my bed? He is mad for you. I have no wish to lose him, milk-faced wench! Go." She raised her hand and brought it down hard upon the stallion's flanks.

The sharp slap caused the horse to bolt, nearly throwing Morgana from its back. It tore out over the desert, hooves flying, sending dust and sand scattering like rain. Morgana glanced over her shoulder as she wrapped the reins more tightly about her hand. Sure enough, Krishna had kept her word. The rest of the horses had taken off in all directions. She bent her face down against the stallion's neck, flattening her body against its back, so that, in all the dust, the nomads might not be able to tell this horse bore a rider. Bhavnagar, she knew, lay to the south. She prayed she was going in the right direction.

The ride was not easy, but then Morgana hadn't expected it to be. She had no food and no water, except when she happened across one of the small oases which dotted the desert. But somehow, after all that had happened to her, it didn't seem so hard. She was able to subsist on the land, thanks to the survival lessons she had learned in her ordeal in Africa and Taylor's training. She didn't panic as she had before, but watched the sky at night to study the stars for direction, remembering Rian's instructions carefully this time. She did not make the mistake of travelling in circles and she kept well away from the nomad tribes, fearful that Hassan would follow her. And when, several days later, Bhavnagar loomed up on the horizon, she was able to smile with pride in herself.

One of the guards recognized her, and by the time she reached the palace gates, Sirsi and Taylor were already standing on the steps. She flung herself from the stallion and, dirty and tired as she was, threw herself into Sirsi's arms, laughing and crying, and calling his name over and over. Too late she saw the sudden understanding and anguish in Taylor's eyes as he dropped his outstretched arms to his sides and walked away. She moved to follow him, but Sirsi stopped her, saying, "Let him go, Morgana."

He kissed her openly, then pushed her back a little so that he could look at her, the warmth, relief, and affection he felt for her plain upon his face. Then all at once Morgana saw his dark eyes grow cold and steely.

"Why, what's wrong, Sirsi?" she asked nervously.

He didn't answer, merely turning her hands over and over again in his: small, slender, and perfect. He swore at her then and flung them away.

"You bitch! Why did you come back? Didn't Hassan come up to your expectations, or did he throw you out when he no longer needed you?"

"Sirsi, I—I don't understand. What are you talking about?" Morgana was genuinely puzzled.

"Get out of my sight!"

The Maharajah turned and walked away, leaving her standing there, sobbing, wondering what had gone wrong. At last, she climbed the steps and found her way to the women's quarters. Sirsi's wives had heard the news and Morgana discovered that they eyed her suspiciously upon her entrance.

"English pig!" Amreli spat. "How dare you show your face here?"

She ran across the room and would have clawed Morgana's face had Jind and Dhoraji not caught her wrists and restrained her.

"Would someone please tell me what's wrong?" Morgana wept tiredly.

"I'll tell you what's the matter," Amreli eagerly volunteered, her eyes narrowed with hatred and cunning. "How dare you come here from the arms of your lover, Hassan, after pulling such a nasty trick on the Prince? Has Hassan cast you out now that my lord has paid such a fortune for you? La! I spit on you, English whore!"

Amreli did spit, right in Morgana's face. In a flash, Morgana was across the room, fingers pulling at the Indian's long, black hair.

"You lying bitch!" Morgana's breasts heaved with anger as she dug her nails into Amreli's face and saw with satisfaction the five bloody streaks she left.

The two women rolled and grappled on the floor, pounding each other unmercifully in spite of Jind's efforts to stop them. Dhoraji stepped away from the fracas, screaming for help. Morgana caught a glancing blow to her nose and it started bleeding, but she had the gratification of punching Amreli's eye and seeing it swell and blacken. She did not know that Sirsi, Taylor, and the palace guards had arrived until she felt rough arms yanking her to her feet and away from Amreli. The two of them stared at each other, panting angrily and looking much the worse for wear.

"What's going on here?" the Maharajah asked coldly.

"That English whore! She tried to kill me," Amreli indicated Morgana with an indignant toss of her tangled mane of hair.

"Why, you lying bitch," Morgana spoke through clenched teeth. "No doubt you're the one responsible for putting such ideas into Sirsi's head."

"What ideas? What are you saying?" he turned to her.

"She said Hassan was my lover, and that we planned everything together. It's a lie! Even now he seeks to arm the nomad tribes and attack the palace. He used me, your swine of a brother. He kidnapped me and would have killed me had I not escaped."

"Don't listen to her false tales, my prince," Amreli broke in. "She wishes to save her neck now that her treason has been discovered. Do you desire to be duped again?"

"Silence, woman! Hold your tongue. I am master here."

"How did she escape then? And why is she missing no finger?" Amreli was not to be put off.

"Yes, Morgana, I should be interested in learning that myself," Sirsi spoke again.

Her voice clipped, Morgana related the entire story, omitting the part about Hassan having forced himself upon her night after night.

"And just why would this nomad wish to help you escape if she was Hassan's woman?" Amreli questioned slyly when Morgana had finished.

"Well, Morgana?" Sirsi glanced at her stony face. "Why are you silent, wench? Speak up."

"Because he—he raped me. Krishna feared he might take me to wife," the words were so soft Sirsi had to strain to hear them.

"You see," Amreli smiled triumphantly. "She was his lover all along."

Sirsi felt a blinding rage sear through his veins. Amreli was right. Morgana had deceived him. She had lain with his brother. She even admitted it.

"Captain Jones, get her out of this palace right now or I shall not be responsible for the consequences. I will make arrangements to have your things brought to the docks. I expect you to be gone from Bhavnagar within the hour."

The Maharajah's face was deadly as he turned and walked away.

Morgana did not watch as the coast of India faded from sight. She sat below in the cabin, sobbing bitterly. Oh, where had everything begun to go wrong? She could not accept the fact that Sirsi had not believed her. He had lain with her and loved her, hadn't he? How could he have cast her out so cruelly? And that bitch, Amreli, Morgana wished she had killed the woman.

Taylor had given the men orders to keep away from her, and he himself did not come to the cabin. She felt utterly isolated, desolated. She would have welcomed even Taylor, would have gladly sat on his lap and pulled his beard, and listened to his gruff, Yankee voice telling her not to worry her head about such matters. Then she remembered his sad, accusing face and knew he was too hurt to come to her. Perhaps he hadn't believed her either. Oh, damn Hassan! Why had he spoiled things for her? She sincerely hoped that he and Sirsi would kill each other and that Bhavnagar would be destroyed. It would serve them right.

She went to the bed and lay down again, a damp cloth over her eyes. If only she could get some rest. She was exhausted from her torturous journey over the hot desert sands, but worry about how she would straighten out the tangle of her life kept her from sleeping. Finally exhaustion won out and she fell into a deep slumber.

Taylor paced thoughtfully on the deck. So, they were true then, the rumors he'd heard at the palace about Morgana and Sirsi. It had been the Maharajah's arms to which she'd run, not his, never his. He could scarcely credit it, had refused to believe it, but now he could lie to himself no longer. She had deceived him. Could it be that Amreli had spoken the truth and Morgana had committed that terrible crime, had plotted with Hassan for the ransom money? God, she had given herself to both of them, the Indian brothers, and all this time she had played the shy, respectable widow with him, never allowing him more than a chaste kiss. Did she think him less than a man? Did she not know how much he desired her, sought to make her his? He had offered her marriage and the best plantation in all of Virginia. But what did it matter if Sirsi or Hassan had promised her a kingdom? Would any woman have refused such a chance, a chance to be a queen? No, Morgana surely would not have let such an opportunity slip through her fingers. Taylor remembered only too well her shrewd, calculating eyes and sharp questions.

She had lied. Was this the first time? After all, what did he really know about this strange, lovely, elusive beauty he had found half-dead on the African savannahs? Perhaps it had all been lies. God, he didn't even know if her name was really Morgana. She could be a common criminal, escaped from some penal colony. Morgana had been very closemouthed about her past, saying only that she had sailed from England with her husband. A mythical husband with a mythical ship, perhaps? Taylor had seen no sign of a vessel called the *Sorceress*. A mythical name, as well?

He swore softly under his breath. In spite of what she'd done or who she really was, he loved her. There was no escaping that. He determined that tonight he would try and talk to her, would try to make some sense out of this sad tangle of events. He couldn't bear to hear that dreadful sobbing, and his crew was staring at him as though he were some kind of ogre.

That evening Morgana was surprised when Taylor knocked softly on the door of the cabin and said he would be most pleased if she would join him for supper. She had lain in bed all day, feeling very miserable and she knew she looked a fright. Taylor, however, made no reference to her appearance and Morgana could only assume he did not care about her feelings. But she agreed to dine with him nevertheless; it was better than being left alone with her thoughts.

She dressed with care that evening, intending to appear as presentable as possible. She would not wear any of the lovely saris from India, nor the bangles or baubles Sirsi had given her. Instead she chose a green gown she'd made herself from the fabric on Taylor's ship. She brushed her hair vigorously, forcing it into the smooth roll she'd worn always before marrying Rian, and wrapped it at the nape of her neck. Finished at last, she surveyed herself in the looking glass and was satisfied. She looked every inch the prim English miss. Perhaps she would be able to convince Taylor that those lies Amreli had told were not true.

Evidently the cook had heard the tale and felt sorry for her, for he served up one of his special dishes in an effort to please. Dinner was rather uncomfortable, however, for neither Taylor nor Morgana could think of anything pleasant to say. The events at Bhavnagar weighed heavily on their minds, and each of them deliberately concentrated attention on the meal. But when Taylor at last pushed his plate away and lit his pipe, Morgana knew that the day of reckoning was upon her. She stared at her hands and waited for him to speak.

He cleared his throat gruffly. "Morgana, I've been doing some hard thinking about what happened back in India. I don't know and don't care what the real truth of the matter is. You're young and you've made mistakes. I just want you to know that I love you, and I still want you as my wife. We'll go on to Virginia and forget what's happened here."

Morgana felt the tears well up in her eyes. She was so ashamed. What a good man Taylor was, and kind. Oh, what should she do?

"I'm no good, Taylor," she sobbed. "Can't you see that? I'm forever falling into one scrape after another. Even you don't know what to believe about me. Everything has happened so fast, from the time I was captured by those Africans that I just don't know what to think. It makes my head ache to try. Please be patient with me; I don't want to make any more decisions right now. I need some time to think, to pull myself together."

"I understand. We'll be in China soon. You can tell me your answer then," he turned and left the cabin.

Chapter Thirty

An atmosphere of restraint had fallen over the relationship Morgana shared with Taylor. Both of them were exceedingly polite, but they no longer lingered over dinner, nor did she pull his beard or sit on his lap in the evenings. And with each passing day, she became more and more convinced that she could not marry him, that she had only been deluding herself. She felt intensely lonely, but she could not wed Taylor now, and she could not bring herself to return to Ireland to the mockery of marriage with Rian McShane. She could not return to England—she would have to stand trial for murder. Morgana was as troubled and restless as the seas over which they sailed.

She decided that men were no good, not any of them, and resolved never to have another thing to do with them as long as she lived. She was curt with Taylor's crew almost to the point of rudeness and they watched her with puzzlement and pity, trying to understand what ailed her.

When the ship finally landed in Macao, the Chinese port occupied by the Portuguese, Morgana had lost a great deal of weight from worry and was strangely subdued. She took no joy in the usual hustle and bustle of the docks, scarcely even noticing the coolies who ran to and fro with goods, and the junks and sampans which littered the harbor. She had no idea where they were going to stay and only nodded when Taylor informed her that a Colonel Davis and his wife would be putting them up. She allowed Taylor to help her into the rickshaw, and sat mutely, staring at the crowded streets as they were carried away.

Colonel Davis was about fifty years of age, paunchy and balding, and puffed up with his own sense of importance and duty. It was his misfortune that he reminded her so much of her cousin Trevor and she could scarcely be civil to him.

His wife, Prudence, was a gossip and was obviously delighted at having a real countess in her house, regardless how haughty and distant that lady might be. She greeted Morgana warmly, her sharp, curious eyes noticing every detail of Morgana's appearance as she showed her to her room.

"It will be so good to have someone in the house to talk to for a change. You've no idea how lonesome it gets here with only these dreadful Chinese. Barbarians, I told the Colonel. I don't know how he could have accepted this post. It's so dreadfully dull, with just the other military wives about," Mistress Davis fanned herself vigorously before throwing open the shutters to let some light into the room. "You'll meet them all this afternoon, I expect. 'Tis my practice to serve tea here at four o'clock every day. As I told the Colonel, just because he saw fit to relegate us to this uncivilized country is no reason we should allow ourselves to resort to primitive behavior as well. No indeed. We must keep up appearances, don't you agree, Lady Keldara?"

Morgana nodded her head dumbly, wishing the woman would go away so that she could lie down with a cool cloth upon her forehead. She seemed to get headaches so often these days.

"There, that's better," Mistress Davis sighed as she plumped up the pillows and ran her hand over the dresser to check for dust. "I declare, I'll have to speak to Draya. Such an untidy girl, but there, 'tis difficult enough to get decent help here."

"I'm sure it is," Morgana felt bound to say something at least.

"Oh, yes indeed," Mistress Davis beamed upon having this trivial remark bestowed upon her. "Why, with the opium dens and those dreadful waterfront bordellos! Really, if I've told the Colonel once, I've told him a hundred times that something ought to be done about it. Why, only last week a young sailor boy was knifed to death right there in the harbor. So shocking! But there, I expect you'd like to get cleaned up and rest a bit. Ocean voyages are dreadfully tiresome. So dull with nothing to do but stand on deck and watch the sea. A horrid business, I told the Colonel, with the storms and all. I declare, I was positively green with sickness on the way over. You'll never guess how fervently I longed for my death."

Morgana thought silently that it was too bad Mistress Davis's wish hadn't been granted and decided that if she heard the word *dreadful* one more time, she would scream.

"I'm awfully tired," she said by way of ending the conversation. "I think I'll just lie down for a bit. You'll call me in time for tea?"

"Of course, my lady. You can be sure about that. I'll say one thing for these barbarians, they do know how to make an excellent pot of brew," Mistress Davis pursed her lips together.

The door closed at last and Morgana sank down onto the bed with a sigh of relief.

The days passed slowly. Morgana seldom went out, although Taylor frequently offered to escort her, prompting Mistress Davis to remark that she should be grateful that she had such a thoughtful fiance. But Morgana didn't care what they thought. She ate all of her meals alone, except for dinner, but dutifully attended Mistress Davis's tea parties, where she was sure she was the object of much speculation.

The Chinese, it seemed, had strict rules concerning foreigners, allowing them to settle only in Macao and Canton, so a cluster of English military men and their wives settled there, as did many sailors and traders. The latter were permitted to bargain only with the monopolists in China, and therefore had no control over the outrageous prices charged for goods. They learned quickly, however, that opium could purchase almost anything, and those who did not wish to deal with the merchants in Canton and Macao turned their ships to the port of Hong Kong.

"My dear Lady Keldara," Mistress Atherton leaned forward in her chair. She was one of the ladies who frequented Mistress Davis's parlor at tea time. "How happy you must be to have a man like Captain Jones. My husband says he's one of the kindest men he's ever known."

"Yes," Morgana raised her teacup to her lips, wondering if it had been wise to present herself as a widow, but what else could she have said?

"Oh, yes," Mistress Langley chimed in. "Ship's captains are hard men usually. Do you remember that dark, handsome one who used to put in here? What's his name, Prudence? Can't for the life of me recall it. He was attractive, in a devilish sort of way if you like that type."

"Oh, I know who you're speaking of, Captain O'Shea, Shannon, something like that anyway, Beatrice," Mistress Davis replied, her face puckered up in an attempt to remember.

"Wasn't he the one who kept that Chinese girl down at the Red Lady's place?" Mistress Granger sniffed. "The one who killed an officer in a duel over her?"

"The very one, Elvira," Mistress Langley paused to sip her tea, blowing on the hot brew to cool it first.

"Wonder whatever happened to him? It has been several years since he was here last."

"Lord knows," Mistress Atherton had tired of the subject. "Probably murdered in some waterfront brawl. I say, Lady Keldara, do you intend to join us at the Officers' Ball next week?"

"Oh, do come," Mistress Granger implored. "Gertude and I should love to have you there," she indicated Mistress Atherton with a slight nod.

Morgana was glad to answer this question, and set her teacup down carefully so that they would not notice that her hands were shaking. Captain O'Shea, Shannon, could it have been McShane? Evidently Mistress Davis hadn't made the connection or perhaps Morgana was only imagining things. But Rian had been in Macao many times. He had bought the Chinese silk here, that shimmering green material he'd tried to rip that night on the beach. What had they said? He had had a Chinese mistress. *I once had a mistress in every port and shall have again if you continue to behave in this fashion,* he had told her once, his eyes hard and mocking as they raked her.

"My dear Lady Keldara. Is anything wrong?" Mistress Atherton inquired. "You're looking quite pale."

"I'm sorry, I'm afraid I haven't fully recovered from the voyage yet. You were saying?"

She answered the ladies' questions about herself, politely sidestepping those to which she did not care to reply, her attention wandering again. She was letting her imagination run away with her. There were dozens of Irish sea captains. At last, she dismissed the thought from her mind.

The Officers' Ball was a dull affair, and Morgana regretted she had agreed to come. None of the young men present interested her in the least and she was glad when Taylor asked if she might like to stroll in the gardens. At least she could get away from those prying women for a time. The smell of fall was in the air. She plucked idly at

447

the blossoms on the small trees and studied the statues of the dragons and other creatures that adorned the area. All of China, it seemed, was inhabited by dragons. The Oriental music drifting out into the night sounded strange to her ears, and she realized from Jeb's training on the guitar that it was all based on a five-note scale. She was silent, wondering when or if Taylor was going to speak. She suspected that he'd called her out here to find out if she intended to marry him. She sighed pensively. She didn't know what to do. If only he weren't so quiet, so kind, so thoughtful. God! Why didn't he yell at her or beat her; it would have been so much easier to deal with.

She thought of the times Rian had threatened to break her neck, his mocking eyes and sardonic mouth cursing her in a heated rage. At least that was something she had understood, his passionate temper, his hard, demanding lips. She did not understand Taylor at all. How could he want her after all that had happened?

"Morgana," he spoke at last. "Have you reached a decision yet?"

"Aye, Taylor, I have," she said softly, knowing that she must give him pain. "I—I cannot marry you, Taylor. We are ill matched. We don't think or feel the same way about anything."

"But, Morgana," he pleaded. "We will adapt to each other in time. I promise you."

"Taylor, it's no use," she almost wailed. "You'd grow angry with me in time, and come to resent me. I'd make you miserable. I come from another world. I need—"

What did she need? Her mind drifted back to when she'd been just sixteen in London, just a poor poet's daughter. She had known then what she wanted. A Corinthian, a Libertine; aye, dark and raffish, a man who dressed well, who mixed with the Ton; a man who would take her places, to the dizzying, bright lights of Drury Lane; who drove a curricle and belonged to the Four Horses Club. A devil, a rake who made her heart beat fast and her mind swoon. Rian's face broke into her thoughts, his demanding lips, the manner in which the top one curled into a snarl before it turned into a kiss, the way in which his green eyes glinted in the darkness. Aye, he had been everything she'd ever wanted in a man, proud, passionate, hard, strong. Why, then, had she not been content with him?

"Don't ever wish for things, Taylor," she said suddenly. "You might get them."

Then she turned and ran back into the house.

"Well, I just don't understand you, Morgana," Mistress Davis said as she leaned over to pour out the tea. "A fine man like Captain Jones. Whatever possessed you to turn him down like that, and at the Officers' Ball besides? I swear he looked like a ghost for the rest of the evening."

"I just don't love him, Prudence," Morgana gazed out of the window wearily.

"Love? My dear girl, you could do a lot worse," Mistress Atherton chided her gently. "Whatever do you intend to do with yourself?"

"I don't know. I haven't given it much thought really. Every time I think about it, my head starts to ache. I suppose I must go home to Ireland, but the prospect dismays me, Gertrude."

"You know, I just had a marvelous idea," Mistress Langley clapped her hands together gaily. "How would you like to be a governess? Oh, I realize it's far beneath your position in society, but just the very thing if you want to stay in China for a while. And you could always go home if you found you didn't like it."

"Of course, Beatrice, I should have thought of it myself," Mistress Granger chimed in. "Dear Sung Lü has been positively distraught over the loss of poor Mistress Whiteby."

"Please," Morgana begged, her interest piqued. "Tell me what you're talking about. I might like being a governess. 'Tis what I originally intended to do after my father died."

"Well," Mistress Langley continued. "One of the

Chinese merchants, Sung K'ang Nan, has a house nearby. You must have seen it Morgana, that huge pagoda with the monstrous dragons out front. His wife was at the Officers' Ball the other evening complaining that this Mistress Whiteby, the governess, had just packed up and left without so much as a by-your-leave. Sung Lü was just beside herself. Her husband absolutely insists that the children be tutored by an English governess, and Lord knows they're scarce enough in Macao. He thinks it will aid his son when the boy takes over the silk business."

"It sounds like something I'd like to do, Beatrice," Morgana spoke excitedly. Here at last was a way out of her dilemma. "Do you suppose she'll consider me?"

"Consider you? My dear girl, if you can read and write, I'm sure the job is yours. I'll send a note over today."

"I'm very happy for you, Morgana, but I still think it's dreadful that you rejected poor Captain Jones so cruelly," Mistress Davis sniffed, getting, as always, the final word.

Morgana arrived at the Chinese mansion early the next morning, being borne there in a rickshaw. Taylor was very dismayed by her intentions and even angrier that the ladies had helped her in the matter, but she remained adamant. She thought the dragons smiled wickedly at her as she passed, but then decided it was just a fancy on her part. She rapped the brass knocker sharply and was finally admitted by a small houseboy. He showed her to a small sitting room which was filled with silk cushions, and bamboo tables, laden with ivory and jade, much of which she realized from Rian's instruction was quite valuable.

She waited for what seemed like an eternity before a small woman with jet black hair that shone almost bluishly in the light came in.

"You are Lady Keldara?"

"Yes."

"I am Madame Sung Lü. Mistress Langley has told

me all about you. I understand you are interested in the position of governess which I have open."

"Yes, I'm interested in the post," Morgana took a seat as Sung Lü asked her to please have a chair.

She studied the Oriental curiously. The woman was probably in her late thirties, although Morgana still found it extremely difficult to guess the age of a Chinese. She had almond-shaped eyes and high cheekbones that seemed to slant in the shadows. She was impeccably dressed and her face was unreadable.

"Lady Keldara, my husband insists that my son be tutored in English. I'm afraid he's a difficult child. Your task will not be easy."

"I'm not afraid of hard work, madam. My father thought schooling was very important. I speak English, French, and some Spanish and Hindustani, as well as a little Chinese I have managed to learn here. I am well versed in English literature, and Greek and Roman history; and I can read, write, and cipher. If it is these things which your husband wishes your son to learn, then I can teach him."

"Very well. You may begin on Monday then. There is also a small girl, my daughter. I would like her to study with my son. You will lodge here, naturally, and shall be paid every month."

Sung Lü named a figure which was far more than Morgana had expected and bid her good day. Morgana stepped out of the house, relieved that the woman had not questioned her about her past experience or asked to see references. But then, as Mistress Langley had said, educated women were a rarity in Macao, whose English population consisted mainly of officers' wives. She rode back to the Davis' house in Sung Lü's carriage.

Sung Lü hoped she had done the right thing. After all, the girl was very young. Still, there had been a look of determination about her. Besides, she probably wouldn't stay long. They very seldom did. Her son hated his studies and generally found some means of disposing of his governesses very quickly. The last one had found a snake in her bed. It was harmless, but it had been the last straw for the governess. She'd departed the same day. Sung Lü sighed and went to inform her husband of the matter.

"You got the position then?" Prudence asked when Morgana arrived back at the house.

"Aye, 'twas not hard at all."

"Well I didn't think you'd have any trouble. Captain Jones is very upset, though. Why don't you go out into the garden and speak to him?"

Morgana soon settled in at the Chinese household. Her room was small, but comfortable. She'd had several trying scenes with Taylor and was glad to get away from him at last. He had asked that he be allowed to call on her, however; and she'd reluctantly agreed, more out of pity than anything else.

Sung Lü showed her the schoolroom and introduced her to the children. The small girl, Sung Ni Yüan, eyed Morgana curiously as she dipped a pretty curtsey, her tiny face grave. But the boy, Sung Hsi Wei, gave her a rebellious stare and bowed only when his mother spoke to him sharply in rapid Chinese. Morgana sighed. He certainly looked like a handful. To her surprise, both of the children spoke English, although it was halting and somewhat broken. They had a great deal of trouble pronouncing her name and she finally suggested they call her Lady Mag, not realizing how much it would disturb her to hear Rian's nickname for her on their lips.

"Well then, Lady Mag," Sung Hsi Wei studied her covertly after Sung Lü had disappeared. "Do you know how many governesses I've had? Seven," he replied, not waiting for her to answer. "I've run them all off and I shall get rid of you, too," he boasted.

"Have you ever been to Africa?" she instantly decided that what he needed was a good spanking. He was much too spoiled.

"No," the boy answered somewhat sullenly.

"Well, I have. Do you know what they do with

disrespectful little boys there?" She didn't wait for him to reply either. "Someday I'll tell you."

He gazed at her in disbelief. "You don't know!" he spat. "You can't teach me anything."

"You shall see," she warned. "Now take your seat."

She almost smiled at the look of apprehension which crossed his face, but she managed to keep a stern countenance as she glanced through the books which had been provided. She had never taught before and really didn't know what to do next, but she was determined not to let the little tyrant know it.

"First of all I'd like you both to read for me so that I may determine where you are in your studies, and then we'll do some mathematics. Sung Ni Yüan, you shall be first," she spoke to the little girl who'd hardly said a word.

"You can call me Ni, Lady Mag," the girl offered timidly, giving Morgana a shy smile, much to her brother's disgust.

Morgana smiled back. "Very well then, Ni."

The child stumbled over many of the words, but she tried hard and was near tears when she could not finish the page.

"That's fine, Ni," Morgana smiled again. "You will learn in time. Here," she handed the book to Sung Hsi Wei. "You try, Hsi."

"My name is Sung Hsi Wei," he said coldly. "And I do not need to read. I already know all that I need to know, Lady Mag."

"Then do you know what we do in England to little boys who don't want to learn? We reinforce their lessons with a ruler," she picked up the ivory rod lying on the desk, beginning to grow rather angry.

"You wouldn't dare. I shall tell my father if you touch me."

"Listen to me, Hsi. When you have weathered the rains of England, climbed the rocky crags of Ireland, made monkey stew in Africa, and seen the Taj Mahal of

India, then you may tell me what to do, and not before, is that clear?"

"Have you really done all those things?" he looked at her with some interest now.

"Yes, I have. You see, you don't know as much as you thought. Now read the page, please."

He pouted sullenly, but did as she asked. So it was that when Sung Lü, not hearing the usual noise from the classroom, peeked in to check on the new governess, she found her children seated quietly at their desks, saying their multiplication tables. She closed the door, not wishing to disturb them, then walked away, somewhat amazed; and was able to tell her husband a short time later that she thought the new governess would do very nicely.

Morgana soon learned that she was considered above the salt in the Chinese household and was expected to dine with Sung Lü and Sung K'ang Nan. The children did not join them for meals, but Morgana was startled the first evening when she sat down at the table and an elderly lady was carried in. The woman was seated in a bamboo chair, her white hair beautifully coiffed, her yellow skin wrinkled with age, and her eyes a piercing shade of blue.

"Lady Keldara, this is my mother, Madame Sung," Sung K'ang Nan introduced her. "Mother, this is the new governess."

"Ah, so you're the bold tyrant who threatened to whip my grandson," the woman eyed Morgana craftily.

Morgana blushed furiously under the appraising stare and the words the woman spoke. "I would not actually have done so, Madame," she began, only to be cut off with a wave of the hand.

"Do not apologize, Lady Keldara. From what I've seen, that child is sorely in need of a good thrashing. My son spoils him," she gave Sung K'ang Nan a piercing glance. "I can see you're wondering how I came to speak such excellent English." Morgana jumped, for she was indeed thinking just that. "My mother was English. Left her people to marry my father, she did."

So that accounted for the woman's sharp blue eyes.

Madame Sung was decidedly frank. Unlike most Orientals, she said whatever happened to come into her mind. Morgana could tell this embarrassed her son and daughter-in-law, but they could do nothing about it. The Chinese held the elders of their society in great respect, deferring to them at all times in all matters. When dinner had ended, Madame Sung asked Morgana to come up to her room, then summoned two of the houseboys to carry her away again. She obviously could not walk. Morgana discovered the reason for this later, after Sung Lü had escorted her to the old woman's room, her face impassive as ever. If she found her mother-in-law distressing, she did not show it.

Madame Sung's feet were very tiny, deformed, bent almost double. Morgana could not help staring.

"An abominable custom, wouldn't you agree? I had them bound when I was seven years old. It was a disgrace then for highborn ladies to be able to walk and still is in many parts of China. Sung Lü is Siamese. That is why her feet are healthy, not withered like mine. And we refuse to allow Ni's feet to be bound in this fashion."

"But, why was it done?" Morgana almost shuddered at the thought of deliberately maiming someone so that she could not walk.

"To prevent wives from taking lovers. If they could not walk, they could not arrange secret assignations, for they would have no way to get there. None of the servants would dare to aid them in such a venture. Ah, I see that you are shocked. Well, each culture has its eccentricities. Please, sit down, Lady Keldara. Tell me of England. It has been a long time since I have spoken with someone from my mother's homeland; and longer still since I set eyes upon it. A very cold, damp country as I remember, but intriguing."

They conversed at some length while Madame Sung poured out the tea, then at last the old woman said she was tired. "You must come back again, Morgana," as she had asked Madame Sung to call her. The old woman smiled wearily.

"I will, Madame," Morgana promised.

The Red Lady leaned back in her chair, a wicked, toothless smile upon her yellow face. So Rian McShane had returned to China at last after five long years. She suspected Taian would be happy. Foolish girl, Madame Kiangsu thought, to have waited for him for so long. She would have been much better off if she'd married one of the stupid sailors who were always begging her to run away with them, or Fang Lai, the swordmaker, who did not care that the girl was a prostitute. Well, well, things should be interesting again for a time.

Rian's ship had not yet put into port, but Madame Kiangsu knew he was not far off the coast. She had spies everywhere. There was nothing she did not know, but very little she ever revealed. One of her agents had spotted the *Sorceress* an hour ago. She puffed thoughtfully on her opium pipe and settled back to wait.

The Earl of Keldara stood on the deck of the *Sorceress* and watched the shore grow larger on the horizon. And although he was still unhappy, he had resigned himself to Morgana's death. All he wanted to do now was finish his trip and go home to try and straighten out the mess he'd made of things. He still felt very bitter at times, especially late at night when he had to face the emptiness of the cabin and the memories it held for him. Often he sat silently strumming the guitar he had given Morgana, recalling the sweet, lilting sound of her voice; or reading the pages of her father's books, remembering the way the shadows played across her face as she recited the poems aloud in the evenings.

He missed the length of her warm body up next to his at night and the feel of her soft hair against his throat. He had difficulty sleeping and many times at night he strolled upon the deck studying the stars. None of the sluts he picked up in the ports could ease the ache in his heart, although they did much for the one in his loins.

It was late when the ship entered the harbor of Macao, finding a spot to drop anchor amidst the junks and sampans. With a sigh, he gave orders to the crew and finally disembarked, calling for a rickshaw. He gave the destination, then settled back against the seat, paying no attention to the drunken sailors who sometimes stumbled out of the bars along the waterfront. When he reached the Chinese bordello, he tossed the coolie boy a few coins and went inside.

It was smoky, as always, and the smell of incense hung heavy in the air. Several Oriental girls lounged about the room, their painted faces barely flickering with interest at his arrival. There was a rustling of bamboo as a screen was parted and an older woman appeared. Known all along the waterfront as the Red Lady, Madame Kiangsu was a woman to be reckoned with. Many believed she was a member of the Society of Heaven's Law, the organization which had once attempted to assassinate the Manchu Emperor, Jen Tsung. Nothing had ever been proved against her, however, but she still bore the scars on her fingertips where the Emperor's men had driven bamboo shoots under her nails when they'd tried to make her talk. Rian had known her a long time.

"Welcome, Captain McShane," she did not appear in the least surprised at his arrival. Rian was not surprised. No doubt she'd learned of his arrival before he ever reached Macao. It was rumored that she had spies everywhere.

"Good evening, Madame Kiangsu," he bowed low, accepting the glass of wine which she offered him.

They would talk for a while, and then, when she had tired of his company, she would allow him to go upstairs to his Chinese mistress, Taian. It was a ritual he would have preferred to forego this night, but he had no intention of insulting the Red Lady, so he settled back in the chair and waited for her to speak again. Her eyes stared at him unblinkingly, an effect Rian knew was caused by the opium she smoked, but it was nevertheless disconcerting. He did not allow his own gaze to falter, however, and was at last rewarded by her slow, toothless smile. An hour later he was permitted to retire.

Taian was very small and delicately boned. Her black hair fell straight and free to her waist and her crimson-darkened lips curved expectantly at his entrance. She did not fling her arms around him, but waited for him to

457

speak to her. When he did, it was merely to tell her to ready his bath water and she turned away so that he might not see the disappointment which showed plain upon her face. Always she was very sad when he left her and always she was very sad upon his return. She loved him very much and kept hoping that one day he would take her with him, take her away from the life of sin she was forced to endure or starve. But he had never said he loved her, and he never told her that he had missed her, even though it was sometimes years between his visits. The other girls laughed at her and said she was foolish to wait for him when another sailor might have taken her, but she did not care.

Her small hands worked deftly, scrubbing his back and massaging the muscles she knew ached most; and still Rian did not speak. Taian sensed that he did not wish to hear small chatter, so she was silent also, except for one shrill cry when he suddenly pulled her to the bed and spread her kimono apart to bare her high, firm breasts.

For a moment when he awakened in the morning, Rian could not remember where he was. Then the sight of Taian's face on the small, curved board she used as a pillow reminded him. He shook her awake and told her to fetch him some breakfast, frowning slightly as she scurried away. He wondered what thoughts lay behind the smooth mask she so steadfastly maintained. She always reminded him of a doll, an inscrutable doll who did exactly as it was manipulated to do. She never raised her voice to him in anger, although he guessed he often made her unhappy, nor was she able to discuss with him any subjects at length which he was interested in. She had been trained well in the arts of pleasing a man, however, and for a time his body was eased of the ache he felt inside. Taian had been thirteen when first he'd taken her. Well, perhaps he would go shopping with her later. That usually seemed to delight her, although her face was always grave when she thanked him.

After breakfast, he did take her to the marketplace, where he bought her a lovely jade bracelet. The cost seemed little enough to him, but the pleasure it gave

Taian was evident in her eyes. Then he left her at the bordello and went out to conduct his business. While he was gone, Taian took great joy in showing off her gift to all of the other girls who did not have so fine a cavalier.

"See," she tossed her proud head indignantly. "He always returns and only to me."

"Such proud words for a girl of the streets," Pengpu snorted. "He will leave again as always; then we shall see if you sneer at the rest of us."

Taian only smiled and jingled the bracelet on her wrist.

Morgana stared at the lizard in her bed. Its tongue darted in and out rapidly as it contemplated her with its beady eyes. It had slick, colorful skin, but it nevertheless reminded her of the snakes in Africa. Slowly she found one of her gloves and, putting it on, grabbed the creature and started down the hall, dangling it by its long tail, a martial gleam in her eyes. She knew the culprit responsible for this prank. Only last week she had found a horned toad in her sea chest. Damn the boy! Would he never learn that such tricks would not frighten her away?

"Hsi!" she pushed open his door angrily without knocking. "Haven't I warned you to be more careful with your pets. I found this creature in my bed."

The boy stared at her in amazement. He'd thought surely the lizard would work. Some of his other governesses had run screaming from the house at the sight. Others had been routed by the horned toad. Lord, would nothing faze this one?

Morgana tossed the lizard at him and he caught it deftly before it could scurry away at such brutal treatment; then Hsi watched as she slammed out of the room. He sighed. He could think of nothing else at the moment to frighten her away.

She knocked on Madame Sung's door, then pushed it open upon being told to enter.

"I swear, Madame, I will lose my temper with that boy one of these days," she said, much agitated.

"Why, whatever has he done now, Morgana?"

"Put a lizard in my bed; yes, and last week it was a horned toad in my sea chest. I tell you, Madame, he needs to be spanked and quite smartly, too."

Madame Sung laughed. "Morgana, I fear my grandson has met his match in you," her eyes twinkled.

Morgana glanced at the old woman fondly, then suddenly laughed herself, seeing the humor in the situation.

"Well, I do think he should have learned by now that I am here to stay. After all, I've been here over two months, and the rest of his governesses never lasted more than three weeks."

"Yes, I do think that tiresome child would have caught on by now," Madame Sung gazed at Morgana affectionately. They had become fast friends over the passing weeks. "Perhaps I should speak to him."

"No, he'll just think he's getting to me. I'll have to try new tactics, that's all. As my cousin, Gerald, who was in the military used to say, if you can't win the battle, retreat and try a new line of attack."

"Very wise, my dear."

"Well, I must admit it was the only intelligent thing I ever heard Gerald say. How are you feeling? Can I get you anything?"

"No, dear, I'm fine. They tell me Captain Jones was here again today."

"Yes, poor Taylor. He just won't take no for an answer," Morgana admitted ruefully. "I fear I've caused him a great deal of pain."

"Ah well. He'll get over it. I've never heard of anyone dying of a broken heart yet."

"I have," Morgana said, remembering the story of Rian's mother and the ghost of Katy McShane. "At home, at Shanetara, we have two ghosts that sometimes appear when the fog sets in and the rain falls lightly. Aye," she lapsed into the Irish brogue she knew delighted the old woman as she told the tale of William and Katy McShane.

"What a beautiful story," Madame Sung spoke when Morgana had finished.

" 'Twas told to me by one of my cousins," Morgana explained, a guilty feeling in her heart. She had not told anyone in the Chinese household that the man she had married might still be alive. They were shocked enough by her behavior and confused over her broken engagement to Taylor.

"You miss it, don't you, Morgana? Shanetara?" Madame Sung's eyes were kind.

"Aye, sometimes I do. It all seems so far away and distant now, almost like a dream."

For a moment, she considered confiding in this old woman whom she'd come to adore, then decided she couldn't burden Madame Sung with her troubles.

"Tomorrow, Madame, would you like to sit in the gardens with me? I have some free time and would appreciate your company. Besides, the fresh air will do you good."

Of late, the elderly woman had seemed to be feeling less and less well, and Morgana was afraid the dark, dreary household did nothing toward improving her condition.

"Of course I would, child. It always delights me to talk with you and the gardens are so pretty this time of year. It will be a pleasure."

"I'll see you tomorrow then," Morgana promised and closed the door softly behind her.

The next day was cool, but pleasant as she had hoped, and Morgana watched as two of the houseboys set Madame Sung's chair down so that she could enjoy the warmth of the sun's rays. She draped the old woman's shawl about her carefully.

"There now, Madame. I vow you'll be feeling better in a trice."

"Thank you, child," Madame Sung patted Morgana's hand warmly. "I don't know what I did until you came. I swear this place has seemed like a different household. Even Lü mentioned it."

461

Morgana felt very pleased, for Sung Lü seldom complimented anyone, being much too occupied with keeping her husband out of the bath houses of the geisha girls, without much success. Morgana was afraid women were second-class citizens in China. She sighed.

"Oh, Madame, do you think the day will ever come when women are not subservient to men; when we will be allowed to have professions of our own?"

"La, child! Open your eyes. 'Tis women who rule the world, though they are too stupid to realize it. Think you. Was it really Caesar who reigned in Rome? Nay, 'twas Cleopatra who turned his head and coaxed him into abiding by her wishes. Twisted Marc Antony's head while she was about it, too. And why did Columbus discover the New World if not to lay his prize at the feet of Isabella of Spain? Look at your own Anne Boleyn. Did not Henry VIII divide the Catholic church to have her? Yes, never underestimate the power of a woman, Morgana," Madame Sung nodded her head wisely. "There's not a man alive who hasn't sought power, conquered kingdoms, or gained a fortune all for the love of a woman, whether it be his mother, his lover, his wife, his daughter, or his sister. When women start thinking and acting like men, it will be their downfall. The two are as different as night and day, and that is how it should be."

"I suppose you're right," Morgana smiled at the old woman thoughtfully.

"Of course I am. When you've lived as long as I have, you'll understand what I'm talking about. There, fetch me a bit of that jasmine. I should like to smell its fragrance, child. Such a lovely scent."

Morgana rose obediently to do as bid. She had reached the plant and leaned forward to pluck one of the flowers when she saw Taylor approaching. She picked the blossom and turned to him.

"Yes, Taylor, what is it?"

"They told me in the house that you were out here, in the gardens, I mean. Morgana," his voice was urgent, pleading. "I mean to set sail today. I've lingered here far too long as it is. I've come to beg you one more time. Change your mind. Come with me to Virginia, please. I love you."

"Oh, Taylor. Why can't I make you understand? I can't, I just can't."

"You mean you won't. My God, Morgana!" He grabbed her suddenly and began to press eager kisses upon her mouth. "I can't stand it. How can I leave you here?"

"Taylor!" she broke away from him, one hand against her lips. "You forget yourself, sir."

"Morgana, please—"

She did not hear. She was already running to the house, and to her surprise, she was crying bitterly. She had quite forgotten Madame Sung, who had witnessed the entire scene. The sight of her brought Morgana up with a start.

"Madame, I beg your pardon," she was instantly contrite as she handed the elderly woman the flower and tried to dry her tears.

"Never mind, child. I saw what happened. You weep, Morgana, yet your heart does not go with him," she indicated Taylor's retreating figure.

"No, Madame, my heart does not go with him," Morgana replied; then quite suddenly she flung herself down on her knees at Madame Sung's feet and poured out her very soul.

She began with her meeting with Rian and told the entire story, sparing herself nothing, holding nothing back. The old woman listened in silence, stroking the bright red hair which lay in her lap, the face, so anguished, glistening with crystal tears. Madame Sung listened for over an hour, and not once did she interrupt, understanding that this was something Morgana had kept locked within her for far too long. The child needed to talk, to get it out of her heart and mind. When she had finished, Morgana continued to sob quietly, making small choking sounds in her throat.

"My child," Madame Sung spoke slowly, thoughtfully. "I have never heard such a sad, foolish tale in all of my life. 'Tis quite a tangle, isn't it? And it's made you terribly unhappy. Well, it's no less than I would have expected from Rian McShane. Such a misguided man, filled with such foolish pride."

"You know my husband, then?" Morgana raised her face curiously at last.

"Yes, I know the Captain. He comes here sometimes to trade with my son and a more arrogant rogue I've yet to meet," she smiled kindly. "He probably loves you very much."

"He does?" Morgana asked unbelievingly.

"Yes. Let me tell you something, child. A very long time ago I knew a proud, arrogant man such as your Rian. He was my husband. Oh, mind you, I had no choice in my marriage; it was arranged by the parents in those days. I never laid eyes on Sung Tsingtao before my wedding day. I was fourteen and innocent in the ways of life and men, but Tsing was very gentle with me. He was twenty-eight and a fine figure of a man. I don't mind saying that I considered myself very fortunate. Some of my friends had been married to husbands as old as I am now, which is very old indeed," her eyes twinkled. "But as I was saying, I was young and impressionable, and right away I fell in love with my husband.

"But he was a proud man and somewhere along the way, he had been taught that men must not have feelings, or if they do, they should suppress them. He was a very sensitive man, afraid of being hurt, afraid of being laughed at, afraid of not being all that a man should be. He did daring, scandalous things, and I thought him the most dashing man I'd ever seen. I did not understand that he did them to seek my favor because he could not speak what was in his heart. It was only when he lay dying that I realized how much he had cared for me all along. You see, he sent me away, child."

"But, why, if he cared for you, madame—"

"Ah, child. He loved me so much that he could not bear for me to see the pain he suffered at the end. He wanted me to remember him always as the bold, brave, dashing warrior who'd captured my heart. And somehow, just knowing that he loved me, although he never spoke the words, has sustained me all these years. I never married again."

"Thank you, Madame," Morgana spoke softly.

"I once read some words written by a very wise old man," Madame Sung sighed. "The verse said, 'Look to your heart and you will know everlasting joy, even as the plum tree blossoms while the snow lies yet upon the ground.' Look to your heart, Morgana."

Chapter Thirty-one

Taylor had seen that everything was finished, his cargo loaded, and the supplies replenished. He cursed Morgana silently under his breath as he walked up the gangplank for the last time. A fancy clipper ship next to his own vessel caught his eye in the darkness, and it sure was nice-looking. He wondered to whom it belonged. His eyes strained to catch the name in the silver moonlight and he drew his breath in sharply. Emblazoned on the side was the word *Sorceress*. With an oath, he turned his back and ordered his crew to cast off.

Taian gazed at Rian's dark face solemnly. "Captain Rian is unhappy, no?" she asked shyly.

"Yes, little Taian, Captain Rian is very unhappy."

"It will heal with time, will it not, this pain in your heart? It is a sadness in your mind, I can see it in your eyes," she whispered.

"Yes, perhaps if one ever stops loving, it will heal with time," Rian answered softly.

"Captain Rian loves?" Taian felt something like a knife twist in her heart and the pain was very bad.

"Yes," he repeated a third time. "Captain Rian loves very much indeed."

"And this woman, who is she?"

"My wife, Taian."

The knife turned deeper.

"And where is this woman, your wife?" she asked, fighting back the tears.

"Dead. Ah, she was heaven itself, Taian, was Morgana. Her hair was like burnished copper and her eyes greener than jade," he was suddenly glad to speak of the pain he felt in his heart.

"I, too, know what it is like to love such as that," she said softly.

"Then why do you not tell this man of your love, little Taian?"

"Do you not know, foolish man?" she cried and ran from the room, tears pouring down her cheeks.

Rian understood her reply but he could not say the words she wanted to hear. He felt very sorry that he had caused the little Chinese girl such torment as he had seen in her eyes.

The Red Lady smoked on her opium pipe. Yes, things were getting more interesting by the minute. She'd found Taian sobbing her heart out, poor thing, and had discovered the reason for it. Now the pieces of the puzzle were beginning to fall into place. So, Rian McShane did not know his wife was alive and right here in Macao, a governess to—what was the name of that merchant—ah, yes, Sung K'ang Nan's children. It could be no other. The description fit too perfectly. Maybe the wife thought Rian dead as well, or perhaps she had run away from him. He could be a devil on occasion. She herself had seen it when he'd duelled with a sailor over Taian years ago.

Madame Kiangsu smiled her wicked, toothless grin and sent for the sea captain.

"What is it, Madame?" Rian asked somewhat angrily. "Have you seen Taian?"

"She's run off, foolish child. I'm afraid her sorrow is

too much for her to bear. She'll be back, don't worry. She has nowhere else to go."

"Well, then, why did you wish to see me?"

"I understand you are in the market for silks this voyage."

"I am always in the market for fine materials, Madame," Rian felt slightly annoyed. His business was none of Madame Kiangsu's affair.

"Perhaps you should visit Sung K'ang Nan. I believe he has something you will be particularly interested in."

She settled back in her chair and smiled again when Rian had gone. Yes, things would be very interesting indeed. She had only to wait now.

Taian wandered aimlessly down the waterfront, her poor heart breaking. She stumbled into one of the many bars which lined the harbor, beckoned by the bright lights and noise. There was a young sailor leaning up against the wall inside. She managed to smile at him gaily through her blinding tears.

"Buy a thirsty girl a drink, sailor?"

She told herself that she didn't care, that nothing mattered anymore as she helped him up the stairs to a tiny room and took off her dress.

Morgana sat quietly telling Ni a story. The child's eyes were big with delight and wonderment as Morgana spun out her tale of being captured by the African natives. Ni scarcely breathed, she was so excited. Morgana pretended not to notice when Hsi crept closer, his head cocked so that he could hear as well, and barely suppressed the smile which touched her lips. He no longer attempted to play foolish pranks on her and seemed content that she was going to stay. When she got to the part about the pit vipers attacking her leather boots, he gasped audibly.

"Weren't you scared, Lady Mag?" he moved to sit beside her on the bed.

"Yes, Hsi, I was," she answered gravely. "I was nearly frightened out of my wits."

"But you didn't get bitten, did you, Lady Mag?" Ni's small face was filled with concern.

"No, Ni. Their fangs couldn't penetrate the leather. I was very lucky indeed, for pit vipers are extremely poisonous and I would surely have died."

"I'm glad you didn't die," Ni said solemnly.

"So am I," Hsi chimed in.

"Why, Hsi," Morgana looked at him surprised. "I thought that I was just another nasty governess; you tried so hard to drive me away."

"Oh," he hung his head sheepishly. "You're not like the others. None of them ever had such grand adventures. I'm sorry I was so mean."

"Shake on it?" Morgana offered him her hand.

"Shake on it," he smiled suddenly, giving her hand several enthusiastic pumps.

"That's my boy," she tousled his hair. "And my girl, too," she didn't want to leave little Ni out. "Very well. That's enough for tonight. You've got lessons in the morning. Time for bed now."

They grumbled goodnaturedly, and presently she tucked them both in, giving each a kiss before blowing out the lamps. Then she went to sit with Madame Sung, who was feeling much better these days. Morgana felt convinced that the sun was good for the old woman's bones.

Two days went by and finally Rian decided that he would call on Sung K'ang Nan. After all, the Red Lady generally knew everything in Macao; and if she thought the Chinese merchant had something worth seeing, it probably was. He was worried about Taian, though. She hadn't returned yet. Pengpu, one of the other girls, told him that Taian had taken up with a sailor she'd met down in one of the bars on the wharf and had moved in with the lad. Well, so much for her broken heart, he thought sourly.

Dusk was falling when he hailed a rickshaw and gave the address, but he had not wanted to arrive while they were eating dinner. Sung K'ang Nan was used to the odd hours Rian kept anyway. He had done business with the man in the past and knew him to be a fair and honest merchant, not like some of the cheats in Macaco. Rian had planned to call on him sooner or later, but he had to admit that Madame Kiangsu had pricked his curiosity.

He was whistling when he rapped on the brass knocker. Wong Chow, the houseboy, smiled when he saw Rian.

"Welcome, Captain McShane," he said in English. He always remembered the Captain because Rian had once saved him from being beaten up by a group of drunken sailors.

"Evening, Wong Chow. Is your master at home?"

"Yes, Captain McShane. I will tell him you're here."

The boy disappeared and Rian studied the hallway interestedly. Sung K'ang Nan certainly had some fine Oriental pieces. Rian wouldn't have minded bargaining for some of them, but he realized that these were Master Sung's private possessions.

"Good evening, Captain McShane," Sung K'ang Nan bowed low.

Rian bowed in return and followed the Chinaman to a small sitting room. "I understand you have some particularly fine silks this year," he said when they had been seated.

"Ah, yes," Sung K'ang Nan's face lit up. He always loved a good bargain and was a born merchant. "Naturally I have many more at the warehouse," he explained. "But the best bolts of cloth I keep here, as you well know, Captain," his eyes appraised Rian shrewdly. "If you care to wait, I'll fetch them."

Rian nodded, tapping his fingers restlessly on one of the small bamboo tables in the parlor during Sung K'ang Nan's absence. From somewhere in the house, he could hear a woman singing. For some strange reason, it reminded him vaguely of Morgana, although the words were Chinese. Then he shook himself mentally. What was he thinking?

"Yes, these are very fine, very fine indeed, Master Sung," Rian stroked the silk bolts of material thoughtfully. They would certainly fetch a good price when he returned to England. "Shall we agree on a price?"

The men haggled for over a half an hour before at last reaching an agreement, each thinking he'd gotten the better part of the bargain.

"You'll have these delivered to my ship in the morning?"

"As always, Captain McShane," Sung K'ang Nan nodded placidly, pleased with himself.

"I would be interested in several more bolts as well," Rian spoke again. "I will leave the rest to your choosing. We can settle the price when they arrive on my ship."

"Fine," the Chinese agreed. He was always secretly delighted that the Englishman had such faith in him and trusted him not to be a cheat as so many of the other merchants were. Consequently he always gave Rian a much better deal than he did any of the other seamen who came to trade with him. "Shall we go have a drink to seal the bargain? I believe that is the English custom."

Morgana wandered idly through the gardens, pausing now and then to smell a flower blossom or study the Chinese statues. She had grown accustomed to the dragons and no longer found them wicked as she had before. She could hear voices in the large salon. Someone come to do business with Sung K'ang Nan, she supposed. The seamen sometimes came in the evenings to the house instead of visiting the merchant at his office during the day. She suspected most of them just wanted a good dinner and better liquor than what was offered along the waterfront. This one, however, if he were a seaman, had not dined with them. She sighed and dipped her hand idly in the pond, sending the goldfish scattering.

"So nice to see you again, Madame Sung Ling Kwan, Madame Sung Lü," Rian acknowledged the presence of the two women. The older Madame Sung did not seem surprised that he was in Macao, but he knew that her sources of information were as good as, if not better than, Madame Kiangsu's.

Madame Sung had indeed expected his arrival after

hearing Morgana's story, but truth to tell she had not known he was already in port. She'd been much too wrapped up in the girl's sorrow to pay a great deal of attention to anything else. Now she concealed her startled expression well, her eyes narrowing. The man obviously did not know his wife was here.

"Captain McShane," she inclined her head in his direction graciously. "Why do you not take a short stroll among the gardens? I believe there is one flower in particular which will interest you there." She was sure she had seen Morgana slip out earlier.

Rian stared at the old woman rather bemusedly. He wondered impatiently why all of a sudden everyone seemed to think they knew what he would find particularly interesting. Nevertheless he did as Madame Sung suggested. It would not do to offend his host's mother.

"To the back of the gardens, Captain McShane," Madame Sung called after him. "By the statue of the dragon near the lily pond."

He found the little winding path with its large stones easily. He had been out here several times before and wondered what new flower blossomed beneath the small, fragile trees.

It took his eyes a moment to adjust to the light, and when he first saw her, he thought she was a ghost. She sat so still on the edge of the pond, her hair unbound and hanging down her back, her almost sheer, white gown like a shroud in the moonlight. She looked sad, pensive, almost wistful, as she stared at the stars. Rian scarcely breathed.

"Morgana?"

He fully expected her to vanish in a shimmering cloud of mist. She turned her dark emerald eyes upon him and he thought he would drown in their depths. She had not heard him come up behind her and he had spoken softly, but she would know that husky voice anywhere.

"Rian," she whispered before she fainted into his outstretched arms.

Morgana was not unconscious for long and when she

473

came to, Rian was bending over her, a look of concern and disbelief upon his face.

"Let go of me," she pulled away from him angrily, not believing he held her in his arms. "How dare you touch me after leaving me to the mercy of those African natives?"

"Morgana!" Rian stared at her uncomprehendingly. "I thought you were dead, don't you understand? I thought you were dead. I searched for you, and the African chieftain told me that you'd escaped into the jungle. I didn't think you'd survived," he gave her shoulders a small shake. "God knows you've given me just as big a shock as I've apparently given you."

"Leave me alone. I—I've got a job here. What will they be thinking of me? I have duties to attend to," she rose from the bench again.

"Morgana, I don't intend to let you get away from me again," he spoke and she saw the familiar mocking light in his eyes.

"Please, Rian. I can't think now," she rubbed her head. It was starting to ache again. "I've got to go inside now. I'll talk to you tomorrow."

Without another word, she turned and ran away from him, pushing aside the jasmine to get by. He started after her, but she had disappeared. At last, realizing that he could hardly drag her bodily from Sung K'ang Nan's household, he returned to the sitting room.

In his absence, Madame Sung had briefly explained the situation to her son and his wife, leaving out much of the story she knew Morgana had intended for her ears alone, telling them only that Morgana had become separated from her husband in Africa and had thought him dead.

Sung Lü was deeply moved. "What a shock this must be for her," she murmured.

"And for Captain McShane," Sung K'ang Nan added.

They had no time to say more, for Rian burst into the room. "You knew, didn't you?" he stared at Madame Sung accusingly. "My God! Why didn't you warn me

474

what to expect? And Madame Kiangsu," his eyes narrowed dangerously. "She must have guessed, too."

"Leave us, please," Madame Sung told her son and his wife, and they moved to obey her at once, shaking their heads over the unfortunate circumstances of what had arisen. "Yes, I knew," the old woman said after they had gone, settling back in her bamboo chair. She had a feeling that she was going to enjoy giving this raffish young man a piece of her mind. "Where is Morgana?"

"I don't know. She ran away from me," Rian dropped defeatedly into a chair, gazing into his glass of forgotten wine.

"Foolish girl," Madame Sung spoke under her breath. "Serves you right. From what I understand, you have used that poor child abominably. No," she raised one fragile hand. "Do not try to deny it. Morgana has told me the entire story. Well," she gave him a piercing glance. "What do you intend to do about the matter?"

"I don't know," Rian repeated. "I thought she was dead. I—I just can't seem to believe that she's really alive. You don't know the hell I've been through." He rose and began pacing restlessly.

"Oh? I thought you would have been glad to get rid of her," Madame Sung suppressed a smile.

"Glad? I was out of my mind thinking that I'd lost her just when—"

" 'Just when' what?"

"When I—when I finally realized that I loved her. I've told myself a thousand times that if I found her, I'd tell her," he ran his hand through his hair, much agitated.

"Rian, you're a foolish young man," Madame Sung said severely. "What makes you think the child will believe you now? She thinks you hate her and with good reason, I'd say."

"I know, I know. I've made mistakes, too many mistakes, but, damn it! She's fought me evey step of the way, and I refuse to be bullied like some callow schoolboy."

"And just when did anything worth having ever

come easy, dear boy? It amazes me that you were willing to risk your neck over a poor Chinese prostitute—oh, yes, I know all about the affair," Madame Sung said dryly— "yet you refuse to take a chance on being hurt by someone you claim to be very much in love with. Selfish, if you ask me. Think, Rian. The worst thing she can do is say she hates you, something I understand she has already done innumerable times before. Try thinking of her for a change instead of yourself. A lonely child, still grieving after her dead father, finds herself in a strange land, married to a man who does not seem to like her and who treats her as roughly as a woman of the streets. How would you have reacted? Naturally the girl wanted to strike out, to hurt him as she'd been hurt."

"You do indeed seem to be aware of all of the details, Madame," Rian spoke with a wry twist to his lips.

"The child was unhappy. She needed someone to talk to, someone who neither wished to applaud, nor condemn, but merely to listen. She needed someone to show her love."

"I mean to take her back to Ireland with me," Rian's voice hardened. "She is still my wife."

"Yes, but this isn't England, Rian, and I rule this household," Madame Sung's face was stern. "If Morgana has no desire to return with you, you shall not force her to go. She is welcome to stay with us as long as she wishes. I've become very attached to her."

"You do not mean to make things easy for me, do you, Madame?" Rian glanced at the elderly woman measuringly. She was one opponent he did not care to cross swords with.

"No, I don't. You may call on the child tomorrow if she wishes to see you. Good evening, Captain McShane."

Rian realized he'd been dismissed and stalked out of the house angrily. How dare that old woman attempt to prevent him from seeing his wife?

Morgana closed the door to her bedroom and found she was trembling all over. He was here! Rian was here!

God! Just the thought of him being so near made her shake like a frightened child. He'd said he'd believed her dead, that he'd searched for her. Could it really be true? He had seemed rather pale and shocked upon seeing her. Could she have been mistaken in him? Oh, how dare he just prance in and demand that she return with him? And, yes, that old, mocking light had been in his eyes and that sardonic smile upon his lips. No, he hadn't changed a bit. *I don't intend to let you get away from me again.* He had spoken those words and meant them. She'd felt the suppressed violence beneath that cool veneer of his. He would force her to go with him. If she refused, he would have no qualms about kidnapping her himself. It was a very long time indeed before she was able to sleep.

She was awakened early by Sung Lü knocking upon the door. The Siamese woman stared at her gravely when she answered and told her that Rian was waiting downstairs for her. There was no hint of curiosity at all on Sung Lü's face and, Morgana marvelled once again at the skill of the Orientals at hiding their emotions. She told Sung Lü that she would be down presently, then moved quickly to dress.

The first thing she pulled from the closet was a vibrant green robe and she put it on hurriedly, trying not to tremble. Thank God there were no buttons or hooks to do up. She didn't think her fingers could have managed it. She tied the sash around her waist, and ran the comb quickly through her tangled locks. There was no time to do it up in the prim bun. She could have screamed with exasperation. Rian would think she had worn her hair down for him. He had always liked it best that way. At last, she was ready. She made a face at herself in the mirror, then went downstairs to receive him.

He was in the sitting room, gazing out of the window, and did not hear her enter, so she was able to study him for some minutes before he noticed her. He looked older, harder. There were lines of strain around his eyes that hadn't been there a year ago. A year. Was it possible. that so much time had passed? He was leaner, and time

477

seemed to have emphasized the restless, hungry, prowling stance he'd acquired after prison.

"I didn't hear you come in, Mag."

His green eyes glittered, still the same splintering shards of glass she remembered. The scar was more pronounced along his cheek. He was, if possible, even more swarthy, like a bronze god.

"No, I guess not," she looked away, unable to meet his searching glance.

Now it was his turn. His eyes raked her boldly in the early morning light which filtered in through the windowpanes. He thought Morgana looked as though she hadn't slept well. There were dark rings under the eyes she lowered against his piercing stare. What was she thinking, his complex wife? He crossed the room to stand before her, but he didn't touch her.

"You are my wife," his voice was low.

"I wish to hell I weren't," she whispered.

It angered him and suddenly he had her in his arms, had twisted her face up to his cruelly, his fingers tightened upon her jawbone, his other arm around her waist, pulling her to him.

"Do you really, Mag? Have you missed me not at all?"

"Nay, I was glad to be rid of you, my lord," she breathed.

He swore. He had come prepared to beg her forgiveness, to tell her that he loved her, and she scorned him, swore at him. He forced her mouth up to his and kissed her savagely, searingly, his tongue riffling the honeyed sweetness he'd missed and dreamed of for over a year. She tried to free herself, but he pressed the length of his hard, muscular body against her, bending her back over until Morgana thought it would surely break. She was shaking. Her knees buckled and she would have fallen had it not been for his arm supporting her. She felt the old fires stir and the burning ache course through her veins. No one, not even Sirsi, had ever aroused her the way Rian did. She wished he would stop, but his kiss went on and on, blazing, exciting. She melted, quivered in his steely grasp, and whimpered the old, familiar cry deep down in her throat. When he finally released her, she could have died of shame for responding to him. He had known! He had always known. Her cheeks were flushed and her body felt as if it were burning up with fever.

He stared at her with that peculiar, searching glance and Morgana thought she saw something akin to pity in his eyes.

"Do you still say you did not miss me, love?"

She opened her mouth to speak and found that no sound came out. Humiliating tears coursed down her cheeks. Silently he offered her his handkerchief.

"Tomorrow the *Sorceress* sails for Ireland. I shall expect you to be aboard."

He left without another word, without touching her again. Once had been enough and he knew it.

The children cried when Morgana said goodbye to them, although Hsi tried to be brave, angrily brushing his tears away, saying that something had gotten in his eye. Little Ni bawled openly and tugged at Morgana's skirts piteously with her tiny hand. Morgana's heart wrenched at the sight of them, as she attempted to suppress her own tears. They must not see her cry.

"There now. You shall both write to me and one day, perhaps when you are older, your father will allow you to come and visit me," she tried to smile.

"May we really, Lady Mag?" Hsi's face brightened somewhat.

"Of course. I shall be very angry if you don't," she promised.

"We'll never have another governess like you, Lady Mag," Ni's voice trembled. "And just when I was learning to read so well, so that you would not be ashamed of me."

"I've never been ashamed of you, Ni. I expect you to keep up your studies, and when you have learned to read

479

very, very well, I will send you some books of poetry that my father wrote."

"I'd like that very much," the girl said.

"And you, Hsi. No more pranks on your teachers, understand?"

"Very well," he spoke grudgingly. "I daresay none of them will ever be as brave as you are anyway."

The parting from Madame Sung was even harder.

"So," the old woman appraised Morgana carefully. "You have decided to return with your husband."

"I really have very little choice, Madame," Morgana sighed.

"You could stay here, but I think you would be unhappy. You must meet life's problems head on, child. You cannot run away from them forever."

"No, I guess not."

"Here," Madame Sung took something from the small jewel chest she held on her lap. "My husband gave me this right before he died. I want you to have it."

"It's lovely, Madame, but I can't possibly accept it," Morgana gazed at the tiny jade ring, so intricately carved and delicately shaped.

" 'Tis the Chinese symbol for joy. Wear it and remember me, child. I shall have no further use for it soon. I would like to know that someone dear to my heart has it. I hope that it will bring you as much happiness as it did me."

"Thank you, Madame, I shall treasure it always," Morgana slipped it onto her right hand, tears stinging her eyes.

"None of that, now," Madame Sung said sternly. "You will shed tears enough in your lifetime without crying over an old woman. Kiss me goodbye, Morgana, then be off with you."

Morgana bent and kissed the withered cheek, unashamed of her tears. The old woman took her hands.

"Courage, child. Remember the plum tree."

"I shall, Madame," she promised.

She said goodbye to Sung Lü and Sung K'ang Nan, thanking them for their kindness to her, then stepped into the rickshaw which was waiting outside for her. Morgana did not look back as the carriage rumbled past the Chinese dragons, still watching over the mansion, and turned through the gates on to the street.

BOOK FIVE

The Shadows

Chapter Thirty-two

Macao, China, 1816

Rian was waiting for her aboard the *Sorceress*. He watched silently, speculatively, as she walked up the gangplank. The crew crowded around her with shouts and cheers as she came on board, each trying to outdo the others with enthusiastic cries of approval, and arguing vehemently over who was to fetch her trunks. Morgana thanked them all warmly for the welcome, hugging Jeb, who could not get over her being alive, and shaking Harrison's hand. At last, upon noticing Rian standing nearby, they dispersed and made ready to sail, and soon the *Sorceress* managed to slip out of the harbor amidst the many junks and sampans.

Morgana stood on the deck at the rail, watching as the port of Macao grew smaller and smaller, unable to meet Rian's eyes. She did not know he was behind her until he placed his hands upon her shoulders.

"I didn't think you would be here."

"And if I had not been?" she turned to face him.

"I would have come for you."

"Aye, I thought as much."

She moved away, knowing instinctively that he would not follow, that he would remain at the helm until eventide. She was right. He did not come to the cabin until night had fallen and Cook was serving supper. She had done nothing all day. She could not keep her mind on the trivial things with which she sought to occupy her time. She had bathed and dressed, choosing a robe of spun gold that accentuated the flecks in her eyes. She let her hair down, fearing to anger her husband otherwise.

He closed the door quietly and stared at her appreciatively.

"The Chinese silks become you, Mag," he spoke softly, remembering the first time he had seen her arrayed in such fabric.

"Will you try to rip this one in half as well, my lord?" she managed a wry smile, remembering also.

She shivered involuntarily. He would do anything he liked as usual and she would be powerless to prevent it.

"If need be," he mocked, his eyes holding her.

"I shall not fight you, Rian," her voice was almost a whisper. "Have me as you will."

To her surprise, he merely said he was hungry and that the meal was getting cold. He pulled out the chair for her, brushing against her lightly as she sat down, then poured the wine. Their fingers touched when she reached for the glass, and Morgana drew back sharply, nearly spilling the contents in her haste. If Rian noticed, and she was sure he did, he gave no sign.

After dinner, he handed Morgana her guitar and suggested she play for him. She stroked it lovingly, glad to have it back again, and began to sing the Chinese lullaby she had learned from the children. When she finished, there were tears in her eyes.

"The children taught it to me. I shall miss them," she said.

Rian took her hand and pulled her to him, laying the instrument aside. "We can have children, Morgana."

Her heart fluttered strangely at his words and her breath came quickly, shallowly, causing the pulse at the hollow of her throat to beat rapidly. He lifted her to her feet, hands untying the sash which bound the robe. Morgana trembled at his touch, but she did not move or cry out as her garments dropped to the floor and she stood before him completely naked. He stepped away, removing his own clothes, tossing them carelessly on a chair. His hand reached out to lift one fiery tress from her breast, brushing against her belly as he found her mouth and began to kiss her gently, tenderly. She had not expected this, and her body quickened with excitement as his tongue teased, explored, and his hands cupped the creamy roundness of her breasts, fingers playing with the flushed peaks.

One arm went around her back, the other under her knees as he swung her into the air and carried her to the bed. He did not blow out the lamps and Morgana found that it was somehow worse that he could see her, could study her and caress her in the flickering light. She turned her head away, not wanting to meet his gaze, but he caught her jaw and kissed her again, harder this time, more demanding.

"How I treasured my memories of moments like this when I thought you dead," he murmured. "And now you are mine once more."

"Nay, Rian. Not yours, never truly yours," Morgana whispered, her heart pounding strangely at that peculiar, searching glance upon his face.

He smiled softly. "You think not? We are two of a kind, sweet, you and I. Grandfather saw it; and no matter how much you try to deny it, I know you in a way no other man ever shall," he muttered, his lips against her temples. "I know you down to the very core of your being. Aye, like must marry like, Morgana; I understand that now, as you will someday. And then you'll never be free of me, just as I am never free of you. As long as you live, you shall carry the image of my face in your mind, the feel of my lips upon your poppy mouth, the weight of my body on your silken flesh, and all that I am in your heart. I swear it."

His mouth travelled to her aroused nipples, leaving wet swirls on them before finding her warm belly and the softness between her white flanks. She moaned as she felt the rising pleasure from his tongue begin, as it crescendoed to a quivering delight, not understanding the things he'd said, but knowing that she could not fight him. In a strange way, she didn't even want to. She lay in his arms and felt as though she were drowning. He had never loved her like this before, giving instead of taking. Always before he had used her even though he satisfied her, mocking her, laughing at her as he'd forced her to respond.

Now he gave of himself, arousing her lithe body with his hands, pressing hot, searing kisses upon her thighs, her belly, her breasts, her eyelids, her temples, slashing across her cheeks and mouth, his tongue probing, searching, finding as her arms went around his neck, drawing him closer as he entered her, driving deeply between her flanks. Morgana cried out then, sobbing his name, arching her hips to receive him, realizing that he wanted to brand himself upon her heart for always as he had said, and that he was doing it.

As long as she lived, she would remember this wild reunion of their bodies upon the high seas, separated from each other for so long, feverish with hungry passion. The feel of Rian's weight as he lay atop her, driving her senses into a heady rapture that swirled up and engulfed in the flickering darkness; her sweet cry of ecstasy proclaiming her surrender as she quivered, trembled, exploded beneath him like a savage wind in a raging storm, tears of joy streaking her face like rain as he spilled his seed within her. As he wrapped her long red hair about his throat and told her that he loved her.

When it was over, she lay quietly, trying to still the rapid beating of her heart within her breast. His hands stroked her lightly, brushing away the fine trace of sweat which lay over her pale flesh, glistening in the lamplight. She saw that his dark chest, matted with black hair, was drenched too, and she could feel the wetness as it trickled down her sides and between her thighs. He kissed her again, wrapping her long copper tresses around his throat, binding her to him, forever.

"I love you, Morgana," he murmured again.

"Don't, Rian, please," she whispered.

"But I do love you, in spite of all the things I've said and done. I have loved you from the moment I saw you at Shanetara, your flaming hair cascading down your back and your cheeks flushed with the wind. Your emerald eyes glittering with honeyed flecks of gold, so proud, so angry as you stared down at me from Copper Lady. Aye," he breathed. "I wanted you, loved you so badly it hurt inside and I took you. You are mine, always mine."

No, it wasn't true, Morgana's mind screamed. It was the wine. Tomorrow he would tell her he was drunk, had forgotten his words of love, had lied. She couldn't believe him, she wouldn't. This dark stranger who awakened such fires in her flesh and wrapped her long red hair about his throat, whispering an age-old language in the hazy lamplight. He was too cruel. How could he torment her like this?

"Don't!" she cried. "I hate you. Don't say this to me."

"I will say it," his voice was suddenly hard, mocking, as the deviltry danced in his passion-darkened eyes. "I don't care if you despise me, Morgana. I shall take you, possess you, bully you, break you, and I shall make you want me. I shall make you love me. I swear it."

He rose and blew out the lamps, and when he returned, he was not gentle with her. No, this time he took her roughly, brutally, as he ground his mouth down hard upon her swollen, bruised lips and forced her to respond again and again.

Morgana awakened to the soft slap of the waves against the hull of the ship and for a moment she didn't know where she was. She tried to stir, saw that Rian had his arm around her, pinioning her to the bed, and then she remembered. Last night. Her body still ached and tingled with the aftermath of his lovemaking. He felt her move and pulled her up next to him.

"Good morning, love."

She gazed into his green eyes, crinkled up at the corners with his lazy smile and the lines of strain around them.

"Good morning," she said softly, waiting for him to admit that last night had been nothing more than a drunken joke.

Instead, he just kissed her and rose from the bed, pulling on his breeches before honing his razor and lathering his face. She propped herself up on one elbow to watch him shave. When he had finished, Rian wiped his face with a towel, then slung it over his shoulder and came to sit on the edge of the bed, his eyes searching her face with that peculiar, cat-like stare.

"Rian," she broached the subject hesitantly. "About last night."

"What about it?"

"Did you mean what you said? I mean, you didn't appear to be—you weren't drunk?" she asked timidly. "Or—or lying?"

"Nay, sweet. I meant all that I spoke. I do love you. But listen well, Mag. Never think that you shall use my love for you as a weapon to threaten me. I'm warning you," he placed his hand against her slender throat. "I still master those things I possess. You may hurt me, yes, but don't think to rule me, sweet, ever."

His voice was low, pleasant, but Morgana was not deceived. There was a fine edge of tempered steel just below the surface of it. He handed her one of her robes, smiling amusedly as she hurried into it, afraid that he might attack her again. She didn't know if she could withstand another onslaught upon her senses as last night had been, and he was surely capable of repeating it.

Strange that he hadn't asked her what had happened

to her in the past year, hadn't wanted to know how she came to be in Macao. She shivered. Perhaps he was only waiting to turn on her later. And what would she say if he questioned her, how could she explain? Oh, did he really love her?

After he'd gone on deck, Morgana bathed and dressed, then went out for her morning stroll. The air was cool. It would be winter before they reached Ireland. She loved the way the wind played among the sails, making them billow gently in the breeze, and the taste of the salt spray upon her lips. She saw her husband at the helm as always, conferring with Harrison and Timmons. Slowly she approached them, and the two men broke off at once, suddenly recalling various pressing duties. She almost smiled as they scurried away, intent on giving her and Rian as much time together as was possible to adjust to each other.

"Rian, will we be home in time for Christmas?"

"That depends on the wind and the weather, sweet. I doubt it." He looked at her crestfallen face and his voice softened. "I'll try, Mag, if it's that important to you."

"Aye, I would like to be there."

She watched his strong hands on the wheel, the muscles rippling in his arms as he steered the *Sorceress* ever forward. He noticed her glance and smiled.

"Would you like to try it?"

"Oh, do you think I can do it?" her eyes shone at this unexpected pleasure.

"Here, let me show you." He pulled her in front of him, placing her small hands on the knobs which stood out on various points along the huge wheel, his own hands over hers. "She's a fine ship, Mag. Just the slightest touch will keep her on or veer her off course in good weather. But if the winds are up or 'tis stormy, she can be a sorceress to control."

"Is that why you named her that?"

"Nay, love. I called her after you."

"That's not true. You didn't know me then," she laughed, but was oddly pleased.

"Now, pick out a point on the horizon and sight it up with the boom. That's right, as long as you keep her in line, she should stay on course."

Morgana felt thrilled at the thought that she held control of the sleek clipper ship.

"Where did you get her, Rian?"

"She was built in the States. I bought her from an American merchant in New York."

"I didn't know you'd been to America." Morgana straightened up her sights again at a sudden gust of wind.

"Aye, years and years ago. I had some modifications made so that she could be armed as she is now. As you've seen, I sometimes sail in dangerous waters and had no wish to be waylaid by pirates."

His body felt warm against her back. He loved her, he had said so. And suddenly she was happy in a way she hadn't been in a long time. Perhaps they could work things out, make something out of this mockery of a marriage. She knew that he loved the sea. He would never be happy tied to one place for long. She suspected that even if they had children, he would pack them all up and cart them off on some mad adventure. Morgana giggled aloud at the thought.

"Having fun, Mag?" he breathed in her ear.

Lord, what was she thinking? What if he suspected her line of reasoning? "I'm—I'm a little tired now, Rian. Will you take her again please?"

He moved obediently to accept the wheel, smiling as she stretched her arms and back.

"I didn't know it pulled one's muscles so," she explained ruefully. "Why didn't you warn me?"

He laughed. "I figured you'd learn soon enough."

"Thank you, my lord. May I sail her again sometime?"

"If it pleases you."

After a time, Morgana drifted away, deciding to go and visit Cook in the galley. This was one part of the ship that was not off limits to her, although the rest of the hold was. She liked Cook and the galley. Cook was a large, roly-poly man with a fine sense of humor. Morgana always suspected that it was because he was too fat to fight and too fat to run away that kept him so agreeable. He was delighted to see her.

"Ah, m'lady. So good to find you alive and well," he beamed.

"I should think so," she told him in a playfully stern voice. "What were you grumbling about when I came in?"

"Oh, some of the potatoes are beginning to rot and the men are sick to death of them anyway. I serve them up fried, I serve them up boiled, and I serve them up mashed, but they still complain. Ingrates, that's what they are. They should count themselves lucky to even have fresh vegetables. I've sailed on some vessels that didn't stock nothing save salt pork and beans."

"Well, why don't you make potato pies, Cook? That would get rid of them and give the crew a treat besides."

"Lady Keldara, I never heard of such a thing," he looked at her skeptically.

"Oh, 'tis very good, Cook, I promise you. Mistress Tinsley, a very old friend of mine, used to do such when her potatoes started to go. Here, I'll show you. Run, fetch those fiendish spuds, Cook," she ordered in her best Irish brogue. "I'll fix them up."

Morgana was soon bustling about, making the dough while Cook peeled the potatoes. She flattened the mixture in the pans, then put the filling in when she had finished it. Now there was nothing left to do but let the pies bake. She glanced at Cook and smiled. There was a smudge of flour on her nose, and her hands were covered with dough, but she felt proud of her accomplishment.

"Well, I sure hope they taste as good as they look," she sighed.

"I'm sure they will," Cook beamed. "Won't the lads be pleased with such a treat tonight?"

The pies were an instant success and many of the crew members sought Morgana out personally to thank her upon learning that it had been she who'd prepared them, causing Rian to remark sarcastically that perhaps he'd better be careful about letting her steer the helm or next she'd be running his ship as well.

Morgana merely laughed. Rian studied her quizzically in the lamplight. She had changed, his wife, and he didn't like it. The shell she had built around herself had hardened over the past year. Now his mocking insults seemed to go right over her head. He wondered what had happened to her, but was afraid to ask, afraid of what he might learn. He couldn't imagine how she had survived in the African wilderness, or why the Ashanti hadn't killed her. Had she believed him when he'd told her he loved her? Rian doubted it. She had her eyes lowered against his gaze. She had learned several new tricks, it seemed, since he had seen her last. A hard mask had settled over her face after her laughter had subsided and Rian found that for the first time in his life he could not read her thoughts when he looked at her. And suddenly it dawned on him that his wife could be dangerous as well. He remembered that he had taught her to fence and shoot, and wondered if she still carried that savage little dagger against her thigh. She had been compliant enough last night, but now she looked as though she had suddenly regained her footing, had gotten over the shock of seeing him again. Yes, he could see that the words he'd spoken last evening had started to sink in and there was a stubborn look about the corners of her mouth. Why, she's laughing at me, he realized suddenly.

"What's so funny, madam?" he asked coldly.

"You are. Why are you staring at me like that? You look as though you still believe I'm a ghost."

"Well you must admit, Mag, it's been quite a shock for both of us. Tell me, how did you manage to survive that Ashanti attack and find your way to China?"

She drew in her breath sharply. So, it had come. He wanted to know. "Why, on my wits and instincts and the skills you taught me, my lord," she managed to say flippantly.

"Damn it!" he swore. "Don't lie to me."

Morgana could see that he was angry now and so,

not wishing to agitate him further, she told him the barest outlines of the story, leaving out the parts about her relationships with Taylor, Sirsi, and Hassan, not even telling him about Hassan kidnapping her, for fear that he would question her too closely for the details of the matter. Rian suspected that she spoke in half-truths and the frown on his face grew deeper when he saw her blush as she said the Indian Maharajah's name. Morgana faltered over the last few words of her tale at his darkening glance and finally fell silent.

"Now, why don't you tell me the rest of it?" he said softly, his eyes narrowing.

"There's nothing more to tell," she ended the conversation abruptly and picked up her shawl.

"Where are you going?"

"Outside to get some air."

"I think not, my lady," he caught her wrist roughly. "Not until I've heard the rest of this remarkable tale."

"I said I've told you everything," she stared at him defiantly. "What more do you want?"

"I want to know the parts you glossed over, Mag. No, don't try to deny it. You forget, madam, how well I have always understood you. What are you hiding from me? What is it that you don't wish me to know?"

"Let go of me," she breathed. "I'll tell you nothing. I hate you and the only reason I'm here is because I know you would have found some means of forcing me to come with you," she tried to pull away from him.

"Why, Mag, I thought you weren't going to fight me," he laughed menacingly.

"That was last night, when I was too tired and confused to even think," she hissed, forgetting her earlier resolution to try and make something out of their marriage. "You're still the same animal you've always been. And those things you said last night and this morning, my lord. Do you think you can deceive me with those lies? I refuse to be a part of any more of your cruel games. Aye, I survived in that jungle when you left me to the mercy of those savages and more. You will find that I do not break easily, my lord," she warned, yanking free of his grasp.

She tried to run for the door, but he was faster and flung himself before it, blocking her way. She backed off, hating him more than ever. Her glance fell on his rapiers lying nearby. Quick as a flash she seized one and brandished it at him threateningly.

"Don't come near me or I shall run you through," she warned.

Rian hesitated for the barest instant, realizing that at that moment she was capable of killing him, then he moved like a panther, reaching for the remaining foil.

"We have duelled before, sweet, you and I," he grinned. "I recall well who was the victor then," he flexed the blade testingly. "On guard."

Morgana gasped. How had he managed to reach that rapier so quickly? She had not meant for this to happen. There was no way she could fight him, hampered as she was by her long skirts and the close quarters. Nevertheless she saluted briefly, then met his onslaught with her flashing blade. He played with her, slashing her skirts time and again so that they fell in ribboned strips upon the floor, twisting about her ankles, causing her to stumble as she moved. She saw with relief that he really did not intend to hurt her, merely to humble her, and she lashed out again in a frenzy after regaining her balance.

They lunged and blades clashed, ringing in the small cabin, scraping and riposting, Morgana's face tense and sweating.

"I'll—kill—you," she panted, becoming more determined than ever at the sound of his harsh laughter.

All the while, he was wearing her down, asking her sharp questions about the past year, and every time she refused to answer or relent in her struggle against him, he renewed his attacks, his blade slashing at her skirts.

Unfortunately for him, Rian did not take her threats seriously and had no real fear of her expertise with the rapier since he knew he could be deadly with his own. He lowered his guard slightly to kick away a footstool which barred his path and Morgana saw her chance. Blinded by her raging fury, she drove her blade home. He recovered in time to stop her from piercing his heart, and the blow glanced off his shoulder, leaving a thin gash upon his arm which soon grew stained with blood. Morgana's foil clattered to the floor as she stood staring at him in horror. His face had contorted into a small grimace of pain, and he was gazing at her as though he had never really looked at her before.

Rian flung his blade away with an oath and grabbed her roughly, shaking her as though she had been a puppet. With his good arm, he yanked the shreds of her tattered gown from her flesh, dragging her to the floor with him as the *Sorceress* suddenly heaved upon the waves and he fell. His blood felt warm and sticky upon her breasts, smearing across her belly as he attacked her violently, swearing at her, crushing his mouth down upon hers with a brutality that shocked and frightened her.

"You're hurt, bleeding," she moaned.

" 'Twas my fault. Once again I have underestimated your talents, my dear," he snarled, lips against her throat.

Somehow he managed to cast away his garments, keeping her pinioned beneath him all the while before he forced her tightened thighs apart and his manhood penetrated her violently in one clean thrust. She gasped at the spasms of ecstasy that shook her, flared within her, blocking out her anger with a desire even more savage; and her arms locked around his neck as she whispered "You bastard!" in his ear, causing him to laugh mockingly before he bit her lip wickedly. She cried out once at his brutal treatment, then his mouth came down on hers again and his hard, deep thrusts drove all thoughts but her need for him from her mind.

Later, when he had dragged all of the answers to his questions from her tortured lips and forced her to lie beneath him twice more, he finally allowed her to rise. She staggered to the bed and fell in it, watching with fright as he cleansed the raw wound on his arm and wrapped a bandage around it tightly to staunch the bleeding. She wondered if he would beat her for that gash. He'd lost a lot of blood. It was sheer willpower and pride which kept him on his feet at this moment. He turned and slipped in beside her, his eyes glittering strangely in the darkness, for he had blown out the lamps.

"So," he muttered harshly. "You preferred the arms of an Indian prince to mine and would have married a common Yankee to escape me."

Morgana said nothing, lying silently as far away from him as possible.

"I think Hassan had a good idea. Perhaps next time I shall tie you to a post as well, you little hellcat."

"Have you no pity for me at all? Does it make you happy to know the depths of my degradation? 'Twas all your fault. If you had not left me in Bobosanga, none of it would have happened," Morgana cried bitterly, accusingly.

Rian had no answer to this because he knew she spoke the truth. Hell! Had he really expected to find that she'd remained faithful all this time? He hadn't exactly behaved like a monk. He didn't really care that her body had been used by other men. It was the fact that she had given herself willingly to the Maharajah that hurt and angered him so. He pulled her to him roughly and slept, his own arms around her possessively.

Chapter Thirty-three

The days passed slowly. The promised fall was upon them now with its cool winds and the air held the sharp bite of the rapidly approaching winter. Morgana seldom walked upon the deck in the mornings now. The harsh sting of the winds was more than her chapped face could bear. Rian was pressing the crew to get the *Sorceress* to Ireland before Christmas, before it became so cold that they could scarcely keep their numb fingers from slipping upon the riggings and the sails froze and stiffened in the wind.

He came in, rubbing his hands together to warm them, and the wind blew the cabin door shut with a slam. She moved quickly to help him out of his wet clothes, for it had rained nearly every day, adding to the misery of the crew. She feared he would catch a chill and fall ill. He accepted the cup of hot tea she offered him silently. Morgana turned away, wishing he would say something. The voyage had been dreadful, either they quarrelled furiously or remained coldly, politely silent to one another. Ever since the night she had told him the story of her capture and subsequent arrival in China, it had been thus.

Occasionally his somber mood would break and he would lie upon her in the darkness, whispering his love for her, but she did not believe it. Lies. It was all lies. She would not allow herself to be duped by him and made to look the fool in this cruel game he played with her.

He watched her as she moved to the fire and picked up the book she had been reading. God knows she must have read it a hundred times by now. She could quote the lengthy passages by heart. Again Morgana asked herself why she did not accept his words of love and try to make something out of their marriage. She knew the answer well. He would hurt her, laugh at her. Her chin went up defiantly. She would not stand for it. She had borne so much. She would tolerate his rape of her, she had little choice in the matter, but never would she allow him to break her pride, her spirit as he had vowed to do.

Rian saw the gesture and sighed. Christ! To hell with the wench! He was determined that he would not let her headstrong, impetuous independence stop him from getting what he wanted. She must be made to believe that he loved her. Madame Sung had been right. His declaration, however, had made no difference to his wife now. His words had come too late. He could not accept it; he would force her to believe him and to return his love if it was the last thing he did.

She wanted him. He knew that. She trembled when he touched her and cried out her surrender to him with a passion that set him aflame with desire. She could not deny that, no matter how she fought it; her need of him hung between them in the heavy silence like a thick fog. He knew that when he was late coming in, she lay in the bed and could not sleep, although she often pretended to be asleep when he slipped in beside her. The sheets would be disordered from her restless tossing and damp with sweat when he finally reached for her, her mouth clinging almost fervently to his own in the darkness. Rian knew, too, that it was this, the weak betrayal of her own body against him, that made her resent him more than ever; those nights when she came willingly to his arms that made her fight so strongly against him the other times.

" 'Tis still raining," Morgana spoke unnecessarily.

"Aye."

He moved to sit beside her, holding his hands out to the warmth of the fire that burned within the little stove.

"Harrison is bringing hot water for your bath," she offered as a means of conversation.

Rian said nothing in return, merely continuing to stare at her with his glittering green eyes. It made her nervous, although at the same time she felt a warm flush of excitement run through her and she shivered slightly.

"Cold?" he asked.

"Nay, not with the fire so near."

"Then why are you shivering?"

Damn the man! she thought angrily, was there nothing which escaped his notice? She refused to answer and he chuckled softly in his throat.

"I will warm you up soon enough, Mag," his eyes gleamed mockingly.

She flung her book away. "Be still, you horrid beast! Can you think of nothing else?"

Harrison came in with his lordship's bath water just then and Rian had no time to reply. When the first mate had gone again, the Earl removed the remainder of his wet clothes and stepped into the steaming water, sighing as he sank in as far as possible. Morgana tried hard not to look at him, for the sight of his bronzed nakedness aroused her, much as she tried to deny it. He saw her embarrassed blush and closed his eyes, a silent smile on his lips.

"Come here, love," he called lazily. "And wash my back."

"Do it yourself," she snapped.

"Shall I get out of this tub and fetch you?" he drawled again, cocking one eyebrow quizzically.

Morgana bit her lip. She knew he would do it if she did not obey him. Angrily, she rolled up her sleeves and walked over to the metal tub. She took the bar of soap from his hand and began to scrub his back, swearing at him under her breath.

"You cad, you lazy wretch, resident of a pigsty," she muttered.

"What did you say, sweet?" he asked softly.

She nearly choked with rage, slopping the water so that it soaked not only his back, but his hair and shoulders as well, sending it trickling over his chest and down his face. Rian swore and turned, splashing Morgana's face and breasts so that her gown was soon drenched.

"Just look what you've done, you insolent creature," she raged.

He laughed and yanked her to him, his fingers closing about her wrist tightly. Then, before she had guessed what he was about, he had pulled her into the water, sending it pouring over the sides of the tub onto the carpet. Morgana sputtered at him wordlessly as the fluid soaked through her dress and petticoats, and her legs hung awkwardly over the sides of the bathtub. She felt his manhood pressed against her through the sodden material and tried to rise, fearing his next move.

"I must get out of these wet things," she informed him indignantly. "I don't know what you can be thinking of, playing such a dreadful trick on me."

"You brought it on yourself, sweet," he smiled at her, not in the least dismayed by her icy tone of voice.

"Oh! You vile, loathsome animal. How dare you treat me thus?"

He waited until she had shed her wet garments and stood clad only in her damp chemise before he rose and seized her, ripping the dripping material easily from her body. Morgana gasped and swore. It was too ludicrous, the two of them grappling naked about the cabin. She broke free of him, trying to reach her wrapper.

"You fool! What if Harrison comes in?"

"No one comes through that door without my permission," he grinned wickedly, attempting to catch her again.

In a flash, she had the table between them.

"Rian, be sensible," she pleaded.

"I would be, if only you'd let me catch you, sweet. Here," he held out her wrapper enticingly. "Come and get it."

Morgana glared at him and attempted to snatch the flimsy robe from his grasp by leaning over the table so that she could keep the barrier between them. To her utter surprise and dismay, Rian hauled her onto the solid object and proceeded to kiss her hungrily. She moaned wrathfully. Lord! To be taken upon a table like a common barmaid. She would never forgive him. Never! She tried to scratch him, but he caught her hands easily, pinioning them above her head, while his free hand stroked her breasts and sought the softness between her thighs. She gasped at his touch and the bold, mocking way he watched her face as he continued his slow, deliberate caresses. Her cheeks flushed and she closed her eyes tightly so that she would not have to look at his triumphant, jeering smile.

"You cad, you rogue, you defiler of women," she cursed and panted angrily after he'd had his way with her. "Upon the very table on which we dine, too."

"And never have I tasted a more delectable feast," he laughed, his passion-darkened eyes surveying her flesh warmly as she attempted to cover herself.

"Oh! You—you brute!" she threw her hairbrush at him stormily.

Rian ducked and it clattered against the wall harmlessly. She turned her back on him in a huff and found that her fingers were trembling so badly she could scarcely fasten her robe about her. He could barely conceal his smirk as he tossed her the hairbrush. Lord, what a hellcat! He couldn't remember when he'd seen her so delightfully frustrated. He'd have to be careful or she'd murder him while he slept tonight.

The weather got colder the closer they came to Ireland, the wind blowing sleet upon the deck of the *Sorceress* so that it became rather dangerous for even the experienced hands. Large icicles hung from the masts and the sky was cloudy and grey. The ship strained and groaned, riding low in the waves because of the heavy cargo she carried. From beneath the deck, Morgana could hear the horses whinnying anxiously in their stalls. She longed to go and comfort Copper Lady, but didn't dare. Rian would kill her if she ventured into that part of the hold. She hadn't seen her small mare since he had so grudgingly taken her below himself right after they'd left China.

The waves broke and crashed over the rails of the ship. Most of the sails had been trimmed as much as possible so that only the topmost of them were spread full against the wind. No one dared try and change them now. The ropes were too slick to keep a grip on and anyone climbing the riggings would doubtless be blown overboard.

Morgana thought it all very dismal and depressing. She shuddered when Rian informed her that the weather around the northern area of the States was twice as bad during the winter. She couldn't imagine anything worse than this sharp, biting cold. She huddled against him at night to take the chill from her body, for he was always much warmer than she, causing him to remark sarcastically that at least the damn weather had been good for something. Thereafter, she had tried to stay away from him, but always the coldness of the cabin drove her into his arms before the night was over.

During the day, she worked on Christmas presents for the family, embroidering clothes for the children. Once she laughed ruefully and told Rian that she didn't even know whether Fionna's babe was a boy or a girl. She would probably not recognize little Maureen. After all, the child had been born very shortly before they'd left Ireland. Morgana made lovely Oriental dresses for the women, although the gowns didn't even begin to approach the scandalous Chinese silk she'd worn so many years ago. There were fine linen shirts for all of the men.

One night she and Rian played with the puzzle box again, working with the intricate locks patiently. They opened box after box within the maze until Morgana began to grow faintly excited.

"Oh, Rian. Do you think we can do it?" she asked.

"I don't know. Hold on. I think it's this one next. Aye, there, you see. Try that one now."

She did as he instructed her, for her slender fingers could work the catches on the boxes much better than his. Still, both of them were extremely surprised and breathless when they finally managed to get to the center. Morgana sprang the last lock and the tiny box flew open with a small snap. Inside lay a small scroll. She lifted it out carefully, unrolling the fragile parchment, giving a cry of anguish and dismay when she saw that what was written therein was in Chinese.

"Oh, Rian. I can't read it," she almost sobbed, for she had not learned that many Chinese symbols from the children.

"Here. Let me see," he took the scroll from her hands. The Chinese characters looked very old and faded, but he could tell they had once been delicately and painstakingly inscribed. "It says, and I can't translate it literally, but in English it would say, 'Look to your heart and you will know everlasting joy—'"

"Even as the plum tree blossoms while the snow lies yet upon the ground," Morgana finished softly.

"Yes, but how did you know?"

"Madame Sung once spoke those very words to me."

"Well, now you know the secret of the puzzle," he refolded the parchment and replaced it in the center box.

Morgana locked them all back up carefully, memorizing the pattern of the boxes in her head so that she would be able to open them again.

It was Christmas Eve. Morgana could have cried. She knew they had to be very close to Ireland now and she longed to be able to spend the holidays with her family. Strange to think that she'd once lived quietly with

505

only her father for company. She couldn't imagine life now without her five brawling cousins underfoot, even if one of them was her sarcastic husband. Still, he'd been very kind to her lately, seeming to understand how disappointed she was. She stared at the presents, already wrapped and tied so prettily with ribbons and bows, and sighed. Well, better late than never at all, she guessed. Her silent musing was interrupted suddenly by the pounding of feet and the yelling of the men. Good Lord! What was going on up there? Quickly she grabbed her shawl and wrapped it about her tightly. It would be cold outside, although much of the slush had dissipated the closer they'd gotten to the coast.

She made her way to the deck and was at last able to make out the cries of the men. Land ho, they'd said. Land ho! She was home! Home at last.

"Rian," she called, running to his side. "Is it Ireland? Are we truly home?"

"Aye, love," he caught her in his arms and hoisted her into the air gaily. "We did it, Mag! 'Tis bound to be some kind of a record."

She laughed and flung her arms about his neck, kissing him wildly in her happiness.

"Well," he said when she finally stopped. "Had I known you would behave in this fashion, I'd have gotten here weeks ago."

"Oh, Rian," she lowered her eyes shyly, determined that nothing should spoil this night. " 'Tis Christmas Eve."

Not even the fact that she could scarcely see the land because of the darkness marred Morgana's homecoming. She was able to make out Brandon Hill, towering in the blackness, but there were faint lights glimmering through the ocean mist from Kilshannon. Kilshannon, where Michael Kelsey lived and worked, where Gerald spent his nights dallying with the barmaids, where Rian's warehouses lined the docks. Oh! She had missed it all; she did not realize how very much until this moment. And, surprisingly, she found that she had missed her cantankerous old grandfather most of all; in spite of the marriage he'd forced her into. It didn't matter. All that counted now was that she was home!

She stood on the deck at the rail braving the cold, and Rian did not tell her to go to the cabin, although he saw that she shivered and chafed her numb hands constantly. He left the helm once to fetch her gloves and she thanked him gratefully for his thoughtfulness, marvelling at how kind he could be at times. After what seemed like hours, the coast of Ireland at last loomed before them.

They docked at the wharf, securing the ship before the men poured off eagerly, seeking the warmth of a hot mug of cider and the comfort of a wench's bed. Rian did not try to stop them, claiming that they could unload later, after the holidays. He and Harrison fetched Morgana's trunks and Rian's own smaller one, then he bid the first mate good night after spying one of grandfather's tenants, who offered to take them to Shanetara. Morgana was glad they would not have to wait until morning to reach the great house and thanked the young man warmly for his kindness. She sat perched upon the high seat of the wagon, tucking her hands in Rian's pockets to keep them from freezing. He glanced at her and smiled, but said nothing.

Mollie O'Malley tottered down the steep stairs of Shanetara most carefully. She'd had a nip or two of the wassail punch and was feeling very good, very good indeed. Still, she grumbled mightily under her breath when the brass knocker rapped sharply and loudly upon the front door.

"Now, who kin that be, I wonder? So late at night, and 'tis Christmas Eve as well," she mumbled aloud.

The entire family had gathered in the large salon, Bridget and Patrick having driven over from Kilshannon Hall, and Trevor and Fionna from Shaughnessy Bay. They'd brought their children as well. Mercy, but Maureen was such a pretty child. And Fionna's lad, Corby, promised to be as good-looking as all of the rest of the McShane men. Heartbreakers, that's what they were,

Mollie sniffed. But she was proud of every last one of them. She crossed the long hall to the door, muttering about Stepplewhite, the butler, leaving his post, and flung it open.

"Faith and begorra! Sure, if it ain't me lord and lady. Oh, me heart's beating so fast at the sight o' ye, I feel I'm nigh to swooning," she cried.

"Don't you dare, Mollie," Rian laughed, while Morgana ran forward to give the old woman a great hug.

"Mollie, oh, Mollie, we're home, home at last."

"Is it ye? Is it really ye after four years?" Mollie dabbed at her tearful eyes.

"Sure, and who else?" Rian lapsed into the brogue playfully.

"What the devil?" Fergus McShane rapped his cane stoutly upon the floor. "Trevor, go out there and see who's causing all that racket. Can't abide noise. Must put a stop to it at once. By God! If Kerr O'Malley's drunk again, he'll feel the bite of my tongue in the morning, even if it is Christmas Day."

" 'Tis only us, grandfather, and, as you can see, we're quite sober," Rian said as he and Morgana entered the large salon.

"By God! 'Tis my own granddaughter and Rian," grandfather roared as Morgana crossed the room and flung herself into his arms. "What do you mean, bursting in on us like this? Trying to give me a stroke?" he bellowed, but they could tell he was pleased as he hugged Morgana and shook Rian's hand.

"I've already told them it wasn't very nice not to even warn us, me lord," Mollie bustled in. "I've sent Kerr out to fetch yer trunks and put ye in yer old room."

"Thank you, Mollie," Rian told the plump woman whose face was beaming. "As you can see, Morgana's not paying any attention, I'm afraid."

And indeed she was not, sitting upon her grandfather's lap and crying lustily while she attempted to answer everyone else's rapid questions.

"But when did you get here? Why didn't you let us know?" Patrick was asking.

"And where have you been? Rian surely didn't take you to Africa, did he?" this from Gerald.

"Probably dragged her off to a Chinese opium den as well," Trevor groaned dutifully.

"Oh, Morgana, we've missed you so," Rosamunde chimed in as she, Bridget, and Fionna begged her to come and tell them about her adventures. "I wish you'd written more often."

"Hold it," Rian practically yelled over the commotion. "One at a time, please. Christ! Is that Maureen?"

He and Morgana both looked at the lovely child who held back at the sight of them, clutching the hand of a smaller, dark-eyed boy.

"Aye," Bridget informed them. "Don't you want to say hello to your cousins, honey?" she asked the little girl.

Rian laughed when Maureen shook her head and hid behind her mother's skirts. "Come on over here, sweet," he coaxed. "I'll bet you don't remember me. You've become quite a little lady since I saw you last. Who's that with you?" he smiled at the lad.

"Corby," Fionna spoke proudly. "My son."

Morgana saw that she looked happier than she had in ages. At last, Rian managed to get the two youngsters on his lap, one in each arm as he sat on the sofa with his wife beside him. He talked to the children for a while, then turned his attention to the adults in the room, dutifully answering their many questions as patiently as possible. Morgana watched him silently with the children and realized suddenly that he would be a good father. She stroked Maureen's bright red curls and took the child on her lap when Rian handed the small girl over. He bounced Corby on his knee and the boy squealed with delight. Neither one of them noticed that Colin had not spoken to anyone since their arrival.

"Aye, it was touch-and-go there for a while," Rian spoke to Patrick, who was sitting on the edge of his chair, shoulders hunched forward to catch his cousin's words. "But I promised Morgana I'd have her home in time for

Christmas, and by God I did," he gazed at her, a soft smile on his lips.

"Lord, Rian. You must have really pushed that ship and your men hard," Patrick marvelled.

"Aye, but they wanted to get back, too. 'Tis no fun at all to spend Christmas upon the seas," Rian replied.

The huge pine tree looked very festive in the lamplight and Morgana felt a slight pang of disappointment that she had not been able to help decorate it, but then she consoled herself with the thought that she was really home.

Four years! It had been such a long time! Grandfather looked older and greyer since she'd seen him last. He appeared quite overcome at the shock of seeing them again, and after talking boisterously for a time, had lapsed into silence. She glanced at him and saw that his eyes twinkled merrily, however. Rosamunde babbled nonstop as usual, her cheeks flushed and her giggle tittering often as her hands fluttered excitedly to her breast. Every so often she would raise her vinaigrette to her nostrils.

"To keep from fainting, my dear," she explained to Morgana. "Such a surprise. I can't get over it. You're really here after all this time."

"Corby's a handsome child, Fionna," Morgana turned to her cousin-in-law after conversing for some length with her aunt.

"I think so," Fionna answered. "Trevor's so proud. I know he thought we'd never have a child, but after Bridget had Maureen, it happened so fast that Bridget said it must be catching," she laughed gaily.

"You'd better hurry up, Morgana," Bridget chided, smiling, as she hoisted Maureen into her arms. "These two have been begging for another playmate. Time for bed, honey," she said to her daughter, who grumbled loudly, but rubbed her tired eyes sleepily.

"You, too, Corby," Fionna called to her son.

"I'll take him up, Fionna," Bridget offered, then disappeared with the children.

"She's been wonderful," Fionna said. "I don't think I could have managed Corby without her."

"He looks like a handful," Morgana replied, remembering little Hsi in China. "He'll be a heartbreaker one of these days."

"Yes, and Patrick shall have to take his pistols to all of the young bucks if he wants to keep Maureen for long," Rian broke in upon hearing Morgana's last remark.

"Huh. You just wait until you have one, Rian," Patrick responded good-naturedly. " 'Twould serve you right to be saddled with a wench, as many fathers as have had to defend their daughters from the likes of you."

Morgana saw a slow flush creep up her husband's neck and realized that Patrick's remark had come too close to home for comfort. No doubt he was remembering all too well the manner in which he'd made her his wife. She couldn't resist digging him just a little.

"Aye, Rian. How would you like that?" she laughed.

"Is that an invitation, Mag?" he countered quickly, and they all smiled as she lowered her eyes from his quizzical stare.

She knew if she looked up again in that moment, he would have that peculiar, searching glance upon his face, and she felt a sudden shiver of excitement run up her spine as his hand closed over hers.

They stacked their presents under the tree for opening in the morning, then bid the rest of the family good night.

Rian closed the door to their room quietly, pouring each of them a drink of good Irish whiskey from the decanter on the dresser. He handed her one of the glasses. She stared at it thoughtfully before taking a sip.

"Thank you," she said softly. "For not telling them the truth about what happened in Africa."

He had been rather evasive when questioned about those parts of their trip, leaving out much of the story entirely. Not one of the family had guessed about their separation of over a year.

" 'Twas none of their business," he answered bluntly. "And I was in no mood to listen to Trevor's preaching. God, I'm tired," he unbuttoned his shirt,

511

pulling it free from his breeches before he dropped into a chair. Morgana saw that a fire had been lit in the grate. It blazed cheerfully, but she lit the lamps anyway, then moved slowly to undress. It was late, well after midnight, but she didn't know if Rian had been serious or not when he'd suggested they get started on producing a child, and she wasn't quite sure of what do do. At last, she just put on one of her nightgowns, and slipped into bed. He finished his glass of whiskey, then blew out the lamps before he slid in beside her. He pulled her into his arms and kissed her gently. Evidently, he really was exhausted, however, for he was sound asleep a few moments later.

Morgana lay quietly thinking for the longest time, then she, too, closed her eyes and drifted off.

They were awakened by the children's excited cries in the morning. Rian, forgetting where he was for a moment, opened one eye groggily.

"What in the devil is that racket? Tell Harrison he'd better take care of it right away."

Morgana giggled and ran her hand lightly over his furry chest. "Rian, 'tis the children. 'Tis Christmas morn," she reminded him. "Get up, you lazy rogue, or they won't wait for us before they tear open their presents. We'll miss everything."

"Oh, very well," he muttered, yawning and rubbing his eyes. "Come on then."

The others were already downstairs, apparently having been dragged out of their beds as well, for they were all still in their nightdresses and robes.

"Corby, I told you to wait," Trevor reprimanded the small lad grouchily. He wasn't very happy at all at being awakened so early.

" 'Tis Christmas morn, Trevor. Mind you don't spoil it for him," Fionna chided her husband, much to Morgana's surprise.

Having a son to defend had certainly brought Trevor's wife out of her timid shell.

Grandfather was in his huge chair, playing the role of Father Christmas with a great deal of enthusiasm. Morgana thought he looked much better this morning.

512

Perhaps he had only been shocked and tired last night. He called to the children and had them pass out each present as he read the name aloud. They handed Morgana and Rian theirs quickly, being somewhat shy again this morning, although they smiled mischievously and Maureen's dimples flashed brightly.

Morgana had made Rian a fine pair of breeches and a waistcoat, and he had a lovely set of jade jewelry for her. They had many presents to open besides because the family had saved theirs for them every Christmas, putting them aside until the couple returned. Morgana thought she'd never seen so many gifts at once in all her life.

Later, they all sat down to Christmas dinner. Morgana gazed at them all gathered around the table in the dining room and decided that nothing had changed at Shanetara.

"Oh, by the way, Morgana," Rosamunde spoke after they'd retired to the sitting room. "Your new maid's name is Peggy. Doctor Kelsey and Kyla were married right after you left Ireland."

Morgana found the news pleased her and was glad for his happiness. She would have to ride into town and congratulate him! The men did not linger long over port, but joined the women right away. She played a quiet game of chess with grandfather, losing as usual, before the talk turned to politics.

"Those damn rebels," Trevor was saying. "Can't they see they're only hurting the Irish cause with all of these escapades? 'Twill do no good to attack the British with these guerrilla tactics. The way to freedom is through the Parliamentary Seat in Dublin."

"Huh," Colin replied sarcastically. "If it's done your way, we'll never be free of English rule."

Morgana watched his excited, flushed face, and saw the sudden hard glint in her young cousin's eyes. She remembered the letter Bridget had sent to her, mentioning the family's fears that Colin had joined up with the Irish radicals. Lord! She certainly hoped he hadn't done anything so foolish. It would bring disgrace on the entire family if he should be discovered in such a rebellious plot. Why, they had almost hanged Rian for suspected involvement with those radicals.

After the holidays, things soon settled back into the old routine. Morgana went riding with Rian, delighted to be in Copper Lady's saddle once again. The moors were covered with a light frost and little clouds formed in the air when she breathed. She would return to Shanetara with her cheeks flushed from the cold and her hair tangled in a flowing mass down her back.

Once, they rode into Kilshannon to do some shopping and to be sure that the cargo was safely unloaded from Rian's ship and stored in his warehouses along the waterfront.

"I dare not take it to England yet, Mag," he explained as he watched the men carrying the many boxes from the *Sorceress*. "At least, not until we find out what has happened there in regard to my escape from prison and the death of Lord Chalmers. I've written to Brad, but it will doubtless be some time before I receive a reply."

The old fear of being charged with murder stirred in Morgana's heart at his words. It had been a long time since she'd thought about being arrested by the British dragoons. She'd learned that while she'd been in Africa, Napoleon had left his exile in Elba and rallied the French once more to his disastrous cause. He was able to rule for one hundred days more before being effectively defeated at Waterloo. He had tried to gain asylum in England, but had been exiled to Saint Helena, where it was said he spent his dreary days writing his memoirs. She shivered, wondering if he would ever return again, or if France was finally at peace at last. She didn't want to think about it. It reminded her too much of Phillipe and his unpleasant death at Rian's hands.

"Do you think the British will arrest us, Rian?" she asked timidly.

"Nay, I'll get this mess straightened out, and I'm sure Brad will be only too glad to help us."

She glanced at his green eyes and was surprised to

find that for once she believed him. After all, he surely had no desire to hang for a crime he hadn't committed.

They were on their way back to Shanetara when they ran into Michael Kelsey. Morgana studied the doctor with interest. He looked older, thinner, and there were streaks of grey in his reddish-blond hair. But his blue eyes still twinkled merrily, although she felt he looked at her questioningly and a little pityingly.

"Hello, Michael," Rian spoke easily from Lucifer's back. "Congratulations on your marriage."

"Thank you, my lord. But when did you return?" the doctor's eyes still searched Morgana's face.

"Only a couple of weeks ago. We've just finished unloading the last of the cargo on the *Sorceress,*" Rian responded.

Suddenly Morgana knew that Michael was worried about her marriage and wondered if she was still so desperately unhappy. It wouldn't do! It just wouldn't do! She could bear anything but someone's pity, especially someone who had been as dear to her as Michael. She would have to allay his fears or he'd seek her out and there might be trouble.

"It was so good to see you again, Michael," she was surprised at how normal her voice sounded. Then she turned to her husband, "Rian, darling, I'm famished. If we don't get home, we shall miss dinner." She looked every inch the loving wife when she glanced at her husband's face.

There was an imperceptible tightening of the muscles around the corners of Rian's mouth, but only Morgana would have noticed. He knew what she was doing and felt angered by it. Nevertheless he did not attempt to destroy her little charade. After all, they had played it often enough for others, he thought grimly. They were so close, their two horses stood almost touching, and he reached across the small space which separated them, catching her gloved hand. He dropped a light kiss in the palm of it.

"As you wish, love. Good day, Doctor."

Morgana thought she saw Michael's shoulders sag

slightly as they rode off and thought again that he had guessed the state of her marriage. She hoped he would not ask her about it. She whipped up Copper Lady and galloped rapidly out of town, Rian hard on her heels. When they reached the stables, he yanked her roughly from the saddle, leaving the horses to Jim's care.

"Rian, darling," he mocked sardonically. "Perhaps I should keep the good doctor around permanently!"

"Stop it, Rian," she pleaded with him. "I just couldn't sit there and let him feel sorry for me."

"And does he have cause to pity you, Mag? Am I such an ogre? I don't enjoy being made to look a fool, madam."

"No, I wasn't trying to make you look foolish, my lord," her voice was low, noting the riding crop he slapped angrily against the side of his high-topped boots. Surely he wouldn't beat her for such impudence.

"You didn't answer my first question, sweet."

"Loose my arm," she spat. "You're hurting me."

"I'll let you go when I get good and ready to," his voice was harsh. "Come on. I want some answers from you."

"Where are you taking me? Let go of me, I say!"

He paid no heed to her protests, dragging her into the stables.

"Get out of here!" he yelled at Jim, who immediately dropped his curry comb and scurried away.

Rian yanked her up the ladder to the loft and tossed her down into the hay. She swore at him angrily, trying to rise.

"What do you think you're doing? I'm cold. I'm going back to the house."

"Don't move," he snarled, unbuttoning his hunting jacket and shirt, his intentions obvious beneath his tight riding breeches.

Morgana attempted to scramble away from him, but he caught her wrist and twisted it cruelly, forcing her back down. Suddenly she weakened against him, leaving him off guard. Then she sank her small, sharp teeth into his hand savagely. He swore, releasing her at once, and she ran toward the ladder, half falling down the rungs. As Rian got ready to descend, she pulled the ladder away from the loft, nearly causing him to fall. It clattered to the floor and she stared up at him mockingly, a triumphant smile about the corners of her mouth.

"What say you now, my lord?" she jeered.

"Put that back up here. I'm warning you, Mag," his eyes narrowed dangerously.

"You're in no position to give me orders, my lord," she laughed. " 'Twill do you good to sit up there and brood for a while. I'll miss you at dinner, love," she drawled sarcastically.

Rian was dumbfounded when she whirled and stalked out of the stables. Surely she did not mean to leave him here? He sat back on his haunches, confident that she would return in a minute to beg his forgiveness and put the ladder back up so that he could get down. Damn the wench! He'd make her sorry for playing such a prank. He'd give her a proper roll in the hay for such a trick. He waited and steamed in vain. Morgana did not return. Upon leaving the stable, she spied the little lad who cared for the horses.

"Jim, his lordship wishes to be left alone for a while. Why don't you run home and see if your mother needs any chores done? You can come back in a couple of hours," she told him.

"Thank ye, me lady," he smiled at her cheerfully and scampered off.

Morgana headed toward the house, laughing all the way. That would serve the arrogant bastard right. He'd be stuck up there for hours. She trembled briefly upon deliberating on what he would do when he finally did come down, then shrugged her shoulders carelessly. He could scarce beat her at Shanetara. Grandfather ruled here and would have Rian horsewhipped if he laid a hand on her. This was one place where Rian was not master.

The longer he waited, the more Rian seethed. He surmised correctly that Morgana had sent the stable boy on his merry way, and that help would not be forthcoming for several hours. Whenever she finally got tired of the joke! Christ! He'd kill her for this. He was determined that she would not gloat over him, laugh at him and how foolish he'd looked. Rian stared at the fallen ladder. There was nothing in the loft with which he might pull it up. He got angrier and angrier. No doubt Morgana was sitting at the dinner table now, a triumphant smirk on her face. Well, she was not going to get the best of him. He glanced down at the drop and wondered briefly if he'd break his neck if he jumped. Perhaps if he lowered himself over the edge, he could swing into one of the empty stalls and the hay layered within would break the fall. It was worth a try anyway. He'd be damned if he was going to spend the night in the loft.

Slowly, he grabbed onto the edges of the loft and eased himself down. It wasn't that difficult, considering the many times he'd had to pull himself up and down the riggings on the *Sorceress*. He could hardly drop in on top of Copper Lady or Lucifer, however, and he had to slide over until he could find an empty stall. Kicking hard, he managed to begin to swing back and forth and hoped grimly that he wouldn't break his back on the front of the stall. With a last kick, he loosed his hold on the loft and flung himself forward. He managed to land squarely in the stall, but the force of his momentum threw him off balance and he fell back against the door with a sharp blow. It pained his shoulder blades for a minute, but he soon recovered. Upon trying to stand, however, he discovered that he'd somehow twisted his ankle. It hurt like the blazes. He gritted his teeth tightly and hobbled toward the house, cursing Morgana every step of the way.

"Damn the lad! 'Tis not like Rian to be late. You say he didn't come in with you, Morgana?" grandfather queried grumpily.

"Nay, grandfather," she lowered her eyes so that he would not see the sudden laughing guilt that lingered there. Poor Rian. She wondered if he were very angry at her.

"Well, we'll just have to begin without him, then. I'll give him a piece of my mind when I see him next," the old man grumbled.

"I hope not," Rian said. "Sorry I'm late."

Morgana gasped as he limped into the room and took his place beside her. How had he managed to get down? She knew Jim could not possibly have returned yet. She gave him a confused and frightened glance, which he returned with a grim, mocking smile that boded ill for her later.

"Where have you been, you insolent pup?" grandfather asked sternly.

"I was pitching hay in the loft," Rian replied, casting Morgana another jeering glance.

"And where was Jim? He's supposed to take care of things like that. That's what he gets paid for," the old man snapped.

"I believe Morgana sent the lad on an errand, and I needed the exercise," Rian shrugged his shoulders indifferently, filling his plate.

No more was said about the matter, but Morgana felt her knees quake under the table. God! There was no telling how he meant to punish her for the deed. His leg. He'd been limping when he came in. Lord! He must have jumped out of the loft.

"Yes, I did," Rian spoke under his breath, guessing her silent question.

She nearly choked and he made a great display of thumping her on the back rather more heartily than was necessary, then offered her a glass of wine. She thanked him icily for his concern, her eyes stinging with hot, angry tears at his rough slaps, and gave his bad leg a sharp kick under the table. Rian winced visibly. Morgana smiled at him sweetly and continued with her meal as though nothing had happened. A short time later she gave a small gasp.

"Is anything wrong, dear?" Rosamunde questioned. "Your face looks quite flushed."

"No—nothing. I'm still a little choked, that's all," Morgana managed to say.

Rian had somehow gotten his hand up under her skirts and was fondling her most intimately under the table, appearing quite nonchalant as he continued to eat with his free hand. She could have died of shame. There was nothing she could say or do to stop him without drawing attention to herself and what he was doing. By the time Rosamunde gave the signal for the women to retire, leaving the gentlemen to their port, Morgana was quivering all over. Damn him! Damn him to hell and back! She'd never felt so angry and humiliated in all her life. How dare he?

She couldn't even meet his eyes when the men finally joined them. He dropped down onto the sofa beside her, one arm flung casually around her shoulders. She stiffened at his touch and he smiled at her leeringly as he puffed on one of the cigars he'd brought back from Spain. She longed to slap that smirk from his face and it was with some difficulty that she managed to control her churning emotions. She stabbed angrily at the sampler she was embroidering and pricked her finger, glaring at him as she stuck it into her mouth to suck off the blood. She was determined to sit downstairs until the entire household had retired. Morgana was terrified of what might happen once they had reached the sanctuary of their bedroom.

He guessed her line of reasoning, however, and before she had a chance to open her mouth, Rian noted loudly that Morgana looked extremely tired, and bid the family good night. The pressure on her wrist tightened warningly when she attempted to protest as he hauled her upstairs; then he slammed the bedroom door shut and bolted it. Morgana backed away from him, the fear evident upon her face.

"What's the matter, Mag?" he laughed unpleasantly. "Having second thoughts about your nasty little prank? Come here. I said, come here, damn you!" he swore when she didn't move a muscle. "By God, if I have to walk across this room to fetch you, I'll beat you within an inch of your life!"

"You wouldn't dare. I'll tell grandfather if you so much as lay a hand on me," she threatened. "You aren't master here, for all that you would like to think such."

"So, you think the old man will save your hide, huh? Well, you're wrong. How many times do I have to tell you before you get it through your head? You belong to me. You're my property," he almost yelled. "And if you go running to grandfather with any tales, I'll pack you up and take you so far away from here no one will be able to help you."

"Oh. You cad! You're just mean enough to do it, too," she snapped. "And just where do you think we'd go? You're a dead man, Rian McShane. The British army intends to hang you, or have you forgotten?"

"And you're wanted for murder, my dear," he jeered. "I'll take you to Keldara, where I am the sole master. 'Tis what I should have done to begin with. Aye," his eyes narrowed. "I'll take you there and then we shall see who rules this marriage."

Morgana turned away, her hand to her mouth to stifle her sobs. Oh, he would do it. God, he would take her there and she would have no one to run to. Keldara was one of the most inaccessible and isolated estates in Ireland. Rian had described it to her often enough. It had originally been a fortress, much as Shanetara had been, but a much more desolated, impregnable one. Set in the wilds of Connaught along the savage coast, Rian had said it was surrounded still by the walls and moat which had once defended it against intruders. If he shut her up at Keldara, she would never be able to escape from him. She felt utterly defeated as she turned to face him again.

"That's better," he breathed huskily from where he sat upon the huge tester bed. "Now take off your clothes. I'm afraid my leg pains me too much to fight with you tonight."

Her fingers trembled as she fumbled with the tiny buttons on her dress, as she removed the gown and the many petticoats beneath it, standing before him clad only in her sheer chemise.

"That, too," he ordered.

Tears welled in her eyes as she took off the last garment. She could not look at him as his eyes roamed her naked flesh, desire flickering in their darkened depths. He let her stand thus a very long time to make sure she felt properly humiliated.

Then he said, "Come here."

This time, she obeyed him, walking toward him slowly on knees that threatened to buckle beneath her.

"I hate you, you horrid beast," she whispered as he took her in his arm

Rian undressed himself slowly, watching her in the darkness, then he bent his head and found her mouth.

"Well, you're willing enough for a change," he muttered against her throat.

"I loathe and despise you."

He laughed softly, mockingly, as he laid his burning kisses upon her temples, slashing down against her cheeks and throat, his hands cupping and teasing her breasts, squeezing the ripe mounds of flesh gently, fingers brushing her nipples until they swelled with passion. Suddenly he rolled over on his back.

"Kiss me, Mag," his voice was hushed. "All over."

"No."

"Do it. You know what I want."

He felt the wetness of her tears against his chest as she moved to obey him, head lowered in the darkness, and he moaned hoarsely when her lips found him. When he could contain himself no longer, he caught her long, copper hair and pulled her back up to his mouth, helping her mount him. Morgana lay against his chest as he arched upward within her, and when she at last exploded inside, she cried aloud a pure trill of joy at the tremors which shook her body, wave after wave of exquisite delight; then lay exhausted, asleep in his arms.

Chapter Thirty-four

"Rian, would you finish hooking me up, please?" Morgana turned her back to him. It was Peggy's day off.

His fingers felt warm against her flesh as he buttoned the last of the hooks she'd been unable to reach. Word of their return had gotten around the county quickly, and tonight Johnnie Gallagher was giving a party in their honor. Morgana surveyed herself critically in the looking glass and decided that she would do. She had chosen a dress of jade green silk she'd brought back with her from Macao. It was a more formal gown than most of the gowns she'd returned with. With it, she wore the lovely jade jewelry Rian had given her for Christmas. Her burnished hair had been brushed up and arranged in tiny ringlets upon her head, Oriental fashion. She had a small reticule and painted fan to complete the effect.

"You look enchanting, sweet," Rian dropped a light kiss on her shoulder. "I've no doubt the Gallant Gallagher will have designs on your virtue."

"Oh, don't be silly," she chided him. "You know

Bridget said that he was about to offer for Sean's sister, Darcie. 'Tis high time, too. The lass has been pining away for him these many years."

"Why, that chit's barely out of the schoolroom. She can't be more than eighteen at the most," Rian laughed.

"Seventeen. And, as I recall, you once said the very same thing about Anne Denby, and that worked out well enough in the end."

"Aye, that may be, but Johnnie's at least ten years older than Darcie—"

"And what of it? You're eleven years older than I am," Morgana reminded him sternly.

"Yes, and just look at the hell I've been through. I'd best warn Johnnie this evening of what a mistake he'll be making."

Morgana glanced at him fearfully for a moment, then saw her husband was only teasing her. "Oh, you rogue," she frowned at him playfully, in good spirits because of the coming festivity. "You'll never forgive me for shutting you up in the loft, will you?"

"I must admit, love, that bit of nonsense was quite a feather in your cap. I concede that round to you; but I intend to win the battle, madam, have no fear of that," he gazed down at her with darkened eyes.

She flushed warmly and looked away. His leg had pained him dreadfully for over two weeks before the limp had at last gone away. And still, he swore he loved her. At night, he held her in the darkness, his hands upon her flesh, making her tingle with desire and excitement as he wrapped her long red hair about his throat and whispered wild words of love.

He did indeed look very handsome this evening. Morgana had to admit that. The ebony of his locks was accentuated by his black waistcoat and breeches, and his white, ruffled cuffs looked like yards of sea foam against his wrists. He had his cravat tied in a waterfall with a diamond stickpin at the throat. Rian never wore wigs, as so many young dandies of the day did. He scorned them as being too hot and stuffy, and a monstrous nuisance in the bargain.

"We'd better go, or we'll be late, my lady," he spoke softly, offering her his arm.

They greeted a sullen Colin at the foot of the stairs. He was very annoyed at having to attend Johnnie Gallagher's party and had attempted to cry off at the last minute. But grandfather had become highly agitated and said that if Colin did not wish to go into the ministry, he'd better attend some parties and find himself a rich bride.

"Perhaps the old man will change his will again, Colin. And this time you'll be the unfortunate recipient," Morgana laughed as Rian handed her into the landaulet.

Her younger cousin merely gave her a blank stare and took the place next to Gerald, who was already in the carriage. Rian climbed in next to Morgana and told Kerr to drive on.

"And were you unfortunate?" Rian asked after relaying instructions to grandfather's hired man, his arm around her shoulders.

"In truth, my lord, I don't know whether I should answer that or not," she said indignantly.

He laughed and tweaked one stray curl which lay tangled across her breast.

"I'd say you were the lucky devil in this case, Rian," Gerald glanced at Morgana appreciatively.

"Aye, I vow 'tis so," her husband replied positively.

They finished the remainder of the ride in silence. Laughlin Hall was a beautiful estate, although it was fairly new by Irish standards, being only one hundred years old. Johnnie's grandfather had built it, and Johnnie had inherited it upon the death of his father some years ago. His mother, a charming eighty-year-old lady, still resided there, and it was she who greeted the entourage as they were admitted into the ballroom. Morgana had met her several times before, but she couldn't help but feel uncomfortable in the Viscountess's presence, and therefore took extreme pains to treat the elderly lady deferentially. The old woman was a tartar!

"Rian, you rogue, I swear you've broken my son's

525

heart by snatching up the prettiest lass in Ireland," the Viscountess gave him a playfully stern glance as he bowed low over her hand.

"Then I must beg your forgiveness, my lady," he replied, eyes twinkling.

Laughing, Morgana intervened, giving the old woman a hug as she dutifully kissed the upturned, withered cheek.

"Oh, be off with you, the both of you," the Viscountess smiled indulgently. "I've no doubt your scoundrel of a husband is able to handle you far better than any other man would have," she told Morgana before they moved away.

"That's the understatement of the year," Rian breathed in Morgana's ear when they were safely out of the old woman's hearing.

"Silence, you cad, and fetch me a glass of champagne."

Rian laughed softly and strolled over to the table which held the refreshments. It took him a very long time to be served because his friends kept interrupting to welcome him home and inquire about the voyage, and by the time he returned, Morgana was already on the dance floor with the Gallant Gallagher. Johnnie was whispering in her ear and she was smiling at him, her eyelashes fluttering coyly. Rian felt like swearing, but instead he lounged against the wall, holding the two glasses, watching his wife. This caused a great deal of comment among those present at the party, for never before had anyone seen his lordship dancing attendance on any woman, and the frank delight was evident upon his face as he gazed at his wife. Lindsey Devlin felt especially piqued by the Earl's behavior. She had never forgiven him for marrying Morgana and had only accepted Sean's proposal out of spite. Now she longed to hit Rian with a poker. How dare he stand there without asking her to dance? She looked at her husband sourly.

"Well, aren't you going to ask me to dance? Or do you intend to drink yourself into oblivion as usual?"

Sean glanced at her with disgust. "If you'd sweeten

your tongue, I wouldn't have to drink to forget what a shrew I married."

"Shrew, is it? I'll have you know I could have married anybody in Ireland, you drunken sot!"

"Oh?" he grinned slyly. "I don't see your old beau over here begging for a dance. He's probably glad to be rid of you."

Lindsey flushed angrily at Sean's crude remarks, damning Rian McShane silently in her mind. How dare the Earl stand over there, ignoring her as if she didn't exist? She turned her back on her husband and picked her way to Rian's side. Sean watched her go, then asked the waiter for another glass of champagne.

"Were you looking for me, darling? I swear 'tis been quite lonesome without you," Lindsey smiled sweetly at Rian.

"No, I wasn't looking for you," he answered softly. "And as for it being lonesome, I understand you married Sean right after I left. Does he not keep you company, Lindsey?"

"Just look at him, he'll be drunk before midnight and I'll have to send him home before he does something disgraceful. May I beg a ride with you later?"

"Sorry, Lindsey. Devlin Way is not on the route back to Shanetara. But I'm sure Max O'Brien would be glad to drop you off," Rian smiled lazily.

"That bore? No, thanks," she bit her lip.

God! She wanted to bed him. She ached all over just thinking about it. She leaned forward so that he might get a better view of her breasts which peeped enticingly from the bodice of her gown.

"Tell me about your voyage. Was it very dull?"

"Nay, quite the contrary, my dear," his eyes surveyed Morgana warmly as she swept past on Johnnie's arm.

Lindsey pouted prettily. "Well, you might at least say you missed me," she sulked.

"I would be lying if I did."

Rian moved away from her. He had no wish to become entangled with Lady Devlin and she was certainly trying to lure him into her bed. He had enough troubles with Morgana without Lindsey causing a jealous scene again.

"Love, here's your champagne," he caught Morgana as she walked off the dance floor with Johnnie. "Hello, Johnnie."

"Rian, you devil. Morgana tells me you two have been back for over a month."

"Aye."

"Well, I'd have had this party sooner, if I'd known. You ought to at least give a man some warning when you bring back the prettiest thing to ever hit Ireland."

"What? And give you blades a chance to steal her away. Not on your life," Rian took Morgana's arm possessively.

She thanked him for the champagne, sipping it slowly. "Whatever did you say to Lindsey, Rian? She's positively glowering at you."

Rian frowned. "I swear I don't know why Sean doesn't beat her."

"She needs stern handling," Johnnie chimed in. "'Tis a sad day indeed when a man can't control his own wife. I never thought Sean would prove so little a man. All over the county 'tis said that Lindsey's been cuckolding him with Max O'Brien."

"Really?" Rian queried. "She just informed me that Max was a deadly bore."

"You don't say?" Johnnie whistled softly. "Must have her eye on somebody else then."

"Well, how can she have any respect at all for Sean?" Morgana asked disgustedly. "Standing over there, drinking himself into a stupor. Doesn't he care how she behaves? Why, if I were a man, I wouldn't let my wife run all over me like a—"

She broke off abruptly, aware of Rian's mocking smile and narrowed eyes.

"You were saying, sweet?" his voice sounded choked with laughter.

"Nothing," she answered shortly. "I'm going to the card tables."

She walked away, horrified by what she'd said. Really, what must Rian be thinking? That she actually enjoyed having him lord over her, master her? But it was true, she suddenly realized. She wouldn't have respected any man who let her walk on him and bully him with her temper tantrums. No, she might detest her husband, but at least she respected him.

The game of the evening was faro, and Gerald held the bank.

"Deal me in, cousin," Morgana spoke as she joined the crowd at the table, opening her reticule to pull out a handful of pound notes.

Morgana wagered heavily, but she found she could not keep her mind on the game and lost several large sums of money.

Gerald snorted. "Rian is not going to like you wasting his money like that, cousin."

She gave him a cold stare. "I assure you, Gerald, Rian does not care in the least how I spend his money. He has never interfered with my finances."

"Really?" Lady Colleen McIntosh gazed at Morgana in awe. "You mean your husband lets you manage your own money?"

"Certainly," Morgana replied with some surprise.

"Well, I never. My Billy scarcely gives me a pittance."

Everyone at the table laughed. Billy McIntosh, the Baron of Killarney, was hardly a pauper. No doubt Colleen's pittance was a considerable sum indeed.

"And he never lets me draw on his account if I run short," Colleen continued after the laughter had died down.

"Which, I suspect, is quite often," Lady Brenna Murphy gave her friend an amused glance.

"Oh, Brenna," Colleen spoke wryly.

"Morgana, your luck is really out tonight," Gerald said as he raked in her cards and wager. "The cards must be running against you."

"It certainly looks that way, cousin," agreed Patrick, who had joined them in the middle of the game.

"Oh, dear," Morgana's face was rueful. "And I've run out of money, too. Deal me in," she told Gerald. "While I go get some more from Rian."

Morgana hurried from the table, not wanting to hold up the game. She spied her husband over at the refreshment table, talking to Sean Devlin.

"Rian," she implored him, smiling. "I've lost all my money at faro and I knew you would not like me to wager away my jewelry."

"And you want me to give you some more pound notes, is that it?"

"Aye."

"Ah, Sean. Did you ever see such a wench? I knew 'twas not my charming self which brought her running to my side," he laughed as he reached into his waistcoat and brought out a wad of money. "Here, love, I'll be over shortly to recoup your losses."

"I'm sure you will," she smiled again and hurried away, sparing a slight glance of concern for Sean, who hadn't spoken one word to her all evening.

"Well, how much did he give you?" Gerald looked at her disbelievingly when she returned to the table. "I declare, I never knew Rian to be so easy with his money."

Morgana counted the notes and almost choked. "Five—five thousand pounds," she stammered.

Even Patrick's eyebrows flew up. "That's an ungodly amount of blunt for Rian to be carrying around. What if he were to be robbed? I swear, sometimes I don't think he has a brain in his head."

"Who?" Rian asked as he sat down beside Morgana.

"You, giving a wench all that money. What's come over you, cousin?" Patrick was clearly bemused by Rian's behavior.

"You see, I'm not all bad," Rian turned to Morgana. "You could have married a miser. If I didn't give it to her," he told Patrick, "she'd barter away that jade jewelry, and then I'd have to sail all the way back to China to get her some more, which would cost me far more in the long run, cousin. Besides, I aim to win it all back anyway. Deal the cards, Gerry."

They played at length and Morgana had an opportunity to watch her husband. He was an excellent card player, seeming to know exactly when to bet and when to hold back, and soon he'd recouped all her losses and held the bank besides.

"No limit on the wagers, gentlemen, ladies," he bowed low to the fairer sex, and the game continued.

They were interrupted almost an hour later by a gang of masked men bursting through the French doors on the terrace. It all happened so quickly, no one was aware of what had occurred at first, then the orchestra stopped playing, and the women started screaming and fainting. Morgana grabbed Rian's arm tightly and glanced at his narrowed eyes fearfully. He pulled her to him reassuringly, whispering in her ear not to be afraid and to do exactly as the men asked.

One of the masked men stepped forward, then, bold and swaggering. "Ladies and gentlemen, hand over your money and jewelry, and we'll have no trouble. Otherwise—"

He deliberately left the sentence unfinished and the crowd gasped audibly as the rest of the men brandished their pistols threateningly. Morgana shrank against Rian's chest instinctively.

"See here. What's the meaning of this? You can't come bursting in here like this," Johnnie Gallagher stepped forward bravely.

"We just did, didn't we?" the apparent leader poked the Viscount in the chest none too gently.

The other men moved deftly through the crowd, pistols out, while they divested the nobility of their purses, watches, fobs, and seals, dropping the loot into soft bags which soon filled to bulging. Morgana's fingers shook as she unfastened the lovely jade necklace from her throat and pulled the dangling earrings from her lobes. Rian reached into his waistcoat, intending to pull the small pistol he always carried when in evening dress. If only he could divert their attention for a moment, the rest of the lords might be able to overpower the masked men. Colin came up softly behind him.

"I wouldn't do that, cousin. You wouldn't want your wife harmed, would you?"

Morgana turned at the sound of Colin's words and saw Rian glancing at the youth intently. "For God's sake, Rian. Colin is right. Please don't do anything foolish."

Her husband shrugged his shoulders indifferently, allowing his hands to drop to his sides and Morgana breathed a small sigh of relief. She'd guessed he intended to fire on the bandits and had been terrified that he might get killed.

When the masked men had robbed everyone in the room, the leader turned to the crowd again. "Ladies and gentlemen, I want you to know your riches go to a good cause. To hell with King George! Long live the Irish Republic!"

And then they disappeared into the night as rapidly as they had come. The crowd stood shocked and stunned for a moment, then everyone began talking at once. Morgana covered her ears at the noise.

"Rian, get me out of here, please," she begged.

He stared at her scared face and did as she asked. Colin had disappeared and Gerald said he'd catch another ride home, so they were alone in the landaulet.

"Keep a sharp lookout, Kerr," Rian called to the old man who sat hunched over the reins. "I'm sure you've heard what happened inside."

"Aye, Lord Rian. We was out in the stables and didn't know about it until it was over or we'd have come to yer aid. Damn Irish radicals! Ought to have their throats slit," he muttered to himself.

"Oh, Rian," Morgana trembled in his arms. "My lovely jade jewelry. Now you will have to go back to China after all," she attempted a tremulous smile through her tears.

"Hush, sweet," he stroked her hair softly and kissed away her tears. "Everything's all right. I'll get it back. I promise you."

"My God! How could such a horrible thing happen? It was the United Irishmen, wasn't it?"

"Probably, love."

"And their leader, he was so—so bold, and the way he looked at me, it sent chills up my spine," she sobbed.

"I don't think that was really their leader, Mag," Rian answered grimly.

She looked at him, surprised, but he refused to speak further on the subject, saying that she was tired and it would do no good to dwell on the matter.

The raid was the talk of the county for many days thereafter. Johnnie Gallagher apologized to everyone for the manner in which the party had ended and offered to reimburse them all for their losses, but no one took him up on it. Grandfather claimed that he hadn't heard of anything so daring since the rebellion led against the English under Wolfe Tone several years earlier. Morgana refused to ride out anywhere without Rian by her side, something which caused him to remark mockingly on her sudden penchant for his nearness. And everyone slept with their pistols by their sides.

The dragoon guards came around and questioned everyone intensely about the matter. This flustered Morgana greatly, but fortunately the British officers who interrogated her and Rian knew nothing of the fact that the Earl had been sentenced to hang for treason and had escaped. Indeed, no one in Ireland seemed to know about it. But one of the dragoons glanced at them sharply and took down their names, an incident which caused her no amount of unrest.

"Oh, Rian. What if they come back and arrest us?" she asked fearfully.

"Don't worry about it, love, until it happens," he replied grimly. "Brad's letter arrived yesterday and all charges against you have been dropped. A clear case of self-defense as far as Lord Chalmers's death is concerned."

"And you?" she inquired anxiously.

"I'm still wanted for treason, although Brad said the

incident with Lord Chalmers did have some bearing on the case," his voice sounded deadly.

"Then I shall be arrested for helping you to escape," Morgana moaned. "Oh, we should never have come back here."

"Hush, Mag," he took her into his arms. And then more softly, "I love you."

That night Morgana tossed restlessly long after Rian had fallen asleep. As always, his lovemaking had left her body sated, but for some reason she could not shut out the thoughts which crept so readily to her mind. There was a clap of thunder outside and the lightning that followed flashed brightly in the room. She could hear the pounding of raindrops upon the roof and the wind whining softly along the balcony. She could barely make out the crashing of the waves in the distance, breaking roughly against the rocks along the beach. A night for witches, surely, or ghosts.

There. She heard it. The soft sound of someone crying. Katy, it was Katy McShane, Morgana was sure of it. She padded quietly from the bed across the carpet, donning her wrapper as a slash of lightning lit the room again. Was it coming from outside? No. It sounded as though it was downstairs. She opened the bedroom door and tiptoed out into the hall, following its winding course to the long staircase. She descended quietly, her feet cold, for she'd worn no slippers. Morgana could hear the sobbing plainly now. It was coming from the library. She hurried to that room, opening the door softly. Her breath caught in her throat and her heart pounded violently in her breast.

The spectre was gazing out of one of the long windows that looked out over the coast. Morgana could see right through the luminous figure. There, tossing restlessly upon the cloudy seas, was William's ghost ship. The spirit did not seem aware of her presence and Morgana crept closer.

Suddenly a door slammed and the spectre faded into a smoky mist that vanished a few moments later. Morgana stood rooted to the floor with fear. Someone had entered the library in the dead of night! A lamp flickered briefly, then filled the room with its glow. Instinctively, she moved to conceal herself behind one of the bookcases. It was Colin. She could see him clearly now. He had on his greatcoat and it was damp, although not dripping wet as it would have been had he been outside in the rain. She stared at him curiously. What was he doing and where had he been? He had something rolled up under one arm. It looked like some kind of parchment. A chart, perhaps? He poured himself a glass of brandy and she became aware of the slow, supercilious smile on his lips. He almost seemed menacing, malicious in the flickering shadows, and some sixth sense warned her not to show herself. Whatever he was up to, it was obvious he had no wish to be discovered. She watched while he concealed the scroll in one of the bookcases, then blew out the lamp. Her heart pounded wildly in the darkness and for one small instant she thought he'd seen her. Then he turned and left the room. She could hear his boots as he moved quietly up the stairs to his bedroom.

Morgana didn't even realize she'd been holding her breath until she released it in a long sigh of relief. Her upper lip was beaded with sweat. Quickly, she slipped from her hiding place and ran to the bookcase where Colin had hidden the parchment. It crackled when she opened it and she glanced up, frightened for a moment, before she looked down at it again. It was nothing more than a map. A map of the coastal area. Why would he want to conceal such a thing? She studied it silently by the moonlight, fearing to light a lamp, but could see nothing particularly interesting about the chart. At last, she rolled it up and replaced it.

Perhaps Rosamunde was right and Colin had become involved with those Irish rebels. But then Morgana remembered that he had been with them at Johnnie's party and had seemed just as shocked as everyone else by the appearance of the masked men. No, that couldn't be the case, then; she sighed, her mind at ease. Maybe he had been smuggling. She knew that many nobles had become involved in such an enterprise when Napoleon had attempted to conquer France. But the war was over now and there was really no need for smuggling anymore. No, that could not be it either.

At last, she decided that she would not accomplish anything by guessing. No doubt Colin had a very simple explanation for the whole thing. She turned to go and her eye was caught by a flicker of white upon the floor. She picked it up. It was Colin's handkerchief. He must have dropped it when he was leaving the room. She studied the red stains on it. Face paint! It looked like the lip stain ladies of the evening used to redden their mouths. Morgana heaved a sigh of relief. That was it then, just as Patrick had surmised. Colin had a girl somewhere and didn't want anyone to know about it. Aye, that would explain everything. A map of the coastal area if he intended to run away with his bride, his odd comings and goings with no explanation to the family. Maybe the lass was of a lower class, and Colin knew grandfather would refuse to allow him to wed her. Morgana remembered only too well how angry the old man had grown upon learning of Patrick's marriage; and Colin had been incensed when grandfather suggested he find a rich bride and be quick about it. Yes, that had to be it. She could think of nothing else. How simple it all seemed now. No doubt Colin had taken advantage of the Irish rebels to cover himself, intending to divert his family so that they would not become suspicious about what he was really doing. Morgana almost smiled. That sly cousin of hers! He'd caused everyone so much worry for nothing!

She took a peek out of the long windows before leaving the library. Just as she had suspected, the ghost ship had disappeared. Quietly, she crept back to bed.

Morgana rose early in the morning, washing her face and hands in the pitcher, trying not to splash so that she would not awaken Rian, who still slept. She went to the dresser to get her brush and stopped short. There, on top of the polished wood, lay her jade jewelry. She gave a squeal of delight.

"Rian! You got it back. Tell me, how did you get it?" she ran to the bed.

536

"Get what? What are you talking about?" he opened his eyes, a wrathful glance on his face.

"My jade," she held out the pieces for his inspection. "I thought that was one promise you'd never be able to keep."

He took the jewelry from her hands. "Where did you get this?" he asked slowly.

"Why, it was lying on the dresser, where you put it," her voice faltered at the frown on his face.

"I don't know where it came from, Mag," he said. "I didn't put it there."

She stared at him, confused. He was lying. She was convinced of it. He must be. "But if—if you didn't put it there, who did?"

"That's what I'd like to know."

And suddenly Morgana felt shaken by the incident. Why, for instance, had Rian promised to retrieve the jade if he had not thought it would be possible to do it? If he had not known, in fact, that he could lay his hands on it quite easily? And why had he said that the one masked man was not the rebel leader? He couldn't have known that, unless—unless he was their leader himself! God! Her stomach turned over at the thought. Had he really had amnesia that time in England, or had it all been just a terrible ruse to deceive her? She recalled now that three of the British officers had positively identified her husband as the radical leader. She felt sick. But then how did Lord Chalmers's story fit into place? Had Rian perhaps bribed the man to tell her the tale in hopes that she would strike the bargain and get him impressed into the navy? And by mistake she had killed the man, causing things to go very much awry. Lord Chalmers had been very sure that she would give in to him. And Rian had been very calm all the way through the trial. He had known all along he wasn't going to hang. He'd planned on Lord Chalmers saving his neck. Brad and Anne must have been in on it, too! But what about Rian attacking her in the coach and duelling with Phillipe? How could he have been in two places at once? Perhaps he had just taken advantage of her accusation to provide himself an alibi.

There were hundreds of men with scars. She might have been mistaken. It had been dark and she had been very frightened. Dear God!

She suddenly became aware that her husband was watching her intently, his eyes narrowed searchingly.

"Is anything wrong, Mag?"

"No, I—I just don't like the idea of someone creeping into this room, that's all," she lied. "We should be more careful about bolting the door."

"I thought I did bolt it last night," he drawled lazily, but she was not deceived by his manner.

Of course he had bolted it. No one could have entered the room last night without breaking the door down, unless, of course, it had been a ghost. A ghost! Someone could have come in while she'd been downstairs, but she could not imagine grandfather or Rosamunde sneaking about in the dead of night. And Colin had gone straight to his room, she was sure of that. Gerald had spent the night in Kilshannon as usual. No, Rian had put the jade there and now he was lying about it, but why? She could not let him know she suspected him. He would kill her. Aye, how many times had he already tried? She tried not to shrink away in horror as he reached for her and his mouth came down on hers, hard.

Chapter Thirty-five

Spring came early that year, and on the grounds of Shanetara bright, green blades of grass were pushing their way up through the light film of frost which still lay fresh upon the earth, reminding Morgana of Madame Sung's plum tree. But there was an uneasy restlessness upon the land, and Morgana was caught up in its breathless, disquieting expectation.

There had been more raids upon the countryside by the Irish rebels, swift, sudden attacks that ended as quickly as they had begun, the masked men seeming to disappear without a trace. Morgana grew sick at heart as she became more and more convinced that Rian was the leader of the daring schemes. He came and went at odd hours, giving her no explanation for his actions which somehow always coincided with the timing of the raids. Two more British dragoons had been killed during the skirmishes.

Captain Vickery closed the door of the inn which served as his headquarters in Dingle. He rubbed his hands together vigorously as he stripped off his gloves and sought the warmth of the fire, for although spring was in the air, the nights were still chilly. He was a young, but determined man, and his recent promotion in the dragoon guards had given him an overwhelming incentive to capture the Irish rebels and bring them to trial for their crimes. The letter which had arrived only yesterday containing his orders was burning a hole in his breastpocket and he took it out to read the contents once again. Although the Earl of Keldara was still wanted for treason, certain evidence, it seemed, had come to light in the matter due to the belated testimony of one Maria Frampstead. Captain Vickery knew the entire story by now of Lord Chalmers's death and its relationship to the Earl's charges. His orders were to make no sudden moves until the dragoons gained further evidence one way or the other in the case. The charges against Lady Keldara had been dropped. Personally, Captain Vickery had his doubts about the guilt of Lord Keldara, but still it was strange that the radicals, oddly quiet for a time, had suddenly begun to be active again. Lady Keldara had engineered her husband's escape from jail. In any case, he meant to wait until he was sure this time before arresting the Earl as a traitor to the Crown. If he bided his time, Captain Vickery was certain the rebels would slip sooner or later, and he would get his man. He'd always said that if you gave a man enough rope, he'd hang himself in the end. But for now, Captain Vickery was content to keep the Earl under close surveillance and wait.

It was quiet in the large salon. Fionna and Bridget were making a new outfit for Corby, who seemed to be growing by leaps and bounds, and Rosamunde was mending some of Gerald's shirts.

"I declare, I don't know how that lad manages to tear so many of these," the older woman sighed as she held up one of the garments for their inspection.

"Brawls in Kilshannon," Morgana spoke without even bothering to look up.

"Oh, Morgana," Rosamunde chided her gently.

"Well, 'tis true. Why, only last week—"

"I don't want to hear about it," Rosamunde pursed her lips together grimly. "I'm sure I don't know where you pick up these scandalous tales. 'Tis most unladylike of you to repeat them."

"Rian tells me."

Morgana got up and paced the room restlessly. It was growing dark outside and the men had not yet come in from their port. She fingered the pieces on the chessboard idly. Someone had left the game before its conclusion, probably grandfather and Rian, and she could tell that black was doomed to checkmate in a few more moves. With a silent smile, she rearranged the pieces, giving the dark men an advantage they had previously lacked. Then she sighed and turned to look out of one of the long windows in the front casement. She wondered if the Irish rebels would be out again tonight.

They had become more daring in their escapades recently. They didn't seem to care whom they attacked as long as they were able to obtain a sizable amount of treasure for their pains. Morgana thought of Hassan and the money he had needed to arm a rebellion. She wondered if he had achieved his bloody ambition, and if, even now, Sirsi lay dead or dying. No, she wouldn't think about it, about gay, charming Sirsi who had turned on her so cruelly in the end. The wound was still too painful.

The loud voices just outside the door proclaimed the arrival of the McShane men. Apparently they were arguing over the estate again. Morgana couldn't remember when they had ever been together that they hadn't quarrelled over the management of Shanetara's lands. Trevor always wanted to evict some of the tenants and plow up their land, while Patrick steadfastly refused, saying it would cause rioting among those who remained. Privately, Morgana agreed with Patrick. Shanetara had enough farmland as it was and besides, the tenants had nowhere else to go. She shuddered to think what would happen when grandfather died and Trevor inherited the estate. No doubt the tenants would burn the great house down about him.

Rian brought her a drink and she gave him a cool glance as she took it, a slightly mocking smile on her face. She knew her attitude annoyed him, but he refused to make a scene in front of the family, merely giving her a jeering grin before he suggested she play something on the guitar to entertain them.

She shivered slightly as his hands brushed her shoulders, wondering again if he really was the rebel leader, if she was married to a thief and a murderer. If anything, she detested and feared him more than ever now, and wondered why he still insisted that he loved her. Surely he would grow weary of this game soon. Yes, as soon as she accepted his words of love, he would turn on her with laughter and mock her for the fool she was. He was cruel and ruthless, and not to be trusted. But she did as he asked, fingers running lightly over the strings of her ebony guitar before she began to play an old Irish ballad. The McShanes claimed this song was about one of their ancestors, but she doubted if it was true.

Her fingers plucked the strings softly as she brought to bear the anguish and sorrow of the young lovers.

One day he went to the forest green
In search of white meat and game.
A young girl smiling with pale green eyes
Stopped to speak to young Shane.

His heart remembered his love so true.
He tried, but he failed to explain.
In silence now, he roams the woods,
And the west wind speaks to Shane.

Fionna, oh, Fionna, our love was without a stain
Fionna, oh, Fionna, oh, you'll never love another,

Poor Shane . . .

Morgana's voice died away slowly in the darkness, then, without a word, she laid aside her guitar and left the room.

She did not know that Rian had followed her until

she heard his boots tramp softly up the stairs. She shrank away from his grasp, but he appeared not to notice, clasping her hand firmly in his as he led her to the bedroom and closed the door.

The wind swept out over the moors as Morgana gave Copper Lady her head, letting the mare carry her swiftly over the ground. She almost laughed aloud. For once, she had managed to escape the house without anybody dogging her footsteps. No groom trailed her, for she had informed Ben icily that she was riding out to meet Rian in the south pasture. Now she turned away from the great house, galloping wildly until it was out of sight, thinking how easy it had been to fool the groom with her simple lie. She had longed to get away for a while, to be left alone with her thoughts, and she relished her solitude like a starving child. She shivered faintly at the idea of coming across the Irish rebels, but then dismissed it, for she knew they came out only at night when the cover of the darkness would hide their masked faces and rebellious activities.

Copper Lady moved almost instinctively over the old path along the moors and soon Morgana came upon the grassy land where she used to spend such warm moments of friendship with Michael Kelsey. She dismounted and lay down upon the grass, remembering. How long ago it all seemed; and what a child she had been! A confused and grief-stricken child, pouring out her mixed-up feelings to a kind man, who had wanted only to help; and now watched her with pity in his eyes. Morgana closed her eyes, revelling in the warmness which enveloped her in spite of the threatening grey clouds in the distance.

She had changed. God, how she'd changed! Rian had done that to her, made her into a passionate woman. He had stripped away the last vestiges of her childhood; released the impetuous temper she hadn't even known she'd possessed. She could see him so clearly in her mind, his mocking wintergreen eyes and sardonic sensuous lips. The wild, shameless feelings he evoked in her puzzled and hurt her. What was this strange fascination she felt for that devil; and why did she behave so wantonly in his arms? Oh, if only she could have married someone else, or not at all, might not things have been different?

"Morgana?"

The word was so softly spoken, for a minute she thought she had dreamed it, then she opened her eyes and Michael was standing there, almost as though she had wished him to that very spot, her mind needing the release of speech.

"Do you come here often?" he asked.

"Nay," she managed to speak at last. " 'Tis the first time since I returned. And you?"

"Aye, I come here sometimes," he dismounted from his horse and came to sit beside her. "Are you happy, Morgana? You don't seem so. I've been worried about you."

"Happy? Do any of us know the meaning of the word?" She laughed a little bitterly.

"Can I help, Morgana? I felt so badly about your child. I—I didn't know what to think after your strange wedding, and then I didn't see you for so long. Does he beat you, hurt you?"

She gazed at Michael, so gentle and kind; and knew in that moment that he would never understand Rian or what it was like to live with such a man. Michael would never be able to comprehend Rian's wild daring, his bold, insulting arrogance, and, yes, his passionate lovemaking which could be so all-consuming and tender at times, so brutal at others.

"Nay," she said. "Not in the ways you think or in a manner you would understand."

"Damn it! You came to me for help once, Morgana. Let me help you now. I know you don't love him. I can see it in your eyes. You never used to close your thoughts off from me."

"Michael, please," Morgana cried. "I don't want to hear these things. 'Tis all over and done with. I'm his wife and he'll never let me go. Surely you of all people know that; you know what he's like. He's—he's changed me,

Michael. I'm not the child I was when I left here. Nay, I'm his woman now."

"Yes, I can see that," the doctor spoke. "There's a hardness about you that wasn't there before; and something else, something vital and alive, and yet something strangely disturbing, too."

"Passion," Morgana whispered. "Do you know what passion is, Michael? 'Tis a beast that grabs your soul and drives it to the brink of madness with its demons of desire. And once it's awakened inside of you, you can't get rid of it. It unleashes things inside of you that you never even dreamed existed. It hurts you, and all the time it hurts you, you keep hungering for more."

She stopped suddenly, aware that he was only dimly comprehending her feelings.

"Go home, Michael. Go home to Kyla and pray that the beast never finds you."

He took her hand and kissed it. "I shall go home, Morgana. But I will pray for you instead, pray that you find the peace of mind for which you're searching."

She turned away from him, mounting her small mare and riding away. Not once did she look back, and Michael saw the old familiar gesture as she squared her small shoulders. His heart wrung with pity as he watched her until she was out of sight, for in that moment he knew far better than she what ailed her peace of mind.

Morgana found that she was crying as she rode away, and the tears tasted bittersweet upon her lips. She brushed them away angrily. Damn you! Damn you, Rian McShane, she swore silently. You've done this to me, made me into this wild, clawing thing with your demons and desires. She galloped on, toward the beach, heedless of the light rain that was beginning to fall. Perhaps she would never go back, would just keep on riding forever.

She did not hear the hoofbeats behind her, did not know that Rian had been witness to the entire episode. It was not until he came alongside of her, the anger plain upon his face, that she saw him. She gave him a nasty glance, digging her heels into the mare's sides roughly, but he kept pace with her until he was able to reach out and grab Copper Lady's reins, bringing the horse to a halt.

"You lying bitch!" he swore. "Damn your cheating heart to hell and back!"

"I don't know what you're talking about," she stared at him coldly. "Loose my reins."

"Don't lie to me! I saw you with Michael Kelsey," his eyes narrowed warningly and the scar on his cheek stood out whitely.

Morgana blanched. "You don't understand, Rian," she began to explain.

"I don't want to hear your excuses," he yelled. "Get down off that horse."

"I will not," she tried to pull free of him.

"Damn you! Do as I say," he ordered threateningly. "Or I'll break your neck."

She had no time to respond. There was a loud clap of thunder, the lightning lit the darkened sky like a million shooting stars, and the rains showered down from the heavens. She screamed, terrified by the violent storm. Rian cursed and muttered angrily, hauling on Copper Lady's reins as he practically dragged them down the beach. The great house was too far away. They would never make it back to Shanetara in the storm.

"The caves," he shouted over the uproar. "Head for the caves."

Morgana followed without a second thought, petrified by the stark white lightning and the roaring thunder. She whipped the mare up wildly in the blinding rain lest she lose Rian's dark figure in the storm.

They were soaked to the skin and the horses were drenched by the time they finally reached the caves along the shore. Morgana clattered in after Rian, breathing a small sigh of relief at finding a temporary shelter so near. He helped her down, anger still apparent on his face, before he turned to calm the frightened horses, tethering them to a rock. Morgana tried without success to wring some of the dampness from her garments, then sat down on a stone to watch the raging wind, not daring to peer farther back into the large cave where the darkness loomed like a black void and spikes of what looked like colored icicles hung from above. When Rian finished with the horses, he stalked over to where she sat.

"Get up!" he spat, paying no attention at all to her frightened, tear-streaked face. "I said, get up."

"Rian, please," Morgana pleaded softly.

He grabbed her arm, yanking her roughly from the rock on which she'd sat, his unpleasant laughter echoing strangely in the hollow cave. He drew his hand back, slapping her hard.

"You lying bitch! This is one time I'm going to treat you the way I should have all along."

He tore off his greatcoat, tossing it carelessly upon the floor of the cave. Morgana saw his intent then and shrank away from him. He swore, ripping the bodice of her dress down to the waist.

"Don't, please, don't."

He slapped her again, then finished tearing off the rest of her clothes before he forced her down onto the coat, his fingers twisting cruelly into her bare shoulders. Morgana lay on the woolen garment, her head spinning. She was dimly aware that he was casting off his own drenched clothes, muttering angrily under his breath. She tried to rise, but his harsh voice warned her not to move, and she awaited his brutal assault like a cornered animal, whimpering in the darkness while the storm raged outside. He towered over her, his demon laughter ringing in her ears.

"Rian," she begged. "Please, not like this."

"What's the matter, Mag? You've spread your legs before and not only for me," his voice was deadly.

"And you'll never forgive me for it, will you?" she sobbed. "You arrogant bastard! You don't understand what it's like to be a chattel, a possession, a thing to be used and tossed aside," her sobs turned into hysterical laughter. "No, you're the master, aren't you, Rian? You whoreson coward! You're nothing! Nothing, do you hear me?" she fought him wildly as he put his hands on her. "I hate you."

"Silence! I'm getting tired of your mouth, woman," he laughed harshly. "Even though it does have some mighty pleasant uses on occasion. That's what I'm interested in right now. You want to play the whore, madam? Well then, let us see how adept you are at the role."

Morgana moaned as he fell upon her, pinioning her to the hard stone floor. She screamed, clawing and kicking, before he twisted one arm cruelly behind her back.

"Move and I'll break it," he warned.

She stared up into his hard, cold eyes and knew that he would do it.

"Now, open your legs, love."

Slowly, silently, she did as he asked, writhing with shame as his hand dropped between her thighs, stroking gently, invading the soft warmness there. His mouth came down over hers roughly, pillaging the inner sweetness with his tongue, searing her like a hot brand. She felt the dizzy, burning ache within her body and could have died at the betrayal of her flesh. His lips blazed her breasts, sucking greedily at the flushed peaks, his tongue tracing tiny swirls, teeth nibbling until her nipples hardened in response. He stared into her emerald eyes, a triumphant sneer on his face as she whimpered like an animal at the sensations he was arousing in her.

"You're a bitch, but I love you," he whispered harshly before he thrust his heated shaft between her white flanks.

She gasped as he entered her and felt him release the arm he'd held so tightly. She felt blind and sick with desire as she threw her arms around him, her nails clawing little furrows into his back as she pulled him to her, sobbing his name. She cried out as he sank his teeth into her shoulder, laughing lowly before he kissed the tiny wound, his lips travelling to her throat and breasts again. Never before had their lovemaking been so brutal, so violent, and Morgana gloried in it as she arched her hips wildly against him, a thousand suns exploding within her, sending shooting sparks of flame through her body; and blaze after blaze of fiery rapture burned through her ravished flesh.

She lay soaked with sweat and shivering when he'd finished with her, her breasts flushed and her lips swollen and bruised from the force of his kisses. She'd blacked out momentarily from the pleasure and pain of his love-making, and still felt slightly dizzy. Rian stared at her naked flesh, the white flanks that had, a moment past, been his.

"Can Michael Kelsey give you that?" he asked angrily, irrationally.

"He did naught save kiss my hand," Morgana spat. " 'Twas only your jealous temper which made you think otherwise, my lord. You know full well we were but friends."

"Aye," he muttered, knowing she spoke the truth. "He's not man enough for you, Mag. Admit it, my lovely witch," the anger seemed to have suddenly drained out of him. "No man has ever made you feel the way I do, when I fuck you, has he?"

"Nay," she whispered dully, hating herself as much as she did him; and silently cursing the beast called passion.

Chapter Thirty-six

When the storm had finally ceased, Rian helped Morgana dress in what remained of her tattered garments, then draped his greatcoat around her.

"What was that?" she asked sharply, cocking her head. She was sure she'd heard a sound toward the back of the cave.

"What?"

"A noise. I thought I heard something. It came from back there," she indicated the direction.

Rian shrugged his shoulders indifferently. "I don't hear anything. Probably just bats. They're all over these caves. You know that."

"Are these the ones that run into the dungeons under the house?" Morgana had a sudden thought.

"Aye, what of it?"

"Nothing, I just wondered, that's all," she turned away to mount her horse so that he would not read her thoughts.

No wonder Colin hadn't been drenched when she'd seen him in the library that night. He must have come in through the cellar, finding his way through the winding passages of the caves and dungeons. No doubt one of them was his hideaway where he met whatever girl he must have fallen in love with. She knew from the ache in her back that it couldn't be very comfortable for them.

Morgana wasn't very happy about riding home in the dark, but they had no trouble after all. Apparently this was not a night for man or beast to wander, even the daring Irish rebels.

Everyone was already at the dinner table when they arrived, and they hurried upstairs to change before they joined the rest of the family. Rian apologized to grandfather for their lateness, explaining that they had been caught in the storm.

"We're all right though, grandfather," Morgana did not allow a trace of her mixed emotions to show upon her face. "We took refuge in the caves along the coast."

"Oh?" Colin glanced at her, one eyebrow raised. "Which ones?"

"The ones that run into the dungeons," Rian remarked coolly, then took a sip of his wine.

Morgana thought Colin's face looked a little peculiar at that moment, but then decided if one of the caves was indeed his love nest, he would no doubt be worried that they might have found it. She hurried to put his mind at ease.

"It was quite dark, so we stayed near the entrance. Besides, Rian said there were bats farther on."

"Yes, well, we certainly wouldn't want you getting lost in them. I'm sure you remember well what happened that time in the dungeons," Colin seemed relieved.

Morgana shuddered. "Don't remind me. I've no wish to explore any of it again. Once was indeed enough."

"By the way, Colin," Gerald stuffed another bite of roast beef into his mouth. "I saw Lucy O'Neal in Kilshannon today. She asked about you," his tone was teasing.

Colin flushed.

"What have I told you about messing around with those slatternly wenches, Colin?" grandfather glared at the youth angrily. "Next thing you know I'll be having a great-grandchild on the wrong side of the fence."

Colin did not reply, merely staring at his plate sullenly. But Morgana was glad to at last have her suspicions regarding her cousin confirmed. Lucy O'Neal. So that was Colin's little secret. She almost smiled.

"You know," she said to Rian when they'd retired to their room for the evening. "I do believe Colin is planning to run away with that girl Gerald was talking about this evening."

"Oh? What makes you think that?" Rian poured a glass of whiskey for himself.

"Well, the other night I heard the ghost crying again, only this time it was coming from the library. So I tiptoed downstairs and while I was there, Colin came in. He had this chart rolled up under his arm and he hid it in one of the bookshelves. After he'd gone, I took it out and looked at it. It was a map of the caves along the shore. I think that's where he and this girl must meet and that's why he didn't want anyone to know about it. And besides that, I found a handkerchief he'd dropped, and it had cosmetic stains on it." She took the linen from a drawer where she'd unthinkingly stuffed it.

Rian set his glass down slowly, examining the handkerchief carefully. "Did Colin see you, Morgana?"

"No, at least I don't think so." She faltered at the sudden frown which had appeared on her husband's face. "And I put the map back just where I found it. I didn't want to interfere if he is planning to elope. I forgot I still had his handkerchief. You know what a fuss grandfather raised over Patrick's marriage."

"Yes, well, I shouldn't worry about it if I were you."

He blew out the lamps and reached for her in the darkness.

It was dark in the caves, but the flickering torches cast light enough. The Irish rebels gazed intently at the

British soldier they'd managed to capture in a skirmish with the dragoons earlier that evening. He was only a boy, about seventeen years of age, and the fright was evident upon his young face.

"Come now, lad," one of the radicals crooned coaxingly. "Surely you're aware of Captain Vickery's plans."

"No—no, sir," the boy stammered.

"We've ways to make you talk," another of the men sneered, unmoved by the youth's fear.

"Please, sir, I don't know anything, really I don't."

"Don't lie to us, boy. Captain Vickery's got a shipment of arms and reinforcements coming in next week, hasn't he?" the harder man spoke again. "Answer me, or by God I'll—"

He struck the soldier across the face, the blow splitting open the boy's lip, sending blood trickling down his chin.

"If I tell you," the youth's eyes were glazed with fear. "You won't harm me? You'll let me go?"

"Of course, lad," the softer-spoken man agreed.

"Well," the boy looked at the men skeptically, recognizing many of the younger sons of the Irish nobility present. "The word is, sir, that we're to receive reinforcements, but I heard that Captain Vickery's orders said we were to do nothing until we had further evidence against the Irish leader," the youth glanced at the tall, dark man in the corner whose face was hidden in the shadows. "There's some story that he was captured in England over three years ago, but managed to escape. Afterwards, new evidence came to light in the case which may prove that it was the wrong man anyway," the boy licked his lips nervously.

"And who was the man arrested by the British?" the meaner man asked coldly.

"Why, 'twas Lord Keldara, sir," the youth gave another anxious glance toward the man concealed in the shadows. "Captain Vickery said he's a sly fox and that we must take him alive, if possible."

"I think we've heard enough," the man in the shadows spoke softly, coming toward the youth. "You can go now, lad," he smiled slowly.

The boy glanced around the small group of men as though he couldn't believe his good fortune, and turned hurriedly to leave the cave. The rebel leader moved quickly, silently. The youth made a choked, gasping noise, then fell forward to the ground, an Oriental hunting knife protruding from the back of his uniform.

"Deliver this little package to Captain Vickery," the leader's voice was hard as he retrieved his dagger and wiped it clean before returning it to its sheath. He laughed harshly, a match flaring briefly as he lit a Spanish cigar, and for a moment, his face was cast in the flickering light. His eyes glittered darkly and the arrogant, aristocratic nose of the McShanes was outlined clearly in the shadows. "Tell him that it will be a cold day in hell before he catches Rian McShane."

He turned, his greatcoat whispering softly as it brushed against the rocks in the cave before he rode away into the night.

Captain Vickery stared at the young face of the dead lad his soldiers had discovered on the step out in front of the inn.

"Young Riley," he muttered. Then, "Damn those rebels!" He slammed his fist against the desk. "Have they no mercy?"

"Apparently not, sir," one of the dragoons cleared his throat.

It was indeed a nasty business and he did not relish his duty in having to inform the Captain of this night's work. No, he did not like it a bit, nor did he desire to repeat the taunting remarks of the masked men as they'd ridden away, but it was his duty and he would do it.

"There's something else, sir," he cleared his throat again.

"Well, speak up, Lieutenant."

" 'Tis the rebels, sir. When they disappeared, we thought we heard them shouting that—that you'd never catch their leader, sir. Rian McShane."

555

Captain Vickery's eyes narrowed thoughtfully. "That will be all, Lieutenant," he replied. "See to young Riley's funeral. I myself will notify his family of the loss of their son."

"Yes, sir."

Captain Vickery rubbed his eyes tiredly. Was it a game? The very audacity of the man. Did he wish to be caught? Lord, Captain Vickery did not intend to be made a fool of again. It was a good thing his lieutenant had been bright enough to jot down the Earl and Countess's names after the rebel raid on Laughlin Hall. Over three years. It had been over three years since their disappearance and now they'd returned to Ireland as bold as brass. Captain Vickery couldn't countenance such arrogance. He hadn't believed that Rian McShane was the rebel leader, but now, by God, he'd get that strutting, sneering cock if it was the last thing he ever did.

The rain was falling softly when Morgana awakened in the morning. The skies were grey with clouds and the wind whined along the balcony with a plaintive sigh. Rian gazed at her warmly.

" 'Tis a day for staying in bed, love," he murmured softly.

"Nay," she whispered as he kissed her throat. "I promised Fionna I'd stay with Corby today. She wants to ride over to Devlin's Way to see Lindsey and can't take the child because Lindsey can't stand him."

"Corby's got a nanny to sit with him," Rian breathed, his lips brushing her temples.

"I know, but he practically begged me to come, Rian, and I can't disappoint him."

To her surprise, he reluctantly released her. "If you insist, love," he said. "I know how much the lad means to you."

It was true. Morgana had grown very fond of the child and was looking forward to spending the day with him. She set out shortly after breakfast, disdaining the use of the landaulet, enjoying the feel of the wind as it whipped through her tangled mass of hair and brought a warm flush to her cheeks. The frost had disappeared, although the weather was still slightly chilly, but the trees had tiny buds on them and some of the early flowers had already blossomed. The lough was grey and its waters choppy as Morgana passed, and she was careful to keep well away from its edge. More than one poor Irishman had drowned in its depths. And the mountainous crags looked particularly menacing against the overcast sky.

She thanked the groom for riding over with her, then dismissed him with a smile before pounding the brass knocker upon the door of Shaughnessy Bay. It was opened at last by the sour-faced butler who was almost as stuffy as Trevor. Morgana couldn't for the life of her understand why her cousin continued to employ the man, but then decided that Trevor and the butler probably got along famously together. Corby came running down the steps, followed more sedately by Fionna.

"Cousin Mag," the boy cried, hugging her knees since that was about as high as he could reach.

She swung him up into her arms. "My, what a big boy you're getting to be."

"Isn't he, though?" Fionna laughed. "Corby, you mustn't run at people like that. Morgana almost lost her balance."

"Fionna, are you sure you want to ride over to Devlin's Way? This is hardly the day to be paying social calls."

"I know, Morgana, but I shall be fine in the barouche and I must talk to Lindsey. Corby, you go on upstairs and Cousin Mag will be there in a minute." She turned to Morgana again once the child had scampered off. "I'm so worried about her, Morgana. She's always been headstrong and, well, I'm sure you've heard the stories about her behavior. Everyone has, it seems," she bit her lip. "Anyway, I promised mother I'd try to talk to Lindsey. Besides, I hate to see Sean turning into an alcoholic. He's a fine man."

"Yes, he is," Morgana agreed.

Morgana watched as Fionna drove off in the barouche, accompanied by no less than three outriders. Ah well, her sister-in-law had always been far more skittish than she. Then she turned and went upstairs to find Corby.

The lad squealed with delight and begged her to play a game with him, ignoring the disapproving glance his stern-faced nanny, Mistress Doty, gave him.

"Very well, then," Morgana laughed, catching him up in her arms. "What would you like to play?"

"I know," Corby gazed at her slyly. "You be the British soldiers and I'll be an Irish rebel. Bang, bang!" he pretended he had a rifle in his hands.

Morgana shuddered, her mind going back over that day three weeks ago when a young British dragoon had been killed and his body dumped at the inn in Dingle. Rian came in late that night, his greatcoat slightly damp, although it hadn't been raining. He glanced at her carelessly as he shrugged off its woolen material, the same coat on which he'd taken her so violently in the cave.

She surveyed him timidly from the bed. " 'Tis late, my lord."

"Pining for my kisses, sweet?" he cocked one eyebrow mockingly.

"Nay," she drew the sheets about her closer. " 'Tis just that—why must you go out so late when you know those rebels stalk the countryside at night? 'Tis well past midnight, my lord. I was concerned for your safety, that's all." She studied him suspiciously.

"Oh? Since when have you ever worried your lovely head about me, Mag?" he sneered sarcastically.

"I've heard rumors," she began.

"You've heard nothing," he crossed the room swiftly, a darkening frown on his face as he grasped her shoulders cruelly. "And you will say nothing, do you understand? Your life depends on it," he jeered softly.

Morgana drew back in fear. He would kill her. It had been Rian all along, Rian who'd left her to die in the dungeons, Rian who'd pushed her down the stairs. Now she was sure of it.

"Don't hurt me," she pleaded, before he smothered her cries with his hard, searing mouth.

Captain Vickery had come in the morning with several of his dragoons. He questioned them at length, one of his lieutenants taking copious notes on a small pad.

"Where were you last night, Lord Keldara?"

"What business is it of yours?" Rian asked calmly, giving the captain a piercing stare. He was sure he recognized the man.

Where had he seen that officer? Ah, yes, he had it now. This was one of the men who'd testified at his trial. Rian's face revealed none of his emotions as he gazed at the man.

"My lord, we know who you are. Let's not play games. You are an escaped criminal, wanted for treason as the leader of these Irish rebels."

"That was never proved," Rian replied softly. "Have you come to arrest me?"

"Nay, my lord," Captain Vickery swallowed hard. "I have been instructed that additional evidence has come to light in your case which may or may not have some bearing on your guilt or innocence. My hands are tied for the time being, but I will ask the question again. Where were you last night?"

"Home in bed," Rian's eyes narrowed. "With my wife."

Morgana blanched when the Captain turned to her.

"Is that true, my lady?"

She glanced at Rian's stony, implacable face and remembered his warning. "Aye, 'tis true," she managed to speak at last.

"Huh," Captain Vickery snorted. "No doubt she would lie to protect you, my lord. After all, it was she who helped you to escape from Newgate Prison. Do you know the penalties for aiding and abetting a criminal, my lady?" he turned his sharp eyes on Morgana again. "Never fear. You'll slip up sooner or later and then I'll get you, both of you," he vowed. "And neither the Prince Regent nor all your fancy friends shall be able to save you."

"Cousin Mag, you're supposed to fall down dead," Corby wailed, bringing Morgana back to the present with a start.

"I'm sorry, Corby," she said. "Why don't we play something else instead? How about a game of cards?"

"Father says gambling ain't decent," he looked at her gravely.

She studied his small face and realized that Trevor had already affected the boy with his pompous seriousness. No doubt Fionna was the only thing which had kept the lad's natural exuberance from being stifled entirely.

"Well, we won't bet on the game, and then it won't be gambling," she told him, glad to see his face brighten at this.

"All right."

Morgana dealt out the cards, choosing a simple game, for after all, Corby, for all his brightness, was not quite three years old. "Are you coming to my birthday party next week?"

"Uh huh, mother said we were all going to get to come. I've got you a present already," he smiled up at her, relieving for a moment the frown of concentration upon his face as he'd bent over his cards.

Morgana surveyed herself in the mirror. Yes, she looked well this evening. She had chosen a gown of gold brocade which made the honeyed flecks in her emerald eyes swim to the surface most enchantingly. The huge sleeves were puffed and trimmed with lace, and the bodice was cut squarely across the front to reveal the slight hollow between her breasts.

It was her birthday. Today she was twenty-six years old. She found it hard to believe that so much time had passed from the day she'd first come to Shanetara. The family was having a small party for her in the dining room, and she found that she was trembling with excitement at the thought. She'd never had a real party before. Always something had interfered with celebrations for her birthday, at most they had been little parties, just she and her father.

"Mag," Rian stuck his head in the door. "They're all waiting."

"I'm coming," she turned away from the looking glass and went to join him.

Things had been more strained than ever between them since Captain Vickery's visit, but she was determined not to let it spoil her party, so she smiled at him waveringly and accepted the arm he offered. The family was indeed already assembled in the dining room, including Corby and Maureen. Morgana gave them each a hug before she allowed Rian to seat her at the foot of the table, a place Rosamunde had relinquished in her honor. The presents were piled high in the center of the table and there was huge cake in front of her, one she knew, from the looks of it, the cook had painstakingly decorated. Rian uncorked the champagne, ignoring Trevor's comment that Corby was not to have any, giving the small lad, as well as Maureen, a glass.

"A toast," Rian raised his glass. "To the loveliest lass in all of Ireland."

Morgana blushed as they toasted her and she felt Rian's warm eyes caress her boldly. They downed the champagne quickly as she cut the cake and passed out the plates.

"I declare, you don't look any older than the day you got here," Rosamunde smiled gaily.

"Here, here," grandfather stamped his cane upon the floor, gazing at Morgana fondly.

She opened the presents one by one, thanking each member of the family in turn, saving a special smile for Corby, who'd gotten her a lovely lace handkerchief, and Maureen, who'd selected a pretty fan. It was not until she had finished, that she realized there'd been nothing at all from Rian. Puzzled, she glanced at him questioningly. He smiled at her mockingly, as though he were well pleased with himself.

"Is something wrong, Mag?" he drawled lazily.

"Oh, don't tease the child, Rian," Rosamunde chided gently. "You know very well you've given her no gift."

"Haven't I? How remiss of me. I'll have to remedy that right away," he jumped up from the table and disappeared.

Before anyone had time to wonder at his strange behavior, he returned, bearing a young Irish Setter in his arms.

"Rian, oh, Rian," Morgana stared at the small puppy disbelievingly. "Is it really mine?"

"Aye," he handed her the tiny bundle. "Careful now, he's lame in one leg, but I didn't think you'd mind."

"No, of course not," she glanced at its little hind paw, which was somewhat twisted. "Can he walk?"

"Oh, yes," Rian reassured her. "He came from Sean Devlin's kennels. It seems the little fellow didn't move out of Lindsey's way fast enough one day and she rode over him with her mare. He's lucky to be alive."

"How cruel," Morgana cried, hugging the puppy to her breast. "Don't worry," she told the little dog. "I shall take good care of you and I won't ever let anyone hurt you again."

"Sean was going to shoot him," Rian explained. "No good for hunting, but I thought you might like to have him."

"Yes, oh, yes, he's adorable. What shall I call him, do you think?"

Rian shrugged. " 'Tis up to you, sweet, he's yours now."

Morgana thought very hard, and at last she decided to name the little dog "Rory," which meant red-haired. And he certainly was that. There wasn't a trace of the usual white on him. Rory seemed to look at her gratefully, his liquid brown eyes sad, and when she bent to hug him, he nuzzled her timidly, licking her face. She laughed and insisted that the little dog he allowed to sleep in her room, something to which grandfather was averse; but at last he agreed that Rory might stay. Morgana thanked Rian warmly for the puppy and went off to make him comfortable for the night. He whined pitifully when they blew out the lamps, and finally she lifted him up into the bed with them, causing Rian to curse mightily under his breath. But she remained adamant and Rory lay cuddled in her arms for the rest of the night.

In the days that followed, Morgana took to walking as much as possible, for Rory could not keep up if she rode. Kerr O'Malley had watched them patiently for a time, then told Morgana gruffly that he might be able to fix a splint which would help straighten out the puppy's leg. She stayed in the stable while he worked, much pleased by the offer. It had been a long time coming, but it seemed that Kerr had finally accepted her. He cut and measured, sanding down the edges of the splint so that they would be smooth, then taped Rory's leg up in the makeshift cast.

" 'Tis the best I kin do, lass," he cleared his throat gruffly again. "But I think 'twill do the little bairn good in time."

To her surprise, there were tears in her eyes. "I don't know how to thank you, Kerr," she said simply.

"Well, 'tis been many years now and the past is best forgotten. Sure and ye've been good fer the old master and I won't be fergetting it. Many's the time he's told me how much yer being here has meant to him. There, run along now, Lady Morgana, and see that pup don't tear the splint off before it has a chance to do some good."

"I will," she promised.

Later on that day, Morgana walked out toward the moors. It looked as though it was going to rain again. The skies were growing dark and there was a clap of thunder far off in the distance. She sighed. Would this endless downpour never cease? She decided that she and Rory would have time to try out the new splint and make it back to the great house before the storm broke, however, and set out slowly, helping the little dog adjust to the brace.

Rory didn't like it all. He dragged his leg and tried to throw it off, and when that didn't work, he tore at the bandages which held it in place with his sharp teeth.

"No, Rory," Morgana couldn't help but laugh.

She rapped his nose gently and finally he seemed to

understand that he was not to remove the unpleasant hindrance. He gazed at her pitifully and she told him that she was sorry, but that it was for his own good.

They hadn't gone very far when Morgana spied a rapidly approaching figure in the distance. For a moment, she panicked, thinking it was one of the Irish rebels, but then she realized it was Colin. He seemed to be greatly distressed.

"Cousin," he sawed on his horse's reins, making his mount rear as he drew to a hasty halt in front of her. "I'm afraid there's been an accident. It's—it's Rian."

"Rian? What happened?" she cried.

"He was in the caves and there was a small rockslide. I'm afraid he's—he's asking for you, Morgana," Colin did not finish what he'd started to say.

Morgana's hand flew to her mouth. "The caves. Oh, I knew something dreadful like this was going to happen. You must take me there at once."

She scooped Rory up in her arms.

"We don't have time for that mutt," Colin snapped.

"I just can't leave him here. He doesn't know his way around and he'll get lost," she insisted.

Colin swore, but allowed her to mount behind him, holding onto the little dog as best as she could. Then he dug his heels sharply into the horse's flanks and galloped toward the coast. Morgana was almost thrown off in her attempt to clutch Rory to her breast, but somehow she managed to hang on to Colin's coat. They reached the caves in a matter of minutes.

"In here," Colin spoke curtly.

Morgana followed him into the caves, blinking rapidly at the lack of light and trying to soothe Rory, who was whining at this unaccustomed treatment.

"Where is he, Colin?" she asked anxiously. "I can't see a thing."

"Take my hand. I'll show you."

She grabbed hold of him, a small cry catching in her throat. What if Rian were dead? "Oh, Colin, shouldn't one of us go for help?" she sobbed nervously as they wound their way through the dark, twisting passages.

"It may be too late," he answered grimly.

Morgana shuddered. "He's dead, I know it. Why didn't you just tell me?" she wailed.

Her cousin didn't answer, merely pulling her along until they reached another open spot. Torches flickered strangely in the walls of the cave and a group of rough-looking men lounged carelessly against the rocks. Morgana stared at their hard faces with concern and puzzlement.

"What's going on here?" she turned to Colin. "Where is my husband?"

"I don't know," Colin grinned at her slowly, wolfishly. "At Shanetara, I would imagine."

She drew back in fear, some instinct warning her. "Then what's the meaning of this cruel trick, Colin?" she managed to ask coldly.

"My dear cousin," he sneered superciliously. "You have just become a prisoner of the United Irishmen. Tie her up," he ordered his men.

Chapter Thirty-seven

Morgana screamed as rough hands grabbed her, binding her wrists tightly, and she stared at Colin, sick and dazed with shock and fear.

"Scream all you want, cousin," he laughed unpleasantly. "There's no one to hear you."

He kicked Rory to one side, causing the little pup to whimper piteously and crouch beneath Morgana's skirts.

"Don't hurt him," she begged.

"Then shut that mutt up!" Colin snapped. "You men, don't let her escape. I'll be back in an hour and then we'll carry out the rest of our plan."

Morgana almost choked on her sobs as she watched her cousin disappear into the blackness of the winding tunnels, leaving her alone with the desperate-looking men. She shrank away at their wolfish glances, recognizing some of their faces. God! Sean Devlin's younger brother was with them. She turned to him pleadingly.

"Kelly, you've got to help me," she tried.

He stared at her as though he'd never seen her before in his life.

"Robert?" she saw Max O'Brien's brother next.

He looked right through her.

"Oh, God!" she sank to the cold floor, a slow numbness invading her very being.

Colin. All the time, it had been Colin. How could she have been so blind? Lucy O'Neal. Love nest, indeed. She laughed hysterically at the thought. Colin was the rebel leader. But if so, what was Rian and why had he tried to kill her?

Colin stalked slowly up the back stairs of Shanetara, taking great pains not to be seen, his pistol concealed beneath the folds of his coat. He'd waited a long time for this and he meant to savor it with pleasure. He opened the door of Rian and Morgana's bedroom quietly.

"Hello, Rian," he said softly.

Rian turned from the dresser in surprise, a glass of whiskey in one hand. "Don't you believe in knocking?"

"Listen to me carefully, cousin," Colin sneered. "Because I'm only going to say this one time. I have your lovely wife prisoner."

"Morgana! If you've harmed her, Colin," Rian lunged at his cousin.

"No," Colin stepped back revealing the little pistol. " 'Twill do you no good to kill me, cousin. My men have orders to murder your bride if I don't return, after they've used her awhile, of course," he laughed.

Rian clenched his fists together tightly. "You son of a bitch! I knew it was you all along. You *are* the rebel leader, aren't you, Colin?"

"Aye. I've been quite clever though, you must admit that. Using your name and your devilish reputation. You know, we look a great deal alike, especially at night. 'Tis almost amazing how easy it's been. You're going to hang, Rian."

"Oh? How do you intend to accomplish that?" the Earl asked slowly, his mind working furiously. "I cheated the rope once before."

"A most unfortunate occurrence. Would you believe

I actually knew nothing at all of the matter until several weeks ago? Still, your arrest has been quite a piece of luck. 'Twill be even more simple to carry out my plan."

"Which is?"

"You know the British ship moored off the coast?"

"Aye."

"Good. She's carrying enough rifles and ammunition for an army. I want those weapons, cousin. Tonight, after dark, I want you to take the *Sorceress* out, manned by my followers, of course, and attack that British ship. You've enough cannons on your ship to sink a hundred like that English vessel and I know it. You get those arms for me and I'll release Morgana unharmed. One other thing," Colin continued coldly. "After my men have gotten away with the weapons, you will—ah—arrange for yourself to be captured and admit to that prig, Captain Vickery, that you are indeed the rebel leader."

"You've got it all thought out, don't you, Colin? And if I refuse?"

"I've told you, I'll kill Morgana."

"She doesn't mean a thing to me," Rian laughed, attempting to appear relaxed.

"That little trick won't work, cousin. I heard you that day in the cave. You're sick in love with the bitch."

Rian drew in his breath sharply. "You won't get away with this, Colin. I'll hunt you down like a dog."

Colin laughed unpleasantly. "I'll remember that, cousin, when I watch you dangling at the end of a rope. Tonight. Come alone."

Rian sank down onto the bed in despair after his cousin had gone. God! He'd known something like this was going to happen, had guessed for a long time that Colin was the rebel leader. He had been spying on them, attempting to find some way to force his cousin into the open so that he would be able to clear himself of the charges of treason against him. Morgana was probably scared stiff. No doubt Colin had her hidden in the caves. It would be foolhardy to go after her. They would know he was coming long before he ever reached her and would have no hesitation about slitting her lovely throat. Rian knew they were desperate. Captain Vickery was getting too close for comfort. He should have warned Morgana, should have told her from the start; but he knew she would not have believed him. He suspected that she thought he himself was the rebel leader and that was why she had seemed so afraid of him lately. There was nothing to do but go along with Colin's plan until he could think of some way to rescue his wife. Captain Vickery would not believe him if he went to the officer with this incredible tale.

That night, Rian left the house quietly, wanting no questions asked about his motives. A shock like this might very well kill grandfather. He whipped Lucifer unmercifully, hauling on the reins and cursing when the confused stallion stumbled in the dark. He rode hard, desperately, over the road to Kilshannon, clattering upon the docks like a madman. He ordered the few crewmen on his ship off, informing them curtly that they would have to find other quarters for the evening. Harrison grumbled mightily about his lordship's strange quirks of humor, but could see that the Earl would brook no argument, so the first mate followed the rest of the disgruntled crew to the inn, intending to get rip-roaring drunk.

"Ain't that odd?" Timmons remarked as they trudged along the muddy road.

"Aye. No doubt the Cap'n has his reasons. Perhaps that red-haired minx has tossed him out of the house."

The two men laughed heartily over this, linking arms companionably as they turned into the tavern.

Rian paced the deck of the *Sorceress* anxiously after they had disappeared. It was not long before he heard the tramp of boots upon the gangplank and was surrounded by masked men. He searched in vain for Colin's slender figure, then realized that his cousin must have stayed behind with Morgana, the cowardly cur! Rian could have throttled him with his bare hands.

The brassy young man who'd given the orders at the

raid on Johnnie Gallagher's party stepped forward and instructed Rian to get under way. The Earl recognized the man at last as Robert O'Brien, Max's younger brother.

"And no tricks, or your pretty wife gets it," Robert snarled.

Rian cursed under his breath. No point in letting them know he had recognized some of them. He did as they told him, feeling all the while that he would most likely get a knife in his back before the night was over.

There was a hazy ring around the moon and a slight mist hung over the waters as they slipped out of the port of Kilshannon, bound for the British frigate. Rian knew if he fired on the vessel, he would indeed be hanged for treason, and he racked his brain desperately for a plan which would foil the venture. The wind caught the sails and the *Sorceress* rocked on the waves as the unaccustomed crew hurried to trim the billowing material. The Earl hoped fervently that they manned his cannons as badly as they did his ship. That way, they'd never be able to hit the broad side of a barn. He laughed softly in the darkness.

"What's so funny?" Robert O'Brien asked. "I wouldn't be laughing if my wife's life were at stake."

Rian sobered quickly enough after that, bringing the *Sorceress* alongside the British ship, hoping they wouldn't notice what he was doing.

"We're too close," O'Brien hissed. "Our shots will go right over her bow."

Realizing that his ploy had failed, the Earl turned the wheel again, sending the vessel farther out on the seas. He watched with a sinking heart as the rebels loaded and aimed the cannons, toppling the main mast of the British frigate with their first shot. Pure luck. It usually took several tries to gauge the distance correctly. There were shouts and the sound of pounding feet from the frigate as the startled crew scrambled about the deck, and Rian realized that the battle was going to be long and bloody. He had to do something, anything!

Morgana heard the shots echoing in the night, rever-

571

berating through the passages of the caves like thunder. She had dozed for a time, but was awake and desperate now. She attempted to loose the bonds which held her prisoner, but they were tied too securely. That was cannon fire, she was sure of it; she'd heard the guns of the *Sorceress* fired before when they'd been attacked by the Barbary pirates and had learned to tell the difference between cannons and thunder.

"What is it, Colin? What's going on?" she stared at her smiling cousin with fright.

"Rian's leading a little raid against the British, cousin," he smirked.

"Rian? But I thought you were the rebel leader," Morgana was frankly confused.

"You still don't understand, do you, cousin?" he spoke softly, the flickering torches giving him an evil leer. "If only you'd married me, Morgana, you wouldn't be here now."

"What—what are you talking about?"

"You see," he gazed off into the distance as though he were envisioning the ongoing battle. "I always wanted to go into the military, but unlike the rest of the McShanes, I didn't have the money. Oh, I know grandfather wanted me to become a minister, but I never had any intentions of doing so. I had originally planned to kill the old man, but then you came. You came with your fiery red hair and your emerald eyes, and you charmed the old fool into changing his will."

"No—"

"Aye, but it didn't really matter. You said you'd marry me and I still had a chance. It was even better that way. I'd be getting a fortune through you, much more than I should have gotten otherwise. But then you wed that bastard, Rian, instead. Then I found out you were with child. You prim little bitch! How did he manage to seduce you? 'Tis of no consequence," Colin sneered down at her. "I'd tried to kill you before, but that child really sealed your fate, Morgana. Don't you see? I had to get rid of you before the babe was born or your brat would have inherited everything. And you, poor fool, thought it was

Rian who was trying to murder you. You thought he'd only married you for the money, just as I would have done. What a stupid idiot you are," Colin continued.

"He's sick in love with you, has been for years, and you've been too blind and stubborn to see it. My first attempt in the dungeon failed because he insisted on searching every corridor down there until he found you. That's when I realized that bold, dashing Rian McShane had fallen in love at last. It was a pure stroke of luck, his finding that torch you dropped. Damn the bastard! He was always there, interfering with my plans. Your mare's stumbling saved you the time I fired at you on the moors, curse my luck again. You're like a cat, my dear, with nine lives. 'Twas I who pushed you down the stairs. Too bad I didn't kill you then. But at least I destroyed your child," he grinned, and Morgana saw that he was absolutely insane.

"But you kept insisting that someone was trying to murder you, and pretty soon Rian got suspicious about all of those accidents. He started asking questions, poking around the countryside. He couldn't prove anything, so he took you away. I thought I'd lost, but then I had a brilliant idea. I joined the United Irishmen and began terrorizing the countryside, posing as my dear cousin Rian."

"It was you who killed those British soldiers," Morgana breathed, numb with fright.

"Aye, I killed them, all of them. They came snooping around here, stirring up trouble. I had to get rid of them. Everything was going fine until you came back. You thought I didn't see you that night in the library, but I did. I knew you read the chart, but I couldn't understand why you didn't suspect me then."

"I thought you were merely using the caves as a meeting place with that girl in Kilshannon," Morgana moaned.

"A break for me then," he chortled. "You allowed your hate for Rian to blind you to everything, cousin. Tell me, why is it that you detest him so?"

Morgana stared at him stubbornly, refusing to reply.

She felt a warm, little tongue at her wrists and realized that Rory was behind her, gnawing playfully on the ropes which bound her tight. Quietly, she attempted to pull away from him so that his tiny teeth dug in deeper, more furiously, praying that Colin wouldn't notice what she was doing.

"I went up to your room and left the jade jewelry, and just as I'd hoped, you believed that Rian was the rebel leader, that he'd taken it back for you. It was simple then. I discovered that he'd been arrested over three years ago in England and tried for treason. I had him then, although I couldn't understand why Captain Vickery didn't clap him in jail, but that young soldier I killed told me they needed more evidence, that something else had come to light after Rian escaped which might prove that he was innocent, so I devised this little scheme to give them absolute proof. I'll wind up a winner in more ways than one tonight."

"What do you mean?" Morgana asked, anything to keep him from seeing what she was doing.

"Why, even now Rian is attacking the British frigate moored off the coast. My men shall divest her of the weapons she carries and then sink her. I'm afraid your husband won't be returning, however. He's agreed to give himself up to the English in exchange for your freedom. Nay, don't get your hopes up, Morgana. You know the truth now. I'm afraid I shall have to kill you after all."

"You're mad," she cried. "You'll never get away with this."

"Won't I? A poor, love-stricken wife discovers that her husband is a murderer and throws herself off the cliffs. No one shall doubt my story when I find you, dear. I promise you I shall be properly shocked and heartbroken."

Morgana pulled sharply and the last thread on the ropes snapped away. She kept perfectly still, hands behind her back so that Colin would not guess she had managed to free herself. She would have to divert his attention, though, or she'd never be able to get the ropes around her ankles undone. She almost cried aloud in anguish at her plight; in fact, the sound must have come from her mouth before she realized it, for a low, sad moan echoed through the caves hauntingly. Morgana raised her eyes and saw the lovely vision of Katy McShane; but what a sight! The ghost had blood streaming from her ears and nostrils and her neck was twisted as though it had been broken. It opened its mouth and screamed.

"The ghost," Morgana whispered.

Colin turned to where she stared and quick as a flash she untied the cords around her ankles, and ran like the wind through the dark passageways. She heard Colin swear and come after her, scrambling in the blackness. She twisted and turned blindly, stumbling, falling, gasping for breath. Which tunnel was the right one? Was she heading for the coast or were the catacombs taking her to the dungeons where she would be trapped? Morgana pressed onward, hands damp from the green slime that covered the walls of the caves until at last she saw, with a small sigh of relief, the entrance. She ran quickly, climbing rapidly over the rocks, looking for the path which led down to the beach, hearing the pounding of Colin's boots as he pursued her. It was no use; she would never find the trail in the darkness. She turned and headed toward the precarious cliffs which stretched out into the moors. In her haste to get away, she tripped and fell, sprawling dangerously close to the edge of them. She screamed as Colin towered above her, his greatcoat flapping in the wind like bat's wings. He yanked her to her feet roughly, his face leering into hers.

"I couldn't have chosen a better spot, my dear," he jeered, a cruel, taunting smile on his face. "Perhaps I'll even rape you first. You'd like that, wouldn't you? You cheap, whoring slut!"

Morgana fought as she'd never struggled before in her life as his hands ripped at her gown, tearing the bodice open to the waist to expose her pale, rounded breasts. Colin hit her brutally with his fist as she clawed and kicked at him. The blow dazed her and she fell back against his arm, scarcely knowing when he began to squeeze her breasts wickedly, forcing his lips upon her unresisting mouth. Then she bit him savagely and saw the blood spurt from the wound. She pressed home the slight advantage, raking her nails down the side of his face.

"You bitch!" he swore again.

He lunged at her, and then they were falling, falling . . .

Chapter Thirty-eight

Morgana regained consciousness slowly. She was dimly aware of the roar of the waves as the breakers crashed against the cliffs and of a sharp pain in her side that told her that she was still alive. She tried to move and almost fainted again. She was lying on a narrow ledge which hung out from one of the cliffs. It was a miracle; she was alive! She couldn't get over it. But she didn't dare try to move again, the precipice was too narrow. If she changed her position, she would surely fall off and die. She examined herself gingerly in the darkness and at last determined that she had no broken bones, but was merely extremely battered and bruised from the fall.

She moaned softly in the blackness, turning her head once to stare down at the crags upon which she would have been lying had fate not intervened. By the hazy moonlight, she could barely make out Colin's broken body sprawled among the rocks. His head bobbed gently each time the tide rushed in, slapped against the crags, and ebbed out again. Morgana shuddered and turned away, sickened by the sight. He would have killed her, the slight, poetic youth she'd once thought to marry and manage so easily. She laughed hysterically at the idea until she again subsided into choked sobs.

Colin had called her a stubborn, blind fool, and he had been right. Morgana lay on the hard, rocky ledge with the wind whipping wildly about her and the rain beginning to drizzle upon her, and thought about his crazy, impossible story. And for the first time in her life, she understood what her husband had tried to tell her, what Madame Sung had tried to tell her, and what her heart had known all along. She was in love with Rian McShane.

She cried bitterly. Now, when it was too late, she knew that she loved him, had loved him all along, from the first moment she'd almost ridden over him in front of Shanetara and he'd gazed up at her with that lazy, drawling smile, those arrogant, mocking eyes, she had loved him. She shivered from the misty rain and felt his warm, strong arms around her, the muscles rippling in his back, and the searing flame of his lips upon hers. He had always been there, had always stood behind her, waiting to back her up when she'd needed him. Oh, she could see it all so clearly now, and she ached with a pain that ripped through her heart and belly like death! He would give himself up for her tonight, would hang, and it would all be for nothing; she was surely going to die on this cliff of exposure before morning. She could not survive a night out in the open; it was so cold, in spite of the early spring. Oh, why had she been so damned stubborn, aye, so damned arrogant, the very traits she'd accused Rian of? She remembered how the corners of his eyes had crinkled with laughter, darkening in their greenness when he'd told her that she acted just like him, that they were match for match. He had known and he'd tried to tell her. Why hadn't she listened?

He had beaten her, and bullied her, and loved her. Loved her with a fierce, wild passion that even time would never dim. Yes, he was hard and demanding, but above all, he was a man. Did she really ever want anything less? No, she wanted no weak, boyish youth whom she could dominate and order about. Such a man would disgust her eventually. Nay, Morgana would have no gentle love. She would turn her ship headlong into the wind and sail the high seas; and she would conquer them or die trying. Could she settle for a man who wanted anything less? No! She wanted her mate at the helm, his warm hands covering her own, helping her, sharing the battle of life with her.

"Rian, oh, Rian, my love, my life," she moaned softly. "Why was I such a fool? Where are you, my love, and where is your bright star to guide our ship home?"

The British frigate fired back slowly, having been taken by surprise, but fight she did. A mast on the *Sorceress* toppled, splintering in the darkness, its sail collapsing on the deck. The rebels loaded the cannons as quickly as possible, returning the assault with more of their own, ignoring the hot, grimy smoke which filled the air, stinging their eyes with its heated fog. The radicals paid no attention to Rian at the helm and suddenly he saw his chance. He turned the wheel hard, exposing the side of the ship to the British frigate's weapons. There was a loud explosion and the hull of the *Sorceress* ripped wide open, heaving violently from the blast, the waves gushing into the bilge with a deafening roar as they sucked at the bottom of the vessel.

"You fool!" Robert O'Brien turned angrily. "You've sunk us."

He pulled his sword, intending to cut Rian down, but the Earl was quicker. He ran for his cabin, slamming open the door and seizing one of the rapiers that lay on the table, one of the foils that he and Morgana had duelled with that day upon the ship. Morgana! His mouth tightened grimly as he swung upon the brother of one of his oldest friends. The duel was brief, the young rebel being no match for the experienced Earl, and Rian ran the lad through, thinking for a moment that it was a sad day indeed when friend turned against friend and brother against brother. He'd have to tell Max himself. Then he stepped over the body into the passageway.

The *Sorceress* was sinking fast. He had to get off or he'd drown, and Rian was one captain who had no intention of going down with his ship. He ran back to the deck. The rest of the rebels were lowering the dinghies and he saw that he was going to have to fight for one. With a snarled oath, he raised his sword, slashing furiously at two men. They dropped the ropes, allowing the small boat to clatter over the side as they faced him. Rian had no patience now for etiquette or the polite duelling he engaged in at Angelo's in London. He severed one man's arm from its socket and slit the other one's throat. Then he threw the rapier away and leaped over the side of the ship. It wasn't far; the *Sorceress* was almost completely under by this time. The Earl grabbed the side of the small boat before it could get away and hoisted himself over the edge. He watched silently as there was a giant sucking noise and the *Sorceress* disappeared into the dark, stormy waters. For one brief moment, he could have sworn that the image of William's ghost ship lingered there in the hazy outline of the moon, but then there was nothing but a swirling of grey mist. Grimly, Rian rowed toward shore.

Captain Vickery was already waiting there, arresting the rebels as they put into port in the tiny dinghies, his dragoons marching the men into the inn at Kilshannon until he could transfer them to Dingle. He smiled triumphantly as Rian stepped from the dinghy. He had the Earl now and this time the man would not escape.

"The game is over, my lord," he approached Rian slowly. "You're under arrest."

The Earl shook him by the shoulders. "Christ, man! You've got to listen to me. My wife is in grave danger. My God!" he roared as two of the dragoons tried to restrain him. "Don't you understand? By God, I'll make you listen, I swear it!"

"Good Lord, Cap'n," Harrison appeared out of nowhere. "The Earl ain't guilty of treason. I swear he sunk his own ship, I saw it."

Captain Vickery stared at the first mate. "And who are you, might I ask?"

"Lord Keldara's first mate, sir. At least give him a chance to explain what happened. I saw him turn the *Sorceress* so that she caught the full blast of that cannon. He wouldn't sink his own ship if he were guilty now, would he?"

And so Captain Vickery was privileged to hear the most incredible tale of his life. He stared hard at Rian when the Earl had finished what promised to be the most scandalous story of the Captain's entire military career.

"I believe you," he said finally. "Guards!"

Rian gripped the Captain's hand tightly. "I won't forget this, sir. If you've need of a patron—"

"I'll remember that," Captain Vickery smiled. "Now, we'd best hurry if we're to save your wife."

The ride to the caves was long and hard, but Rian pressed on relentlessly, not caring if he killed his black stallion in the attempt; but Lucifer was strong, and although the horse was lathered and winded, it did not falter. The rain was coming down hard as the Earl flung himself from the stallion's back and ran toward the caves, the dragoons following with their torches which sizzled and spit in the wetness.

"Morgana!" he called hoarsely. "Morgana!"

Captain Vickery came up alongside of him, gasping for breath. "Which way?"

"Stick by me," Rian's mouth tightened whitely about the corners. "I know these caves like the back of my hand, but your men might get lost in them."

They traipsed through the winding passageways, Rian calling his wife's name desperately, but still there was no sign of her.

"What was that?" the Earl asked sharply.

"I didn't hear anything," Captain Vickery gave him a penetrating glance. "Don't let your imagination run away with you, my lord. I know how upset you are, but you must keep your head."

"No, there it is again," Rian told the officer. "A whining or something, like a child crying."

He raced hurriedly through the corridor until he reached the clearing in the cave where the rebels had held their secret meetings.

"Rory," he picked up the small puppy. "They're gone," his face was grim as he stared at the guttering torches and the ropes upon the ground. "Come on."

Rian led the dragoons back through the damp tunnels, out into the night. Not knowing what else to do, he set the dog down. "Where is she, Rory? Find Morgana for me."

The puppy gazed at him, confused for a moment, but like all Irish Setters for centuries, he had an inbred hunting instinct and he was frightened. He wanted the only person who'd ever treated him with kindness, and after a minute, he ran toward the cliffs, dragging his little splint behind him.

"My God! Colin's thrown her over the cliffs!" Rian felt his heart lurch sickeningly inside. "Morgana! Morgana!" he screamed hoarsely. "Get those torches over here."

The Earl stared down over the breathtaking drop and saw Colin's poor, broken body, the head still bobbing gently in the waves.

"Morgana!"

She heard him. Over the roar of the sea and the rain, she heard him; and her heart leaped with a joy she'd never before known in her life. He had come! Incredibly, Rian had come; he had always been there. The tears trickled down her cheeks, their salty taste mingling with the misty rain.

"Rian!" she cried. "Rian, I'm here!"

She saw his worried face from far above, the torches blazing in the night like a million candles.

"She's alive," he said, grabbing Captain Vickery. "Christ! She's alive! Hang on, love, I'm coming."

"Rian, you fool, you'll be killed," she called weakly. "Wait until morning."

"And have you freeze to death? Will you never learn, woman? I'm the master of us two. Stop giving me orders," he yelled as he tied a length of rope snugly about his waist, fastening the other end securely to Lucifer's saddle. "When I get down there, you back my horse up and pull us up," he told Captain Vickery.

"I think you're crazy." The Captain looked at him in disbelief. "You're likely to lose your footing and kill yourself."

"If it were your wife, what would you do?"

Captain Vickery glanced at the Earl's determined, stricken, love-filled face again, noted the hard lines about the corners of his eyes and mouth, and the white scar slashing across the left cheek. He smiled. "Good luck, my lord."

Morgana watched her husband drop over the edge of the cliff and her heart leaped in her throat. "Rian, don't!" she screamed. "You'll be killed."

"Faith and begorra, lass," he called in his best brogue. "Have ye ne'er heerd o' the luck o' the Irish? Fer shame, lass, and ye an Irish wench wi' a temper to match at that. Sure, an I've got a leprechaun on me shoulder now, telling me tales o' the lovely pot o' gold at the end o' this rainbow."

Morgana didn't know whether to laugh, or cry, or box his ears for being so silly as he inched his way slowly down the face of the cliff, step by step, hand over hand, feet grappling for a hold in the darkness, slipping and sliding toward her. She had never loved him more than she did in that moment when he conquered the rough, wet crag to reach her side, his eyes glittering greenly in the blackness.

"Are you all right?"

She nodded her head, not trusting herself to speak as the rain fell down upon them, as the past faded like mist and she put her arms around his neck tightly. Morgana wept, the sobs wrenching in her throat in small chokes.

"I love you, Rian McShane."

She saw that queer, hurt, mocking glance come over his face as his splintering green shards of eyes searched her face intently. It was the last time in her life that Morgana was ever to see that peculiar look. Then slowly, softly, he smiled and it was as though she had suddenly reached across the chasms of her life to find the other side of her soul.

"Pull us up," the Earl shouted hoarsely, his arms tight about her waist.

Eager hands helped them over the edge of the cliff, pulling them both back onto the solid ground of the moors. Morgana leaned against her husband's strong chest tiredly, a wan smile on her face at the cheering cries of the dragoon guards, the pain in her side dulling to a slight ache.

"Colin is—is down there," she looked at Rian, the pain and sorrow evident on her winsome face.

"I know," he answered softly.

"He was—he was quite mad. He tried to—to kill me."

"I know," he said again. "Don't think about it now."

She felt a warm, little bundle fling itself happily at her ankles. "Rory, oh, Rory," she bent to scoop the puppy into her arms.

" 'Twas Rory who told me where to find you," Rian spoke gently as he patted the dog's ears fondly. "Come on, let's go home, Morgana."

He helped her into the saddle on Lucifer, then mounted behind her, one arm fastened tightly around her and Rory.

"Lord Keldara," Captain Vickery rode up beside them. "I'll need your testimony to clear this matter up. I'll be around in a few days. I'm sure all the charges against you will be dropped. Lady Keldara," he nodded to Morgana. "I owe you a profound apology."

"Accepted, Captain. Thank you," she smiled.

"We'll be here," Rian promised, meeting the Captain's eyes in the kind of understanding shared only by the bravest of men, then he dug his heels into Lucifer's sides and headed toward the long shadows cast by the great house in the light of the mist-ringed moon.

Morgana cried as Colin's casket was lowered into the ground and she heard the first clods of earth being shovelled in. She turned away hurriedly. It was bad luck to witness the sight. Colin, strange, brooding, poetic Colin. He had been her cousin, had once wanted to marry her, and in the end, had tried to destroy her.

" 'Tis best this way, Morgana," Rian took her arm as she stumbled, unable to see the way back from the cemetery through her tears.

"Aye."

She wondered what he was thinking, this tall, dark stranger who was her husband; and she knew that sooner or later they were going to have to talk, to come to an understanding of this love that had tortured them both with its tender fury.

They had barely spoken since that night when he'd rescued her. He seemed afraid to talk to her, afraid that she might mock him as she had thought once he would laugh at her, as though she might take back her words of love, claiming they were spoken in haste and despair.

But he had loved her that night. He had put his hands upon her and made her feel that old, familiar desire, that hot, searing flame of passion, and she had given herself to him willingly, understanding at last what love really was. It was not only a burning ache to be eased with kisses and strong hands. It was caring, sharing, and it was pain.

The charges against them both had been dropped. They were free now, free to begin again. Grandfather was a broken old man; he'd wept and cursed, his chin trembling with the shock of the heartbreaking news; but then he'd stiffened his jaw determinedly, squaring his bent shoulders with the same gesture his granddaughter had inherited, summoning the pride and dignity he'd instilled in all of the brave, arrogant McShanes. And Morgana had known then that he would conquer this sorrow too in time.

The county had been properly shocked and scandalized, but no one came to gossip or stare. Some of the oldest and best of the proud Irish families had lost their sons to the ill-fated rebellion. Many had died when the *Sorceress* went down, and those who remained were being shipped back to England to stand trial. Captain Vickery had promised to speak on their behalf if they returned the stolen goods, for Colin had been the only one who'd committed murder among them. They were young and impressionable youths, searching for glory and excitement. A stint in the British navy would teach them a lesson. The British frigate had suffered only minor damage, thanks to Rian, and no one aboard had been killed.

But Morgana knew that the minor rebellion, which would never be recorded as an important event in history books, was only the beginning. She gazed out over the lush green land and knew that someday, somehow, Ireland would be free.

Chapter Thirty-nine

Morgana awakened early; the sun was not even up. She glanced across the bed. Rian was gone. There was only a slight indentation in the pillow to tell her that he had even lain beside her at all.

She rose and dressed, creeping quietly downstairs so as not to awaken the rest of the household. Somehow, she knew where he had gone. She let herself outside, savoring the fresh, clean bite of the spring air in the early morning mist under a sky still untouched by the dawn.

Copper Lady snorted and pawed the ground eagerly as Morgana coaxed a bridle on the mare, not bothering to awaken Jim for the saddle, mounting the mare bareback and astride instead. She turned the horse away from the great house, toward the sea, toward the wild, raging greenness of the white horses which called him, would always call him.

He was walking on the beach, his dark figure tall and proud against the horizon, his demon stallion standing quietly beside him, and she knew that he was thinking of the *Sorceress*, of his wanderlust. She rode toward him slowly, her heart pounding in her breast. He gazed at her a long time as she approached and dismounted, walking toward him slowly, her eyes never leaving his face.

"I knew you would be here," she said softly.

"Aye."

She paused. "There will be another ship, my lord."

"Aye," he spoke hesitantly. "But it won't mean a thing without you by my side to share it, Morgana."

She reached out and took his hand, instinctively understanding that she must meet him halfway if they were to begin again.

"I want to be there, Rian. I love you." She raised herself on tiptoe and placed her mouth on his gently, feeling the fire blaze deep down inside of her. "Aye, I've been a fool, but I do love you, my lord, my life. Take me home, Rian. Home to Keldara so that your son may be born there."

"My son?"

"Aye, already he grows within me, brave and strong like his father."

She could tell him now, now that she was sure of it. His son, conceived in wild, passionate abandonment on the cold stones of the caves, lay safe inside her warm belly. Strange that a fall had taken one child and left another.

"Oh, Morgana, I love you so," he kissed her deeply. "And we've wasted so much time—both of us too proud, too stubborn—"

She gazed into his green eyes and saw the old mocking smile touch his lips, but it held only love for her, the love that had always been there if only she hadn't been too blind to see it.

"We have a lifetime to share, Rian. To grow old together. To watch your child become a man."

"How do you know 'tis a son, sweet?"

"Why, because you ordered it so, my lord."

They laughed together, shakily, hesitantly, but it was a beginning. A beginning on which they would build their love and life together. The sun came up behind the great house, as though a careless artist had swept his paint-brush across the sky, awakening the world with the pale, hazy colors of the rose dawn. And Shanetara cast no shadows then, nor ever again.

Desperado

Rebecca Brandewyne

Araminta Winthrop dreads her wedding night. Then a band of black-clad desperadoes bursts into her wedding reception and the green-eyed beauty finds herself captive of her husband's bitter enemy. But the darkly handsome Rigo del Castillo heats her blood like no other man: The notorious *bandolero* has awakened a passion within her. Soon Araminta finds herself aching for Rigo's sweet kisses and yearning for his tender caresses. For when the brazen outlaw steals her from her life, he carves out a future filled with love for them to share.

___52376-0 $5.50 US/$6.50 CAN

Dorchester Publishing Co., Inc.
P.O. Box 6640
Wayne, PA 19087-8640

Please add $1.75 for shipping and handling for the first book and $.50 for each book thereafter. NY, NYC, and PA residents, please add appropriate sales tax. No cash, stamps, or C.O.D.s. All orders shipped within 6 weeks via postal service book rate.
Canadian orders require $2.00 extra postage and must be paid in U.S. dollars through a U.S. banking facility.

Name_____
Address_____
City_____State_____Zip_____
I have enclosed $_____ in payment for the checked book(s).
Payment <u>must</u> accompany all orders. ❏ Please send a free catalog.

Heartland

Rebecca Brandewyne

After her best friend India dies, leaving eight beautiful children in the care of their drunken wastrel of a father, prim Rachel Wilder knows she has to take the children in. But when notorious Slade Maverick rides onto her small farm, announcing that he is the children's guardian, Rachel is furious. Yet there is something about Slade that makes her tremble at the very thought of his handsome face and sparkling midnight-blue eyes. And when he takes her in his arms in the hayloft and his searing kiss brands her soul, Rachel knows then that the gunfighter Slade Maverick belongs to her, body and soul, just as she belongs to him.

___52327-2 $5.50 US/$6.50 CAN